A DANCE OF SILVER AND SHADOW

A RETELLING OF THE TWELVE DANCING PRINCESSES

MELANIE CELLIER

LUMINANT PUBLICATIONS

Luminant Publications
PO Box 203
Glen Osmond, South Australia 5064

melaniecellier@internode.on.net
http://www.melaniecellier.com

Cover Design by Karri Klawiter
Editing by Mary Novak

For Adeline Kate
who brings joy and love and laughter

ROYAL FAMILY TREES

DUCHY OF MARIN
Duke Philip
Duchess Aurelia (sister of King Edward of Trione)
Prince Jonathan
Princess Lilac
Princess Hazel
Princess Marigold

KINGDOM OF TRIONE
King Edward (brother of Duchess Aurelia)
Queen Juliette
Prince Theodore (Teddy)
Princess Millicent (Millie)
Princess Margaret (Daisy)

KINGDOM OF PALINAR
King Nicolas
Queen Ruby

Prince Dominic
Princess Adelaide

KINGDOM OF TALINOS
King Clarence
Queen Sapphira
Prince Gabriel
Prince Percival (Percy)
Princess Pearl
Princess Opal

KINGDOM OF ELDON
King Leopold
Queen Camille
Prince Oliver
Princess Emmeline
Princess Giselle

KINGDOM OF ELIAM
King George
Queen Alida
Princess Blanche (Snow)

MAP

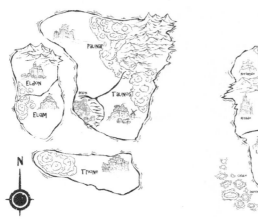

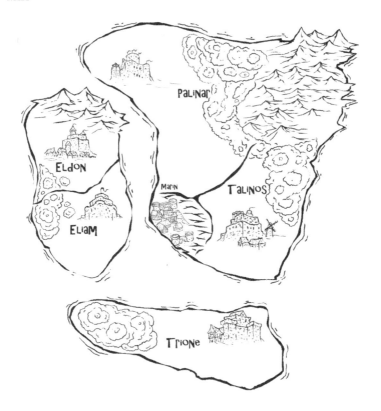

PART I
THE PRINCESS TOURNEY

CHAPTER 1

*B*right banners and flags flew from masts and the tops of buildings. Everywhere I looked the sun glinted off a riot of color. I gripped the rail in front of me as the ship rocked gently, pulled along by lines attached to two smaller rowing boats. The harbor already looked full, with several ships anchored further back in the deeper water, so I was glad we weren't attempting to enter under sail.

The Duchy of Marin, the city-state we were entering, was a center of trade. At least according to the Marinese Emissary who had brought us here. But I still hadn't expected it to be so busy.

Look! I didn't bother to open my mouth as I called my sister's attention to a ship with rainbow sails. Our traveling companion, Princess Celine, had gone to see something from the other side of the ship, so neither courtesy nor secrecy demanded we speak aloud.

How delightful. I've never seen such a thing before. Sophie's projected voice rang in my mind with childish delight. She hung over the railing, her golden curls blowing about in the light wind, a wide grin on her face.

I wasn't sure if the enthusiasm was for the exotic-looking

port, or the end of our long sea voyage. It would certainly be a welcome relief to feel land under my feet again. And I hadn't even been seasick like my twin.

I glanced across at the Emissary and frowned. His eyes were roving over the many ships in the port, and I found the surprise on his face disconcerting.

I narrowed my eyes and stepped toward him when a loud voice hailed us all from the pier. I swung reluctantly back toward the dock and found Sophie alternating her gaze between me and the Emissary. After seventeen years, we were attuned enough that she could guess a lot of my thoughts, even if I didn't speak them into her mind.

He looks a bit odd, doesn't he? Are you worried? Sophie projected. Outwardly, she had stepped back from the rail and assumed a demure smile for the welcoming party on the pier.

I don't know. But he's the person who gave assurances about our safety. I don't like to see him looking surprised.

We haven't even stepped off the ship, and you're already worrying about our safety. Why am I not surprised? Sophie's mental tone swung between exasperation and amusement. *You know that's the Baron and Baroness of Lilton's role, right? They're the Arcadian delegation heads.*

On the outside, I maintained the same courtly façade as my sister. But, internally, I sent her a mental image of my shaking head. *You know I trust Gregory and Helena, but that doesn't mean I won't stay alert.*

I know. Sophie sent the ghost of a laugh along with the thought. *You're hopeless. But one day you'll have to realize that we're not on our own anymore. And that my sickness was a long time ago now.*

I sent her an apologetic grimace. She was right, I couldn't help myself. Our parents had distanced themselves emotionally from us as children, and I could understand the complex dynamics behind that now. After five years of being secure in their love, I could even sympathize a little. They had meant it for the best. They never imagined that you could grow up lonely when you lived in a palace full of people. And, in a way they were right. We hadn't been lonely, not exactly. Because we'd always had each other.

How many times had we told each other as children that it didn't matter if our parents loved us, because we loved each other? Two halves of one whole. It didn't matter if we were weak on our own—as long as we had each other we were strong.

I drew a deep breath, almost shaking at the memory of how close I'd come to losing her. To facing it all alone.

I'm sorry, Lily. Sophie's apology came quickly. *I didn't mean to bring it back up. There's enough going on right now.*

I forced myself to smile. *Don't be silly. I'm fine. You're right—it was a long time ago.* So many years ago, in fact, that many of the details had faded away.

My mother had even recently assured me that I was remembering it all wrong. That Sophie had never actually been dangerously ill. A normal childhood sickness, she'd called it.

But I knew better. While the facts might have disappeared, as early memories do, the emotions still burned clearly. I knew if I closed my eyes, I could bring them rushing back, as powerful as ever. Fear for Sophie. The certainty that no one saw the danger but me. And the utter terror of being left alone.

But I couldn't afford to dwell on those emotions now. I was no longer either helpless or a child. Sophie and I would be eighteen this summer, and I had spent years learning as much about healing as the palace doctors were willing to teach a princess.

I had no time for clouded judgment, I needed all my wits about me. Because we had finally arrived in this foreign land, and something was wrong.

And for all she had laughed at me earlier, Sophie's next projection showed that she shared at least some of my concern.

Has it seemed to you like the closer we get to Marin, the more nervous the Emissary has become?

I bit my lip. *It doesn't quite fit with the idyllic picture he's been painting of his beloved duchy, does it?* I noticed the slightest tremor in my sister's clasped hands and stepped to her side.

Do you think we should have let Father send more guards? she asked.

I shook my head almost imperceptibly. *No, Alyssa was right,* I projected, referring to our brother's wife, a favorite with us both. *What would be the point? They have six kingdoms full of guards. If it comes to a fight, we wouldn't have a chance.*

But it won't come to a fight. Sophie's answering smile seemed more genuine than her previous attempt. *The Emissary has made it clear Marin wants a trade alliance with Arcadia. They wouldn't do anything to endanger our new ties.* Sophie sounded confident now, her tremble gone.

My soft-hearted sister was brave and determined—she sometimes just needed to be reminded of it. A service I was always on hand to perform. Just as she was always around to remind me that I wasn't responsible for everything.

Celine sidled up to us. "Is anyone else getting a bit of an odd feeling?"

"Absolutely." I didn't take my eyes off the people waiting on the dock. The sailors had nearly finished securing our vessel, and the Emissary had already stepped off to consult with the newcomers.

"Sounds like an adventure to me." Celine bounced a little on her toes. "It has to be better than four weeks at sea at any rate."

Sophie grinned at our friend. "It's a relief to see land again, isn't it?"

I listened with only half an ear to their comments on the unpleasantness of being cooped up for so long on a moving ship. The Emissary was now involved in some sort of heated dispute with the committee on the dock. And he looked increasingly unhappy about it.

The Emissary had led the deputation from Marin that arrived unexpectedly in our kingdom of Arcadia. He had requested that an Arcadian delegation return with him to his home. When he heard Sophie and I were considering accompanying him, he had given personal assurances to our parents of our safety in his land. I found it unnerving to see him so quickly discomposed upon our arrival. Perhaps we had been foolish to put our trust in his authority.

But the chance had seemed too good to miss. Old stories held that inhabitable lands existed beyond the Four Kingdoms, but no one in living memory had managed to find one. Any ships that tried to sail westward eventually encountered an impenetrable wall of storms of such severity that they were forced to turn back. So our surprise had been great when, two months ago, an unknown ship sailed into the harbor of Arcadie, the capital of my kingdom of Arcadia.

The Emissary explained that he came from a duchy nestled amongst another set of kingdoms. That all their attempts to sail eastward had previously been foiled by storms as well, until several fishing boats had recently reported calm seas for as far as they dared sail. His people wasted no time in outfitting their largest ship and sailing into the unknown in search of new kingdoms with whom to establish diplomatic ties.

It had all sounded exciting and romantic. And it seemed as if the High King himself must have sent his godmothers to open the way between our two lands. He ruled over all the kingdoms from his Palace of Light, helping us to keep the darkness at bay, and his laws decreed that a kingdom ruled by true love would prosper. Several years ago, the Four Kingdoms had seen a run of royal marriages that had been assisted by the godmothers and fueled by love, with the consequence that we were currently in an historic period of peace and prosperity. So, it had seemed only natural that the High King would clear the seas to the fabled other lands.

Sophie and I had begged to be included in the return delegation, and after much discussion, it had been agreed that we should go. Our southern neighbor, the kingdom of Lanover, was also sending a delegation that was to include our friend Celine, the youngest Lanoverian princess. No one had stated outright the reason for our inclusion, but none of us were foolish. We knew we were the only three unmarried princesses left in the Four Kingdoms. And a marriage alliance was the strongest bond two kingdoms could forge.

Well, the only unattached princesses of marriageable age, I conceded. Sailing away from my new niece, possibly the cutest button of a baby to ever exist, had been the hardest part about leaving home. Sophie and I had been so excited when the second child of our brother Max and his wife Alyssa had been a girl.

Three figures emerged from below deck and came to stand behind us. I felt my muscles loosen a little at their solid presence. The middle-aged couple and the older woman carried the same sort of reassuring authority as a parent. If something was wrong, they would see it put right.

Gregory and Helena, the Baron and Baroness of Lilton, were the official head of the Arcadian delegation, and the Duchess of Sessily led the Lanoverians. Sophie and I had been strictly enjoined to follow their direction in all things. The duchess was a highly respected negotiator throughout the Four Kingdoms, and everyone knew that Lanover never considered a new treaty without her input. In fact, so great was my parents' admiration for her wisdom and shrewd intelligence, that they had instructed us to take careful note of any directions she might give Celine, and to match our behavior to any restrictions she chose to bestow on her own charge.

The Emissary, who was still on the dock talking with the group who had come to greet the ship, noted the arrival of the delegation heads and hurried back onboard. He bowed low before launching into a speech that only made me more nervous.

"I'm afraid there has been an unforeseen occurrence. Entirely unforeseen, I assure you." He paused and rubbed his hands together.

"I'm sure, whatever it is, we can find our way through it together." The duchess' calm tones should have given anyone confidence, but the Emissary simply threw her a wary look.

"Yes, yes, certainly. Of course, we will do all we can. Our greatest desire is to see a profitable alliance established between our two lands and we would never willingly do anything to jeopardize that."

I caught Celine's eye roll just as Sophie projected, *Gracious, he's not good at getting to the point, is he?*

Apparently our guardians shared this opinion. "Perhaps you might enlighten us as to this new development," said the baron with admirable restraint.

"Yes, indeed. It has all happened in my absence, you understand. I had not the smallest inkling. How could I?"

"How indeed?" said Helena, the baroness, with apparent sympathy. No doubt our parents had hoped we would learn from her example when they had chosen her as a joint head of the delegation. She hadn't been born to her station, as we had, but she carried herself with more dignity.

The man who had originally hailed the ship strode on board. "I'm afraid we really can't wait any longer." He cast an exasperated glance at the Emissary. "Their Highnesses will need to accompany us immediately."

"Excuse me?" A lining of steel appeared around the duchess' calm.

The man gave her an apologetic look. "You are welcome too, Your Grace, of course. But we only have room in the carriage for three. We didn't realize there would be so many. Another carriage is on its way. But we cannot wait for it. The ceremony is about to begin, and we don't know what will happen if Their Highnesses aren't present."

"What ceremony?" Baron Lilton stepped forward as if to shield Sophie and me with his body. I appreciated the gesture, but I also noticed a group of guards standing uneasily on the pier. Our small Arcadian honor guard looked equally uncomfortable, hanging back on deck and awaiting some sort of direction.

"The opening ceremony of the Princess Tourney," said the Emissary unhappily. "Apparently it is beginning even now."

The Princess Tourney? That sounds ominous. Sophie had her eyes on the Marinese guards as well.

Tourneys had long gone out of fashion in the Four Kingdoms, but our great-grandparents had apparently been fond of them. I had never heard of one with princesses, however. *They can't possibly mean us to joust with each other, can they?* I tried to picture it and failed.

"The Princesses need to come with us now." The newcomer reached forward and gently gripped my upper arm, attempting to lead me off the ship. "The Emissary will remain to explain everything. And you may follow as soon as the extra carriages arrive."

I dug my heels in and glanced back at the baron and baroness. They both looked concerned, but I could read the truth in their eyes. They could do nothing against the might of this entire land. Even the ship we stood on was theirs. We would have to acquiesce and hope for the best.

I stopped resisting and gripped Sophie's hand, dragging her along behind me.

Don't worry, Lily, you know they can't separate us. Not truly. Sophie looked at me knowingly, and I felt a renewed sense of justification for keeping our secret.

No one in all the kingdoms knew about our connection. Not since Nanny had passed away the previous year. She alone had known the true effect of the gift our godmother had given at our

Christening. *A greater bond than ever twins have shared before.* And she had always advised us to keep it to ourselves.

"Your special secret," Nanny had told us as children, and "Your special weapon," as we had grown older. "It will unnerve others, unnecessarily," she had warned. "You have no need to speak of it."

I had wondered, sometimes, if she was wrong. If we should have told our family at least. But now I tucked the knowledge of the secret close. There was no way anyone in Marin could have heard of our connection so, whatever happened, we had one unexpected advantage.

The Marinese herded Celine along behind us and within moments had bustled us all into a waiting carriage. Their attempts to shut the door were hampered by Celine's outstretched foot. "Wait," she said. "Where are we going?"

"To the Palace, of course, Your Highness," was the reply, before the door was forcibly closed. Celine collapsed back onto a seat, and I took her place, peering out the window.

The carriage jolted and started to move, and I watched the distant figures on the ship recede farther and farther away. Was it only minutes ago I had been comforted by the presence of the older nobles? It looked like I wasn't going to be able to rely on them to fix things, after all. My earlier instinct had been right. If we wanted to stay safe, we would have to rely on ourselves.

CHAPTER 2

"So what do you think about this ceremony?" asked Celine. "Are they carting us off to be innocent sacrifices? Ooh, or maybe we're going to be part of a coup?"

"Celine!" Sophie sounded shocked. *She's ridiculous,* she projected, apparently not wanting to offend our friend by saying the words aloud.

I had no such qualms. "You seem rather buoyant if you think we're about to become maidens sacrificed to a horrible beast, or some such. And I can't imagine what good we would do anyone in a coup."

"Speak for yourself, Lily." Celine smiled over at me before positioning herself at the opposite window. "It's big, isn't it?" She watched the city rolling past.

"The Emissary said the whole duchy is one giant city," said Sophie, attempting to peer over my shoulder. "There must be a lot of people here with all those ships in the harbor."

"I suspect they've come for this Princess Tourney," I said. "That would explain why the Emissary looked so confused at seeing them all."

"What in the kingdoms do you think a Princess Tourney involves?" Sophie looked a little nervous.

"Sword fights? Jousts? Hey, maybe they'll have an archery competition. Marie's been helping me with my aim." Celine's older sister-in-law had become something of an expert archer in recent years, but I didn't have the same confidence in Celine's skills.

"I hope not. The Emissary never said anything about all their princesses being expert warriors." I frowned. "Of course, he didn't say anything about a tourney either."

The numerous stone buildings of the city seemed clean and prosperous, as the Emissary had described. But I received the inescapable impression of age and fatigue. Curtains, clothes, awnings—everything looked a little faded. Only the flowers maintained their bright cheerfulness.

The people themselves seemed excited, however, flocking through the streets in droves. Many were headed in the same direction we were—toward the palace. But others were occupied selling their wares, and still others stopped to point at our carriage and exclaim loudly or whisper to their companions.

"There must be a lot of people going to this opening ceremony," said Celine, still gazing out the window.

I pulled back. "Do the people seem...happy to you?"

Sophie pushed past to take my place. "Not exactly. It doesn't have the same air that a celebration in Arcadia has. It feels almost..." She glanced back at me, her eyes wide with concern.

"Apprehensive," said Celine, the light-hearted humor from earlier replaced with grim seriousness. "Excited but a little bit afraid would be my assessment."

"Look," Sophie pointed out the window. The palace had come into view.

The imposing stone building looked older than the rest of the city but also lighter somehow. Its towers soared over the duchy in graceful spires, bright with flags. Somehow the sight of it drove away some of my anxiety. "It's beautiful."

"At least we should know what's going on soon enough," said Celine, apparently unimpressed by the elegant structure.

"Since I'm a year older, you'd better let me go in first," she added, as the carriage rattled through the palace gates and into the courtyard.

I snorted. "Yes, because that extra year definitely makes you more fit to face coups and sacrifices."

Sophie smiled at our friend. "That's very brave of you, Celine. But whatever is coming, we'll face it together."

Celine sighed. "You know I have six older siblings, right? You could consider letting me have my moment of glory."

Sophie looked down, biting back a smile. "If there's any glory to be had, I promise to step briskly to the side."

Celine looked at her, a twinkle in her eye, but her voice grave. "Thank you, Sophie, I appreciate that." She pushed open the door of the carriage and stepped out, waving away the assistance of two footmen who rushed forward.

She looked backwards over her shoulder. "Come on twins, it's time to show these people what princesses from the Four King-doms are made of."

We followed her as a throng of waiting officials ushered us into the palace. Our arrival appeared to have produced a wave of relief and a great deal of noise. The man from the dock had led us to the palace, and he now rushed us through the building and into a small receiving room.

I had only a brief impression of smooth stone, long corridors, intricate tapestries and elegant furniture before the door closed, shutting us in. The room held nothing but a slightly threadbare rug that looked as if it had once been plush. But a bevy of women awaited us, their moving limbs and lowered voices making the space appear crowded.

They descended on us immediately, exclaiming with relief and smoothing our dresses and hair.

"We've been in such a panic," said the one who appeared to be their leader, as she patted at my windswept curls. "Word arrived this morning that the Emissary had reached the harbor, and that he had brought a foreign princess with him."

"Who could have dreamed it would be *three* foreign princesses!" interrupted another. "Such unfortunate timing."

"What do you think would have happened if they had arrived the day after the opening ceremony?" One of the women paused in her useless flitting.

A momentary stillness swept through the room as the other women considered this question. Then the leader shook her head and returned to her task. "Perhaps they would have been free of the whole thing. Or perhaps they would have brought down curses on all our heads. That doesn't matter now, though, because they're here."

Curses? Sophie projected, wisely refraining from attempting to speak above the babble.

Well, she did say if we didn't *arrive today,* I pointed out. *So, hopefully that means we're safe from curses.*

Sophie met my eyes. *And maybe it means the Marinese really are being forced into this, whatever it is. Maybe they do have our best interests at heart, like the Emissary keeps saying.*

Then why don't I feel heartened? I raised an eyebrow, and she shook her head back at me. I was glad to see her sense of humor remained intact.

In the distance, a trumpet fanfare sounded. A side door swung open, and a footman stuck his head in. "The first of them has already been announced," he said to the room at large.

"No time for more, then, they'll have to go as they are," said the leader, sweeping her arms out in a clear command for the rest of the women to move away from us.

"Thanks for the vote of confidence," muttered Celine. "And

here I was, thinking I'd worn one of my best gowns for our arrival."

I shook my head. "You know perfectly well you look stunning in that dress, Celine."

"I do, don't I?" Celine flashed a satisfied smile at us as two of the women thrust her out of the room.

You know I love her, but she's a bit much sometimes, I projected.

Sophie disappeared from the room, propelled by the leader of the women. *She wouldn't be Celine if she wasn't,* she pointed out, her voice sounding in my head as if no distance separated us. We had tested it when we were younger and had yet to find a physical limitation that affected our ability to communicate.

The remaining women gestured for me to follow my sister. I found myself in a large stone hall facing a tall double doorway. The trumpet fanfare sounded again, and a loud voice proclaimed, "I present the eleventh contestant—Her Royal Highness, Princess Sophia of Arcadia."

I could see Sophie's back as she stepped through the doorway and began to walk down a long, red carpet. A large crowd on both sides of the aisle pressed forward, whispering loudly to each other.

Whoa, Lily, there are a lot of people! Sophie sounded amused. *Don't forget to smile.*

I had barely registered the truth of her words before the fanfare sounded again, and the herald announced, "I present the twelfth and final contestant—Her Royal Highness, Princess Liliana of Arcadia." A hand in the small of my back thrust me forward, and I stepped through the open doors.

Are there really nine *other contestants?* I kept my pace steady and my expression confident. *How many princesses do these lands have?*

It's the princes I'm more interested in, Sophie replied with a giggle.

A moment later I advanced far enough to see the front of the great hall. The crowds were packed in with standing room only, but two thrones faced the crowd with a row of chairs extending to either side. The occupants of all of the chairs, including the thrones, were standing facing me as I moved toward them.

An older couple wearing circlets, presumably the duke and duchess of Marin, stood in front of the thrones. My eyes skated over another older couple standing to the duke's right with a child beside them. They then travelled across to the left of the duchess and snagged on four young men. Four handsome young men wearing circlets of their own.

The princes all looked tall and strong but otherwise nothing alike. How many different kingdoms did they represent? Was I destined to make a marriage alliance with one of them?

I was hoping there might be twins, Sophie projected.

You never know, I replied, *they could be non-identical.*

Maybe. She giggled again in my head. *I like the look of the one on the end.*

I could understand why. He had a contemplative, melancholy look sure to appeal to Sophie's soft heart. *Let's not get ahead of ourselves,* I projected back. *We have to survive this Tourney before we can think about alliances.*

Sophie sent me an image of rolled eyes. *I wasn't thinking about alliances. I was thinking about how handsome he looks.*

I was about to scold her, when my eyes caught on the prince standing next to the duchess. He had broad shoulders and chestnut hair that looked as if it was about to flop into his eyes. But it wasn't his unquestionable good looks that caught my attention. It was the expression of unmistakable horror in his warm brown eyes as they rested on me.

I almost recoiled. I might look a little mussed from our mad dash to the palace, but I couldn't imagine anything about my appearance worthy of such a response. I met his gaze with a glare, while calling out silently for my twin.

Sophie! Is there something wrong with my dress? Or my face?

I had reached the end of the aisle and found a line of richly dressed girls spread out at the front of the crowd, facing the duke and the other royals. I took my place next to Sophie, and she turned slightly to examine me.

No, you look fine. Why?

I didn't reply because the duke had started to speak, and I didn't want to miss my chance to find out what was going on.

"Welcome fair contestants of the Princess Tourney of Prince Dominic of Palinar."

I glanced at the row of princes again. Was one of them Prince Dominic?

"It is our honor to host this Tourney on behalf of Palinar. I, Philip, Duke of Marin, commit to housing all contestants, and their retinues, for the length of the competition. I remind you all that anyone who attempts to interfere with, or in any way disrupt, the fair running of the Princess Tourney shall forfeit their life. So say our laws."

"So say our laws," echoed the crowd behind me. I glanced uneasily at Sophie and Celine. I didn't like this talk of forfeiting lives.

The duke scanned the row of girls in front of him. "By standing before me, you have bound yourselves to complete this Tourney. The winner shall be declared on the first day of summer…"

That's weeks away! Sophie's surprise echoed through my mind.

"…and the winning princess shall immediately be bound by legal betrothal to Prince Dominic of Palinar."

Ah. I should have guessed. Why else would there be a competition of princesses? But what kind of kingdom was Palinar? And what kind of prince was Dominic? I needed more information before I knew whether this was a competition I wanted to win. Or perhaps my duty to Arcadia meant I should attempt to win regardless. We had come here to make alliances, after all.

CHAPTER 3

$\mathcal{A}$n hour later, I stood in another small room flanked by Sophie and Celine. A modest gap separated us from the nine other princesses who mingled and whispered amongst themselves. Plenty of glances were sent our way, but none of them seemed to know what to make of such unexpected late arrivals. I took the opportunity to examine them.

"They're so young!" said Sophie quietly.

"Too young." Celine's grim voice had reappeared.

I had to agree. Another set of identical twins looked barely thirteen and terrified. They clung to each other and barely spoke. And at least two of the other girls looked almost as young. Looking from face to face, I suspected that Celine at eighteen must be the oldest.

"We can't compete against children," said Celine. "Where's the integrity of that?"

"You heard the duke." I shook my head. "We are all legally bound now. And they don't seem to take interference lightly." I gave her a significant look.

Two girls with particularly cold expressions stood alone and silent to one side of the room. One of them looked barely more than a child, but the other didn't look much younger than us. Something about their expressions irritated me, and I admitted to myself that I wouldn't mind beating either one of them in some sort of contest.

Another older girl also stood apart. But her beautiful face held such a heartbroken expression I wanted to give her a hug rather than a lesson. The remaining four girls stood in a tight huddle, glancing our way much more frequently than the others.

"Do you think they'll let us speak to the baron and baroness soon?" asked Sophie, looking around for some sort of official or servant. I just hoped our delegation heads had made it to the palace.

"Tradition requires that the contestants speak to no one between the opening ceremony and the opening ball. Except for each other, of course." The oldest looking girl from the huddle had approached us, the other three trailing behind her, their faces open and curious. "But you'll be free to speak to whomever you like at the ball. And I'm sure your delegations will be there."

She dropped a small curtsey. "I'm Princess Millicent of Trione, by the way. But everyone calls me Millie."

We all gave return curtsies and murmured our own introductions.

I like her.

I had to agree. Millie's friendly smile was a welcome sight after the madness of the last couple of hours.

"This is Lilac, Hazel and Marigold of Marin," she added, pointing to the three girls behind her in what appeared to be descending order of ages. Seeing the three princesses in closer range, it was obvious they were sisters. But even the oldest looked barely mature enough for a betrothal tourney.

"Isn't Marin a duchy?" asked Celine.

"Yes," spoke up Lilac, the eldest of the sisters. "But the children of the ruling duke and duchess are given the honorary title of prince or princess. I used to be glad, but now..."

"You don't want to be a princess anymore?" asked Sophie.

"Only princesses have to compete in the Tourney," explained Hazel, the middle sister.

"And you don't want to compete?" Sophie sounded sympathetic.

"Only because it's Prince Dominic! He's scary," whispered Marigold, the youngest.

Hazel elbowed her in the side. "You're too young, anyway. You shouldn't have to compete."

"I wouldn't mind if it was Prince Gabriel." Marigold giggled. "He's cute."

"None of the princes looked scary to me," I said, hoping to reassure her and allay my curiosity at the same time. "Which one was Prince Dominic?"

"Oh, he wasn't there," said Marigold, her eyes wide. "No one's seen Dominic for *years*. But everyone knows he's a monster. The rumor is that he's cursed, and his whole kingdom with him." She leaned toward us and lowered her voice. "They call him the *Beast*."

"Stop it, Marigold!" Millie glared at the younger girl. "Lily, Sophie and Celine are our guests, and they've barely been here for two hours. There's no need to scare them with silly fairy stories."

Marigold turned her wide-eyed gaze on the older princess. "But you told me half of those stories yourself. You said they were true!"

"Marigold!" Millie glanced at us guiltily.

I really do not like the sound of this, projected Sophie.

I wished I could disagree with her, but she would hear the insincerity in my thoughts. The whole situation seemed to get worse by the minute.

"Hazel, take her away," ordered the oldest sister.

I tried vainly to remember her name. They'd all been named

after colors, or was it flowers? I glanced helplessly at Sophie, and she hid a smile, not needing me to spell out my confusion.

It's Lilac, Hazel and Marigold.

That's right. Lilac. I had always been hopeless with names, an unfortunate defect when travelling to a new kingdom.

Hazel and Marigold both appeared to be contesting their banishment in whispers, but Lilac stood firm, giving Hazel a stern look that the other girl seemed to understand. With a sigh, she dragged her still-protesting younger sister away.

"Sorry about that," said Lilac, turning back to us. "Marigold is only fourteen, and she gets a bit excitable sometimes."

I glanced with amusement at Celine. Sophie and I had first met her when she was fourteen, and excitable would have been a good description.

"Don't underestimate a fourteen-year-old," said Celine, apparently thinking along similar lines. She glanced after the retreating girls. "Although it does seem too young for an event like this."

"Yes, much too young." Millie sighed. "I'm the oldest here at seventeen. Even Lilac is only sixteen." She looked at us speculatively. "Unless you're all older?"

"We're seventeen as well," said Sophie. "But we'll be eighteen in the summer, and Celine is eighteen already. And she was just complaining to us about always being the youngest." She glanced at our friend. "Hopefully you can enjoy your chance to lead a group at last."

Celine surveyed the young girls spread throughout the room. "My sympathy for my older siblings is growing by the minute." She sighed and then looked at Millie and Lilac. "I have six older siblings."

"Six!" Lilac winced in sympathy. "I only have one older brother, and he's bad enough."

"I have an older brother, but only by nine minutes, so I hardly think it counts," said Millie. "My sympathy is with your siblings,

I'm afraid. I have an eight-year-old sister who's even more 'excitable' than Marigold."

"Oh, you're a twin too!" Sophie sounded pleased. We didn't know any other twins amongst the nobility back home in the Four Kingdoms.

"Yes." Millie smiled. "Not identical, obviously. My parents and little sister were to the right of the king, and my brother, Theodore, was the one on the end."

The cute one, I projected to Sophie.

She blushed and glared at me.

Hey, I didn't say it out loud.

And you'd better not! That was for your ears only. She paused and a small smile slipped onto her face. *Not ears, exactly, I suppose.*

We could never stay angry at each other for long. *My lips are sealed,* I assured her.

I noticed Lilac was giving us both a strange look, and I wondered about our expressions. We normally made an effort in company to speak aloud and to avoid long, awkward silences. But the new location and all the unexpected happenings had thrown us off.

"Ignore them, they're odd sometimes," said Celine, apparently aware of Lilac's confusion as well.

I hadn't realized she'd noticed. Sophie carefully kept the guilt coloring her tone from appearing on her face. *She's never said anything.*

We'll have to try harder.

Celine continued. "I want to know more about this supposed curse and beastly prince. And this whole Princess Tourney, really. No-one's paused to explain anything to us. And I, for one, don't appreciate being legally bound into a competition, and potentially a betrothal, without the slightest explanation."

Millie wrung her hands together, her eyes flitting between each of our faces. "Oh, yes. I understand, of course. We all feel terrible about the whole thing. The duke and duchess have been waiting with such eager anticipation for the delegation's return. When word came this morning that the ship had been sighted on this of all days…" She shook her head.

"The timing seemed terrible even before we discovered that the Emissary had brought foreign princesses with him. It was panic, I assure you, when we realized you would be forced into the Tourney with the rest of us. Everyone is afraid that your kingdoms might take offense. My kingdom of Trione is closely allied with Marin—the duchess is my aunt—and my father spent the afternoon closeted with the duke discussing the potential ramifications. I imagine they're explaining things to your delegation heads right now and assuring them that we wouldn't have included you in the Tourney except out of dire necessity."

Lilac nodded her agreement. "My father is greatly concerned that this will destroy any chance of an alliance. Or even precipitate a war."

"We can all hope not," I said, but my heart sank. Just how bad was this Tourney going to be?

"Yes, indeed. Hopefully not war!" said Millie. "There really was nothing we could do. The law is clear. All eligible princesses in the land must compete. There's no provision for visitors."

"Why would there be?" asked Lilac. "We've never had visitors from other lands before."

"But isn't your father the duke?" Celine looked confused. "Couldn't he just change the law?"

"Oh, it's not Marin's law," said Millie. "It's part of the ancient laws. The ones from our founding that govern all the land."

"Oh," said Sophie. "You mean the High King's laws?" *Surely it can't be so bad if it's the High King's law,* she added to me. *Maybe we should ask our godmother about it?*

"I…I suppose so." Lilac looked between us uncomfortably. "They're certainly upheld by magic. None of the kingdoms dare break them, for fear the whole kingdom will be cursed."

There's something wrong with this place. Sophie's voice sounded quiet in my mind. Once again I couldn't disagree with her.

"I don't like all this talk of cursing," I said aloud. "I think you'd better tell us exactly what the old laws say about this Princess Tourney."

Millie and Lilac shared a look, and then Millie took a deep breath. "Any ruler, or his heir, has the right to call a Princess Tourney to choose his bride. Every eligible princess in the land must compete, and the winner is betrothed to the one who called the Tourney."

"And what makes a princess eligible?" asked Sophie, her eyes on the young twins still huddled in the corner.

"It's every unattached princess over twelve, I'm afraid," said Millie. "They're very old laws. And I know Pearl and Opal don't look it, but they just turned thirteen. Historically, the young ones don't usually win, though. And, if they do, they have a long betrothal. The actual wedding can't take place until the princess is at least sixteen. The laws are clear on that as well."

"Well, that's something I suppose," said Celine, under her breath.

"And what does the Tourney involve?"

"No one knows," said Lilac. "Only the princesses attend, and they are bound to secrecy. The history books say their lips are magically sealed on the subject."

"The history books?" I surveyed the room again. "There seemed to be plenty of princes in the throne room. Surely some of you, at least, have competed before? Or your mothers?"

Millie shook her head sadly. "There hasn't been a Tourney called for more than two generations. That's why it never even occurred to us..."

"The last one was called by our grandfather's father," said Lilac. She gestured at Millie. "That's the grandfather we share. A previous king of Trione."

Millie grimaced. "My mother told me that the rulers didn't

like having the control of alliances taken out of their hands by the Tourney. They began the practice of betrothing their daughters before they turned thirteen. Only three princesses competed in that last Tourney, and no-one has called one since. It's been so many years...I suppose the kingdoms all assumed the practice had fallen into mutual disfavor. No one bothers with early betrothals anymore." She spread her arms wide. "So here we all are."

Sophie and I frowned at each other. Celine put her hands on her hips. "So why has this 'beastly' Prince Dominic called a Princess Tourney then?"

Millie bit her lip and glanced toward Marigold, who was pouting in a corner. "I'm afraid no-one knows. No-one has spoken directly to the Beast since he and his kingdom were cursed. None of us could have been more surprised when we received the news."

"He sent my father a letter," said Lilac. "Marin has always hosted the Tourney, and my father had no choice but to call it once he had verified Palinar's seal. It is unusual for the person calling the Tourney not to attend, but it is not required."

"Marigold said no one has seen the Beast for years," said Sophie. "And you're saying no one has talked to him. How can that be? Don't your kingdoms trade with each other?"

"We used to." Lilac's face drooped. "Our duchy is the trading center for all the kingdoms. Trade is the whole basis of our prosperity. And Palinar is the largest, and oldest of the kingdoms. But something changed there several years ago."

Millie leaned forward and lowered her voice. Perhaps she felt guilty for the tales she had told the younger princesses previously. "First we noticed that no one had come out of Palinar for weeks. Then weeks became months. The travelers and merchants who attempted to enter the kingdom turned back with tales of desolate wastelands roamed by wild animals. Wolves and bears."

She lowered her voice further. "Only Palinar never had any wastelands. Or packs of hungry animals, either.

"The last group to attempt to enter turned back after rescuing a man who had been mauled by a bear. The man was gravely injured and seemed confused in his mind. They brought him back to Marin and managed to heal his physical hurts. But his mind still wanders even now. He speaks often of a curse and a beastly prince. When asked about the king and queen, or about Princess Adelaide, Dominic's sister, he says only that they are gone."

She pulled back, her eyes fixed on our faces, waiting for our response. I could see a small part of her relished the dramatic story, and I could imagine the response she normally got from the younger girls.

None of us spoke. Sophie's shocked silence rang in my mind as loudly as any words.

"It's obvious what happened," said Lilac at last.

"Is...is it?" Had I fallen asleep on deck, and the last few hours had been one long dream? It seemed much too far-fetched to be real.

"Palinar must have broken the ancient laws," she said. "It is the only way an entire kingdom could be cursed. And it's why we had to pull you into the Tourney. No one wants to see Marin cursed in the same way."

Sophie finally found her voice. "So, you're telling us that whoever wins this Tourney will be engaged to a prince known as the Beast? A prince who did something so terrible that his entire kingdom has been cursed. And this unfortunate girl will have to venture off into a wasteland full of wolves and bears."

Celine snorted loudly. "So, what you're really telling us is that this competition will be a race for the bottom rather than a race for the top?"

"Oh no!" Millie sounded horrified. "You heard the duke.

Interfering with the competition requires a life be forfeit. That includes us as well."

"But how would anyone know?" I asked. "I mean, no one here can have any idea of our abilities, for instance."

"It's the ancient laws," said Lilac, her eyes glassy. "The magic knows. The second to last Tourney before this one was called by the heir of Marin. A couple of princesses felt that being a duchess would be beneath them. They didn't try at all. Each of them lost a family member to illness before the end of the competition."

Millie looked at us sadly. "And it was someone back in their home kingdoms, too. So not even the three of you are safe."

Sophie turned to stare at me. *Max and Alyssa!* she projected, naming our brother and sister-in-law.

My stomach churned. *Little Harry and Rose.*

At the mention of our young nephew and baby niece her face went pale. She turned back to the others. "So we all must do our very best to win the Tourney and condemn ourselves to this awful fate."

"No wonder your fathers were worried about war," said Celine. "Welcome to Marin, hey."

A tear slipped out and ran down Lilac's cheek as she looked at us. She was the oldest of the Marinese princesses, and her family's Emissary had brought us here. Did she feel responsible, or just afraid of the consequences?

I surveyed the room, half-full of children, again. A sinking sensation made me reach out wordlessly in my mind for the comforting feeling of my sister. I felt her reaching out for me as well and wished we could extend the same support to Celine. Because I had a bad feeling that one of the three of us was going to win this Tourney.

CHAPTER 4

I forced myself to rally. None of this was Millie or Lilac's fault. And they seemed the most likely candidates to win after the three of us. They were fellow victims, and I appreciated the information they had shared.

"So you're telling us we're not going to see anyone until this ball tonight? No hope of any food delivery then?"

Millie smiled at me gratefully. "No, I'm afraid not. But the ball should be starting soon, and there will be plenty of food there."

I smiled back at her.

Could you really eat right now? Sophie sounded shocked.

No. But I couldn't think of anything else to say.

We should get her to tell us about the others. She turned to Millie. "Who's that girl on her own in the corner? She looks so sad."

Both of the local princesses turned to look. "Oh, that's Snow," said Lilac.

"Princess Blanche of Eliam," Millie added.

"She's usually fairly good fun." Lilac sighed. "She and Hazel are friends. They're both fifteen and were born only days apart."

"Is she sad about the Tourney?" I asked.

Millie shook her head. "It's her father." Her forehead creased.

"He's been sick for over a year, and the doctors think he won't last much longer. She's an only child and very close to him. He was too sick to travel, and she's heartbroken to be forced to leave him. We're all hoping he'll last until the summer. I can't see her winning, given her state, so hopefully she'll make it back in time to say goodbye."

"Oh, how sad." Sophie looked like she might cry. I reached over and squeezed her hand. "She's so beautiful, too!"

I wasn't sure what bearing that had on her sorrow, and Celine seemed similarly unimpressed. "Beautiful, yes. But too pale, if you ask me. I can see why you call her Snow. You should see my sister, Celeste. No one in any kingdom is more beautiful than her."

I smiled apologetically at Millie and Lilac. "It's true, I'm afraid. A Christening thing."

The Marinese and the Trionian exchanged a glance I couldn't interpret. "You all got gifts at your Christening, did you?" Lilac sounded half curious, half envious.

"Not me, unfortunately." Celine sighed. "Most of my older siblings did, and Celeste even got three. But her Christening went rather spectacularly wrong, so everyone felt it was best to avoid gifts after that."

"Well, Snow's beauty is natural, as far as we know. And everyone says she grows lovelier every day." Lilac sounded a little wistful. "She even cries beautifully. Unlike me. I get red and blotchy."

"Just be glad you don't have anything to cry about like she does," said Millie.

"Nothing to cry about?" Celine raised an eyebrow. "It sounds like we all have something to cry about. Unless any of you like being forced into secret competitions with potentially deadly outcomes."

Both girls looked at her, and then Lilac's lower lip wobbled.

I glared at the Lanoverian. Lilac might be older than half the girls here, but she was still younger than us.

Celine looked a little guilty and quickly pointed at the two cold-looking girls standing aloof. "Who are those ice queens?"

Millie patted Lilac on the shoulder before turning to look. "That's Emmeline and Giselle of Eldon. Their older brother, Prince Oliver, is just as bad. You might have noticed him at the ceremony—he was the haughty looking one."

I didn't want to admit to anyone, even Sophie, that I had been too busy looking at the brown-haired prince with the horrified expression to notice much about the others.

"Oh, yes, I saw him," said Celine. "The fair one. They do all have the same look, now that you mention it. Like you're not worth the effort even to look at."

"Eldon is the northern kingdom across the strait," said Millie. "They say it's winter there for ten months of the year. The climate must rub off on them." She managed a small laugh. "I wouldn't hold out any hope of friendliness from that direction."

"Maybe one of them will win," said Celine, hopefully. "Emmeline looks old enough."

"Yes, she's sixteen, like me," said Lilac, at the same time as Sophie exclaimed, "Celine!"

Celine grinned wickedly at my soft-hearted twin. "Hoping doesn't change anything. I'm free to hope whatever I like."

I shook my head but couldn't resist a small smile. Until my eyes fell on the other twins in the room. "Just as long as neither of those two win." I could still hardly believe they were thirteen—they looked so young.

Millie followed my gaze. "Not much likelihood of that, thank goodness. Poor Pearl and Opal. They're only just thirteen and were scared of their own shadows before any of this even started. Their whole kingdom is like that, to be honest, so I don't think we can blame them."

"Maybe we should go talk to them." Hesitation sounded in Sophie's voice, and it was certainly hard to imagine what sort of comfort we could offer. As long as the competition itself remained a mystery, we had no actual way of knowing who would win.

Thankfully, just at that moment, the door swung open, and a herald announced the start of the ball. Millie directed us all to line up and file out of the room, the three local princesses in the lead, and down a long corridor to the entry of the ballroom.

Once again we were announced individually with a trumpet fanfare. Apparently our arrival at the opening ceremony had locked in some sort of official order, so I stood at the back of the line. It took a long time to announce eleven princesses.

By the time Sophie disappeared into the ballroom, I was starting to think maybe I was hungry, after all. The herald announced me, and I stepped forward onto a landing. An elegant stairway descended before me into an enormous ballroom lined with tall windows and filled with brightly dressed nobles.

The other princesses had already disappeared into the large crowd, but Sophie had waited for me. She linked her arm through mine, and I heard a murmur run through the crowd.

I thought we'd better make a proper first impression, since we were in a bit of a rush last time.

I couldn't help grinning. Individually we were beautiful enough, as princesses always seem to be, but together we did tend to stop crowds.

I straightened my shoulders. After the day we'd had, we could do with the confidence boost. And, regardless of what else was going on, we were still here to represent our kingdom. We needed to impress people as much as we could. When this Tourney was over, there would be other alliances to be made. I just hoped both of us were still free to make them.

As soon as we stepped down onto the dance floor, a young man approached us. He bowed low and introduced himself as a local Marinese nobleman. He asked for a dance but looked a little lost, as if he wasn't sure which of us he was asking. I suppressed a sigh. It was always like this when we first arrived in a new place. No one knew quite how to differentiate between us.

I'll go, offered Sophie, *I don't mind.*

She disappeared onto the dance floor, and I looked around for the promised food table. I had barely taken two steps toward it, however, when a tall figure blocked my path. I looked up into a face I recognized. Any traces of hunger fled.

"I'm Prince Jonathan of Marin," he said. "Welcome to my home."

So, he was the heir to the duchy. No wonder he had been placed beside the duke and duchess at the opening ceremony. No trace of his earlier horror remained. Instead he watched me intently, with an expression I could best describe as hopeful.

"Will you dance with me, Princess Liliana?"

The name sounded foreign on his tongue. At home my full name was only used on the most formal occasions. The entire kingdom knew me as Princess Lily.

"It's Princess Lily," I told him. "No one has ever called me Liliana. And my sister is Sophie."

"My apologies. Princess Lily, will you dance with me?"

For a moment I wanted to say no. It had been a long and tiring afternoon, and it promised to be an equally long evening. I still didn't understand his reaction at the ceremony, and I wasn't sure I had the emotional energy to deal with someone who seemed so volatile.

He saw my hesitation and took a small step closer, holding out his hand. "Please?"

This close, I could see the gold flecks in his brown eyes, and their pleading expression looked too genuine to deny. I put my hand in his and pretended I didn't feel the spark of connection at the contact as he led me onto the dance floor.

Plenty of eyes followed us, and many of them didn't look pleased. With royalty gathered from all the different kingdoms, I could imagine how many had flocked to the duchy with alliances on their mind. I had grown up in a court. I knew how they worked, and how unwelcome a foreign princess could be.

I reached out to Sophie in my mind and felt her reassuring presence. I didn't need friends at this court. I had brought my best friend with me.

Prince Jonathan's arm drew me close, our hands tightly clasped. I said nothing, reminding myself that he looked handsome and welcoming now, but he hadn't looked that way the last time I had seen him.

After several silent revolutions, he spoke. "My sister, Lilac, told me you know everything about the Tourney. It's no wonder that you look at me so warily."

I continued to say nothing. The madness of the Tourney was simply another reason to tread carefully around this foreign prince.

He swung me around in the dance, and his hands tightened momentarily. "For you to arrive on the day of a Princess Tourney. And the Beast's Tourney, too! It's the most wretched luck."

He sounded so genuinely upset that I caved and gave him a smile. "The ladies who prepared us for the ceremony seemed to think if we had arrived any later and missed the opening ceremony, our presence in Marin might have cursed you all as Palinar has been cursed. So perhaps it was the best of good fortune, after all."

He looked down into my eyes, and for a moment I forgot to breathe at the depth of emotion there. "Perhaps," he said. "But not for you."

"No." I drew a careful breath. "Not for me."

I barely felt my body swirling over the dance floor, so lost did I feel in his gaze. The moment stretched out, and then his expression turned dark. I stumbled, remembering my first sight of him, and he steadied me.

He straightened, drawing back a little. The horror had disappeared and been replaced with a sort of determined formality.

"I have a confession to make Princess."

"A confession? But we've only just met."

He drew a deep breath. "I'm the one you should blame for being forced into this tournament. Whatever happens to you now is my fault."

"Your fault?" I regarded him through narrowed eyes. "Did you call it yourself? Perhaps you're secretly Prince Dominic?"

A laugh escaped him. "Definitely not." His expression sobered. "I didn't call the Princess Tourney. I just called you here."

"Me?"

"All of you. I wanted to show initiative and help our duchy. I pushed for a ship to be sent when we received word the storms had disappeared. I chose the Emissary myself, and I spoke to him without my father's knowledge. I told him that if he found any other kingdoms, he should press for a delegation to return with him. And that he should bring back any unattached princesses that he could." He looked away and muttered his final words, as if to himself rather than me. "I wanted to speed things up..."

I frowned. For all his frank confession, there was something he wasn't telling me. Was it the same thing that had caused the Emissary's unease? Something to do with the difference between the stories he had told to lure us here and the faded reality before us now. Why did Marin need the Four Kingdoms so badly?

He shook his head and looked back at me. "I didn't even hear about your ship's arrival until I was waiting for the ceremony to start. I had been occupied with greeting our many guests and preparing for the Tourney. My mother only had time to whisper to me that the Emissary had returned, and he had brought foreign princesses with him. By the time you walked in the door —the *third* princess brought here only to be trapped into the Tourney—I had realized the consequences of my instructions to the Emissary. I never thought he would succeed so well."

"How did the news of our presence on the ship reach the duke at all?" I asked.

"You must have seen how busy the harbor is at the moment with all the visitors for the Tourney. We used to regularly host events on behalf of all the kingdoms, so it was once a common sight. It can take hours for the rowboats to ferry all the bigger ships in and out. Your captain called down word of your arrival to one of the smaller vessels, and it was passed along to the city long before you were secured to your berth. Only no-one thought to tell me."

He grimaced, and now that I understood his look of horror was *for* me, rather than *about* me, I found it oddly endearing.

"And worst of all was seeing your ages." His voice lowered and became truly pained. "I'm so sorry, Lily, but I think there's a good chance one of you might win."

Since I had already come to that conclusion, his words hardly came as a shock. Instead I couldn't help focusing on the fact that he'd dropped my title in the heat of his concern. Despite everything that had happened to us, this foreign prince seemed to truly care. And he had three young sisters in the Tourney. He should have been celebrating their likely reprieve.

In fact, I couldn't help questioning him on it. "That must be a relief to your family, given your sisters' involvement." I kept my tone level.

He flinched back from me. "No, of course not!" Then he frowned. "Not that I want them to win either, of course." He paused before growling in frustration. "I don't know what to think. I don't want anyone to win! But I know Marin invited you here, and our representative gave you assurances about your safety. And he did it under my instruction. As your hosts we owe you that safety. And we want good relations with your kingdom. If we could have done anything, anything at all, to have you excluded from the competition, I assure you…"

He pulled me to a stop in the middle of the dance floor, gripping both of my upper arms. "You do believe that, don't you?" He sounded almost frantic. "We never intended any of this."

Even more eyes were on us now. *Lily? Is everything all right?*

Yes, it's fine. I reassured my sister first. *Prince Jonathan is Lilac's brother. I think they're still nervous our families are going to lead a flotilla of attack ships across the ocean because of this whole Tourney situation.*

Oh. Well, hurry up and put him out of his misery, then. He's just as cute as that other one.

I hoped the smile in her voice meant she was enjoying the dancing in spite of everything. *How would you know? Have you been spying on me?* I loaded my question with outrage, playing up our usual joke.

Lily! Seriously! Stop talking to me. He's going to think you're a half-wit.

I focused back on Prince Jonathan who did seem to be growing marginally more panicked. "Relax, Your Highness," I said. "There's not going to be any armada heading in your direction. Our families are more reasonable than that. As long as you do your best, within your laws, that is enough."

He smiled and swept me back into the dance. "You are as gracious as you are beautiful."

"Thank you, Your Highness," I said demurely. But he looked so relieved that I couldn't resist grinning up at him. "You should know that particular compliment means a lot less when there are two of us. You could be dancing with Sophie right now and telling her how beautiful she is, and it would make no difference whatsoever to you."

"Oh, I don't know," he said. "I don't think you're that similar."

I gaped at him until he chuckled, and I realized he was joking. I shook my head, grumbling to myself.

"But, in all honesty, I'm not making my apology to you out of chance, you know."

"Really?" I looked at him skeptically. "Sophie is generally

considered the softer-hearted of the two of us. Look at her smiling at that poor young man right now." I pointed across the room to one side of the refreshment table. She was seated on a chair against the wall, examining the hem of her gown, which had been torn. A young man, dressed formally but surely not more than fifteen, appeared to be stammering and stuttering his way through an apology.

Prince Jonathan winced in sympathy before returning his gaze to me. "But exactly," he said.

I gazed at him blankly.

"If you're truly sorry, you don't go for the easy apology." He leaned in close and whispered in my ear. "I wanted the twin with fire in her eyes."

CHAPTER 5

ily! Rescue me—now! Sophie's order jerked me out of the shock of the prince's words.

I dropped a quick curtsey, ignoring his outrageous comments, and excused myself to aid Sophie. He cheerfully volunteered to accompany me, his demeanor giving no hints that he had said anything out of the ordinary mere seconds before.

I allowed him to lead me off the dance floor and directed him in a quiet undertone to get rid of the poor adolescent responsible for the clothing disaster. I knelt at Sophie's feet and examined the damage as Prince Jonathan deftly steered the young man away.

Oh, thank goodness, he looked so embarrassed and wouldn't stop apologizing. The whole thing was hideously awkward, I thought he would never get the hint and leave. Do you think it's fixable? I don't know if any of our other gowns have made it off the ship yet. She leaned forward to try to see what I was doing.

"Sit back," I scolded her out loud, remembering that we needed to keep up appearances. When we were children others had found our silences when we played together unnerving.

"Here's a pin." She held it out, and it only took me a moment to use it to fix the hole.

"That should do for now," I said, levering myself up into the chair beside her. "And I'm sure Helena can have it mended properly later."

Sophie looked at me closely for the first time. *You look flushed!* she accused.

Well, I was just bending over, fixing your dress, remember. Thank goodness she could only hear the thoughts I projected to her and couldn't actually read my mind. I hadn't decided if the prince's words were a compliment yet, but I feared Sophie would be offended either way—on my behalf, or her own.

Prince Jonathan returned before she could question me further. He had succeeded in losing Sophie's previous dance partner but appeared to be dragging another young man over in his stead. His new companion also wore a circlet, and I didn't need an introduction to guess his identity.

The newcomer strolled along behind Prince Jonathan, his languid air proclaiming that the whole thing was beneath his notice, but not actually worth the effort of protesting over. He had to be Oliver, prince of the northern ice kingdom the other princesses had told us about. What had been his sister's names?

That must be the Eldonian prince—Oliver, right? Sophie projected before I could even ask. *Emmeline and Giselle's brother?*

Absolutely! Eldonian prince. Emmeline and Giselle.

She looked over at me with amusement in her eyes. *Do you have any idea what we're talking about?*

Of course I do! I tried to look offended and failed. *Great piles of snow and all that.*

She shook her head at me before rising and smiling at the two princes. I followed more slowly, less inclined to show politeness where it was so obviously unappreciated.

"You must be Princess Sophie. I'm Prince Jonathan of Marin." Jonathan bowed over her hand. "And this is Prince Oliver of Eldon." He gestured toward the other prince. "Oliver, these are Princesses Lily and Sophie of Arcadia."

The Eldonian prince gave a small movement that might have been considered a bow but said nothing.

Charming.

Perhaps he's concerned about his sisters. Sophie didn't sound like she actually believed that, so I felt no need to protest.

"It's a pleasure to meet you, Prince Jonathan, Prince Oliver." Sophie gave a small curtsey.

"Please, call me Jon."

She inclined her head. "Then you'll have to call us Sophie and Lily."

Jon looked at me. "If neither of you mind…"

For a wild moment I wanted to say no. To insist he continue to use my title before my name. To attempt to put up some sort of wall between me and this prince who somehow managed to get under my skin. I was going to have enough distractions with the Tourney.

Lily!

I smiled quickly. "Of course."

Jon turned expectantly to Oliver, but he said nothing. He appeared to be gazing at a spot on the far wall, as if he hadn't even noticed our conversation.

Jon sighed. "And you can call him Oliver, too. The young royals here don't tend to stand on too much formality with each other. This isn't him being formal, it's just him being…Oliver."

I wanted to ask what was wrong with him, but I didn't think that would be polite. I cast around for some other topic of conversation while Jon fetched us both drinks from the nearby refreshments table.

"Your sister, Lilac, said that no one knows what these Princess Tourneys involve," I said when he returned. "It seems like a rather strange way to pick a wife."

Lily! That's not polite! Sophie gave me her public remonstrance smile.

So much for that, then. Our sister-in-law, Alyssa, had spent a

41

long time transforming us from the wild children we had been when she first arrived at our castle into polite and proper princesses. I had never taken to the lessons as well as Sophie and was much more liable to forget them under pressure. I did try, though, because Alyssa was right. Subtlety was an admirable trait in a royal.

"Although it has been many years since the last Princess Tourney, it is the traditional way in this part of the world." Jon looked torn between defending his home and his obvious discomfort with the Tourney.

"Do you not have marriages of alliance in the Four Kingdoms?" Although Prince Oliver asked a question, his tone betrayed no curiosity.

"If the situation allows, we take advantage of it," I said, when I had recovered from the surprise of hearing him speak. "But marrying for love is more important for the well-being of the kingdom. Everyone knows the High King has ruled it so." I looked up through my lashes, hoping he wouldn't read any offense into my probing statement.

"You follow the High King, then, in Arcadia?" Still Oliver betrayed no actual interest in the conversation.

"Of course! Don't you?" Sophie, however, sounded genuinely surprised. "I thought he ruled over all the kingdoms. Certainly the Four Kingdoms would have fallen to darkness long ago without the aid of his godmothers."

"So your godmothers keep the evil at bay, do they?"

Sophie shifted beside me, and I didn't need to hear her thoughts to sense her unease. I chose my words carefully. "That is their role, is it not?"

"I suppose it is." He glanced down, and an awkward silence enveloped us.

Jon watched him for a moment and then glanced ruefully at us. "I will confess, if Oliver is reluctant to do so. It has been many long years since we have seen a godmother in these kingdoms.

Some still possess a godmother item—relics of the past—but we have received no aid from them in my lifetime."

Oh dear. Sophie's dismay came through clearly in her projection, despite her understated words.

A young girl appeared at Jon's side. I thought I recognized her as the prince's youngest sister, one of my fellow contestants. The one who had first told us about the beastly Dominic. She whispered in her brother's ear while I racked my brain for the girl's name, and Sophie waited politely.

Marigold. A hint of amusement sounded in Sophie's thought.

I smiled at her. Thank goodness Sophie had a head for names.

"Please excuse me," said Prince Jonathan. "My parents need me." He bowed respectfully before allowing his sister to drag him away.

Prince Oliver made no effort to follow suit. He gazed away across the crowd as if he hadn't even noticed Jonathan's departure.

I tried to pick up the conversation where it had been interrupted, forcing some enthusiasm for my sister's sake. "It sounds like it's a good thing we've come! We will call on our godmother and see what she has to say about the situation."

Oliver started, as if he had forgotten our continued presence, and glanced between us. I couldn't read his expression. "By all means," he said at last. "You are certainly welcome to try."

He gave a small movement that could have been a bow and strode away, leaving us alone in a sea of strangers.

Lily...what have we gotten ourselves into?

I gripped my glass so tightly I feared it would shatter. *I only wish I knew.*

"Lily! Sophie! There you are." Celine appeared out of nowhere and grabbed both of our hands, towing us along behind her as she wove through the crowd. "I've been looking for you everywhere."

"We've been having a slightly disconcerting conversation with the haughty Prince Oliver," said Sophie.

"Tell me about it," said Celine. "There's nothing but disconcerting conversations to be had here."

She pulled us to a halt in the far corner of the ballroom.

"Apparently the contestants aren't allowed to leave the ball, so this is the best we could do." The delegation heads from Arcadia and Lanover were partially shielded by a large potted bush. They had stationed several of our ceremonial guards in strategic locations around the nook to ensure we weren't disturbed.

"I'm afraid this is the closest we can get to a war room, my dears," said Helena.

I smiled at the baroness. She was an old family friend and felt like a welcome piece of home. "We're just glad to see you at all. We weren't so sure there for a while."

"The Duke and Duchess of Marin have filled us in on the situation. It is..." The Duchess of Sessily paused ominously. "...less than ideal, shall we say."

"The Marinese prince, Jonathan, spoke to me," I said. "He seemed very concerned that we might doubt his family's intentions."

"We cannot condone this Tourney," said the baron, glancing unhappily at his wife. "But it seems we have no choice. We have consulted at length with the relevant officials, and you are all bound to compete."

"It is certainly an unfortunate situation," said the duchess, "but I am convinced the local kingdoms hold no ill will toward us. It is beyond apparent that they feel the same reluctance toward their own daughters' participation as we do about yours. Yet they feel we all have no choice. We must be guided by their understanding of their own laws and hope for the best. I'm not sure I put much credence into these stories of well-timed deaths, however. People do die from illness, in the natural course of things. I think we must consider whether you aim to lose this Tourney."

Sophie was already shaking her head vigorously, so I knew I spoke for both of us. "We're not willing to risk it."

The duchess turned to Celine, who indicated her agreement. "I was afraid you would say that. I have examined the other contestants, and I have never been so disheartened to see an opponent's inferiority. A couple of them show promise, however, so all is not lost."

"Thanks...I think." Celine glanced back toward the rest of the ballroom. "Despite this Tourney, the Marinese certainly seem excessively enthusiastic about an alliance, so we can't fault the Emissary on misleading us there."

"Yes," said the baron. "Even if he wasn't entirely honest about the reasons why."

I nodded. "It seems fairly clear that he might have...*overstated* Marin's prosperity."

The duchess smiled approvingly. "That puts us in a strong position, as long as the three of you can escape this Tourney unscathed. By which I mean, unbetrothed. I cannot imagine either Lanover or Arcadia seeking an alliance with this cursed Palinar." She shook her head. "Some of the other kingdoms show promise, however. For now we will proceed with negotiations under the assumption that a local girl will win the Tourney."

"And if they don't?" asked Sophie.

The duchess frowned. "We shall cross that bridge only if we are forced to do so, my dear."

A loud bell rang through the ballroom, and a hush descended in its wake.

"It seems it's time," said Helena, looking distressed. She gave Sophie a hug and then moved on to me.

"Time for what?" asked Sophie, meeting my eyes over the baroness' shoulder.

"Did no one tell you?" The duchess gazed in surprise at our confused expressions. "My apologies, I thought you knew. The Tourney begins tonight. Apparently it is always conducted at night. It seems you are expected to dance half the night away before competing."

"Now?" Sophie's voice faltered. "We're competing *now*?"

CHAPTER 6

*M*arinese officials hurried us all toward the far side of the ballroom. The nine other princesses were already gathered there next to a simple door. A child in an elaborate gown clung to Millie, babbling too fast for me to understand her words. I recognized her as the girl from the front of the room at the opening ceremony. Millie's eight-year-old sister, I think she'd said.

As soon as we arrived, the duke gestured for the door to be opened and directed the contestants to file inside. The girl moved along beside Millie, until one of the princes stepped forward and tried to pull her away. She resisted, but Millie said something quietly that made her let go. She let the prince lead her away with much sighing and backward glances at her sister. As he towed her past me, I heard her complaining, "But it's not *fair*! I want to go, too!"

I shook my head. Clearly the young girl had no idea what the Tourney truly meant. Surely she didn't want to find herself betrothed at eight years old.

Once all twelve contestants had entered the room, the duke

addressed us. "Welcome to the first event of the Princess Tourney for Prince Dominic of Palinar. Good luck."

And he closed the door.

For a moment silence gripped us as we all looked around the room. The plain walls and empty floor gave no indication of what we were supposed to do next.

"Perhaps we're now supposed to fight to the death," said Celine.

Millie chuckled, and the sound released the other girls from their silence. Whispers and the rustle of movement filled the room.

"Surely they can't mean for us to stand here all night," said Emmeline. I hadn't heard either of Oliver's sisters speak before, but she sounded just as haughty as he did.

A small scream attracted our attention toward the far wall. One of the younger twins, either Pearl or Opal, I couldn't tell them apart yet, pointed toward the floor. I thrust my way through the small crowd in time to see a trapdoor slowly opening.

It rose up, as if pushed from underneath, but I couldn't see any sign of a person through the rapidly widening hole. As the door fell back against the floor with a clatter, a large square opening confronted us. Pearl and Opal drew back, but I stepped forward and peered down into the darkness. A ladder descended down from the edge of the trapdoor.

"I'm guessing we're supposed to go down there." I looked over at Lilac and her sisters. "Did you know this was here?"

Hazel shook her head, her eyes wide, and her lips pressed shut. Marigold looked equally nervous, but she spoke up anyway. "We're not allowed in here normally. No one is."

"Of course you aren't." I sighed. "Traditions and ancient laws and all of that." I looked around at all the others. "Well, unless anyone has a better idea…" I waited a moment to see if anyone would protest but, when no one did, I crouched down and

48

turned around, feeling blindly backwards for the first rung of the ladder.

"Lily, wait!" Sophie called from the back of the crowd. She burst out from behind the other princesses. "I'm coming with you."

I smiled up at her. "You'd better be." And then I began to descend the ladder.

When my feet hit the ground, I moved away to make room for Sophie and looked around me. The light was dim, but clear enough to see my immediate surroundings. I stood in an empty space, large enough that the walls and ceiling were lost to the surrounding darkness. A path stretched away from the ladder and wound through what appeared to be a grove of...

"Are those trees?" Sophie stared at them in confusion. "Inside?"

"They look like trees." I crossed over to examine one more closely. "Extremely odd trees."

The other girls had all now descended the ladder, Celine stepping down last of all. She came straight over to us.

"Since you two were bravely leading the way, I figured I'd better bring up the rear. And a good thing too, I practically had to push those two down the hole." She gestured at Pearl and Opal who still cowered near the ladder, although the rest of the girls had started to spread out. "I think they'd forgotten about the consequences of not taking part."

She turned her attention to the branch I had been inspecting. "Are those...silver?" she asked, reaching out to brush her fingers along a leaf.

"They appear to be, yes," I said, trying to keep my voice level, as if this was a perfectly ordinary occurrence.

"Is it actually alive, do you think?" asked Sophie, leaning in to observe a leaf more closely.

"Goodness knows." Celine turned to look down the path. "I guess we're supposed to head down there."

"I can't see what else we could do."

"Come on everyone," she said, raising her voice. "Let's get this over with." She paused and surveyed the others, her gaze latching on Lilac. "Lilac, can you make sure there aren't any stragglers?" Her eyes flicked to the younger twins. "I think it would be best if we stick together."

"I'll help." Millie moved to stand beside her friend. "I can't imagine any of us want to wander off on our own down here, anyway."

"I don't suppose any of you know anything about 'down here'?" I asked without much hope.

"Nothing at all, I'm afraid," said Lilac. "I've never even heard so much as a rumor about an underground level to the castle like this." She turned to her sisters. "Have you?"

They both shook their heads, and I sighed. "I thought as much." I fell into step beside Celine. "I guess we'll have to explore it for ourselves then."

As it turned out, the youngest girls showed no inclination to linger or fall behind. Our group moved along the path in a tightly packed mass, passing through trees that all bore the same mysterious silver leaves.

I still hadn't seen either walls or ceiling. We could see well enough in our immediate vicinity, but when I tried to look into the distance, the scene gradually faded away, as if swallowed by a dark fog. After a short walk, the trees dropped away, only to be replaced by a second grove. For a moment, I thought the air had started to lighten, but then I realized the effect came from the new grove of trees. The leaves of these trees sparkled like gold, reflecting a warm light through the branches.

I looked back to check the whole group had kept up and noticed Lilac eyeing the leaves. I hoped no one was foolish enough to try to take anything from this place. Who knew what would happen.

A minute later we exited the second set of trees, only to enter a third grove. These trees seemed even lighter than the ones before, the light refracting into rainbows everywhere I looked.

"There's no way those leaves could actually be made from diamond!" exclaimed Celine. "I don't care what it looks like."

Sophie stepped over and touched one of them. "They certainly feel hard enough."

"Let's just keep moving," I said. Even with all the excitement and fear to buoy me up, I could sense weariness creeping in. We had all had a long day and then danced for the early part of the evening. How long would this event last? Not all night, I hoped.

When the trees next fell away, no new ones rose to take their place. Instead, the path led us down to the edge of a large lake. The water lay completely still, swallowing the rest of the path.

"Is there seriously a lake under this castle?" Celine shook her head.

"I don't think we're under the castle. Not really," said Sophie. We both looked at her. "Remember Queen Ava?"

"Who's Queen Ava?" asked Millie, coming up beside us, her eyes on the lake.

"She's one of the queens in the Four Kingdoms," I explained. "And she once visited the Palace of Light."

"What? *The* Palace of Light?" Millie turned to stare at me. "Where the High King rules?"

I nodded. "She said you can't get there by any normal means. This must be a place like that. A place apart from the normal world, a magical place."

"That's all very well, but how are we supposed to get across?" asked Emmeline, regarding the water with disfavor.

"Maybe we're supposed to use those?" Marigold pointed toward the surface of the lake, to the left of the path.

A group of small, empty boats floated toward us on the otherwise still lake.

"Goodness, this place is creepy," muttered Celine. I threw her a look. The younger girls were scared enough without her making it worse.

"There are twelve of them," announced Sophie. "And they don't look like they would fit more than one person each. We must be meant to use them."

"Great." Celine looked down at her dress. "First we have to climb down ladders, and now we have to go clambering in and out of boats. In our ball gowns. And dancing slippers." With a sigh, she stepped to the edge of the water and then into the closest coracle. It wobbled dangerously, and she sat down fast.

It gently drifted away from the edge, making way for another boat.

"Well, that didn't look so hard." I turned to Pearl (or possibly Opal). "I can lift you in, if you like." I didn't wait for her to agree, since I wasn't sure she would, but instead gripped her under both arms and swung her into the nearest boat. She squeaked but didn't otherwise protest. I lifted her sister in to the next one, and then Sophie told me to hop into one myself.

I obeyed, managing the feat successfully, despite making my boat rock even more wildly than Celine's had done. One by one, the rest of the girls clambered into a boat, only Hazel slipping and ending up with one wet slipper and a wet hem. I looked around the bottom of the boat but could see no sign of an oar. Apparently we weren't to have any say in our destination.

As soon as all the coracles had been filled, they began to float across the lake away from the now-distant path. The boats spread out a little as they travelled, so that we would have had to raise our voices to be heard by our neighbors. Silence reigned except for the soft slap of water against the hulls.

It's quite a relaxing mode of transport, if you take everything else away, projected Sophie.

That's quite a big if.

"I can see the other side," called Celine, whose boat was in front. I craned forward in an attempt to see and then straightened abruptly when the small boat began to rock again. But it wasn't the shore that gripped my attention moments later.

Rising from the gloom ahead, a large castle came into view. By the time my coracle nudged against the land, most of the other princesses had already disembarked. I scrambled out, my attention still on the stone building a short distance ahead.

We all moved toward it together, led there by the path which continued on this side of the lake. Lilac and Millie walked with their heads together, conversing in whispers with their eyes glued on the castle.

When we stepped through the large, open doors. Lilac exclaimed, "It is! I knew it."

We all turned to stare at her. "Look around." She gestured around the entrance hall. "Does it look familiar?"

I frowned and looked around. She was right, it did look vaguely familiar.

"It's the reverse of our castle. Just the same, except everything is on the opposite side, like a mirror image. I thought I recognized it on the outside, and now I'm sure."

Since I had only managed the most hurried glimpse of the outside of the duchy's palace and its entrance hall, I had to trust her judgment on the subject. But she must have been right since her younger sisters, Hazel and Marigold, both exclaimed in astonishment and agreed with her assessment.

"Well, since you know the building then, where do you think we should go?"

Lilac frowned and glanced at her cousin. Millie swept her eyes over the various exits from the entrance hall.

"The throne room, perhaps?"

Celine and I shared a glance. I shrugged.

"As good a guess as any," she said. "Lead the way."

Millie and Lilac strode ahead, the rest of us following behind, still tightly packed together as we had been on the path. The light seemed slightly better inside, although I still couldn't see where it came from.

I recognized the throne room, although it looked different without a full crowd of people. The thrones occupied the same space, but the middle of the room had been filled with a long table of dark, polished oak. Six tall, cushioned chairs lined each side.

"Twelve again," said Sophie. She walked over to one of the middle chairs, pulled it out and then sat down. The rest of us followed suit.

"Wasn't there supposed to be some kind of contest?" Celine asked me under her breath as we made our way to the last two chairs. "This place just gets stranger by the second."

The table had been set with twelve plates and twelve goblets, all of which appeared to be made from gold. I really hoped we weren't expected to eat a meal down here. I suspected nerves would prevent quite a few of the contestants from keeping down any food. I was nearly five years older than the twins, and I still found this strange place unsettling. And that was assuming there wasn't anything wrong with the food.

As the last chair scooted in to the table, I saw a folded piece of parchment resting on my golden plate.

"Where did that come from?" asked Hazel, staring at an identical parchment.

Marigold blinked down at the one on her own plate. "It just appeared."

I ignored them, picking up the parchment and unfolding it.

RULES OF THE PRINCESS TOURNEY

1. All contestants must present themselves every third night in the ballroom of the Marinese palace for the competition, which will culminate on the first day of summer.

2. Once returned through the trapdoor each night, the contestants may not speak of the events of the Tourney, even amongst themselves.

3. The Tourney shall be conducted in three stages.

The first stage shall involve a series of collaborative exercises. Points will be awarded to each contestant based on the value they provide to the exercise.

The second stage shall involve a series of individual challenges. Points will be awarded based on success in each challenge.

The final stage shall involve a group competition to be held on the final night of the Tourney.

Leaning over I checked the parchment held in Sophie's hands. It looked identical.

"Collaborative exercise doesn't sound so bad," said Sophie. Looking around the table I saw relief on several faces.

"We still don't know what skills we're supposed to be demonstrating." I read the words again. "What sort of 'exercises' and 'challenges' is it referring to? Are we going to be embroidering cushions, or shooting arrows?"

"I guess we're about to find out." She pointed to the middle of the table where another piece of parchment had appeared.

Leaning over, Celine grabbed it and read aloud. "In the highest keep of this castle, you will find twelve necklaces fit for a queen. Together you must ascend to this tower, and each princess must claim a necklace. Only then will the boats return you to the other side of the lake."

She looked around the table. "Well, that sounds unexpectedly easy. What are we being tested on? The elegance of our necks?"

She had no sooner finished speaking, than a large piece of stone broke from the ceiling and smashed onto the middle of the table.

CHAPTER 7

*S*hards ricocheted in all directions as Pearl, Opal and Hazel screamed. A second piece of roofing smashed behind my chair.

"Under the table!" I yelled, and a mad scramble ensued.

Within seconds we were all huddled beneath the solid wood. Several more crashes sounded in quick succession, including another one that landed on the table, shaking the wooden frame.

"We need to get out of here," gasped Millie. "The whole castle is collapsing. Do you think we can make it if we run for the door?"

I met Sophie's eyes and knew she was thinking the same thing I was. We knew each other so well that we often didn't need to project our thoughts at all.

"I don't think we can do that," I said, speaking loudly enough for all eleven girls to hear. "The parchment said the boats wouldn't take us back until we're wearing those necklaces."

"But that was before the castle started falling apart," said Lilac. "Surely…" Her voice trailed away.

"Exactly," I said grimly. "Do any of us really think it was coincidence that the first stone fell just after Celine had read out our task?"

"*This* is our task." Celine nodded her agreement.

"Could we leave the younger ones here and make a dash for the tower without them?" asked Sophie. "We could bring their necklaces back down for them."

I bit my lip, considering it. "Have you still got the parchment, Celine?"

Some rustling and a quiet ouch sounded as Celine crawled toward me through the crowd of arms and legs under the table. "Here it is."

I read the words again. "It says, *together you must ascend to this tower, and each princess must claim a necklace.* It sounds like we all need to go. And even if it would let a few of us collect all the necklaces…"

"We have to think of our families." Sophie sounded tired and worn, so I sent her a small burst of mental warmth, and she gave me a faint smile. She looked around at all the other girls, focusing on the smaller ones. "I know it's scary, but we each have to at least try. That's the way the magic works, right? We each have to do our best."

Pearl and Opal shared a look, and then both nodded. I wanted to hug them for leading the way. No one else protested after that.

"Hazel, Marigold and I know this palace inside out," said Lilac. "We can lead the way to the tallest tower."

"We don't know what state the rest of the building is going to be in." My mind raced through all the potential dangers. "And there are a lot of us. I think we should split up and go in smaller groups. We may end up needing to use different routes."

I could see in Sophie's face that she didn't like the idea of splitting up, but she didn't say anything. "Millie, why don't you go with Lilac."

Millie nodded. "I know the Marinese palace pretty well, too. We can take the twins."

"Sophie, you go with Hazel."

"We'll go with them," said Emmeline decisively. Her input surprised me. I had almost forgotten her presence.

"All right, then. That leaves Blanche, Celine and me to go with Marigold." I smiled at the younger girl.

Marigold looked proud and terrified at the same time, and I felt a rush of anger at a system that tormented young girls.

The largest crash we'd heard yet sounded directly above our heads, and the wood of the table creaked ominously. "I think that's a sign it's time for us to get moving."

"We'll go first." Millie gestured for Pearl and Opal to join her at the end of the table.

"Wait!" said Sophie. "I've been watching the falling stone. It seems to come down in a pattern. First on the left, then on the right, then in the middle."

Thank goodness Sophie was just a little more thoughtful, and a little less reckless, than me. I hadn't thought of watching for patterns in the stone.

"Thanks," said Millie, too focused on the room in front of her to turn back toward us. She waited for the next crash and noted its position. "That way," she yelled pointing to the left, and the four of them dashed out toward the doorway.

Hazel, Sophie, Emmeline and Giselle crawled forward to take their places at the end of the table. A moment later they had disappeared as well.

I crawled forward and saw them racing away, their heads down, and their hands clasped over their necks. They moved in a sort of rhythm, moving from side to side in response to the crashes, following the directions Sophie had given to avoid the falling stone. Piles of rubble had accumulated all over the floor, so they often had to swing wide around the obstructions.

Marigold crouched beside me. "They sort of look like they're dancing," she whispered.

I smiled down at her. "Exactly! That's the way to think of it.

We're just going to dance our way across to the other side of the room. Now, let's go!"

I dashed forward, mimicking the protective pose the others had adopted. A piece of stone smashed to the floor in front of me, and I flinched away, leading the others to the right as the next piece fell far to the left.

I skipped around a large pile of rubble that looked like it contained several falls' worth of debris, veering back toward the left. I glanced under my lifted arm, checking the other three still followed me.

I reached out to Sophie, needing to know she was safe. *Did you all make it out?*

The entrance hall isn't as bad. I got the impression she was puffing, although a projection never actually sounded out of breath. *Just...messy.*

I forced my mind back to the throne room as I swung to the right again. We would see the entrance hall for ourselves soon enough.

I burst through the doorway, head still down. But when no further falling stone appeared ahead of us, I slowed and let the others catch up. I had expected to see at least one of the other groups at this point, but there was no sign of anyone. Probably because the large space was now filled with huge piles of gravel. The mounds rose and fell across every part of available floor space, obscuring my view.

"What in the kingdoms...?" muttered Celine.

I ignored her. "Which way?" I asked Marigold.

She bit her lip. "Lilac and Hazel will have taken the main stairs, I'm sure. But I think we'll go faster up the servants' stairs."

I had no choice but to trust her. "Well you're our leader, not them. So lead away."

She nodded, a look of determination on her face, and scrambled up the pile of gravel to our left. We all followed. After less than a minute, I understood why Sophie had sounded tired. Scrambling uphill through gravel was exhausting work.

We're going a back way, I told Sophie.

Good idea. She sounded shaken. *Because the main staircase just collapsed behind us.*

I gasped aloud, and Celine looked over at me questioningly. I shook my head and pressed forward. I could only hope this second staircase wouldn't collapse behind us, too, or we'd all be trapped on the upper levels.

All of our lovely dresses were covered in gravel dust by the time we reached an unadorned side door. Marigold pushed it gingerly open before I could stop her, but no fresh danger rushed through.

"Oh, good, it's clear," she said, reaching her foot toward the first step.

"Wait," I said, remembering Sophie's words. "Test each step before you put your full weight on it. That goes for all of us."

"I can go first," said Celine, stepping forward.

Marigold shook her head, "No, I can do it." She bit her lip before carefully testing the first one.

Slowly we made our way up the stairs without mishap. My pulse continued to race, however, and I couldn't let myself relax. We climbed up four flights before Marigold led the way out another door and into a long, narrow corridor.

"It's that door at the end." She pointed toward it. "One last flight of stairs and that's the top keep."

"Nearly there then," I said, forcing a smile. "Well done." I examined the corridor carefully but couldn't see any threats. "Let's move quickly."

We all took off racing down the corridor only to come to a sudden halt when something whizzed past our heads.

"What was that?" asked Blanche in a breathy voice.

"More stone. Get down on the ground." Celine dropped flat as she called the instruction, and we all mimicked her.

Looking up, I saw another small piece of masonry go flying past. The pieces seemed to be launching themselves from the walls and flying almost horizontally across the corridor before colliding with the opposite wall. They all seemed to be above waist height, though.

"We'll have to crawl," I said, pushing myself up onto my hands and knees. Slowly we advanced along the floor, hampered by our long skirts.

I found myself crawling beside Princess Blanche. I thought she came from Eliam, but I didn't dare project to Sophie to check. She might need her concentration right now. I glanced sideways at the other girl.

If I had thought her nickname of Snow fit before, it was nothing to how she looked now. I had never seen someone so pale.

"My father made me promise that I would come back to him." She spoke softly, squeezing her eyes shut for a moment.

I reached out and briefly patted one of her hands. "Of course you will. This is all just a contest, remember? I'm sure we can't actually be hurt." Was I trying to convince her or myself? "No one is going to die. Look—" I paused. "I think the stones have stopped."

I had no sooner said the final word, than a loud rumble shook the corridor, and a cloud of dust erupted around us. A scream pierced the air, laden with pain.

CHAPTER 8

I leaped to my feet and ran forward blindly. Not far down the corridor, I almost tripped over Marigold and Celine. A large section of corridor wall had collapsed, pinning Celine's right foot and lower leg.

She was sitting up, but only with Marigold's support, and she leaned heavily against the younger girl. She had stopped screaming, but her breath came in sharp pants, and her eyes remained tightly shut.

"Quick!" I said to Blanche, who had followed me more slowly. "Help me get her free."

Together we pushed and pulled, dragging the pieces of stone away from Celine's leg. As soon as her foot came free, she pushed herself backwards, away from the remaining pile of rubble, gasping loudly as her leg dragged against the floor.

I knelt beside her and touched her ankle lightly. She groaned. I looked up, and this time she met my eyes. She knew of my interest in healing and was mutely asking for my opinion on the injury.

"I'm sorry, Celine. I think it's broken." So much for my theory about none of us being hurt. I felt my heartbeat race faster, something I wouldn't have thought possible. What if the wall had collapsed onto her head?

There were twelve of us in this palace, and it could still happen. I looked at the other two girls who both watched Celine with horror. "I don't suppose either of you know anything about setting broken bones."

They both shook their heads silently. I hadn't expected anything else. Our doctors in Arcadia had never appreciated having a child or a princess underfoot, and I could only imagine the medical staff here felt the same way. I had only spent so many hours in our infirmary because my brother and sister-in-law had friends amongst the doctors and nurses. Friends who let me help when I could safely do so. But even with my experience, I still didn't trust myself to try to set an ankle on my own.

"I'm sorry, Celine," I said again. "I don't think there's anything we can do for you before we get back to the palace."

She took a deep breath and nodded. She closed her eyes for a moment, then opened them and attempted to push herself to her feet.

"Whoa," I said, but she sank back down on her own before I could intervene.

She shook her head and met my eyes. "There's no way I'm going to be able to make it up those next stairs. You'll have to bring my necklace down for me."

"Of course." I touched her hand as comfortingly as I could manage. "Don't worry, there's no way the Tourney could fault you for not trying."

I hated to leave her on her own, but none of the rest of us dared risk our families by staying behind with her. "We'll be back soon," I promised, gesturing for the other girls to follow me as I ran for the door. I didn't look back. I couldn't bear to see her lying there alone in the dirt.

We ascended the next set of stairs more quickly than was probably safe and burst into the large room at the top. All eight of the others stood grouped around a large table. I counted them and then counted again.

"Is everyone all right?" I counted a third time for good measure.

Sophie waved me over. "We're fine, although only just. Giselle was standing on the stairs when they collapsed, but Emmeline managed to catch her."

I looked at the Eldonians, impressed. They looked as impassive as ever.

"What about you? Wait…" Sophie's eyes roamed over us again and then flew to the door. "Where's Celine?"

I shook my head. "She couldn't get up here. It's her ankle. I think it's broken."

A sharp hiss of indrawn breath pulled my eyes toward Millie. She was wincing. "I broke my arm once." She rubbed at her left elbow.

I looked down at the table. Twelve necklaces—large, ornate and covered in jewels—lay scattered across the surface. They looked identical except for the color of the gems. "She's on her own down there. Let's hurry." I grabbed the first chain my hand landed on and shoved it over my head. Then I grabbed a second one for Celine.

The rest of the princesses followed, looping the gold and gems around their necks. The bright jewelry looked ridiculous against our tired faces and dirty gowns. I turned back to the door.

We raced back down, eleven of us now in a long line. Celine lay where we had left her, flat on her back, her eyes closed. I feared she had fainted, but she opened her eyes at the sound of our arrival and struggled into a sitting position. One of the younger twins whimpered at the sight of her.

"The main staircase collapsed," said Millie. "We'll need to use the servants' stairs."

"We came up that way," said Blanche. "They were fine when we left them."

"Millie, Lilac, you take the others and get out of here as fast as you can," I said. "Sophie and I will help Celine."

"Lilac and Hazel can lead the others. I'm staying to help you." Millie met my gaze defiantly.

I considered arguing, but I didn't have the energy—and we might actually need the help. "Fine. But let's get moving."

Lilac paused for a moment, as if torn, so I gave her my best glare. She grimaced, and then rushed down the corridor calling for the others to follow her. Hazel brought up the rear, glancing back at us with concern.

I took a deep breath before kneeling beside Celine. "This isn't going to be pleasant," I warned her.

She forced a small smile. "Has anything about this place been pleasant yet?" No one asked her whether she meant the Tourney or Marin itself.

Sophie knelt on her other side, and we positioned ourselves under each of her arms. Directing a steady string of projections toward each other, we managed to time our movements, rising smoothly to our feet and bringing Celine up with us. She swayed, her damaged leg held up off the ground, and her face full of strain.

"Good job. That's the way." I murmured a stream of quiet encouragement to her, paying no attention to the particular words. Millie, who had taken the extra necklace off me when I crouched down, thrust it over Celine's head.

Slowly we started toward the stairway. I hadn't heard any loud crashes yet, so I was hoping to find it still intact. When we reached the top, Millie darted around us, offering to go in front. I understood her unspoken intent. She would test the stairs and try to catch Celine if any of us tripped.

It seemed to take an interminable time to descend all four flights, Celine's hops becoming smaller and more exhausted as time went on. She didn't complain, or scream, but I could read the pain on her face and hear it in her frequent gasps and hisses.

When we reached the bottom, I nearly collapsed in relief. Until I saw the piles of gravel still filling the entrance hall. I wanted to scream. They had been hard enough to scale without an injured princess in tow.

I looked over at Sophie. She looked just as defeated as I felt. But what choice did we have? Slowly we began moving again. I could see no sign of the others, and I hoped they had long since made it safely out of the castle. No new danger had appeared since we had taken the necklaces, and I took that as a good sign.

Within seconds it became clear that Celine wasn't going to be able to hop her way up a giant mound of gravel, and we weren't going to be able to carry her on the unstable surface. We stopped, lowering her gently so she could sit. She stretched out her injured leg, but pulled the other knee up and buried her face in it.

There's only one way I can think of to do this, projected Sophie. I didn't need to see her expression to know how unhappy she was about it.

I sighed. *You're right. It's the only way.*

I knelt beside Celine. "We're going to have to drag you, Celine. If you lie back against the hill, we'll pull you along by your arms. Try to keep your ankle up, if you can." I was afraid she wouldn't have the strength to do it, but I hated to think what state her ankle would be in by the end of the process if she couldn't.

We started up the first hill. The three of us took turns, two at a time, pulling one of her hands each and advancing slowly backwards up the slope. Celine fainted before we made it off the first mound, and we all felt nothing but relief.

We could move slightly faster when we didn't have to worry about causing her more pain, but I still worried about her ankle. We turned Millie's short cloak into a small cushion to place under Celine's injured foot, but it didn't seem like nearly enough.

By the time we reached the great doors at the entrance to the palace, I could barely stand, every part of me trembling from exhaustion. Lilac, Hazel and Blanche all rushed forward as soon as we appeared and helped us carry Celine a few steps away from the building. I didn't look back. I had no wish to see the mirror palace ever again.

We rested briefly, all of us too shocked and spent for talking. Sophie eventually stirred, looking toward the lake. "The boats are back."

"We need to try to wake Celine," I said. "We won't be able to carry her the whole way."

"I'm awake," said a shaky voice, the words slightly slurred. I wanted to ask if she was all right, but I didn't really want to hear the answer, so I remained silent.

Once again Sophie and I crouched down on either side of her. This time we wobbled as we rose to full height, our fatigue hampering our movements.

Millie had shepherded the other girls ahead of us and most of the boats were full by the time we arrived at the edge of the lake. As carefully as we could, the three of us lifted Celine into a coracle, our feet splashing in the eerily warm water.

Once Celine had been safely placed inside, I collapsed over the edge of the closest boat. I lay there, not bothering to sit up, just watching the murky darkness overhead as I floated along. Perhaps I would just lie here forever.

All too soon, I felt the bump as I hit the other side. Forcing myself up, I saw with relief that Lilac and Blanche had enlisted Emmeline's help and already lifted Celine from her boat. Sophie and I stepped forward and took up our places under each of her arms, and the whole group started back down the path.

Somewhere in the golden grove, Celine slipped into a partial swoon. She remained on her feet but only just. We pushed on.

All the older girls were helping younger ones now. Lilac and Hazel flanked their younger sister, Marigold, who appeared to be crying. I hoped she didn't feel guilty for what had happened. It wasn't her fault.

I limped along in my threadbare dancing slippers, my shoulders aching from Celine's nearly dead weight. I kept mindlessly counting the girls in front of us, making sure, over and over, that we hadn't left anyone behind.

The ladder appeared at the end of the path, at last, and Millie began to help the youngest girls to climb. Pearl and Opal drooped from fatigue, their feet slipping on the rungs. Lilac stepped forward to help them, leaving Hazel to support Marigold on her own.

Finally, they all made it up, and Millie returned to help us with Celine. I eyed the ladder with profound misgiving. How in the kingdoms were we going to get her up those rungs?

"Lily?" Sophie's voice interrupted my musings.

I turned my head slowly to look at her. Perhaps she had an idea.

She didn't bother to speak again, merely pointed wordlessly past my head. I turned back around and saw that the last tree, the one closest to the ladder, had a branch that stretched out toward us like a reaching hand. And on the end of the branch, tucked into a small cleft in the wood, was a folded piece of parchment.

I leaned over, nearly unbalancing us all and eliciting a moan from Celine, and grabbed it. Opening it, I scanned the contents. A neat table had been drawn up in glistening black ink. Sophie, Millie and I were listed first, with equal points. All three Marinese princesses were close behind. Celine's name came last.

"Our scores," I said shortly.

Millie shook her head in disbelief. "I'd sort of forgotten it was a contest."

I sighed. "Let's think about that after we get Celine up the ladder."

"I can do it," Celine said between panting breaths. She seemed to have come out of her half-swoon.

"One way or another, you'll have to, I'm afraid."

We half carried her to the ladder and placed her hands on the rungs. "We'll come up behind you."

The ascent was slow and far from graceful, but somehow we all ended up once again in the small room at the top of the ladder. Millie had gone in front again, and pulled Celine up the last steps.

As soon as I stepped back, the trapdoor swung closed, disappearing into the floor. I stared down at it. Even knowing exactly where it was, I could see no sign of it. I looked around and noted that our necklaces had disappeared, along with the dirt and dust and gravel that had clung to our dresses. In fact, our clothes had returned to their original state. I glanced over at Celine but, from the grimace of pain on her face, the same restoration hadn't happened for her leg. Apparently our bodies could be harmed down there, even if nothing else could.

Lilac thrust the door of the room open, and princesses poured out.

A small group awaited us in the now empty ballroom. All traces of the party from earlier in the night had disappeared, efficiently removed by the servants, I presumed. The first hint of dawn shone through the long windows, but the waiting crowd still carried lanterns and candles. Had they stayed up for us all night, or had they risen early?

Lilac had been first through the door, and her calls for a doctor had already been taken up by other voices. When Sophie, Celine, and I finally emerged, the Duchess of Sessily, the head of Celine's delegation, rushed to our side, her face pale.

"Where has she been hurt?" she asked, gesturing for us to lay Celine down.

We did so gladly. Sophie sat beside her, holding her hand and talking to the duchess, but I stepped away, ceding my place to the doctors and nurses who poured into the ballroom.

I stared down at the parchment still clutched in my fingers, and then fisted my hand, scrunching the elegant paper. Looking up, my eyes fell on Prince Jonathan and sudden rage filled me with a burst of energy.

I strode over to confront him, not even noticing his far superior height. In my anger, I felt six feet tall. "You!" I poked my finger into his chest. "I am done with games. I want the truth, right now!"

"Truth?" He looked completely bewildered by my unexpected attack. He focused down on my face, and his eyes turned pleading. "We've told you nothing but the truth. I swear I would not lie to you."

"Well, then. Tell me this truth. How many princesses have died competing in this Tourney of yours?"

"Died?" He turned pale and glanced over my shoulder at Celine. "What are you talking about? No one has ever died!"

I deflated a little. He seemed genuinely shocked by my question. His strong hands reached out to grip my arms, and I could feel him shaking, the tremors passing through to me from the contact.

His eyes looked desperate as they bore into mine. "Lily! Are you all right? What happened to you down there?"

I opened my mouth to tell him exactly what had happened, still too angry to consider the rules. But nothing came out. I tried again. Still nothing.

Sophie! Try to tell the duchess what happened.

But Lily, the rules!

I don't care. Just try.

A moment of silence.

Oh.

Yes.

Another moment of silence. *You really shouldn't have tried, you know. Think of our family.*

I didn't reply, hit by a sudden wave of guilt. I couldn't let myself get out of control like that. Now, more than ever. Now that I had seen for myself just how deadly serious this competition truly was.

I pulled myself out of Jon's grip. "I'm sorry," I said quietly. "I'm not allowed to say."

He stepped forward and pulled me into his arms. For a moment I resisted, and then I melted against him—glad, just briefly, to rely on someone else's strength.

"No, Lily," he said, his voice thick. "I'm the one who's sorry."

CHAPTER 9

*J*think I might have actually drifted off for a moment against the safety of Jon's chest, because I wasn't sure how much time had passed when Sophie called to me. I started and pulled back, too tired to even flush at the way I had been clinging to him.

Sophie's expression told me that there would be questions later. But she was far too tired to ask them now. With Celine in the care of the duchess, I handed the parchment of scores to Jon's father, not bothering to flatten it out, and allowed our own delegation head, Helena, to guide us to our rooms. The baroness' eyes expressed her sympathy, but thankfully she refrained from questions. Whether she knew we couldn't answer them, or she just recognized our fatigue, I didn't know. I appreciated it either way.

She had requested a shared guest suite for us, and I imagined the palace staff had been happy to oblige. Marin already seemed full of visitors, and accommodating so many unexpected and high-ranked newcomers with no notice couldn't have been easy.

I felt too tired to even project to Sophie, but her presence comforted me nonetheless. We helped each other unlace our dresses, hurrying into the nightgowns that someone had lain out for us. Collapsing into my bed, I passed out within seconds.

~

Awareness returned slowly, my head groggy and my body aching. It took me several long moments to remember why. When the memories finally hit, I rolled onto my back and stared up at the canopy overhead. Far too many unlikely things had happened to be quickly or easily understood. I reached out with my mind, testing if Sophie was awake.

Good morning, she projected back.

Oh, good, you're awake. Did all that really happen?

I think so. I heard her yawn and move beneath her blankets, as if stretching. *What time is it?*

I rolled over onto my side, facing toward her bed, which lay between me and the window. *No idea. Those are effective curtains.* The heavy velvet reached all the way to the floor, blocking all light from entering the room. *Either that, or we slept the entire day and it's already night again.*

I hope not! I want to see the sun.

Feel free to get up and open the curtains, then.

Ha, you wish! Why don't you get up?

I flopped over onto my back again and resumed staring at the canopy. *Not a chance. I think I may never move again.*

Sophie sighed. *Except that we have to go back there again in three days.*

I shuddered.

I've been lying here calculating it, she continued.

How depressing.

She ignored me. *The duke said the Tourney ends on the first day of summer. And the rules said we have to be in that room every three days. So that means we have* fifteen *more events.*

Did I mention how depressing you're being? We were both silent for a moment. *My feet hurt.*

My everything hurts.

We both broke out into sudden laughter. When the giggles finally subsided, I wiped the tears from my eyes. "I think we needed that." I forced myself to sit up. "What *is* the time?"

"Mid-afternoon," said Helena, gliding into the room. "I thought I might find you awake at last."

She had brought two maids with her, each carrying a heavily-laden tray of food. I leaped out of bed, suddenly discovering motivation to move, and devoured it gratefully. I could barely remember when I had last eaten.

She sat with us while we ate, updating us on Celine's condition—her ankle had been set, and the doctors had given her medicine to ensure she slept all day—and telling us that we had the day off and were under strict orders to do nothing but rest.

"There will be time enough for official meetings and receptions tomorrow, when you've had another good night's sleep. And the day after. And then that night, there will be another ball as well."

"Another one already?"

"Apparently you will compete every three nights, and every competition will be preceded by a ball."

"Seriously?" Sophie groaned. "Because competing in a ball-gown and dancing slippers is such an ideal scenario."

I winced at the thought. I could only hope not every night would be as physical and exhausting.

Once we had eaten and dressed, we asked a servant to direct us to some greenery. We discovered extensive gardens spread behind the palace, full of gravel paths, bright flowers and well-sculpted bushes. The sun felt comfortably warm, and a cool breeze blew past our faces. We sat on a well-placed bench, enjoying the view in silence. Surrounded by living, green trees, I felt a world away from the strange underground groves.

"Good afternoon," said a warm, deep voice. I recognized it easily and then wondered why. We had only spoken twice before.

Prince Jonathan approached us with two young men at his side. Thankfully Prince Oliver was not among them. I recognized them both from the opening ceremony, though. I could hardly believe the formal event had been only this time the day before. It felt like a world ago.

"This is a happy coincidence." He smiled down at us. "Gabe and Teddy have been dying to meet you."

"Thanks, Jon," said one of them, shaking his head. He turned to us. "I promise neither of us is as desperate as that makes us sound."

Jon laughed, looking entirely unrepentant. "That scapegrace is Prince Gabriel of Talinos."

Prince Gabriel bowed while I tried to remember what, if anything, I knew about Talinos. *Does he have sisters in the Tourney?*

You really are hopeless you know. Sophie tutted at me in her mind.

Yes, yes, I know. But does he?

The other twins, Pearl and Opal. Talinos is the southern one to the east of here.

Ah, of course. I remembered now. The Emissary had told us all about the various kingdoms on our voyage here, showing us maps and teaching us their names. Although I was gradually starting to realize how much he had left out.

The city-state duchy of Marin shared a land mass, and borders, with the large, northern Palinar and the almost-equally-large, southern Talinos. Across the strait, northern Eldon and southern Eliam were both smaller. As was the southern island kingdom of Trione.

Sophie was busy saying all the proper things and covering up my confused silence. I noticed Jon was watching me, a question in his eyes, so I forced myself to join in the conversation.

I turned to his other companion. "And you must be Prince..."

Theodore.

"...Theodore," I added, smoothly. "Millie's twin." *The cute one on the end.*

Sophie kicked my foot, her movement hidden by our large skirts. *He's a little young.*

What do you mean? Millie's the same age as us.

Exactly!

I chuckled to myself at her apparent new-found interest in older men.

Prince Theodore bowed politely, but the slightly dreamy look I had noticed the day before gave him an abstracted air. Even so, he didn't have the coldness of Oliver.

"I have to apologize for my brother here," said another familiar voice. Millie rushed down the path and dropped onto the bench beside us. "I've been looking for you everywhere, by the way." I wasn't sure if she meant us or her brother, but she kept talking, so I didn't have the chance to ask. "Teddy used to be a lot more fun. But he had a bit of an accident on the voyage here."

"Yes." Jonathan laughed. "We've been hearing all about it."

Millie rolled her eyes. "I'll bet you have. Not that there's that much to tell."

"I hope it wasn't a serious accident," said Sophie.

"Less of an accident," Theodore assured her earnestly, "and more of a divine encounter."

Millie groaned. "Just listen to him!"

I grinned. "Now I'm really curious. Tell me the whole story."

Theodore opened his mouth, presumably to oblige, but his twin cut him off. "Absolutely not. We'll be here all day. And I'm sure Gabe and Jon have heard enough about it. I'll tell it."

She turned slightly to face us. "Trione is an island, so we had to sail here. Our whole family decided to come as it's been forever since we visited Marin. That meant Daisy was with us. Our younger sister," she broke off to explain. "Princess Margaret, really, but don't bother calling her that, she won't know who you're talking about."

"She's a handful," said Gabriel, with a chuckle.

"Poor Gabe should know," said Millie, with a grin. "He fostered with us for eight years—the result of some alliance-strengthening treaty—and she hero worships him."

"I'd like to meet her," said Sophie with a smile of her own.

Would you really?

Sophie sent a laugh back. *She sounds like us when we were children.*

"Anyway," Millie continued, "a storm came up on the way and Daisy became frightened. She'd been filling her head with terrifying stories about the Beast and the Princess Tourney, so she was already on edge. Teddy started playing around, acting like a fool to show her there wasn't anything to fear."

"I don't remember the word 'fool' coming into the story we heard," said Gabe, elbowing his foster-brother in the side.

"The best mistake I ever made," said Teddy dreamily.

Millie coughed. "To keep it short, in his efforts to show her how safe it was, he managed to prove exactly the opposite by falling off the side of the ship. Everyone panicked. It wasn't a very big storm, but we thought he was gone for sure." She shook her head, and I saw a remnant of real fear in her face. I shivered. I could swim well, but I had never liked deep water because I didn't like not knowing what might be lurking beneath my feet. A storm only made it worse. I would have been terrified in either of their places.

"Only somehow he managed to resurface," Millie continued, "and he hadn't been swept away from the ship, either. We threw him a rope and hauled him back on board."

"That sounds unpleasant. But I'm glad it had a happy ending," said Sophie.

"If only that were the end of it," said Millie. "Apparently, while nearly drowning, Teddy here didn't have the good sense to see his life flashing before his eyes. Instead he hallucinated a beautiful girl swimming through the water and saving his life."

"Hallucinated?" I asked.

"No!" Teddy exclaimed. "It wasn't a hallucination. That's what I keep telling everyone. She was real. She was young and beautiful, and she saved my life. She even sang while she did it, and I've never heard such a lovely voice." He looked over our shoulders and seemed lost in his memory, or dream, or whatever it was.

"So now he's determined to find this magical girl of the sea," said Millie, finishing her tale. "And to make us suffer through endless descriptions of her beauty and grace and bravery and…" She sighed. "I keep hoping he's going to snap out of it."

I considered the strange story. "How did she survive the storm? And what was she doing in the ocean? And why didn't she come on board the ship with you? And how on earth could she be *singing* while swimming through a storm and dragging a man behind her?"

"All excellent questions!" Millie spun around to face her brother, placing her hands on her knees and leaning forward with fake expectation. "Perhaps you'd like to enlighten the fair princess as to the answers?"

"I have no answers, you know that," said Teddy, shaking his head at his sister. "But I intend to find them, however long it takes."

"Believe me, he cannot find them quickly enough for my liking," Millie muttered in our direction. Her next comment was directed at the princes. "But that's quite enough of that topic of conversation. It's been far too long since I've had the chance to see the gorgeous rose gardens here, and Lilac tells me they're in full bloom. So I expect an escort." She turned back to us. "Would you like to see them? They truly are exquisite."

Sophie nodded and stood up, but I shook my head. Sophie loved roses, but my liking for flowers was only middling. Their attraction didn't override the ache in my feet, and I had no desire to wander too far afield. Gabe offered his arm to Millie and, after a poke from his sister, Teddy offered his to Sophie.

"I'll stay here with Princess Lily," said Jon.

Sophie raised an eyebrow at me as she began to move away. *Don't think I've forgotten last night, either,* she warned. *The two of you were looking very friendly. We're going to need to have a talk, you and me.*

There's nothing to talk about, I protested, although I knew I wasn't getting out of it that easily.

Mmhmmm, she projected dismissively as they all disappeared down the path.

I stood, feeling awkward sitting now that Jonathan was the only other person present.

"Don't stand for me," he said, with a gallant smile. "I'm perfectly happy to sit."

"Do you mind if we move onto the grass?" I asked. "I know it's not the most decorous thing to do, but I'd like to feel something alive and growing beneath my fingers."

"Certainly." He led the way to a large, sunny patch of grass just off the path.

I sat, just as music started up somewhere out of sight. The charming, lively melody floated through the air from the direction of the city.

"It sounds like someone else is enjoying the beautiful weather." Jon sat beside me, tapping his foot to the rhythm. "They must be dancing in one of the market squares."

"Ugh. Not me. I've had enough dancing for now, thank you very much." I leaned back, bracing myself with my arms and turning my closed eyes up toward the sky. The sun beat warmly on my face. "I'm trying to stay off my feet today."

I could hear Jon lie down on the grass beside me. His informal posture reminded me of the way he had held me the night before. I forced myself to keep my eyes closed and not look at him. Why did I need to keep reminding myself that I hardly knew this prince? I wished he didn't have such an effect on me.

A pause followed before he spoke. "Is that what you all were doing in there? Dancing?" I cracked an eye open and noticed that his expression didn't quite match his casual tone. "We didn't hear a peep the whole time you were gone, you know. Rumor is that there must be some sort of secret passage in there, but no one has any idea where it could lead. And the servants said all of your dancing slippers were worn completely through. Did Celine break her ankle dancing with some handsome prince?"

I wished I could tell him about the deadly dance we had all been forced to perform. "Why?" I asked instead, keeping my voice light. "Are you jealous?"

He propped himself up on one elbow and met my eyes. "Of Celine's dancing partner? No."

I looked away, a faint flush creeping up my neck.

CHAPTER 10

*W*hen I had myself under control again, I looked back up to find he had also turned away. Did he realize he had made me uncomfortable? Did he regret his words?

Perhaps so, since he immediately changed the subject. "It's been a long time since we had representatives from all the kingdoms here." He still didn't meet my eyes. "Everyone except Palinar has sent someone for the Tourney, so we've already scheduled a number of meetings for tomorrow. So, in that sense, at least, you can take advantage of the timing of your arrival." He didn't sound happy about it.

I don't think Marin's too pleased that we turned up just in time to meet royal delegations from all the kingdoms, I projected to Sophie. *I think they were hoping to get in first and lock us into an alliance before we saw our other options. Which makes sense if they're not too prosperous.*

Oh, for goodness sake! Sophie sounded half-exasperated, half-amused. *You're sitting in the sun on a beautiful day with a rather attractive prince. You should be flirting, not talking politics!*

Is that what you're doing over there amongst the roses?

Of course! Marigold was right, Prince Gabriel is charming. A mental giggle accompanied the words, although I suspected she was merely teasing me.

I didn't respond because I knew she would take issue with me if I did. Sophie and I had always done everything together, we were the ultimate team. But, ever since her illness as a child, Sophie had been more prone to sickness than me. And our only brother was eight years older, so from as early as I could remember, I had known that we needed to look after ourselves. For years the two of us were wrapped up in our own world, and the only thing I worried about was keeping her well.

Then Alyssa, now our sister-in-law, came along and showed us that our responsibilities as princesses extended beyond ourselves. She had taught us how to fulfill our roles properly, but now Sophie thought I'd taken the lesson too far. That I'd just extended my efforts to care for her into an attempt to care for everyone. But what was wrong with that? Wasn't it a princess' job to care for everyone?

And that had never been truer than now. Between my family, my kingdom, the Tourney and my sister, I had too many responsibilities to think about flirtation. Especially now I knew how this land approached marriages of alliance. From the sounds of things, one way or another, love didn't play much of a part. So, what was the point in letting my mind dwell on romance?

Jon seemed to take my abstraction as disapproval. "But, my apologies, I don't know what I'm thinking to bore you with such topics on such a lovely day."

I shook my head. "You take your role and responsibilities seriously. That's a good thing and nothing to apologize for."

"Yes," he grinned over at me ruefully. "I often have lovely young ladies lining up to compliment me on my responsibility. A truly attractive quality."

I laughed. "You don't? You shock me. What's wrong with Marin?"

I had meant the comment as a joke, but a shadow passed over

his face at my words. I wanted to kick myself for being so clumsy. I could have sworn I was usually more deft.

"It seems like a lovely place," I said, trying to regain ground. "I've actually never been in a city-state before."

He brightened. "Would you like to see it? I would love to show you around one day. And your sister as well, of course. I'm sure Gabe and Teddy and Millie could be convinced to join us. Do you ride?"

"Oh, yes!" I sat up straight at the thought of riding again. "It feels like an age since I last went out." My thoughts turned wistfully to my beautiful riding mare at home. The Emissary had offered for me to bring her, but I hadn't wanted to subject her to the journey when I didn't know how much opportunity I would even have for riding.

"Then it would be my pleasure to give you the opportunity. I might not be able to find a free day until next week, but I'll do what I can."

"Thank you," I said, just as I spotted the others in the distance. We stood, waiting for them to reach us, but were accosted by a footman before they arrived.

He bowed low. "Your Royal Highnesses. I have been sent with a message for Princesses Liliana and Sophia."

"Princess Lily and Princess Sophie, please," I said absently, as I took the folded note and skimmed its contents. Sophie hurried over and peered around me. "It's Celine. She's awake, and she wants to see us."

"Please take her our condolences and wishes for a speedy recovery," said Jon, and the other two princes chimed in with their agreement.

"I'm coming with you," said Millie, abandoning her brother and striding over to us. "I want to see how she is."

As the three of us moved out of earshot, Millie added, "And we need to have a conversation without the boys." For a moment I thought she meant to chide me on Prince Jonathan as well, but a glance at her face disabused me of that idea. She looked far too serious.

"The Tourney?" asked Sophie.

Millie nodded but didn't elaborate. Our pace picked up, and we arrived at the door to Celine's suite within minutes. Celine's delegation head was clearly keeping a close eye on her condition, since it was the Duchess of Sessily herself who let us in before excusing herself at a significant look from Celine.

The Lanoverian princess looked tired and pale, propped up in bed with her leg stretched out on top of the coverlet. Sophie rushed over, while Millie and I approached more slowly.

"I told the duchess I needed to speak to you alone," said Celine, before any of us could greet her. "I know there's not much we can say—I've already tested it out—but we still need to talk. And I suspect it will be a lot easier when it's just us."

"I hope you don't mind that I tagged along," said Millie.

"No, of course not," said Celine. "You were down there too and are as much involved as any of us."

"But tell us your news first," said Sophie. "What have the doctors said about your ankle?"

Celine's shoulders slumped. "A break, of course. And made a great deal worse by the delay in treatment."

I winced, remembering the way we had been forced to drag her across the hills of gravel.

"I passed out early in their examination, and they managed to set it before I came around, thank goodness. It's bound with a splint now, and I've been ordered on complete bed rest."

Sophie winced. "You poor thing. Not for the whole six weeks of healing, I hope!"

Celine's face, which had been looking grim ever since our arrival, darkened even further. "No, indeed," she said. "Impossible, in fact, since in two nights' time, I will need to present myself in the ball room once again."

"What?" Sophie looked outraged. "They can't possibly expect you to continue in the Tourney!"

I glanced over at Millie who held her bottom lip between her teeth, her gaze fixed on the ground. She looked pale but not surprised.

"Let me guess." I tried to keep the resentment out of my voice for the sake of our new friend. "They were full of apologies, but the rules must be followed. And the rules make no allowance for injury."

"Got it in one," said Celine.

"But...your ankle," said Sophie in a whisper.

"The doctors have bound the splint in starched bandages to keep the ankle as immobile as possible." Celine shifted on the bed uncomfortably. "And they have promised to make me a pair of crutches. But, one way or another, I must be in that room when the time comes."

We all stared at her with varying degrees of discomfort.

"Have you tried calling for your godmother?" I asked. "This Tourney is putting you at serious risk."

She winced. "I tried. She didn't come."

Sophie grimaced. "I tried, too." I stared at her in surprise, and she shrugged. "Nothing happened."

Why didn't you tell me?

It was first thing after I woke up. You were still sleeping. When she didn't come, there didn't seem any point mentioning it. I would have told you later, it just didn't seem like cheery morning news.

"I wish I had a godmother." Millie sighed.

"It wouldn't do you much good given they seem to have an aversion to this land," said Celine. She forced a small smile and shrugged. "The doctors still believe the prognosis is good. But they have warned me to place as little stress on it as possible."

"I don't understand!" Sophie burst out. "Who would set up such a competition? What sort of way is this to pick a bride?"

Instinctively, I reached out for her in my mind. The warm

companionship of her presence washed over me, neither of us able to change the situation but glad to be in it together.

"I don't think that it was like this in the past," said Millie, finally speaking up. "I've heard people say that the Tourney changes depending on who called it. Its purpose is to find the perfect wife and queen for that specific ruler, after all. They say each Tourney reflects the man behind it." She looked at us with wide eyes. "The rumors must be true. Prince Dominic is a monster." She shuddered. "Perhaps the Tourney is only fulfilling its role—perhaps only the strongest of us has a chance of surviving the Beast."

The fear that shone in her eyes also roiled in my gut. I pushed it aside. "It's no good thinking about the end of the Tourney yet. After what happened to Celine, we need to focus on the competition itself. For the collaborative phase, at least, our one goal has to be to keep everyone alive."

For a moment there was silence, and then Sophie took a deep breath and nodded. "The younger girls, especially Pearl and Opal, aren't going to make it without us. They need to be our focus." Her eyes met mine, and she didn't need to project any words for me to understand her thoughts.

We had once felt young and alone, and an older girl had put herself at risk to protect us. Alyssa was our sister-in-law now, a beloved family member, but she had owed us nothing back then. And when I looked at tiny Pearl and Opal, still children, really—and even Marigold and Giselle—I saw our younger selves. Sophie might think I had taken my sense of responsibility too far, but I knew she saw us in these young girls, too.

Celine, unaware of our silent memories, nodded. "And I'm afraid I'm not going to be much help. I'll be worse than dead weight, in fact. I'm going to need your assistance just to get up and down that blasted ladder. Which means it's all on the three of you. Lilac should be some help, but I didn't notice that Emmeline putting herself out too much."

"Try not to worry too much, Celine," I said. "You'll go crazy cooped up in here, if you do. We'll have to lead them, certainly, but you saw Marigold last night. Just because they're young doesn't mean they can't help themselves, too. Remember when you were fourteen."

The ghost of a smile crossed her lips. Celine was proud of her own adventures at fourteen. I remembered her complaining at the time about her older sister shutting her out of the action. Perhaps she understood her sister's perspective better now.

A knock sounded on the door, and the Duchess of Sessily entered without waiting for an answer. "Princess Celine needs her rest, Your Highnesses. The doctors have left strict instructions."

"Of course." Sophie rose from where she had been sitting on the edge of Celine's bed. She looked down at our friend. "We'll come back tomorrow."

Celine managed a smile. "I don't envy you sitting through all those boring meetings." As Sophie began to move away, she reached out and grabbed her arm. "Make sure you do come back to visit me." I could read panic in her eyes. "I don't cope well with inactivity."

I suppressed a smile. After spending weeks on a sailing ship with her, the admission hardly came as a surprise.

"Of course we will," said Millie. "And I'll let the other girls know, too. They can bring some books and games for you. It will be good for them to have something to focus on other than fear for the next event."

The duchess glanced at her sharply but didn't say anything. I didn't know her well enough to guess if she was reacting to the prospect of an invasion of her sick room, or to the mention of the Tourney. As someone used to always being one step ahead, it must gall her not to have access to any information about the events. But, for once, she could do nothing about it.

~

While the diplomatic meetings the next day weren't as boring as Celine had feared, I did find it hard to focus. Thoughts of the following evening with its ball and its Tourney event kept looming. And I clearly wasn't the only one obsessing over the Tourney. It lingered in the background of every meeting, affecting every discussion, every proposed alliance. In the end, only one kingdom would be affected by the Tourney's outcome, but until we knew who, everyone was affected.

Some of the other young royals hadn't bothered to attend the meetings at all. And, of those who did, only the direct heirs had seats at the table. The rest of us were relegated to 'seats of honor' against the walls. Such conduct hardly surprised me. Seventeen-year-old girls had never been highly prized as negotiators or diplomats, regardless of our royal standing. At least I knew the baron and baroness respected Sophie and me enough to consult us and keep us informed between sessions.

The meetings between the various rulers and delegation heads from the represented kingdoms were followed by a series of meetings with important Marinese merchants, craftsmen and nobles. Each group proved eager to know more of life in Arcadia and Lanover and, in particular, what trade might usefully be established and what skills and knowledge we might possess that they did not. And, of course, our own delegations were eager to know the same information from them.

The final session broke off in time for the evening meal, with promises to resume the next day. I resolved not to attend. Though unspoken, it was clear that no firm agreements would be made until the end of the Tourney, so I no longer felt guilty about devoting my energy to the competition.

Prince Jonathan had attended every meeting. He participated actively, showing respect for all, regardless of station, and a keen sense of diplomacy. My eyes were continually drawn back to him during the discussions, and I had to keep reminding myself that he actually held a junior position compared to many of those present. I found it easy to forget given his confidence and intelligence. A couple of times his eyes met mine across the room, and I wished I had something useful to contribute, instead of being relegated to the wall in an honorary position.

But some of those present seemed to dismiss Jon because of his age. One man in particular, a merchant, spoke to him with barely-concealed contempt. Jon maintained his calm and his diplomatic smile, but I fumed on his behalf. How could anyone fail to see the value Jon brought to the discussions? And that was without taking into consideration the respect that was due him as a member of the host royal family.

Listen to that man! I projected to Sophie. *You would think Jon was ten, not nineteen, from the way that merchant is talking.*

Sophie seemed calmer about the whole thing. *Yes, but that particular merchant seems to talk to everyone that way. At least everyone from his own duchy. He's respectful enough to our people.*

Ugh. I shivered slightly. *Listen to him now, oozing charm all over the baron and baroness. Do you know who he is? I don't want Arcadia making any deals with him, but I didn't catch his name.*

Of course you didn't, was there any chance you would? Sophie seemed to find this more humorous than it warranted.

Well, did you? And don't say 'Of course, I did'!

Of course I did! Sophie's placid reply almost made me laugh out loud.

Well, then? I prompted her.

Sir Oswald. Apparently he was recently knighted for his services to the duchy.

I sent her a mental grimace. *Why do I get the feeling that means he made a large financial contribution to some project or other?*

Maybe because he seems like that type?

"An excellent point, Your Grace," said Sir Oswald to the Duchess of Sessily. "I myself have frequently recommended to our own duke that we adopt such a system. I have great hopes to see it implemented yet."

There you go, projected Sophie, *he isn't just disrespectful to your Prince Jon. He's even disrespectful to Jon's father.*

Pompous idiot. I frowned at him. *And he's not* my *prince.*

The Lanoverian duchess had responded civilly, if a little dampeningly, and the conversation moved on. I had my eye on Sir Oswald after that, though, and I didn't like what I saw. It only made me more determined not to attend the next day.

As it turned out, I had less free time than I had hoped. The traditions of this land had once again reared their heads and insisted that we attend the ball that evening in full formal attire. The only thing I could think was that Millie must have been right and that previous Tourneys had been a great deal less physically demanding. But we could hardly explain the true situation to those insisting tradition be maintained.

"The duke seems determined to ensure that his duchy cannot be faulted on any aspect of their running of the Tourney," said the baroness in our rooms that afternoon.

"It must be costing him a lot, hosting so many visitors and festivities." I glanced across at Helena, and the baroness nodded her agreement. "I wonder if it's a problem for them? If we're right about their lack of finances, that is."

"Never mind finances or their lack," said Sophie, her head buried in one of our wardrobes, "whatever are we going to wear tonight?" She pulled herself out and turned to glare at me. "That's a far more immediate question."

The dancing slippers were an unfortunate requirement, but we could do nothing about them. "If you continue to wear them through at such a rate, we shall have to ask the duchy to supply more," said Helena.

I hoped it wouldn't come to that. Surely every night could not be as demanding as the first had been? I just didn't see how we could survive an endless run of such events.

"What about this one?" asked Sophie, holding up a dress.

Helena and I both considered it.

"The skirt is a little on the large side." I frowned at it.

"Yes, but I thought it would give me freedom of movement," Sophie replied.

It took a great deal more such conversation before we settled on a dress for each of us, and Helena left with a large pile of gowns and promises to find the palace seamstresses. If we were to attend a ball and a Tourney event every three days, we would need some adjustments made to our wardrobe.

As we entered the ballroom, I glanced across at Sophie. She looked stunning in pale gold, the tight bodice blossoming into a full skirt. I matched her perfectly in pale blue, our favorite colors.

Who were we fooling? We didn't pick the most practical dresses after all, did we? I shook my head at our foolishness. *We just picked our favorites.*

Perhaps our greatest need was for a little extra courage? Sophie suggested. *That has its own practicality.*

Impulsively I reached over and squeezed her tight. *Thank goodness you're here, Soph. I don't think I could do it on my own.*

No, you probably couldn't. She grinned at me. *And I'm glad you occasionally remember it. Don't think I don't know you're trying to protect me still, even after all these years.*

A tall figure called our attention back to the ballroom. Prince Jonathan stood in front of us, his wide-eyed gaze moving between us before settling on me. "Dance with me?"

CHAPTER 11

*W*hat was that about him not being your prince again? asked Sophie as Jon led me into the dance.

That's called a lucky guess, I told her. *It could just as easily be you dancing with him right now.*

She just laughed at me.

Jon spun me around, still raptly gazing at me. "You look stunning, Lily."

I blinked. Was it possible it hadn't been just a guess? "You really can tell us apart?" He had said he'd chosen me specifically last time we danced, but I now realized that I hadn't fully believed him. "Most people find that difficult, unless they know us well."

"Maybe that means I know you well."

I raised both eyebrows at him.

He laughed. "Fine, I'll tell you my secret…Sophie has brighter hair than yours. It's more gold."

He was right, but I was a little surprised he had picked up on the subtle distinction. *Apparently Jon can tell us apart, he's noticed that your hair is brighter,* I projected to Sophie across the dance floor.

A moment later she whirled past in the arms of Gabe, giving me a stern look when our eyes met. *Don't read too much into it, Lil. I'm sure he doesn't mean to insult your hair.*

As usual Sophie had seen straight through me. I sternly reprimanded myself for the disappointed pang. I had already decided I had no time for flirting, and now my heart needed to fall into line. What did it matter that there were two small differences between us—one more flattering to each of us, and that Jon had noticed the less-flattering difference to me? It really made no difference at all.

"Very observant," I said, trying to keep my voice light. "I award you all the points."

He smiled at my attempted Tourney humor, but his eyes looked all too knowing. He leaned in close and whispered in my ear, "That and your eyes are deeper. Bluer."

Heat crept up my cheeks, and I told myself I did not feel a thrill shooting through me at his closeness and the feel of his warm breath against my face. But I didn't seem to be listening.

When the music changed, neither of us pulled away, and I let him draw me into a second dance. And somehow the second became a third. But I retained enough sense to remove myself from the dance floor after that.

Jon left to find me a drink, and I positioned myself near one of the tall windows, fanning my face. The main Marinese ballroom was the largest I had ever seen. I imagined size was a necessity when you hosted combined events for six kingdoms. The large crystal and gold chandeliers reminded me of the wealth I had expected to find in this duchy. If Marin were struggling now, it had certainly not always been so.

"I suppose you have much finer chandeliers at home," said an unfamiliar voice beside my elbow. I turned and my mind went blank. I scrambled to place the vaguely familiar face but came up empty.

Sophie! I called in a panic. *I've got nothing. I'm against the windows.*

A pause that felt like forever, but probably only lasted a couple of seconds ensued.

Oh, I see you. But I can't recall a name either. I don't think we've met her.

But she looks familiar.

Probably because she spent a large part of the last ball glaring at us, if I remember correctly. Sophie sounded less than pleased. *Watch your step.*

"Oh no," I said, keeping my face neutral, "these are quite the finest examples of chandeliers I've ever seen."

The girl looked torn between pride and disgust. She was tall and willowy, pretty although her features were too thin for classical beauty.

"Lanover might have something similar, though," I suggested, "they're wealthier than Arcadia." I couldn't immediately call to mind the lighting in the Lanoverian ballroom, so the statement was true enough. And Lanover *was* the wealthiest of the Four Kingdoms. I merely failed to mention that my kingdom was also enjoying a time of heightened prosperity. Given her apparent preoccupation with fancy decorations, I hoped the insinuation that Arcadia was poor might drive the girl away.

I felt a little guilty for sending her in Celine's direction. But the other princess, who had just made an appearance hobbling on two wooden crutches, was flanked by the formidable figure of the Duchess of Sessily, so I figured she was safe.

The disgust on the girl's face grew at my words and then quickly fell away. I turned to follow her gaze and saw Jon returning with two drinks. The girl dipped into a deep curtsey, but something about the way her eyes lingered on the prince seemed less respectful. If I had to put a name to it, I would have labeled it as hunger.

I shifted slightly, and Jon seemed to pick up on my discomfort. He gave the girl a small bow and a smile. "A pleasure to see you, Corinna, but I'm afraid I must steal Princess Lily away. State business, you understand."

The girl, Corinna, looked disappointed, but she could hardly protest. I took Jon's arm, and we hurried away.

"State business, is it?" I raised an eyebrow at him, a smile lurking on my lips.

"I'm the prince, remember." He directed an unrepentant grin at me. "Anything I do is state business."

"I could almost feel sorry for her," I said, but he quickly shook his head.

"There's no need, I assure you. Corinna is Sir Oswald's daughter, and he's the second richest merchant in Marin. And now a knight as well." He sighed. "I shouldn't be so harsh, perhaps, but the whole family is rather insufferable."

"From the little I've seen, I recommend you stay far away," I agreed promptly. "Unless you have a particular interest in chandeliers."

"Chandeliers?" He looked adorably confused.

"Never mind." I shook my head. "Now, were you planning to actually hand that drink over?"

"What? Oh!" He looked down as if he had forgotten all about the glasses he held. I compared his laughing expression now with the day before as he patiently ignored Sir Oswald's snide remarks, and I wanted to go back and give Corinna a piece of my mind. I refrained, but it was a close thing.

What's got you steaming at the ears? Sophie glided up, her hand resting on Teddy's arm, now, although Gabe and Millie followed close behind.

I'll explain later, I said. Then couldn't help adding, *That was Corinna, Sir Oswald's daughter.*

Ah! Sophie gave me a knowing look, her eyes drifting significantly toward Jon.

I shook my head at her. *Now is not the time. There's something a bit more important going on tonight, remember.*

She instantly sobered, just as a loud bell chimed through the packed ballroom.

"That seems early." I glanced around at the locals.

"I don't think it has a set time." Millie glanced nervously toward the small door in the side wall. "I believe each ball is different."

"Well, I'm glad not to be forced to wait around," I said, and Sophie nodded her agreement.

"We should probably get going, before the officials come to round us up again."

The princes followed us across the room, the crowd parting before us. When we reached the door, we found the other princesses gathered. Only Celine was missing, and I could see her hobbling through the crowd.

As soon as she arrived, the door opened, and we all filed through in order. One of the Talinosian twins drew a breath that sounded suspiciously like a sob, but everyone else remained quiet. What horrors awaited us tonight?

CHAPTER 12

*A*fter the destruction of the mirror palace during the previous event, Sophie and I had speculated that the trap door might lead us somewhere different tonight. But the ladder deposited us back in the same grove of silver.

We decided to lower Celine down by her arms in the end—Millie and I at the top, and Sophie and Lilac at the bottom. Celine bore the whole ordeal with grace, and we were soon making our way down the path once again.

"Do you think we'll be doing the event in the ruins of the palace?" asked Hazel.

"How would we know?" Marigold rolled her eyes. "That's a stupid question."

Sophie grinned across at me. *Little sisters, right?*

I sent back a chuckle. *We were pretty obnoxious, weren't we?*

Obnoxious, but lovable, Alyssa assures me, she projected solemnly.

The silver leaves gave way to gold and then to diamonds, before dropping away to be replaced by the still lake. Within seconds, the twelve small boats came into sight, their appearance that of aimless drifters, but their path sure.

I strained my eyes forward as we floated across the water, trying to catch a glimpse of the other side. When the shore came into sight, the castle looked exactly as it had on our previous visit. I tried to remember whether the outside had been damaged last time. I couldn't remember.

The other princesses all exchanged wary looks, but no one spoke as I led the way up to the great palace doors. Peering inside, I looked around in astonishment. The entrance hall appeared untouched. Quiet exclamations and whispers broke out from the small crowd behind me.

"Like our dresses," someone said, and I realized they were right. Our restored dresses had been the clue that should have led us to this conclusion.

I sighed. "Well, come on then, let's get this over with." I led the way to the throne room, much more confident in my steps now that I had explored the true palace. Once again, the heavy wooden table with the twelve chairs awaited us.

We seated ourselves and stared expectantly at our empty golden plates. They remained empty. When we exchanged confused looks, we saw the single parchment that had once again appeared in the middle of the table. Celine made no move to retrieve it, so Emmeline did so instead.

"The boats have gone and will not return you to the other side of the lake," she read out. Both of the twins gasped. "You must work together to find your own way back across."

She placed the parchment back down on the table in front of her and regarded us all. No one said anything.

After a moment, Hazel spoke. "At least this task sounds safer than the last one turned out to be."

"Yeah," said Celine, "until our makeshift raft sinks in the middle of the lake, and we all drown."

One of the twins—I really needed to learn to tell them apart—gasped again, and Celine grimaced. "Sorry. The pain from my ankle makes me grumpy. I'm sure we'll manage to make an excellent boat."

"Of course we will," said Sophie, a little too brightly.

Really? I asked her.

Well, we have to, don't we? So we will.

I admire your spirit.

She rolled her eyes at me.

"I can't swim." Giselle glanced at her sister, Emmeline, who said nothing. Giselle didn't seem particularly perturbed, she simply stated it as a fact. Thankfully the thought that we might all swim across hadn't even occurred to me. The lake was wide, and I had to assume it was deep. It wouldn't be much of a challenge if it wasn't.

"What about this table?" asked Marigold. "We could turn it upside down and sit in it, like a boat."

This time Hazel was the one delivering a withering look in her younger sister's direction. "That's a terrible idea. It's far too heavy."

Marigold opened her mouth to respond, so I rushed in before things could devolve into a fight. "I'm afraid Hazel is right. I don't think the table would have enough buoyancy." I cast my eyes around the rest of the throne room. Other than the thrones themselves, it was empty.

"I'm happy to say there's a noticeable lack of falling masonry this time around. So I vote we spread out and look through this palace, see if we can find anything useful."

A couple of the younger ones looked reluctant, but Millie smiled at them. "We'll stick together in twos or threes."

This seemed to alleviate their worst fears, and I quickly found myself wandering through the rooms with Sophie. Millie had taken the young twins under her wing, and Blanche had volunteered to help Celine. Emmeline and Giselle had stuck together, as always, and Lilac, Hazel and Marigold, the local princesses, had also chosen to go exploring together, despite their earlier tiff.

All of which resulted in me and Sophie finding ourselves unencumbered.

It didn't take me long to realize we had a problem. The layout might mirror the real palace, but none of the furniture had been replicated. The rooms were all empty. I stuck my head into the fourth room we had encountered and then withdrew it with a sigh. The windows didn't even have curtains, so there was no point going in.

Sophie peered into the next room and then paused and stepped inside. I followed close behind, hoping she'd found something. Another empty room greeted us, except that this one had rows of tall cupboards built into each wall.

You never know... Sophie walked all the way down to the end of the room to open the furthest cupboard first. Perhaps she just wanted to prolong any small hope.

I saw her shoulders slump before I received her projection. *Empty.*

We checked each cupboard, just in case, but every shelf turned up bare. We met in the middle of the room.

What do you think will happen if we can't get across?

I didn't even want to think about that option, but if we didn't find something soon, we were going to have to consider it. Another head appeared around the doorway.

Blanche's gaze locked on to us. "Oh, you're already here." She looked up and down the room and then back at us hopefully.

We both shook our heads, and she seemed to shrink a little. "Nothing here either," she said to someone, presumably Celine, outside in the corridor. "Well, except for Lily and Sophie."

I sadly surveyed the closed cupboards. If only they had held something of use. I paused and looked at them again.

"Actually," I said. "I might have an idea."

"Really?" Blanche stepped into the room, and Celine appeared behind her.

I pointed at the cupboard doors. "Do those look like pine to you? Do you think we could get them off?"

All three of the others turned to stare at the cupboards. "I think we could," said Celine slowly. "And there's plenty of them."

"Let's give it a try." Sophie was almost rubbing her hands together in anticipation.

The three of us who were uninjured took to the destruction of the room with enthusiasm. Celine watched our efforts a little enviously before hobbling out into the corridor. She started calling loudly for the other girls to gather.

It ended up taking the combined efforts of Sophie, Blanche and me to pull a single cupboard door free. As the other girls trickled in, Celine explained the situation, and they all attacked doors of their own. The twins made almost no impact on their chosen cupboard, but Emmeline and Giselle managed to remove one.

A great deal of bickering sounded from the cupboard being demolished by the three Marinese princesses, but they all appeared extremely pleased with one another as soon as it came free. I shook my head and hid a smile. One benefit of mind-to-mind communication was that Sophie and I had been able to hide a lot of our petty squabbling from others.

Each group of girls removed a second door, and then we took a break to survey the results of our efforts. My arms ached, and I rubbed my shoulder which I had wrenched a little pulling the second one free.

Look at poor Pearl, projected Sophie.

One of the twins was staring at the detached doors and shivering violently. Her sister put an arm around her, but she didn't look much more confident herself.

"I want to be brave," said Pearl, her voice small. "But I'm scared. I can't swim either; what if I fall off and drown?" Her eyes flicked briefly to Celine and then away again. "What if my door drifts away from everyone else's?"

"Oh, Pearl." Sophie crossed over to put an arm around her. "We'll help you." She looked down at the doors. "And I think they're big enough for two of us. So you won't be on your door alone."

"She raises a good point, though" I said, trying to put a positive spin on her words. "We need to think about how we're going to steer and propel ourselves."

"And stick together," said Sophie. "Maybe we can come up with a way to tie ourselves to each other, so no one floats away."

A mischievous smile crept over Celine's face. "There's really only one solution. And it's a good thing we're all girls because I'm afraid it's going to be rather indecorous."

"Oh dear," I said, guessing where she was going.

She grinned at me. "We'll have to kick our way across, and they'll only hamper our movements anyway."

"Hamper our..." Emmeline's voice trailed off as understanding hit. "You want us to remove our dresses. Absolutely not."

Celine glared at her. "What other option do we have? We can still wear our underthings, of course. I don't much fancy getting a splinter halfway across the lake." She grinned at the rest of us, and Millie half-laughed, half-groaned.

Emmeline's face hadn't responded to Celine's glare or her grin. "I am not worried about drifting away from the group."

Opal whimpered, and I strode up to Emmeline.

"I don't care what *you're* worried about," I whispered at her. "I'm not exactly worried either. We're doing it for the sake of the younger ones. This is a collaborative exercise, remember? We all need to make it across, and we all need to make an effort to participate."

She stared at me for a moment, then looked away. "Very well."

I rocked back on my heels, swallowing my next argument. I hadn't expected her to be so easily convinced. I glanced at Celine who shrugged. Her expression suggested she understood the two icy Eldonian princesses as little as I did.

I sighed and turned back to the others. "Well, that's settled then. We'll use our dresses. If we position the doors sideways…" I knelt down to measure the length of the wood with my hands. "We can lay them flat on the water with the longest side facing forward. Then two of us can lie across them, side by side."

"How will we move forward?" Marigold frowned down at the cupboard door in front of me.

"We'll lie with our stomachs and chests on the board, but our arms hanging over the front and our legs dangling off the back. That way we can still paddle and kick." I looked up at them all. "If we get into pairs and tie two dresses together, we can use them to connect our rafts, like ropes between us. We won't have enough length to tie them on, but one girl can hold the end of the dress connecting them to the raft in front, and one can hold the dress connecting them to the raft behind. I actually think this might work."

"No might about it," said Sophie. She rubbed Pearl's arm. "Good thinking, Pearl."

Turning Pearl's fear into a helpful suggestion was a nice touch. Hopefully it might convince the magic of the Tourney that the young twins were doing their best to contribute.

"Let's get these down to the lake, then." Millie leaned down and lifted the end of one of the doors. Blanche stepped forward to help her. Emmeline and Giselle made no move to help, but Hazel and Marigold, the two younger Marinese princesses, managed a door between them. Pearl attempted to help Lilac but wobbled awkwardly as she tried to lift her end. Opal stepped forward to join her and, between them, they got it under control.

I looked toward Emmeline and Giselle, only to discover they had already left the room. Three doors remained, along with Sophie, Celine and I. Celine grimaced down at her crutches. "Sorry, twins."

I shrugged. "We can lift three." We stacked them on top of each other, and picked them up. I staggered for a moment before properly balancing the weight.

Thankfully the room had been on the ground floor, so we didn't have to navigate any stairs. I had a nightmarish vision of Pearl or Opal losing their footing and tripping down an entire flight, only to be squashed by their dropped cupboard door.

"At least the water's warm," said Sophie. "It could be worse, really."

I winced. "Don't say that. I'm still waiting for the ceiling to start falling in."

No collapsing stone impeded us, however, and we reached the edge of the lake without incident. Everyone put down their burdens and then stood around awkwardly. Sophie turned her back to me. "Can you undo my laces, Lily?"

I worked as quickly as I could, glad to see the others all following Sophie's lead. As soon as we had both scrambled out of our dresses, we went to help Celine who was struggling to balance while she tried to pull her gown over her head. Soon we all stood in our underclothes and petticoats.

"I hope the dresses come out unscathed again," said Sophie. "Since this is one of my favorites."

"Just as long as we don't drop any into the lake," said Celine. "It would make someone's arrival back aboveground a little awkward."

A quiet snort that might have been a hidden laugh drew my eyes to Giselle. I thought that might have been the first sign of emotion I had seen from the younger girl. When she met my eyes, I smiled, but she just looked away. I sighed. Like brother, like sister.

Sophie and I knotted our dresses together, using the three-quarter length sleeves. I tugged at the knots. "I think they'll hold. Especially once they're wet."

"I'll check the others," said Celine, clearly eager to be helpful.

Within minutes we had six makeshift rafts, each with their own lifeline.

We don't actually need six lifelines. Sophie sent me an image of the six rafts in a line across the lake. *We only need five.*

I know. But I don't want anyone wearing a dress if they lose their grip and end up underwater.

Sophie's eyes flew up to meet mine, her face slightly pale in the strange light of our underground kingdom. She didn't say anything, though, so I turned to the others.

"I think Blanche and I should each take a raft with one of the twins," said Millie, clearly not speaking about Sophie and me.

I ran my eye over everyone else, counting in my head. The Eldonians would stick together, as they always did. "Marigold, why don't you go with Sophie," I said. "And Celine and I can lead the way and set the pace."

Celine sent me an apologetic look. "I can kick with one foot."

I shook my head firmly. "Absolutely not. You can't risk further injury, remember. You can hold our lifeline, and I'll do the kicking. That's why I want us in front. We'll set the pace, however slow that is. It doesn't matter how long it takes, just as long as we all arrive on the other side. The water's warm, so we won't have to worry about that, either."

"Let's get going then," said Emmeline, dragging one of the doors toward the water. Her sister moved to help her.

Between us, we dragged the six rafts into the water. The ground dropped away gradually, so we were all able to stand in a clump, nearly up to our waists in water, with the rafts floating between us. It was impossible to see through the water, even at this shallow depth, and I suppressed a shiver. Anything could be down there. I sternly told myself not to think about it.

Instead, I helped Celine to drape herself across the closest raft, and then placed her crutches horizontally, tucked between her chest and the wood. It didn't look comfortable, but she didn't complain. Her face looked determined as she gripped the raft with one hand and our lifeline of dresses with the other.

I pushed her a little way away from the shore, and fed the other end of the makeshift rope to Lilac. With some squirming and splashing, she and Hazel managed to get themselves into position, and Sophie handed Hazel a second lifeline.

Emmeline took the other end, and I left Sophie to help the others get into position while I pushed our lead raft further into the lake to make room for the line to form behind us. Hoisting myself up onto the raft, I tried not to jostle Celine. Her crutches poked into me, and she apologized and attempted to move them out of the way.

By the time we had both stabilized again, only my head remained dry. The warm water made my underclothes stick uncomfortably to my skin. I tried to ignore them, kicking us gently out into the lake and only stopping when the dress clutched in Celine's hand pulled tight. Looking back, I saw Lilac and Hazel following us, with Emmeline and Giselle behind them. Next came Millie and Pearl, and then Blanche and Opal. Right back at the shore, Sophie helped Marigold position herself on their door. I kicked forward a little further, and the line of rafts bobbed after me, giving Sophie a bit more room.

We're ready. You can go now, she projected after another minute.

I started kicking again. *Can you keep an eye on our direction? Let me know if I start veering off.* A more reliable way to keep a straight course would have been preferable, but I still appreciated the ease with which Sophie could direct me from the back.

Our progress was slow, and it took a while for us all to find a rhythm, so that we didn't constantly pull at each other. I appreciated the distraction since my mind kept coming back to the question of what might lurk unseen in the water beneath us.

Every few minutes, Sophie would project, directing me back toward the left or right. She also called out occasionally to one of the other rafts. I trusted her to direct us, instead focusing my efforts on moving forwards. Propelling a cupboard door, two wet girls and a heavy weight of wet material on my own proved to be hard work. Soon I could see nothing but water in every direction. Only the splashing from my own feet and the rafts behind me let me know we were moving forward at all.

As time wore on, my legs began to feel as if they had been weighted down with rocks. Kicking became more and more of an effort. My arms complained, too, about their awkward position on the raft and the strain of holding me in place. I guessed it must be worse for Celine who had the crutches and lifeline to contend with as well.

More time passed, and I heard soft murmurs from some of the girls behind me. I didn't waste my breath talking, limiting my comments to projections in Sophie's direction. I had started to stare ahead of us, convinced I would catch sight of the shore at any moment, when a squeal rang out behind me.

Wave! Sophie's silent warning screamed in my mind just in time for me to fling one arm around Celine, locking us both in place as a surge of water threw us helplessly up and then dropped us down again.

Celine grunted in pain, but she remained on the raft, so I ignored her and twisted around to examine the rest of the group. Two rafts behind us, Giselle had dropped her end of her dress lifeline, so that their raft, along with the ones attached behind them, had come loose from the leading two. She seemed to have recovered, however, because she had joined her sister in kicking their raft back toward Lilac and Hazel who had managed to keep hold of their end of the lifeline.

My eyes skipped straight to the back of the rafts to find Sophie, but she didn't meet my eyes, focused instead on something between us. I followed her gaze, counting heads as I did, and stopped when I reached the raft two in front of Sophie. I could only see one head.

Millie, now gripping both her and Pearl's lifelines, was looking frantically around at the surrounding water. I saw her shift, as if about to let go and dive under, but her hands were full with their raft and both lifelines. "No one move," I yelled, as Pearl resurfaced, spluttering, only to sink back under the water again. I abandoned my raft to Celine and kicked off hard in Pearl's direction.

Opal didn't listen, reaching out to try to help her sister. When Pearl resurfaced again, however, she blindly grabbed at Opal's reaching hand and pulled her twin down with her. Opal screamed and let go of her end of the lifeline.

"Blanche!" I called, but the pale princess had already snatched the soggy clothing from the water. *Sophie!* I projected. *I'm not going to be able to pull them both back up.*

I'm already on my way. I saw her then, rushing toward me through the water from the other end of our line of rafts. *Marigold has our raft in hand. And thankfully there don't seem to be any more waves behind us. I wasn't watching backwards, so I didn't see that one coming.*

I kicked harder. I hadn't even thought about another wave, although I should have. Such a clearly unnatural event might come again out of nowhere.

We met up at the spot where the twins had gone down, and I waited for them to resurface. But neither did. For a brief second my eyes met Sophie's, and then we both took a deep breath and dived, cold washing over us despite the warmth of the water.

CHAPTER 13

The dark and murky water made visibility impossible. I quested out with my arms, hoping desperately to encounter a petticoat or a hand. And hoping equally strongly that I didn't touch anything slimy. It took every bit of courage I had to dive down away from the surface.

I've got one of them! Sophie sounded triumphant.

My breath was running out, so I twisted in the water, swinging my arms out wildly. My foot bumped against something, and I twisted again. Please be the other twin, please be the other twin, ran through my head like a litany.

One of my hands encountered fabric, and I kicked toward the surface, dragging it behind me. Pain blossomed along the shoulder I had wrenched earlier, but I pressed on. My lungs burned, and I burst from the water, gasping wildly. I pulled up the dead weight behind me, and one of the twins appeared. She gulped down air and grabbed at me, nearly sending us both back under.

"Whoa, whoa," I called between splashes. "Calm down, I've got you."

Slowly she stopped fighting and floated in the water, letting me support her as she continued to gasp in air. I saw that Sophie was already helping Opal retake her place next to Blanche, so it must be Pearl I was supporting. I towed her toward Millie.

"Oh, thank goodness." Tears streamed down Millie's cheeks. "That wave caught me by surprise, and I didn't even see her go under."

"It caught us all by surprise." I clung to the edge of their door, my legs already long past exhaustion.

"Do you think you can hold on if there's another one?" I asked Pearl as I hoisted her into position on the wood.

She nodded. "I'll hold on tighter the rest of the way." Her teeth chattered, but her grip did look secure. "Do you...do you think there'll be another one?"

I glanced at Millie. "I hope not."

"Don't worry," she said. "I'll be ready, too."

I nodded to Millie and kicked off toward the next raft, using it to propel me toward the next one. Thankfully, while I had been occupied with Pearl, the others had managed to reform our line. All too soon, I had retaken my place.

"Are you all right?" Celine eyed me.

A shudder ripped through me. An aftereffect of the shock, I supposed. "Has the water gotten colder?" I shivered again.

"Not that I've noticed." Celine frowned at me.

"Never mind. Let's keep going. I want to get out of this water before the Tourney decides to send another wave in our direction." Somehow I forced my leaden legs to kick again. Bit by bit we inched forward through the water.

"There!" said Celine. "I think I can see the land."

The effort of lifting my head to look overwhelmed me, so I stayed down, my face only just clearing the surface of the water. We were nearly there, and that was all that mattered. I just had to keep kicking, one leg after the other. One leg after the other.

"I can touch!" I felt Celine's weight lift off the door. I stopped kicking and let her hop along, pushing us in. I knew I should tell her to stop, that she might hurt her ankle, but I couldn't find my voice.

I rolled off the door and onto my hands and knees in the shallows. Slowly I crawled forward until I could flop onto my back on dry land. Now that my wet body was entirely out of the water, I trembled with continuous shivers. I could hear the other princesses around me, coming in to land, and then a familiar figure lay down beside me. She scooted in close, and our arms touched, the shivers passing back and forth between us.

Is everyone...?

I did a head count. Even Sophie's projection sounded exhausted. *Twelve.*

Good.

We lay there for another minute. Finally I forced myself to sit up. Celine had marshalled the others to unpick the knots in our dresses. Some had finished, but others still hunched over the sodden material. Several of the rafts had been beached, but others had floated away. No one seemed inclined to stop them.

Pearl and Opal both looked miserable. They sat together slightly apart from the others, attempting to pick apart a bundle of knotted material, although they both shook too hard to make much headway.

I tried to motivate my legs to move in their direction until I saw Blanche and Millie approach them instead. Within minutes, the last of the dresses had been separated, and Sophie and I staggered to our feet, clutching each other for support. No one talked much as everyone found their own gown from the pile.

We stumbled through the groves, our wet dresses clutched in our hands. When we reached the bottom of the ladder, we scrambled back into them. I secured Sophie's laces half-heartedly, not bothering to tie them too tight. Hopefully we would be changing into dry clothes within minutes.

A deep shudder rocked me as I noticed the last tree again bore a folded parchment. This time the paper held two tables. One gave the scores from the event, the other the cumulative totals. Celine, Sophie and I had all done well in the event, but Celine's dismal results from the previous event meant she remained at the bottom of the overall table. Another shudder made the parchment shake in my hand.

"Come on," said Sophie. "We need to get Celine up the ladder."

The task proved slightly less difficult than on the previous occasion, since Celine was more alert and in less pain. I, on the other hand, felt almost as tired as I had after dragging Celine from the palace. And I nearly slipped while helping her up several times because of my shudders. At last it was my turn to climb up into the room.

The water evaporated instantly from my dress as soon as I stepped off the ladder, but the chill that had gripped me from the moment my head slipped under the lake did not. By the morning it had turned into a fever.

I could hear Sophie tossing and turning on the bed next to mine, calling out in her sleep. Our minds reached for each other, so that I couldn't tell where her fevered dreams ended and mine began. Time passed.

When I finally opened my eyes, certain that dreams no longer gripped me, I found sunlight pouring into the room.

"Oh, thank goodness!" Helena rushed to my side. I tried to make sense of her tired, pale face.

"What's the matter?" My voice came out scratchy and rough. I coughed, and she sat on the bed and helped me to sit, holding a glass of water to my lips.

"You've been asleep for two days and two nights." Her quiet words were laden with meaning.

"You mean…tonight…" Sophie's wispy voice came from the next bed.

An older lady I didn't recognize rushed forward with water for her as well.

"Yes, I'm afraid so. We've all been extremely concerned you wouldn't wake."

I tried to assimilate the news that we would be back in the ballroom within a matter of hours. "What's the time?"

"It's still morning." Helena sounded eager to offer even the faintest piece of good news. "You have most of the day still to recover."

Oh good, how lovely. I didn't want to offend Helena, who had been caring for us all this time and bore no blame, so I didn't speak out loud.

It's not her fault.

I know.

Sophie finished her glass. *I think it was the water of the lake. I began to feel strange as soon as my head went under.*

Me too. And now we'll be going into the next challenge weakened.

Sophie met my eyes. *You think the Tourney is punishing anyone who went under during the challenge?*

I shrugged slightly at her. *Punish probably isn't the right word. More like disadvantage. Like Celine. Except hopefully our weakness will pass more quickly than her broken ankle.* I spoke my next thought out loud. "How are the twins? The other ones, from Talinos."

Helena and the unknown nurse exchanged a glance. "How do you know...?" Helena must have realized I couldn't answer since her question trailed away. "They've both been ill as well, but they woke up last night."

"Oh, good."

"That they're awake, she means," Sophie clarified on my behalf. I wanted to roll my eyes but couldn't be bothered. "Not that they were sick."

"Of course, Your Highness," said the nurse with a small smile.

Sophie glanced over at me. *Have you noticed the prohibition on talking about the events doesn't seem to extend to our projections?*

That could prove useful. It already has during the two events so far.

Good, that gives us an advantage, then.

I didn't like the implications of her comment—wasn't this a contest we wanted to lose?— but my mind struggled to keep pace with the conversation, so I let it drop. I felt groggy and still slightly confused. I also felt...

"Hungry. I feel hungry."

"Me, too."

"Well, no wonder, when you haven't eaten for more than two days." Helena gestured for the nurse to pull a long golden cord hanging against the wall between our beds. "We'll send for the servants, they've been standing ready to bring you food as soon as you woke."

"Thank you," I managed before falling back against the bed. I would just rest a little before the food arrived.

I started awake when the door opened and two maids entered. I glanced around in confusion before remembering what had happened. I felt slightly better than I had the last time I awoke, but I hoped I hadn't lost too much more time. I had slept away enough already.

"His Highness said to pass on his well wishes and his relief at your recovery," said one of the maids, as she deposited a tray on my lap.

The other one giggled. "He's been lurking out in that corridor a lot the last two days. And looking awfully worried."

"His highness?" asked Sophie politely. But I could hear the mischief lurking beneath.

"Oh! Our prince, we mean—Prince Jonathan I should say."

Ha!

I took a sip of the warm broth. It tasted delicious, so I tore off a chunk of bread and dunked it in. *He feels responsible for our safety. He's the one who invited us here.*

Mmhmmm.

"He also said to tell you that he'll have some comfortable chairs carried outside for you, if you'd like to get some fresh air and sun this afternoon. It's another lovely day."

"That would be perfect, thank you," said Sophie. "If our nurses allow."

"Certainly," said Helena. "An excellent idea." I noticed her amused gaze lingering on me also, and I glared around at the room at no one in particular.

But when the maids left, I acknowledged that some time in the garden actually sounded quite appealing. But the company had nothing whatsoever to do with it.

～

Sophie and I both insisted on walking out to the garden. In a matter of hours, we would have to do a lot more than walk a few steps, and we wanted to test ourselves. It scared me how much the minor activity tired me.

How are we going to get through tonight? Apparently I wasn't the only one concerned.

"I'm so glad to see you up!" Prince Jonathan waited for us both next to a collection of comfortable-looking chairs. "I wasn't sure which one you would prefer, so I had them all carried out." I told myself it was only my imagination that his concerned gaze lingered on me. I didn't want to feed the all-too-rapidly growing attraction I felt for him. Our illness only proved I needed to keep my attention focused on surviving the Tourney.

Sophie and I each chose a seat, and Jon took one of the remaining ones. His next comment was lost as Prince Theodore and Prince Gabriel arrived.

"Teddy. Gabe." Jon nodded at them both, his voice serious. They took seats without further invitation, their faces equally serious.

Why do I feel like we've just been ambushed? I eyed the princes uneasily.

Because you're wise beyond your years?

Flatterer!

Jon leaned forward, resting his elbows on his knees and clasping his hands together. I could see the earnestness shining from his eyes. I shifted uncomfortably. Whatever was about to happen, I didn't feel at all well enough to face it.

"I'm worried." He tipped his head toward the others. "We're all worried."

"We appreciate your concern." I hoped my cool tone would put him off.

It didn't.

"There have only been two events, and already five of you have come back ill or injured. No one knows where you go, but your dancing slippers were ruined again." He glanced at the others as if for support. "All of them. They were soaked through and coated with mud."

I looked at him hopelessly and shrugged. I wished I could tell them what was going on, but I had no choice.

"All three of us have sisters in the Tourney," said Gabe, leaning forward as well. "We can't sit idly by while you're all in danger."

I sat up straight, sudden energy burning through the lingering fog in my brain. "Just what exactly is that supposed to mean?"

Gabe glanced at Teddy and then over at Jon before shrugging.

"There's nothing you can do. You know that, right?" I looked at Jon. "Right?"

"But maybe there is…" I didn't like the eager light in Jon's eyes.

"No, absolutely not!" A more panicked voice than mine rang out, and we all swiveled around in surprise. Millie emerged from some bushes and stormed toward us. She stood over Teddy in his chair and glared daggers at her twin and his friends. "I knew you boys were planning something. But I can't *believe* you would bother Lily and Sophie right now."

She swiveled around to face us. "I'm glad to see you up, by the way." She turned back to the princes. "You are the heirs of three different kingdoms. You cannot afford to be idiots right now."

"Or ever," I muttered.

"Thank you!" She didn't turn away from the angry stare she had trained on her brother. "Or ever."

"Relax, Mill," said Teddy. "We just..."

She put her hands on her hips and stared at him. "Well?" she asked after a moment. "We just what?"

Jon ran his hand through his hair and looked at the ground. None of them met her eyes.

"Exactly! You know the rules of the Tourney better than anyone. If you try to interfere, your lives will be forfeit."

"But, Millie..."

She rounded on Gabe. "Don't 'but Millie' me. It doesn't matter that you're princes. The rules of the Princess Tourney apply to everyone. The magic knows no distinction, you know that." This time she skewered Jon with her glare. "Do you want to break your family's hearts? Not to mention causing who knows what sort of crisis amongst the kingdoms."

I leaned forward as well. "You're just going to have to trust us. We can look after ourselves. We might be a little battered, but everyone's come through so far." I tried to pour far more confidence into my words than I actually felt. At this point I had no idea what events the Tourney might throw at us next, or how well we would be able to survive them. But I did know that any interference by the princes would be disastrous.

I snuck a glance at Jon. He worked so tirelessly for his people, they couldn't afford to lose him. A small voice whispered in the back of my mind that I didn't want to lose him either. I shooed it away. I hardly knew him.

"I'm not so sure my sisters *can* look after themselves." The frustration in Gabe's eyes made me wince. I could definitely see his point. He must be terrified for Pearl and Opal.

"You'll have to trust us to look after them," said Sophie softly. "We are completely committed to seeing all those girls make it safely through the Tourney."

Gabe looked mutinous, but Millie stared him down. "I know you, Gabriel. And this isn't a problem you can fix with your bow and arrow. This isn't a time for your bravery."

He met her eyes for a moment before looking away in discomfort.

A giggle sounded in my mind. I looked at Sophie in surprise. The situation didn't strike me as particularly humorous.

Sorry. Another giggle escaped. *It's just so funny seeing Millie facing them all down. Every one of them is taller and stronger than her, but she looks like she's about to spit fire. And they all look like they think she actually might.*

I looked at the scene before us again and suppressed a smile. Now that she said it, they did all look rather cowed. *Millie is pretty fierce.*

This time, Sophie's giggle slipped out of her mouth. All of them, including Millie, turned to look at us. The sound of Sophie's laugh and their astonished faces proved too much for me. I giggled too.

Sophie looked over at me and burst into louder peals. I followed, each of us feeding off the other, until we were leaning back in our chairs, tears running down our faces.

"Sorry," I managed to force out between chuckles. "It's a twin thing."

Millie raised an eyebrow, and I remembered she was a twin too. I shrugged helplessly, seized by a fresh paroxysm. Finally she gave her own small chuckle and shrugged at the bemused princes. Looking around for a spare chair, she plonked herself down.

I shook my head as the final giggle died away. "I think I needed that."

"Are the two of you all right?" asked Millie. "We've all been worried."

"Some of us more than others," said Gabe with a significant look at Jon.

Jon glared at his friend, and I blushed. To my surprise, Sophie refrained from joining the teasing, even in my mind, and rescued me instead with a change of topic. The conversation moved on and didn't come back up until we returned to the palace.

Jon and Gabe escorted us back to our suite, and as he said goodbye, Jon leaned in close and whispered, too quietly for the others to hear, "He was right, you know. I was worried. Next time I don't care what they say, I'm coming in to sit by your bedside."

I swallowed. "Let's hope there isn't a next time."

"Yes. There'd better not be."

I couldn't decide if it was a promise or a threat in his eyes, but it haunted me long after the door had closed. I liked these new friends who had welcomed us into their land. And, if I liked some, or one in particular, more than others, I couldn't help that. Certainly none of them deserved an untimely, magical end. After our conversation in the garden, I couldn't help but be afraid. Apparently it wasn't only the princesses of these kingdoms that needed our rescue. The princes needed rescue from themselves.

CHAPTER 14

*T*hat night, we arrived at the ball as late as we dared. Helena had helped lace us into our simplest gowns, and had provided yet another new pair of dancing slippers without comment. She had also summoned a footman to help each of us down to the ballroom, and I had shamelessly leaned on his arm the entire way. I figured I should conserve what strength I could for when no such convenient support would be available.

As soon as we stepped through the doors, Jon appeared in front of us.

Almost as if he's been lurking next to the door all evening waiting for us. Sophie sounded far too smug, so I didn't deign to reply.

I shook my head at him. "No dancing tonight."

"You have to dance, at least once." He continued to hold out his hand. "It's…"

I groaned. "…tradition, right?"

He tried to hide his grin. "No spinning, I promise."

I sighed and put my hand into his. A surge of energy shot through me at the contact, and when he pulled me into his arms, and we began to sway, I almost enjoyed the sensation. Except my legs still felt a little leaden, and I kept thinking longingly of my soft pillow.

"I'm sorry about this afternoon." He sounded sincere. "I just hate feeling so helpless."

I softened and smiled at him. I had learned independence and responsibility far too young. I recognized those same qualities in Jon and knew all too well his welling frustration of helplessness. People like us felt it the most.

I imagined spending every third night waiting on the other side of the door while Sophie and Celine disappeared through, the way that he was forced to watch his sisters, Lilac, Hazel and Marigold. I shivered. However unpleasant it was to be trapped in the Tourney, at least as contestants we were free to help each other.

And, of course, that didn't even take into account the curiosity. I wasn't sure I could have borne it in his shoes. Imagine not knowing where or how we all spent our nights?

"What is it?" he asked, having felt my shiver.

"I'm just wondering how you manage it," I said, wanting to keep the conversation light. "The curiosity, I mean. Don't misunderstand me—if given the choice, I would have opted out of the Tourney. But I also might have died of curiosity by now."

His face darkened for a moment, and I suspected his mind had gone to the impotence of the nights spent waiting, as mine had. But he chose to stay light as well. "I will admit it's quite difficult. Everyone has a theory, of course, each wilder than the last. Gabe comes up with the most exciting suggestions, but Teddy's are cleverer."

"And yours?"

He chuckled. "Mine are entirely too practical. Or so I'm told." The cloud passed over his face again. "Although the state of your slippers—and yourselves—is making it increasingly hard to convince myself of any boring, sensible suggestions."

"Sensible doesn't have to be boring, you know." I smiled,

trying to take his mind off his frustration, and all the questions I couldn't answer.

He shook his head. "Maybe not. But it does tend to lead to fewer broken bones. You only have to compare my childhood to Gabe's to confirm that."

"I'd love to hear about your childhood sometime," I said. "Even if it was disaster-free." I laughed up at him with my eyes, inviting him to join my lighter mood.

He looked down at me, and I could see his face softening. "And I would love to hear about yours."

"I didn't break any bones, but I'm afraid there were disasters. I'd hate to shock you," I said with mock solemnity.

His eyes crinkled in suppressed laughter. "Don't worry, Lily." He somehow kept his voice grave. "I have three sisters, remember. I'm not so easily shocked."

A bell chimed through the ballroom, killing my response. Annoyance crossed Jon's face, and his hands tightened as if he didn't want to let me go. I wished for a crazy moment that he would ignore the bell and continue to hold me close. I felt more energy with his arms around me than I had since waking up from the fever.

But he let me go, and I hid my irrational annoyance, pretending I hadn't noticed his embrace at all. "Goodness, that was quick tonight." I reminded myself an early start was a good thing. I wasn't optimistic about how long Sophie and I would last.

The twelve of us had become efficient at lining up and descending into the mysterious realm belowground, although Pearl and Opal looked unusually pale.

I hoped they had recovered enough from their own illnesses not to collapse partway through whatever event we faced. I didn't have the energy to carry either of them—however light they were.

A knot of tension grew between my shoulder blades as we

passed through the diamond-leaved grove. Would the boats return now that the last challenge was complete? I could read the same question in some of the eyes around me, but no one spoke it out loud.

When the small coracles bobbed toward us across the water, several quiet breaths released. Still no one spoke aloud, however. Minutes later we once again entered the mirror palace and took our places at the heavy oak table. My eyes fastened immediately on the only difference in the room—a small sandglass in the center of the table. I tried to guess how much time it would measure. Five minutes, maybe? Ten?

My tension had only grown, despite the smooth arrival of the boats. Just walking through the three groves had left me tired, and my eyes kept drooping shut of their own accord.

Once again Emmeline retrieved the note from the middle of the table and read our instructions aloud. "You will be presented with a series of riddles. You must work together to solve them. Once you have determined the answer, write it on the piece of parchment provided."

Tears welled in my eyes from the relief. A non-physical challenge. In fact, this one really didn't sound so bad at all.

Except Emmeline hadn't finished. "Each failure to supply a correct answer before the sand runs out will result in the loss of one of your number. Do not attempt to leave the table until all twelve riddles have been completed."

The beginnings of my smile dropped away. *The loss of one of our number? What exactly does that mean?* I had meant to merely project the thought to Sophie but, in my exhaustion, I spoke the words aloud. The briefest glimpse up the table, however, showed that it didn't matter. I had only said what everyone was thinking.

"I don't like the sound of that, at all." Celine frowned.

"We'll just have to make sure we get them all right, then," said Sophie. "There are twelve of us, surely we can do it." She looked up and down the table. "Any keen riddlers present?"

"Hazel is quite good at them," said Lilac. Her younger sister blushed at the praise and tried to look modest.

"Emmeline and I have some skill," said Giselle. It still astonished me whenever either of them spoke. I didn't understand how anyone could be so emotionally disconnected from the ordeal of the Tourney. But, it made sense they would be good at riddles. They seemed to have the necessary objectivity.

"Oh!" Marigold's exclamation made me jump slightly in my seat. She was staring down at her golden plate which now contained a folded parchment. She scanned the other plates, but they all remained empty.

"It looks like you're supposed to go first, Marigold." Hazel leaned in from the next seat to peer over her younger sister's arm.

Marigold, who sat on the same side of the table as me, but at the opposite end, looked less than excited about the idea. I could hardly blame her. Unfolding it, she read out, "I was not born, and I cannot die. Yet I bring all things low and death inevitably follows in my wake."

"Cheery," muttered Celine.

"It seems they've started with an easy one," said Emmeline. "Hopefully they will all continue that way."

"Yes." Hazel nodded eagerly. "This one isn't difficult at all."

Ugh! Could they be more smug? Please tell me I'm not the only one who doesn't see the answer! I projected.

Sophie sent me a grimace. *It feels as if my head is full of cotton balls.*

I forced my brain to focus. It had been years since I had done any riddling, but the others had said this one was easy...

The answer came to me just as Giselle spoke it aloud, "Time."

Marigold glanced around to see if anyone wanted to dispute the solution. Greeted with a row of nodding heads, she wrote the answer on the parchment with the pen that had appeared in front of her.

We all looked around warily. Nothing happened.

"Try putting it on the plate," suggested Lilac.

As soon as the parchment hit the gold, it crumbled into dust and was somehow absorbed into the plate. After another pause, I forced a smile. "I guess that must have been the right answer, then."

As if to prove me right, a second parchment appeared on Hazel's plate. Apparently we would be taking turns around the table. She picked it up quickly. "I am circle without end, square without corner. Nothing can grasp me."

She bit her lip and frowned, her eyes running over the page again. Eventually she looked up. "That's it." I could see her disappointment at not immediately seeing the answer. She looked questioningly at Emmeline and Giselle, but they wore the same confused, thoughtful expressions.

I tried to think. Circle. Square. Corner. What was the rest again? I closed my eyes and had to force them to reopen. I kept thinking of my pillow which interfered with my attempts to find an answer. Wheels are circles...Goose feathers are soft...Books are square—well, not really...I often *grasp* at the coverlet in my sleep.

As the seconds of silence lengthened, the discomfort around the table grew. More and more eyes fixed upon the sandglass. Surely we hadn't all been defeated by the second riddle. I tried to bully my brain into working, but it wasn't paying attention.

The glass looked dangerously low. "We should make a guess, at least," said Sophie. "Any chance, however small, is better than none."

No one spoke, but I saw Lilac open her mouth and then close it again.

"Lilac?" I asked. "Do you have a suggestion?"

She frowned. "It's probably not right. I'm sure it's not."

"What is it? Quick!" Hazel gripped the pen tightly in her fingers, her eyes on the final disappearing grains of sand.

"The stars."

Hazel dashed down the words and then dropped the parchment onto her plate, just before the final grains flowed through to the bottom of the glass. For a moment, we all held our breath, waiting for the parchment to dissolve. Only, when it did, a whoosh accompanied it, and both Hazel and her chair disappeared.

Marigold and Lilac screamed, and Lilac, who sat on Hazel's other side, dropped down almost out of sight below the table.

"Hazel!"

"What happened?"

"Where is she?"

Voices all spoke over the top of one another. It had happened almost too fast to register, and several girls made as if to stand to get a better view.

"No! No one move." My harsh command caused everyone to drop back into their seats. "Remember what the instructions said. Who knows what disaster will befall us if any of us try to leave our seats before the riddles are finished." I rushed out the words as quickly as I could, craning in my chair as hard as any of them in my attempt to see past Sophie and Millie, who sat between me and Lilac.

"Careful! Don't let go!" Marigold, the only one with a clear view, sounded terrified. She was staring at the empty gap in the table next to her where her sister had been sitting only moments before.

Millie, who sat on the other side of Lilac, leaned over and appeared to grasp hold of her friend. Whatever assistance she was offering must have worked because, a moment later, Lilac straightened in her chair. As she came back into view, Hazel also appeared, dragged up by her sister.

Scooting to the side, Lilac made room for them both to sit on her wide seat. Hazel still hadn't made a sound, but they both trembled violently.

"What happened?" asked Celine.

"It…it's just gone." Lilac's voice trembled, as well as her body.

"What's gone?"

Marigold answered for her older sister. "The chair. The floor. Everything. It's just a gaping hole." She was still staring at the gap in the table between her lone chair on the end and the chair that now held both of her sisters.

I swallowed. Hard.

Lilac tried to speak, stopped, and then tried again. "I was paying extra attention—I guess I was on edge because I had given the answer, and I was sure it was wrong. If I hadn't been, I never would have caught her arm as she fell…"

"Well done, Lilac," said Sophie. "And now we're prepared." She looked around at everyone with a forced smile. "When you write your answer, make sure you grip one of the people next to you before you place the parchment on the plate."

As she spoke, the next parchment appeared on the plate in front of the chair that now held both Lilac and Hazel. Millie, Lilac's only remaining neighbor, looked from the parchment to the two girls on the seat and went pale. I couldn't blame her. We would have to get this one right, at least.

I scanned the table. I sat on the end of our row, and could rely on Sophie to catch me. But Blanche sat directly across from me, with only the fourteen-year-old Giselle as a neighbor, and Celine sat on the other end, diagonally opposite me, with only Pearl as her neighbor. Which meant there were actually several we would have to get right.

"Quickly!" I said, proud that my voice didn't shake. "The sand has started."

Lilac read out the riddle in a low mumble.

"You'll need to read louder," said Emmeline.

Lilac cleared her throat and tried again.

"Another easy one," said Giselle, giving the answer.

"But are you sure?" I pressed, not taking my eyes off the disappearing sand.

"Emmeline?" Giselle turned to her sister for confirmation.

"Absolutely. That is the correct answer." I didn't like having to trust in the two icy Eldonian princesses when they showed no fear. Did they even understand the gravity of the situation? But I had no choice.

Lilac took a deep breath, wrote the answer on the parchment, and then held it above her plate.

"Wait," said Millie. "Let me get a firm grip." Both girls clasped each other's forearm, locking their hands as tightly as possible. Hazel clung to her sister's other side as Lilac dropped the parchment. It floated down and settled on her plate.

We all held our breath for a second that seemed to go on and on. I blinked, and a pile of dust disappeared into the plate. We all waited another long second before releasing a breath of relief. Millie and Lilac shared a wobbly smile.

Millie read out her riddle and once again my brain refused to engage. This time because I was too busy considering who stood in the most danger. Sophie sat between Millie and me, but Millie must be as heavy as Sophie, so catching her wouldn't be an easy feat. I decided to grip Sophie's other arm, to anchor her in case Millie's seat fell away.

But Emmeline managed to puzzle out the correct answer, so Millie was safe. My relief mixed with an unreasonable frustration. It galled me that we were so beholden to someone who seemed entirely disinterested in the process.

I didn't even hear Sophie read out her riddle. I knew I should be helping to think of an answer, but my fuzzy brain kept circling back to the dropped chair and the approaching danger to my sister. I gripped Sophie's arm harder than I had ever done before.

But a shaken Hazel managed to give the correct answer, and then it was my turn. To my surprise I recognized a favorite riddle from my childhood. "My dress is the envy of maidens," I read out. "Another simple one."

I looked over at Sophie, and we smiled at the same time. I had always loved it because of my name.

"White calla lily." Sophie looked around the table. "Because it looks like a wedding dress."

No one disputed it, and I quickly wrote the answer on my parchment. I was certain we were right, but...

"I should hold your arm, anyway," said Sophie. "Just in case."

We gripped forearms as the other girls had done, as I dropped the parchment on my plate and watched it dissolve into dust. I smiled at the others. After four correct answers in a row, my heart rate had slowed down. Until my eyes caught on Blanche.

Sitting across from me she looked even paler than usual and kept casting surreptitious glances at the smaller Giselle, her only neighbor. My anxiety spiked again.

When the next parchment appeared on Blanche's plate, she read it in a shaky voice. Like earlier, my concern for the consequences made it too hard for my tired mind to focus on a possible answer. I kept measuring the relative weights of the two girls in my mind. Blanche couldn't be *that* much heavier than Giselle...

Thankfully, given my inattention, Hazel knew the answer, and Blanche wrote it down with a shaking hand. She gripped Giselle's arm, and I held my breath as the parchment seemed to drift lazily through the air onto her plate.

It dissolved and disappeared, and I breathed again. I slumped back into my chair as Giselle read out her riddle. My eyes ran down the table. We were past half-way now, making our way down the opposite side of the table. But we wouldn't be safe until we had finished. Not with Celine on the far end with only Pearl to catch her.

I refocused on the table in time to see Emmeline and Giselle exchange shrugs before Giselle wrote something on her scrap of parchment. They seemed less sure than usual. I didn't feel too concerned, however. Emmeline, older by two years, also looked considerably stronger than her sister and should have no trouble holding her weight if needed.

I watched the parchment hit the table, already wondering if the reverse were true—would Giselle be able to catch Emmeline if we got the next one wrong? Giselle would need to be ready to try, since tiny Opal sat on Emmeline's other side.

It took a moment for my mind to register the whooshing sound, or the empty place where Giselle had been sitting. As with Hazel and Lilac earlier, Emmeline almost disappeared from view, yanked down by her grip on her sister.

I waited for her to reappear with Giselle in tow, and it seemed to take forever for her to straighten. When she finally did, however, there was no sign of her sister.

PART II
THE DUCHY OF MARIN

CHAPTER 15

"*G*iselle?" I managed to squeeze out the word, my eyes darting between Emmeline and the empty space next to her.

"She slipped."

Marigold and Opal both screamed, but everyone else seemed stricken silent. Shock had stolen our voices. Emmeline's face looked completely blank, and I suppressed a mad urge to shout and rail at her.

Did that really happen? Sophie sounded hesitant and confused. *Or is this a dream? Have I fallen asleep at the table?*

"Can...can you see her?" Hazel's voice quavered, and I guessed she was remembering her own terrifying drop.

Blanche, on the other side of Giselle's missing seat, peered over the side of her chair, before shaking her head. "I can't see the bottom of the hole. It's just darkness."

Several audible breaths sounded from around the table.

"She'll be all right, though, won't she?" asked Lilac. "I mean she can't be..."

No one answered her unfinished question, and the young twins started crying.

I looked at Emmeline who still showed no emotion. *She can't really be so uncaring.* I sent Sophie an image of Emmeline's empty face. *She must be in shock. Surely?*

Surely! A pause. *You don't think she could possibly have...* Sophie's projected whisper faded away.

Why would she wish her sister harm? I couldn't believe it to be possible. Even of Emmeline.

Yes, of course. You're right.

Emmeline cleared her throat and began to read aloud from the parchment that had appeared on her plate. I wanted to snap at her to be silent and remind her that her own sister had disappeared. That she might even be dead. To tell her she should be an emotional wreck, and we couldn't calmly continue riddling.

And yet, the sandglass had begun its inexorable trickle. Calmly or not, continue is exactly what we had to do, unless we wanted more of our number to fall. Emmeline's voice didn't falter, but she looked up afterwards with a confused face.

I looked at Sophie, wondering if she had caught the riddle. I had missed it completely in my shock.

Hazel squeaked before clearing her throat and trying again. This time she managed to get out the word, "Books."

"Ah yes, of course." Emmeline wrote down the answer without waiting for confirmation from anyone else. She had placed her parchment onto her plate before I remembered that with Giselle gone, only Opal remained to catch Emmeline, hardly a feasible option.

But Emmeline didn't turn to the younger girl for help, obviously confident in her answer, and a second later her parchment had dissolved and disappeared. A new one appeared in front of the still weeping Opal.

I knew I should encourage her to read it, but my mind kept catching on Giselle's empty place.

She can't really be dead. Sophie met my eyes. *The Tourney wouldn't* kill *one of us!* I bit my lip. I wished I shared her confidence.

Celine leaned forward to look around Pearl. "Come on, Opal. Read your riddle. The sandglass has started." She pointed at the running grains and Opal gasped, choked on a sob, and picked up her parchment.

Her voice trembled too much for us to understand, so she had to start again. "Up and down, round and round. I travel freely where I will, and not even the largest army can restrain me. And yet, neither can even the smallest baby feel me."

Staring at Opal's terrified, tear-stained face gave me a shot of energy that partially cleared my mind. Clearly we couldn't rely on Emmeline to catch her. Hazel had started shaking again, so the others directed their hopeful gazes at Emmeline. She remained silent, her lips pressed into a thin line. Another one she didn't know, then. I wished I could help but my thoughts kept circling endlessly around the loss of Giselle, and how we could save Opal.

Wait! "Thoughts!" I called out the suggestion with excitement. "I know mine go round and round. No one can tell you what to think, but no one can feel thoughts either, unless they're acted on."

I can feel your thoughts sometimes, when you send them to me. I could tell Sophie's quibbling didn't represent a serious objection, but it still made me nervous.

Slow nods around the room gave me a buoyant feeling that collapsed as soon as I thought about what would happen if I was wrong. It was a lot of pressure.

"Never mind," I said quickly. "That's probably wrong."

"No." Emmeline shook her head slowly. "It does fit. And who was it who said any answer is better than none?"

I looked hopefully around the table. Surely someone had a better answer. Surely someone was about to recognize the riddle from their home kingdom. No one spoke.

"Go on Opal," said Pearl. "I…I'll catch you if you fall." It was the bravest thing I'd heard her say, and I wanted to applaud her.

Opal scratched with her pen against her parchment and took a deep breath before dropping it on her plate. I waited with my own held breath. If she fell now, it would be my fault.

But her chair stayed in place, and small smiles blossomed around the table, although they were quickly extinguished when eyes fell on Giselle's empty place.

"Don't worry, Pearl," said Celine bracingly as the second-to-last riddle appeared on the young princess' plate. "I won't let you slip if we get this wrong."

Celine easily had my confidence, but the reverse was certainly not the case. If we got Celine's riddle wrong there was no way Pearl could take her weight. Celine would fall.

I couldn't bear the thought. Especially not given her existing injury. There might not be a soft landing at the bottom of the drop. I refused to let my mind think about the fact that the hardness of the surface wouldn't matter if the fall was long enough.

I suddenly realized that Pearl had already returned her parchment to her plate. Whoever had given the answer had been right, since her chair remained in place.

Celine took a deep breath and read out her riddle. "Many dream of me, but none can have me." Another short one. She looked around at us all enquiringly.

Surely someone knew the answer.

But only blank faces greeted her. Everyone had visibly begun to tire, our nerves on edge from the constant tension and strain, and from our underlying shock and fear about Giselle's unknown fate. My mind came up blank. And apparently, so did everyone else's. No one could come up with any but the most unlikely guesses.

Eventually Celine shrugged, swallowed and chose an answer to write on her parchment. Pearl extended her slight arm toward Celine, the limb visibly trembling. Moisture filled my eyes. Her action was even braver than her earlier words to her sister, since Celine would surely pull Pearl down with her rather than being saved herself.

Celine smiled at the younger princess but shook her head. "I'll grab onto the edge of the table. I should be able to hold myself briefly." She looked over Pearl and Opal's heads toward Emmeline, the closest of the older girls. "As soon as I put this down, we'll have finished all twelve riddles, so be ready to leap up. If it's wrong, you'll need to dash over and grab me."

The answer was definitely wrong. I poised my body to leap from my chair. I was the furthest possible from Celine, at the opposite diagonal of the table, but after what had happened to Giselle, I didn't trust Emmeline to save her. I wanted to squeeze my eyes shut, but I didn't let myself. I needed to be ready to run.

Celine dropped the parchment and gripped the table in the half second it took to float down onto the plate. Every single one of us, with the exception of Emmeline, held our breath as the parchment disappeared.

And every single one of us, with the exception of Emmeline, flinched violently when Celine's chair disappeared with a whoosh, and her body dropped out of sight. As I leaped from my chair, I noted with relief that her fingers gripped the edge of the table. I ran around toward her, Sophie two steps ahead of me, both running at full pace despite our exhaustion.

My twin came to an abrupt halt, and I collided with her back. Peering around her, I saw Celine lying on the ground, her face grim, and Emmeline kneeling beside her.

So the other girl had followed through after all. Had she been attempting to redeem herself for letting her sister fall? I saw no evidence of such emotion in her face.

The others gathered around us, all understandably anxious to vacate their chairs. Only Blanche stood apart from the group, staring down into the hole that had swallowed Giselle.

She looked up and met my eye. "What do we do?"

I walked over to join her and peered down myself. The opening was only just wider than a chair and disappeared into darkness much sooner than I would have thought possible given the light in the room. As little as I liked Giselle, I still hated the thought that she might be lying at the bottom of it, hurt or worse. But that didn't change the fact that we had no rope and no way to lower someone down there to check.

Sophie came to stand beside me. "Perhaps it curves once it's out of sight and becomes like a slide. It might have simply deposited her outside the building."

I nodded, grateful for the suggestion. I didn't want to leave without hope, but there was no way I was going down that hole, or helping anyone else to do so, either.

Now that my fear for Celine had faded, my earlier exhaustion had returned, heightened by so much emotional turmoil and our mad dash to our friend. Warm, familiar arms, like an extension of myself, wrapped around me. *Come on, Lil. Waiting here won't help anything.*

I nodded and turned toward the door. The rest of the princesses joined us, sped along by our desire to be gone from this terrifying place, and the small hope we still held for Giselle. Marigold and Lilac both clung to Hazel, and the twins clung to each other, but everyone else walked single file.

When we reached the lake, no one moved for a moment.

"There are only eleven boats," said Celine.

"The Tourney knows she's dead," said Marigold, and the younger twins began crying again.

"Or she's already crossed ahead of us," I suggested, hoping to calm them.

Their tears did stop as everyone considered the possibility, but I still heard the occasional sob as they climbed into their coracles. No one spoke as we floated across the water. I was as emotionally drained on this return journey, as I had been physically drained on the last two. And my body drooped from the fatigue of my recent illness. Would every Tourney event be so devastating? How many of us would be left at the end if they were?

"Look!" Celine pointed ahead of us as we approached the other side. I followed her finger and saw a single boat floating in place. I blinked and rubbed my eyes, but when I looked again, I could still see it. For the first time I began to actually believe that I might have been right about Giselle crossing before us.

We all walked quickly, almost jogging through the groves, although no one spoke the reason for our haste aloud. As we stepped out of the silver-leaved grove, Marigold, who walked next to me, shrieked.

"Giselle!" She shrieked again and took off running.

I told my feet to hurry after her, but they didn't respond. The relief of seeing the familiar figure waiting for us at the bottom of the ladder seemed to have drained the last vestiges of my energy.

I made my slow way toward her. Marigold babbled questions at Giselle, but she didn't answer. She briefly met her sister's eyes, and I saw no sign of recrimination or relief on either side. Yet the girls usually stuck to each other's sides without fail. Surely they must care for each other in some way?

"What are you doing here?" I asked her, unable to form a more coherent question.

"I thought I would come ahead and wait for you here," she replied.

I stared at her. Was that really all she had to say? After what must have been a terrifying experience for her. What had been a terrifying experience for the rest of us.

Marigold continued to ask her questions, but she just shrugged.

"Come on," I said, too tired to fight Giselle for answers. "Let's go."

I didn't notice who helped Celine up the ladder, but somehow we all arrived in the room at the top. I looked down at my nearly pristine dancing slippers. That was new. My eye caught on a bare foot. And then a second and a third. Apparently Hazel and Celine had both lost a slipper to the holes that had swallowed their chairs. And Giselle had lost both. I pictured the slippers falling endlessly down into darkness, and thought about how much worse the night could have turned out. How much worse it had seemed only moments before. I was nearly sick into the corner of the room.

Sophie gripped my arm, frowning at me in concern. I shook my head at her, not trusting my voice. And then the door opened, and Helena was there. She must have guided me after that because the next thing I knew, my head finally made contact with my pillow.

"Wake me in a decade," I croaked and was lost to unconsciousness.

～

When I opened my eyes again, I saw Sophie sitting at a small table beside our window, eating from a tray piled high with food. The light streaming onto her looked like morning sun.

Please, please tell me I haven't slept away another two days!

She shook her head. *Only one. Apparently we both slept for a whole day and night, but that means the next ball isn't until tomorrow night. And, I don't know about you, but I feel amazingly better.*

I considered her words. I did, indeed, feel remarkably recovered. My head was clear, and I would almost describe myself as full of energy. I joined Sophie at the small table, even more famished than when I awoke from the fever, if such a thing were possible.

Helena entered the room and wished us both a good morning. A sudden thought struck me. "Helena, did anyone bring up a parchment with our scores?" I had forgotten all about checking the branch for it.

"Indeed," said Helena. "Princesses Hazel and Emmeline performed strongly, but neither of you lost ground overall."

None of us met each other's eyes, and Helena quickly moved the conversation on to other things. Apparently Jon had proven true to his word, and we were to have a riding tour of the duchy.

Riding through the city two hours later, I felt more happy and relaxed than I had since arriving in Marin. Jon had found two amiable and lively mares for me and Sophie, and Teddy, Gabe, and Millie had all decided to join us.

At the last moment, Teddy and Millie's younger sister had come rushing from the palace demanding to be included. After a short dispute with her siblings, a groom was dispatched to saddle her pony as quickly as possible.

I used the time to get to know my new mount, attempting to keep my mind off my own pony. Sophie and I had been gifted ponies of our own at a young age and had loved them passionately. Although we had long ago graduated to full-sized mounts, we had still regularly visited the ponies until they had been struck down by a disease the previous year. Thinking about the sweet-tempered animals still brought moisture to my eyes. They had been our closest friends—with the exception of each other, of course—during our loneliest years.

Daisy seemed as full of energy as Millie had warned, and I noticed her eyeing me inquisitively throughout our ride. Jon led us down through the wide cobbled streets, pointing out buildings of interest and markets as we passed them. Many of the people stopped to watch us. Some looked unhappy at our intrusion, but most smiled and waved in our direction. The stone buildings had all been decorated with a profusion of window boxes holding bright spring flowers, and it made the city look alive, despite the mass of stone.

Before we arrived, I had imagined that a duchy consisting of a single city must be grey and dull. But the colors and the plants made it feel vital in a way I hadn't expected. And although, in reality, the people were all strangers to me, their friendly greetings felt warm and welcoming.

Our own capital city, Arcadie, was considered large, but this city-state dwarfed it. A wall encircled the city on all sides except for where it met the harbor, and it seemed to take the longest time for us to reach it. Past the walls, hills rose steeply in all directions, covered in green grass and the occasional clump of trees. I could see a couple of distant flocks with attendant shepherds, but otherwise the land was empty.

"The pastures on this side of the hills belong to the duchy," Jon explained. "But everything on the other side of the peaks belongs to our neighbors."

I pictured the maps of this land in my mind. The southern half of Marin bordered Talinos, a kingdom that raised my curiosity. Millie made it sound as if the entire kingdom were as scared of their own shadows as Pearl and Opal, while their prince, Gabe, was daring and impulsive. Was it just because he had been raised in Trione with Millie and Teddy?

But the northern half of Marin bordered the cursed Palinar, a kingdom I had no desire to see. "We're close to Palinar, then?" I glanced at Millie, but it was Jon who answered me.

"The wastelands don't start for a full day's ride north. We have nothing to fear here."

I nodded and forced myself to smile. In only a few weeks, one of us would be travelling north toward those wastelands. I turned my mind from the thought. The green that met my eyes in all directions was far too appealing and cheerful a sight for such dreary thoughts.

As we started up the hill, Daisy angled her pony toward me. "I'm Princess Daisy. You're Princess Liliana." She tipped her head to one side and regarded me curiously.

I smiled at her. "I am. But I prefer to be called Lily."

She nodded solemnly. "Daisy isn't my full name either." Her sideways glance warned me she knew she would be scolded for whatever question she intended to ask next. "Do you eat with a knife and fork?"

I bit back a smile and responded seriously. "I do indeed, why do you ask?"

"Oh!" She paused to digest the information and then gave me an impish smile. "Back home, I heard one of the maids say that if the Emissary's ship found other lands, the people would most likely be barbarians who don't even eat with a knife and fork."

"Daisy!" Millie threw me an apologetic look. "You should know better than to listen to such talk. Does Lily look like a barbarian to you?"

Daisy examined me consideringly, and I waited with equal parts curiosity and amusement for her assessment.

"I don't know," she said at last. "I've never seen a barbarian. Have you?" she asked me with a hint of hope.

I suppressed another smile. "I'm afraid I have not."

"That's something we have in common," said Daisy. "I think that means we can be friends."

"Thank you," I said gravely, and then couldn't help adding. "What about Sophie?"

Daisy looked over at my twin. "Have *you* seen a barbarian?"

"No, sadly," said Sophie. "I hope that means we may be friends also."

"I suppose so," said Daisy. "I have a lot of friends, you know."

"I'm sure you do," said Sophie.

Daisy nodded and then directed her horse toward her brother without another word.

"Goodness." I laughed. "She must keep you all on your toes."

Millie rolled her eyes. "You have no idea."

"Spare a thought for our poor brother," said Sophie with a chuckle. "He was in your position only reversed—us young ones were the twins, and there was only one of him."

Millie shuddered dramatically, and we all laughed. The unbroken blue sky and bright sun had put more than just me in a good mood it seemed. It made the dim underground gloom of the Tourney feel like a different world. Riding along with the breeze on my face, I found it hard to believe we would be down there again so soon.

An escort of guards and servants had accompanied us, bringing a picnic meal. Jon directed them to spread it out on one of the highest slopes, giving us a stunning view down over the whole city. From this height I could see no sign of the faded air that had struck me when we first entered the city all those days ago. Only the grandeur and the size and the life showed from up here.

"It's incredible," I said to Jon when he came to stand beside me. "We don't have a city like it in the Four Kingdoms."

"Marin is older and larger than any of the other capitals. Despite our lower rank, our family has always been well-respected amongst the kingdoms."

I nodded. "A trustworthy neutral ground. It's a great honor to your family and your people."

He smiled at me, and I felt a pleasant shiver at the warmth in his eyes. "There's an even better view from just over there." He pointed to the peak of the hill behind us. "Would you like to go take a look while the servants set up the food?"

Our attendants were in the process of laying out a carpet of rugs, and the closest one smiled at me. "We'll be a few minutes yet, Your Highnesses."

"We might as well then," I said to Jon who called our intentions to the rest of the group.

Do you want me to keep them all away? asked Sophie.

I have no idea what you're talking about.

She shook her head. *You're hopeless.*

Jon and I started ahead, but most of the rest of the group began to drift along behind us. I told myself I had meant what I said to Sophie and had no desire for a tête-à-tête with Jon. I wasn't quite convinced, however.

Millie and Sophie both stopped to pick wildflowers, but Daisy ran ahead of them to catch up with us.

"Don't you want to pick some flowers, Daisy?" I asked.

"Nope," she said as she raced past. "Flowers are for ninnies, I'm an adventurer." She reached a large rock and began to scramble up it, heedless of her embroidered skirts.

"Do you think that's safe?" Not having any younger siblings, I wasn't altogether sure what sorts of things you were supposed to let them do.

Jon shrugged. "You heard her, she's an adventurer." He looked over and must have read real concern in my eyes. "Daisy has been a little monkey since the day she learned to walk. She won't come to harm on a rock like that."

I bit my lip, embarrassed by my worries. Did he think me an overcautious fool?

"This is the spot here." Jon stopped and turned. I joined him and sighed happily at the view. From this angle we could clearly see the entire city, the large palace and the sparkling ocean stretching away to the horizon.

"Lord of all you survey, hey?" I smiled at him, and he grinned back.

"We're proud of it. Although Palinar was the truly magnificent kingdom, back before…" A dark shadow crossed his face, and he didn't finish the sentence.

The thought of Palinar and the Tourney crept across the scene like a blight. I could feel it looming menacingly at my back, and had to resist the urge to turn around and check behind me. I frowned and rubbed my arms.

Millie called something out to us, but Jon's name was all we could catch. "Just a moment," he said. "I'll be right back."

He moved back down the slope toward the others, and I looked around for Daisy. I hadn't heard her in the last minute or so.

She had disappeared from the rock, and I could see no sign of her. I moved a few steps to the left, and then to the right, trying to increase my field of vision. I didn't want to be alarmist, but I'd feel better if I at least had her in view.

I didn't spot her until I reached the highest point and finally looked down the other side. My heartrate picked up a little. Daisy had crossed over into Palinar.

It looked surprisingly normal from here, this side of the hill visibly no different from the Marinese side. Still. Everyone had made it clear that the whole kingdom was cursed and unsafe. Only the magical nature of the affliction kept the danger safely confined within its own borders. Which made stepping over that border seem like a bad idea to me.

"Daisy!" I called to her, but she either ignored me or didn't hear her name. I half turned back to call to Jon but paused. He had said the wastelands were far away, and that we had nothing to fear. And he had shrugged off my anxiety for Daisy earlier.

If I went after Daisy myself, I wouldn't need to admit my, probably unnecessary, concern to anyone. I started down the far slope, stepping carefully to avoid loose rocks or hidden burrows.

Daisy darted back and forth, moving downwards, away from me, apparently looking for something or playing a game with herself. When I got close enough I called to her, and she looked up with a wave and a smile. I gestured for her to come back up to me, and she started skipping in my direction.

But at the last second she must have spotted whatever she was searching for, because she veered off to the side.

"Daisy!" I called to her again.

"Wild honey," she called back, pointing at a tree. As she turned back to it, however, a large shape rose, seemingly from nowhere, to tower over her.

She screamed and, without conscious thought, I took off running toward her.

CHAPTER 16

he low, deep growl provided the ultimate counterpoint to Daisy's scream. The dark, shaggy fur of the bear looked out of place against the cheerful colors of the hill. It lumbered two steps toward Daisy who seemed to have frozen in fear.

"Run!" I screamed at her. "Run!"

She still didn't move.

As I flew down the slope, no longer minding where I put my feet, I called to Sophie in my mind. *Bear! Bear! Bear!*

Launching myself forward, I grabbed Daisy's thin wrist and thrust her behind me. The bear seemed confused by my wild approach and, for a second, I hoped it would back up. But, instead, it rose to its hind legs and roared.

When it dropped back down to all fours, it charged forward. As it neared, it lifted a clawed paw ready to swipe at us.

Spinning I wrapped my arms around Daisy and flung us both flat to the ground, shielding her with my body. I waited to feel pain tearing up my back, but it never came. Instead I heard a deep yell and then a thwack. I recognized the sound. It was quickly followed by a second and then a third. Another roar from the bear cut off suddenly. A loud thud followed.

Cautiously I raised my head and looked up the slope. Gabe stood there, a bow in his hand, his eyes fixed on something behind me. I twisted my head to follow his gaze. Jon, a sword gripped in his hand, stood panting over the body of the bear stretched out on the ground just behind us, three arrows protruding from its fur and its head severed.

I looked back up at Gabe in time to see Sophie and Millie push him aside in their rapid tumble down the hill. They both dropped to their knees beside us and tried to pry us off the ground. Their efforts were more hindrance than help but, after a chaotic scramble, we all managed to get back to our feet. Sophie gave me a tight squeeze before we both turned to check on Daisy.

Millie had wrapped her arms around her little sister but kept pulling back to look at her instead. She cupped her face in her hands, opening her mouth as if to yell at her. But, instead, she started crying, pulling Daisy back in for another hug.

"Oomph, errgh, get off me," said Daisy, fighting her way free of Millie's grip. Her gaze locked on her brother, and her eyes lit up. She pointed at the dead bear. "Look, Teddy! A bear! It nearly killed me."

Teddy looked queasy, his gaze moving from Daisy to the bear to Millie. "You sound entirely too gleeful about that."

Millie shook her head. "You're just fortunate Lily was here. And that Gabe keeps his bow ready."

"And that Jon had his sword." Gabe walked over to get a closer look at the bear. He whistled. "It's a big one. No wonder my arrows were barely slowing it down."

"Thank you," I said, my voice wobbling a little. "Thank you both."

Jon finished cleaning his sword and returned it to his scabbard. He took one of my hands in both of his. "Are you unharmed? Are you sure? This is entirely my fault. I shouldn't have left you alone without even a weapon. But it never occurred to me that Daisy would cross the border."

For someone with younger sisters, that seemed like a startling oversight in perception. He had obviously forgotten what eight-year-olds were like. But it was an accident, and his prompt reaction had prevented disaster, so I couldn't find it in myself to be angry with him. Especially not when he seemed so very contrite. And so very close to me.

I told myself the shaking was the aftereffects of nerves and had nothing to do with the fact that an attractive prince had just saved my life and was now holding my hand while gazing into my eyes with concern. Nothing whatsoever.

"We're both fine," I said. "That's what matters. Although I'd feel a great deal more comfortable if we could cross back over onto Marinese land."

"Yes, of course." Jon ushered me and Sophie back up the slope. I caught him exchanging worried glances with Gabe. "That bear shouldn't have been here. No one has reported any dangerous animals this close to Marin. If I had had even the least suspicion, I wouldn't have brought us so near the border."

"Honestly," I said. "I'm merely shaken. And Daisy appears to be delighted." The young girl had rushed ahead of us all, pulling her brother along with her and chattering rapidly about her recent adventure.

"She's certainly resilient." Sophie shook her head in admiration.

"I should have called you from the beginning," I said to Jon, "rather than going off alone and unarmed. I knew I was entering Palinar. I'm merely thankful the two of you acted so quickly."

"We heard the scream, of course," said Gabe. "But it was Sophie here who told us to grab our weapons and run." He looked at her. "I don't know how you knew."

Uh oh. I carefully avoided looking at her, not wanting to fuel any possible suspicions.

"Just a twin's connection, I guess," said Sophie. "I had a bad feeling as soon as I heard the scream." *That's true enough,* she added in my mind.

"Good instincts," said Gabe, but he seemed satisfied.

Our small retinue of guards must have been coming to our aid, because they had made it most of the way from the picnic site. However, they had stopped and now milled around in confusion as Daisy regaled them all with her story. The highest-ranking guard approached Jon.

"What would you like us to do, Your Highness? I take it you've dealt with the animal."

"We'll pack up the picnic, of course," said Jon. "And get these girls to a doctor."

"What? No!" Daisy dashed toward us, apparently having over-heard the conversation. "The cook told me she packed my favorite pies. And I'm starving!"

"What are you doing talking to the cook, you rascal?" asked Teddy, ruffling her hair. "You know you're not supposed to be bothering the servants. They're busy enough with all the Tourney festivities without having you underfoot."

She stuck her tongue out at him and danced out of reach, fixing her pleading eyes on Jon. "Please. Please."

"There really is no need for a doctor," I said. "I've spent count-less hours over the years assisting in the palace infirmary in Arcadia, so I know what I'm talking about when I say I'm unharmed. But, if you feel any concern for our ongoing safety ..."

Gabe shook his head before I could finish talking. "One bear may have wandered so close to the border unnoticed, but the shepherds up here would have seen if there were more of them roaming around. They don't move in packs like wolves, so I'm sure this one was on its own."

"Plus, we're safe enough here," said Jon. "The girls told you this plague on Palinar is magical, did they not? It won't cross our border."

"Let's eat then," I said. "Daisy isn't the only one who's hungry." I smiled as winningly as I could and saw the moment he capitulated.

"Well, if you're absolutely sure you weren't injured..."

"Absolutely." I nodded.

It wasn't exactly the relaxed meal I'd been expecting, but the attack had lent the occasion a sort of thrill. I toasted Gabe and Jon as heroes, and everyone seemed extra bright and witty, our relief going to our heads. We talked over what had happened from every possible angle, and Jon dispatched most of the guards to do some scouting. "Stay in pairs," he ordered. "And don't go far."

When we finished the meal, the servants who had been conducting their own little picnic not far away, began to clean up. The guards still hadn't returned, and Daisy wanted to go looking for them. Both of her siblings refused, point-blank, but she wheedled and pleaded until Teddy relented and said she could go a little way, but only in his company and definitely not across the border.

She took off with a whoop and Teddy followed.

"That child clearly needs more than one pair of supervisory eyes," said Millie with a sigh. "I'd better go too."

"I'll come and keep you company," offered Sophie.

Gabe leaped to his feet to help her rise, and the three of them wandered away, eyes fixed on Daisy and Teddy who were fast disappearing.

After the encounter with the bear, I had no desire to wander up the hill. But, after a moment, I realized I was in the servants' way and took myself a short distance away to a patch of soft grass that offered a clear view of the city. As I sat, someone else dropped down beside me.

"It seems to me that you're the true hero," said Jon, after a moment. "There aren't many people who would rush *toward* an attacking bear.

I shrugged. "I can't really take any credit for bravery. I didn't think at all, it was pure instinct."

His eyes didn't waver from my face, and I dropped my own down to the grass. "Then that is even more admirable," he said. "Surely your instincts in such a situation demonstrate your true self."

Glancing back at him through my lashes, I thought he looked like he wanted to continue but then thought better of it. I wished I knew what he had been about to say.

After a long silence I decided he wasn't going to say more on the topic, so I changed it. "You mentioned a plague. But I thought no one knew what had happened in Palinar?"

He sighed and turned his face toward his city. "No, not a literal plague." Leaning back on one arm, he stretched a leg in front of him and propped up the other knee. I watched him through my lashes, distracted by the strength of his muscles and the way the sunlight brought out the gold in his hair and eyes. This quiet moment felt entirely removed from the earlier terror of the bear. Had that fear unbalanced my mind? I couldn't think of any other reason I had suddenly become obsessed with the line of his arm and the fall of his hair.

"Like I said earlier," he said, oblivious to my scrutiny, "Marin may only be a duchy—and a city-state, at that—but we have always been well-respected amongst the kingdoms, serving as a neutral meeting place, and even as adjudicators on occasion. I suppose that's why we host the Princess Tourneys." He paused and plucked a long blade of grass, twirling it between his fingers.

"We are the true center of these lands, both in culture and in trade." He pointed toward his distant home. "Our palace is considered to be the oldest building anywhere. The first permanent structure our ancestors built when they came to these lands."

He sighed and threw the grass away. "But we have all of us fallen on bad times."

"I'm sorry," I said, unsure what else to say.

He glanced over at me and then away again. "It seems like a lifetime ago that we met, although it's only been a few days. I promised full honesty to you then, in everything, and I will give it. I will not hide our true state from you."

He sighed. "Palinar's fall was a significant blow to us all. And Talinos responded badly. The borders remain intact, but they're still terrified that the taint may creep down into their land. They've refocused all their resources to their border with Palinar, and the rest of the kingdom falters, too neglected to thrive.

"Meanwhile, the winters in Eldon seem to get longer every year. Oliver and his sisters used to be good company, but they seem to have frozen alongside their kingdom. It's been some time since Eldon was able to produce any sort of harvest. And we have no fields of our own. Just this small ring of hillside pastures around the city.

"We're a trading hub. If the other kingdoms aren't prosperous and trading with one another, it puts us in a desperate situation. We're living off stored gold and foodstuffs from better times as it is. And now that we have to host this Tourney, the supplies are draining fast."

"What about Trione?" I asked. "They seem prosperous and, from the way Millie talks, you sound like close allies. Your mother is her father's sister, right?"

He sighed again. "Trione have pulled back from us lately, but I don't think Uncle Edward and Aunt Juliette have told their children. They're making decisions as king and queen, not as brother and sister-in-law, and they probably guess Teddy and Millie will be unhappy about it. I know my mother is upset."

He stopped and ran his free hand through his hair. "But personally, I can't blame them. There's a darkness creeping down from the North, on both continents, and it makes sense for them to try to save their own kingdom."

"A darkness?" I shivered despite the bright sunlight.

"My father doesn't seem to see it, but it's quite clear to me. Palinar is completely lost, and Talinos is crippled by fear. Eldon will soon be entirely swallowed by ice, and Eliam..."

He glanced over at me. "You've heard about Snow's father? He won't last much longer, they say. And his wife—that's Snow's stepmother—is an...interesting character. I can't like the idea of her ruling one of the kingdoms."

"Won't the kingdom go to Blanche if he dies? She's an only child, right?"

"It should, of course, but she's not of age yet which complicates things. And if her stepmother doesn't want to cede power, who's to make her? Us?" He laughed, but there was no humour in the sound. "As I said, this is a full confessional. We're in a bad way here. All of us."

"Except for Trione?" I tried to cling to some shred of positivity.

"Yes, which is why I understand their withdrawal. They're an island, so maybe they have a chance, too." He looked at me sideways. "I'm sure Teddy will forget about his mystery ocean girl soon. He's a nice enough fellow generally. And Trione would make good allies."

He looked miserable. And, his expression made my tension at his words melt away. In fact, it made me want to smile. But I suppressed the urge. It didn't matter if I had no intention of marrying Teddy, something far bigger stood between me and Jon. "There is no point in thinking of alliances until we are through this Tourney. Anything might happen still."

"Yes, of course. You might win, after all." His voice sounded a little odd, but I couldn't see his eyes because he kept them trained away from me toward the sea. I did, however, see his free hand slowly clench into a fist.

CHAPTER 17

*A*s soon as we were back in our suite, Sophie turned on me. I'd seen it coming in her eyes ever since she'd returned from her walk and interrupted my conversation with Jon. I didn't always need projections to know what she was thinking.

That's it! No more putting me off. She faced me, her hands on her hips. *You two have been making eyes at each other ever since we arrived. But this afternoon the tension was so thick between the two of you, I could practically touch it. I want to know what's going on. What did he say?* A small smile crept over her face. *And, more importantly, what do you think of him?*

I sighed and sat on the edge of my bed. *I'll tell you what he said, of course. But it isn't anything like you're thinking. We weren't talking about us. Or, at least, not directly. He actually gave me insights on all the kingdoms—things you should know. And they serve as a reminder that I have far more important things to worry about than a personable prince.*

I proceeded to relate everything Jon had told me. About Marin, about Palinar, about the encroaching darkness. Halfway through, Sophie sat beside me, all humor gone from her face. We had sensed something wrong with these lands from the beginning, but neither of us had expected the situation to be so bad. When we had sailed away from our homes, aware that we faced possible marriages of alliance and might, therefore, never return, we had imagined this land quite differently. So far, only the friendly young royals had lived up to our expectation. And our connection with our new friends only made the insidious threat worse.

When I finished, we sighed in unison and then smiled weakly at each other.

So you see, I explained, *I could talk about the fact that, no matter how much I try to deny it, there's something in his gaze that makes me feel...special. And I could admit that it took all my self-control this afternoon not to reach across the short space between us and touch his arm. But what would be the point? I can't afford to indulge the luxury of such thinking. Not with the Tourney. And maybe not even without it. From the sound of it, even Jon thinks Teddy would make a better choice.*

Sophie took a deep breath and then spoke aloud. "No, you were right in what you said to him, Lily. There will be time enough to think of alliances after the Tourney. We should just focus on getting everyone safely through the events. When it's over we can think about other things."

I could easily read the concern in her eyes, and the way she wanted to distract me from the unpleasant truth. To put off as long as possible the likelihood that the end of the Tourney would mark the first of the alliances between the Four Kingdoms and this land. Even without Marin's troubles, I was unlikely to be free to follow my heart.

I hated the heavy feeling that had settled between us, so I smiled and spoke slowly, trying to cheer her up. "Although, surely it can't do any harm to spend just a moment dwelling on those muscles. He must be strong. Did you see him take down the bear? I was too busy cowering on the ground, unfortunately. If I'd thought a bit more quickly, I could have pretended I'd twisted my ankle, and then he would have had to carry me up the hill."

"Lily! You're shocking. You would never!" Sophie pushed me lightly and then collapsed back onto the bed, laughing.

I dropped back to lie beside her and stare up at the canopy. "Maybe not, but a girl can dream." I used my most innocent voice. "I'm sure I would have been light as a feather to him."

"Not the point," she said between giggles.

I smiled, upwards. Mission accomplished.

She propped herself up on one elbow so that she could see me. "He is rather attractive, of course. I agree with you completely there. It's something about that hair, and those eyes..."

"...those arms," I interjected, and she giggled.

"I can understand why you're drawn to him. But..." She paused and wrinkled her nose, trying to find the right words. "He's a little too...dutiful for my taste.

I rolled over to look at her in surprise. "What do you mean?"

"I don't know exactly. It's hard to describe, just a feeling, really. Maybe he comes across as just a little too constrained? Don't you want to be romanced? You said it yourself, in fact—you want to be swept off your feet."

"Mmmm, yes." I flopped back to stare upwards again. "Only I meant that quite literally you know."

Sophie snorted.

"But, in all seriousness?" I frowned as I thought over my words. "I like that he takes his responsibilities seriously. It shows that he truly cares. For his family and his people." I knew I sounded a little defensive, but I couldn't help myself. "That's an attractive quality."

Sophie laughed softly. "And that's probably why you don't notice it—you're too much alike. Except he keeps forgetting he's not the duke yet, and you keep forgetting I'm not sick anymore. He's not solely responsible for his people, and you're not responsible for me." She sighed. "I keep hoping one day you'll realize that."

We lay there for a moment in silence. A part of me agreed with her, but another part of me knew that she didn't really understand. I had never come close to death, which meant she had never stood on the edge of solitude, gripped by fear. I didn't just take care of her for her sake. I also did it for mine. Because I couldn't bear to lose my other half. What would I be without her?

"Do you remember all the other girls back home?" Sophie asked eventually. "All the courtiers and the commoners who thought being a princess must be lovely?"

"Being a princess *was* lovely back home. I've been lying here remembering how we begged our parents to let us accompany the delegation."

"Yes, our lives would be a lot simpler if we'd stayed in Arcadia." She turned her head to look at me. "Less exciting, though."

I rolled my eyes. "And thus, our downfall."

~

The next evening, Sophie and I entered the ballroom together as we always did. Jon had been occupied all day with his father, and I had told myself to be glad for his absence.

And yet, as usual, my mind refused to behave, and I found myself looking for him as soon we stepped through the doors. If he was still occupied with his duties, he might not have time for balls and dancing. He didn't spend his days looking handsome and socializing, like Teddy and Gabe. He cared for his people and poured his time into them, which made every minute he took off to spend with me that much more meaningful. I had no right to expect he would always be awaiting our arrival, as he had done at past balls.

And yet, sure enough, he approached us immediately. His eyes flew to me, as they so often seemed to do, but for once he didn't smile. He looked determined, and a little cold, as he turned to Sophie instead.

"Dance with me, Princess Sophie?" His friendly smile appeared as he looked at her.

"Oh! I…" She looked at me.

What are you waiting for? Go! I tried to make my projection as nonchalant as possible and to keep my eyes off them as they swept away.

But when Gabe reached me, I agreed to dance without knowing what I said. And my attempts to keep my eyes from straying to Sophie and Jon as they circled the dance floor failed miserably.

Had this been the real reason for my determination to push Jon away? Perhaps, somehow, underneath everything, I had been waiting for this. Eventually Jon would get close enough to see my weaknesses. To recognize how incomplete I was as an individual. It had only been a matter of time before Jon saw the truth and lost interest.

Back home it had never been an issue, because we had never had any real suitors. The only men who courted us were interested in the power and position that such a marriage would bring. They didn't differentiate between us, since any princess would do for the purpose. And none of the young men amongst our friends at court had ever tried to court either of us. My brother and his wife claimed it was because we were too close to each other. The boys had always seen us as a single unit rather than two individuals.

But our family was blinded by their love. They didn't see the reason everyone saw us as a single unit, the essential closeness that kept us both functioning. Our godmother had gifted it to us, and we had no idea how to change it. And no desire to do so, either. After all, our families didn't know our true connection, or how impossible it would be to temper it.

And yet, somehow, right from the beginning, Jon had seen us

as distinct. He had never once confused us. I had started to believe he truly saw us as two separate people. I didn't know why I hadn't recognized the inevitable consequences of his unexpected insight.

My dance with Gabe ended, and another young man took his place—a Marinese nobleman whose name I instantly forgot. Sophie and Jon had disappeared from sight. Had they moved to the other side of the dance floor? Or had they left to search for refreshments?

Before I could make up my mind, Jon spun past. Except now he was dancing with Millie. A minute later I spotted Sophie watching me from the side of the dance floor, a glass in each hand. She shook her head at me pityingly, and I excused myself to my partner so that I could cross the floor to join her.

She handed me one of the drinks. *I thought if I let you stress a little it might make you acknowledge your true feelings a little more openly, but you looked so pathetic I don't have the heart to continue.*

I bristled. *I don't know what you're talking about.*

Uh huh. She smiled at me knowingly. *Then I'm sure you have no interest whatsoever in the fact that Prince Jonathan has been reprimanded by his father and reminded that, as a host of the Tourney, it is his duty to dance with all the contestants.*

Oh. I could feel the flush rising up my face. Sophie was right. When had I become this pathetic?

"Here take this." She thrust the glass at me. "But drink quickly. We need to show Jon that he's not the only one in high demand."

I stared at her. *I thought we'd agreed to put schemes of romance aside until after the Tourney?*

She tossed her head. *No, we agreed to put thoughts of alliances behind us until after the Tourney. Personally, I wasn't thinking of them much to start with. And since Teddy's good looks are rather spoiled by his moping, and Gabe is a little too daring for my tastes, I have yet to decide where my own romantic efforts should fall. Which means we need to focus on you.*

"Sophie!"

She ignored me. *Jon seems to think Teddy his most likely rival, so we should start there.*

"Sophie!" I tried again, and this time she turned to glare at me. A struggle, since her smile kept trying to shine through.

Her projection dropped to a quiet whisper. *Aren't you curious to see if we can break through all that responsibility and restraint? Just a little bit?*

I... I had intended to tell her off, but she seemed to take my hesitation as agreement.

"Excellent, then." She slipped her arm through mine and dragged me toward the refreshment table. "Teddy!" she called as we barreled up to him. "You're just the person we need..."

When the bell finally rang, I still hadn't danced with Jon. But I'd danced with five other handsome and eligible young men, and I had been silently complaining to Sophie for the last two. *Remember how we still have to compete in an event after this? We should be conserving our strength.* I glowered over at her. *No, scratch that, I should be conserving my strength. You're doing just fine.*

Sophie had taken a seat against the wall and gathered a small court of admiring locals around her. She had turned down all offers to dance and had kept them busy bringing her food and drink instead. *We didn't even need our feet for the last event. And, anyway, some sacrifices are worth it. Love is pain, and all that.*

I believe that's beauty *is pain, sister dearest.*

Oh! Is it? Her projection dripped with surprise, but I knew the emotion was feigned.

I didn't know why I was still arguing with her if she was in this mood. Love is pain. I shook my head and startled my dance partner by chuckling out loud. Sophie was the last person to appreciate pain in any form. She was just being ornery and outrageous on purpose.

Thankfully the bell rang before I had to think of an excuse for my oddly-timed levity, allowing me to excuse myself and hurry away.

We princesses were a silent group as we made our way through the groves and floated across the lake. After the outcome of the second event, I had since made special care not to let even a toe touch the water.

When we arrived in the throne room, everyone seemed equally reluctant to approach the table which once again had twelve chairs. Sophie's earlier good humor had dropped away. A glance at her pale face made me step forward, ignoring my own nerves.

"There's no reason to think the chairs are unsafe. The castle was collapsing on our heads in the first event, but I haven't seen so much as a piece of gravel come away since. None of the events seem to affect future events."

"Except for this," Celine grumbled as she pointed at her bandaged leg.

"Well, yes, except for that." I grimaced at her sympathetically. "But that doesn't change the likely safety of our chairs."

When no one else moved or responded, I sighed, and stepped forward to take the chair that had collapsed under Giselle. When nothing happened, I glared at the others and they came over to take seats of their own.

Parchments appeared on all our plates the instant the last princess sat down. Almost as if the Tourney had shared my impatience. I eyed the parchment uneasily, but Emmeline picked up hers with the utmost unconcern. Steeling myself, I unfolded my own.

The first stage of the Tourney has been completed. The second stage will now begin. This stage involves a series of individual challenges where points will be awarded based on success. Each challenge will begin with the sound of a bell, and will only finish once at least one of you has successfully completed the task. Once the bell sounds, your lips will be sealed until the task is completed.

My eyes flew to Sophie. She looked as surprised as I felt. We had only had three tasks, and we were already moving to the individual phase? There must be twelve more still to come before the final group competition on the last night of spring. We had both expected the two stages to be more equal in length. Pearl squeaked, and Marigold looked almost as scared although she remained silent.

I looked at them both uneasily. During the collaborative phase, I hadn't had to choose between protecting them and completing the task. Things had just become a whole lot more complicated.

"What's the challenge?" asked Hazel, clearly attempting— somewhat unsuccessfully—to sound grown up and not at all nervous.

Emmeline retrieved the parchment from the middle of the table and read it out. "It is the responsibility of a ruler to see value in her kingdom, wherever it lies, and however hidden the treasure may be. The first of you to uncover the hidden treasure will win the challenge. You may begin the search as soon as the bell rings."

There was a moment of silence.

"That actually doesn't sound too bad," said Celine. "Even I have a chance at winning a treasure hunt. It's sort of like a riddle without any plummeting trapdoors."

I nodded slowly. "Just remember your families, everyone. Don't give in to the temptation to let yourself lose. We all need to at least try."

Slowly the other eleven heads nodded. No one looked pleased, but they all looked determined. Except for Hazel who leaned over to Blanche, sitting next to me, and whispered, "Maybe you should try to lose, Snow. With any luck, the Tourney will strike down your stepmother."

"Hazel!" I tried to keep my voice low since most of the other girls were too busy talking amongst themselves, or examining their parchments, to have heard.

She looked over at me guiltily. "I'm just joking. I know Snow would never really do something that might put her father at risk."

"She's only trying to cheer me up," said Blanche. "She's a good friend."

I frowned at the parchment in my hand. Just how bad was Blanche's stepmother? What was it Jon had said about her? An interesting character. I had assumed he mainly meant incompetent, but there must be more to it than that.

I shook my head to clear my thoughts. I didn't have time to think about Blanche's family, I needed to try to win this competition for the sake of my own.

A familiar bell rang through the mostly-empty room, the sound distorted in this strange, mirror world. The scrape of twelve chairs followed, and we all ran for the door.

CHAPTER 18

I brought up the rear, partly from a lingering protective instinct, and partly because I needed more time to come up with a plan. *What do you think?* I asked Sophie. *Any ideas what this treasure might be?*

I thought our lips were supposed to be sealed. Her projection sounded amused.

Do you see my lips moving?

She laughed silently. *The only treasure I can think of is the leaves in the grove. I've never seen silver or gold, let alone diamond, formed into such delicate shapes.*

But it's not exactly hidden.

No, true. She sighed. *And the same goes for our golden plates and goblets.*

Apparently we weren't the only ones whose thoughts had gone to the groves. Almost half of the other girls went straight to the boats.

Should we join them? Or stay here in the mirror palace. Sophie watched them clamber into the coracles.

I considered the question. *There must be a clue in the wording of the challenge. Surely we're not supposed to stumble around blindly until one of us trips over it?*

It just said we needed to 'uncover the hidden treasure'.

Hmmmm. We could check that room with all the cupboards. Maybe that would count as hidden.

It didn't seem like a great idea, but we both started walking in that direction. The cupboards, not surprisingly, proved bare. I bit my lip and tried to focus.

What about the word 'uncover'. It could mean simply 'discover'. Or it could mean it's actually under a cover of some sort.

I looked around the room. Like all the other rooms I had seen here, it was devoid of decoration. No tapestries, no curtains, nothing that could cover even the smallest of treasures.

Just as I was despairing of coming up with a single idea, the bell's chimes rang through the palace again. For a brief second, Sophie and I stared at each other. And then we both took off running for the entrance hall. It had only been minutes but, somehow, impossibly, someone else had already found the treasure.

Celine had managed to hobble back into the entrance hall ahead of us, along with Blanche, Pearl and Opal. They were all looking around in confusion, though, so it obviously hadn't been any of them.

I did a quick count in my head of the girls who had already taken the boats. Only one other was missing.

"Hazel," I said, just as she walked into the entrance hall. She looked up at us, dazed, and then held up a small leather pouch. It jingled as if full of coins.

"I...I won." She didn't sound happy.

"Where was it?" asked Pearl.

"It was down in the kitchens. I think it's full of gold coins... but it wasn't when I found it."

"What do you mean?" asked Blanche. "What was in it when you found it?"

Hazel flushed slightly. "It was full of salt. I found it down in the kitchens, and I remembered hearing cook talking about how important it is. We don't produce our own food in Marin, so our stored food is particularly valuable to us. The bell sounded as soon as I took it out of the kitchen, and then it started jingling. It looks like it's full of gold now."

"It was a good idea," said Sophie. "All of our kingdoms would be lost without salt."

Hazel smiled slightly at the praise before her face fell again. How had she known to look in the kitchens? Or had it simply been a lucky guess? I bit my lip. Or, rather, a not-so-lucky one. Her face certainly suggested she knew the undesirability of a win.

"How did you know to look in the kitchens?" I asked, wanting to understand.

"It was the words of the challenge," she said. "And what Celine said about it being like a riddle. *Uncover* stood out to me, so I kept trying to think of all the possible meanings. There isn't really anything in this whole place that could cover something else. And then I remembered that when my mother is planning a formal dinner, she and the servants talk about the number of covers." She looked around to check we all knew what she meant. "The place settings at the table. We'd just come from the only table in this palace, so I thought I would check the kitchens…"

"That's very clever," said Sophie.

Hazel nodded sadly. "Nearly falling down that awful hole threw me off the other night. Usually I really am quite good at riddles."

Celine looked around the large hall and then over at me and Sophie. "It seems hard to believe it could be over already, but I suppose it must be. So, we might as well head for the boats. I, at least, have no desire to spend my whole night down here if I don't have to."

"No, indeed!" agreed Blanche with a shiver.

We had all drifted into a tight clump during our conversation, so we moved out the door together. Blanche put her arm around Hazel's shoulder, supporting her friend, who still looked a little shaky.

Seven of the boats still remained, so we soon reached the other side of the lake. Emmeline and Giselle were waiting for us on the shore.

"We heard the bell," said Emmeline. "Who found it?" Her eyes darted between me, Sophie, and Celine. She obviously thought us the most likely candidates. Did she care about the results, after all? After her success in the riddles, she sat fairly high on the charts. A less than desirable placement.

"I did." Hazel held up the pouch.

I saw a shade of surprise on both their faces, but they didn't ask her where, or how she had worked it out. Maybe they were smart enough not to want to gain even such a small insight into the Tourney. It was a strange dynamic, this competition where everyone had to try their best, but everyone wanted to lose.

In the diamond grove we found Millie and, a moment later, Lilac and Marigold came running out of the golden-leaved trees.

"What happened?" called Marigold as she approached. "Who won?"

"Is it really over already?" Lilac shook her head in wonder. "That was so much shorter than the others."

"I guess the Tourney didn't count on Hazel being so clever," I said.

"H...Hazel." Marigold turned a horrified face on her sister. "You won, Hazel?"

Hazel nodded wordlessly, and Lilac ran over to give her a comforting hug.

Not exactly normal victory celebrations, are they? Sophie sounded sad and tired, but I still couldn't help comparing how much less tired I felt than on all our previous trudges back to the trapdoor.

When we reached the ladder, Emmeline and Giselle began to ascend immediately, but the rest of us paused. Everyone's eyes followed me as I removed the parchment from the branch and unfolded it.

I stared down at the numbers, not wanting to read them out. But I couldn't delay forever. "Only Hazel scored highly for tonight's challenge." I looked up at her. "And since you also did fairly well with the riddles, you're now in the lead overall."

Hazel's face went completely white, and Lilac and Marigold didn't look much better.

"Don't worry," Blanche whispered audibly to her friend. "There are still twelve more challenges. I'm sure you'll fall behind again soon."

Hazel nodded and pulled up a tremulous smile just as her knees buckled. Blanche gasped and managed to half-catch her, helping her regain her balance. Hazel still looked unnaturally pale, leaning against her friend, and her sisters rushed over to hover close. I kept back, giving them some space, confident it was just shock and not anything seriously wrong.

Emmeline's head appeared at the top of the ladder. "Are you coming?"

"Yes," I called up to her. "Move back."

Lilac and Blanche supported Hazel as she climbed, and then I ushered all the younger girls up. Sophie, Millie and I helped Celine, so that soon we all stood together in the small room. Normally someone moved straight for the door, but tonight we all paused and stared at each other, thrown off by how differently the event had gone.

"Oh!" A soft gasp from Hazel drew everyone's attention. She was looking down into her hands.

"What is it?" asked Marigold, crowding in close beside her.

"The pouch. It didn't disappear." She opened it and peered inside. "The gold hasn't either," she added in an awed voice.

"It must be your prize," I said. "For winning."

A murmur swept through the small crowd of princesses. It

seemed that lots of things had changed now that we had entered the individual phase.

"I'm tired." Giselle pushed open the door and left, her sister close behind her.

Slowly the rest of us filed out to be greeted with surprise by the faithful group that awaited us. Of course, none of us could explain anything to them, although Lilac told her parents they needed to get Hazel to bed.

The ducal family moved off together, grouped around Hazel and talking quietly. Jon, however, hung back, turning to meet my eyes. I couldn't bring myself to smile given his sister's state, and I couldn't interpret the turmoil in his gaze. A moment later, he was gone, and Helena was ushering Sophie and me to bed.

We climbed into our nightgowns, and slipped obediently into bed, but as soon as she was gone, Sophie sat up. *Lily.*

I sat as well, crossing my legs and facing toward her. She mirrored me, and we stared at each other in the near darkness.

Tonight was different. Sophie sounded thoughtful.

Everything's changed. I paused. *At least it seemed a lot safer.*

I've been thinking about something Marigold said on our first night.

Oh? I tried to remember what the youngest Marinese princess had said after we arrived, but I couldn't remember much other than her mention of the Beast.

She said how she wouldn't mind the Tourney if Gabe had called it. I've been thinking about how different it would be if it was his Tourney. From what Millie said, even the events themselves would be different.

I thought about it. *He's fun and friendly, but also daring. So there might still have been some scares to deal with. And he's an excellent archer. Maybe Celine would have gotten her wish and we'd all be shooting targets down there.*

If only. Sophie sighed. *I just keep picturing Hazel's face as she came out of the throne room. And when you told us about the scores.*

Yes, everyone would feel a little differently about winning if it was

Gabe rather than this Dominic. And a pouch of gold as a prize would only excite everyone more.

She nodded sadly. *From what you said, her family could do with the gold, too. Everyone would be competing with enthusiasm if it was Gabe...*

I bit my lip and closed my eyes. I had known from the second I saw the rankings what had to be done. Had known it from the beginning, really. But saying it made it feel too real. I hesitated a moment longer and then drew a deep breath.

"We have to win." I said the words out loud, trying to make myself accept the awful finality of them. "We've got the younger girls this far, we can't abandon them now when we know it means facing something even worse than any of these challenges. We should be able to succeed, too. We're the oldest except for Celine. And, even with all the will in the world, I can't see her winning at this point."

I shook my head. "We should have won tonight, though. You were even on the right track. But I don't think we were truly trying. I guess, if I'm honest, I just assumed we would win, so I didn't feel any great hurry."

"You're right, we should have been able to work it out." Sophie looked half guilty, half sad. "If for no other reason that we're able to talk to each other and work together, when none of the rest of them can."

"So we just need to try harder next time." I tried to sound confident for her sake. "Because we're fighters, and we have each other. Which means we have the best chance of surviving this Dominic. I simply couldn't bear to send one of those girls off to Palinar alone."

Sophie sighed again. "Agreed. So it sounds like our goal has changed. We can stop worrying about keeping the others alive in the events, now we need to start worrying about winning."

"I have confidence in us," I whispered.

"Yes." Sophie lay back down. "That's what scares me."

I lay down too and rolled away from her. I had said *we* needed to win, but that was only to forestall an argument. I had no more intention of letting Sophie face this Beast than I had of letting the younger girls do it.

~

It felt strange to wake up after an event and find it was only morning of the next day. It gave me a light, buoyant feeling, despite the heavy realization of the night before. The next ball seemed such a long time away.

The bright sunshine lured us out into the garden again, and we passed many of the other princesses as we wandered up and down the paths. We hadn't seen Hazel or the other Marinese girls, though.

I was just about to comment on this to Sophie, when a loud voice from behind hailed us. Turning we saw Gabe, Teddy and Jon, with Millie trailing behind. She looked a little irritated, but brightened when she saw us, and rushed forward to catch up.

"Good morning." Gabe seemed particularly cheerful. "Not a scratch on any of your slippers this morning, I'm told. And you came out with a bag of gold. Things seem to be looking up in this Tourney."

Jon didn't seem to share his excitement. "Except that *Hazel* is now in the lead. My sister. Don't forget that." He shook his head.

"Oh." Gabe looked crestfallen. "I hadn't heard that actually. And she's only just fifteen, isn't she?" He looked mutinous. "Much too young to be having anything to do with Dominic."

Sophie and I exchanged glances.

Jon ran his hand through his hair and looked at me sideways. "All the girls are too young."

"Hey! We'll be eighteen just after the Tourney finishes," said Sophie.

"It sounds to me like age has nothing to do with it." I jumped in before anyone could start fighting over the acceptable age for involvement in the Tourney. "No one of any age should have to deal with this Prince Dominic, or Beast, or whatever you want to call him. But someone has to." I took a deep breath. "But there are still twelve events to go. I hardly think it's time to be despairing for Hazel."

"Maybe we should make sure of that," said Gabe, with a significant look at the other two princes.

"Whoa, slow down there, genius." Millie's grumpy face had returned. "We've discussed this before. None of you are going to be throwing your lives away by interfering in the Tourney."

I stepped up beside her to show my support. "Absolutely not. And, as I already said, it's far too early to be worrying anyway. We're all fine, as you saw last night. Not so much as a scratch on any of us. We have weeks still to go. There will be time enough for worrying about who's going to win later."

Gabe looked mutinous, but Jon clapped him on the shoulder. "They're right, you know."

Since Jon was Hazel's brother, Gabe could hardly protest further, and the conversation turned to lighter topics as the two groups merged and wandered down the path together. But I couldn't help but notice a certain defiant look in Gabe's eyes, and I decided I'd better start paying more attention to him at the Tourney balls. If he intended to do anything foolish, I intended to stop him. I owed him my life after his quick intervention with the bear, and I had every intention of paying back my debt, whether he liked it or not.

CHAPTER 19

*A*s we walked, we fell into pairs, and somehow Jon ended up beside me. So much had happened since we had last spoken during our picnic outing, I couldn't immediately think of what to say. And the longer the silence continued, the more blank my mind became.

Finally he spoke, glancing sideways at me. "I was sorry not to have the opportunity to dance with you at the ball last night."

More silence.

He glanced my way again. "You seemed very popular." As soon as he said it, he shook his head quickly, as if annoyed with himself. "Of course you were. Ignore me."

An actual flush appeared to be creeping up his neck, but I tried to ignore it. Tried to pretend I had no interest in the potential success of Sophie's romantic plans on my behalf at the ball. Not anymore. Not now that I had truly accepted how this Tourney was going to end. It would be best if Jon stopped thinking about me altogether.

"You seemed well occupied yourself," I said. "I hope you had an enjoyable time."

"Oh, yes. Well, that is, I mean…" He rubbed the back of his neck, and I hid a smile. He was usually much more confident.

He glanced at me ruefully. "I don't seem to be able to say the right thing this morning. Of course, I enjoyed all my dances. My duty as a host is clear, and I am more than happy to fulfill it." He gazed away across the bushes that bordered our path, and then quickly back at me, before moving his eyes forward again. His next sentence was delivered so quietly I almost missed it. "But I've never felt so torn in my duties before."

Now I was the one flushing, but I ruthlessly suppressed it. Silence settled over us again. Jon's eyes had locked on Teddy who walked ahead of us arguing with his sister in low tones. "At least Teddy was free to oblige you."

The fire in his tone made my eyes fly to his face. He looked ahead, not meeting my gaze, his face carefully controlled. But his hands had once again formed into fists.

Part of me wanted to snap at him that he didn't have a monopoly on my dances. The other part felt guilty for joining in on Sophie's scheme to break through his restraint. It was hardly fair given I was actively trying to win the Tourney which would force me into a betrothal with someone else.

Either way, I didn't know how to respond to his statement. There were too many words that could not be said between us. I needed to change the subject.

"At least you all didn't have to wait up most of the night for us this time," I said. "You must have appreciated the good night's sleep almost as much as we did."

He smiled, but the gesture didn't reach his eyes. "A pleasant surprise, certainly. But I'm afraid everyone in my family had a hard time settling once we saw the latest scores."

I wanted to kick myself. Where had all my usual poise gone? Of course it hadn't been a good night for Hazel and her family. I needed to do better.

"I greatly enjoyed the tour and picnic the other day," I tried. "Thank you for organizing it."

He smiled a little incredulously. "In spite of the bear?"

"Well, that bit certainly wasn't the high point of the occasion, I'll admit. But I loved seeing Marin."

"I'm glad. I've always thought it a beautiful city. I enjoyed sharing it with you...all."

I ducked my head and pretended I hadn't noticed his hasty addition. "Have you seen Daisy? Is she fully recovered from her scare? I had some concern that she might find herself covered in bruises yesterday from where I pushed her to the ground."

Jon chuckled. "Daisy is as irrepressible as ever. She does have a couple of bruises, but she's wearing them as badges of honor and telling anyone she suspects of noticing them about her fight with a bear."

I grinned at the thought of all the poor people subjected to the tale. "She reminds me of the mischief Sophie and I got up to as children. But she seems so much more secure than we were at that age."

He glanced at me with curiosity, and I remembered his earlier interest in my childhood.

I shrugged. "For reasons I didn't find out until I was much older, we were left to grow up a little wild. All we wanted was love and attention from our parents, of course. And we received it in the end, but..." I shook my head, not wanting to go into the whole tale. I forced my tone to become more cheerful. "But we always had each other, of course."

"You've always been this close then?" His eyes followed Sophie who had abandoned Gabe and joined Millie and Teddy in an effort to break up their dispute.

"Yes, always." I watched him surreptitiously but could see nothing but curiosity and a mild friendly interest on his face as he watched my twin. I still couldn't quite believe that I might have met someone who could distinguish between us and saw us as two separate individuals.

"My family has always been very close," he said. "But nothing like the two of you. It's almost uncanny how attuned you are to each other."

I bit my lip. He had no idea. And yet, here was another thing he had noticed about us. Perhaps we needed to be more careful.

Jon gave a sudden, soft exclamation of annoyance. When I looked over at him questioningly, he indicated a path ahead of us that joined with ours a short distance ahead. "Talking about duties that need to be performed regardless of desire, there are two subjects I'd rather not meet right now."

A young man and woman strolled along the other path, on an intercept course with our group. The woman looked vaguely familiar, and for once I managed to dredge a name from my memory. Corinna. The unpleasant daughter of the unpleasant Sir Oswald. I could understand Jon's irritation.

As they drew closer, I examined her companion. The tall young man, dressed like a nobleman, appeared to be a couple of years her senior. For some reason it surprised me to see them together. Perhaps because she hadn't looked like someone with a sweetheart when she looked at Jon.

"I've met Corinna," I said. "But who is her companion?"

Jon grimaced. "That's Cole, her older brother. And he's even worse I'm afraid, although in a different sort of way."

Ah, a brother. That explained it.

Their pace slowed, ensuring that when the others ahead of us passed the intersection between our paths, Corinna and Cole were only close enough for polite nods. When Jon and I reached the spot, however, they fell into step beside us.

"Your Highness, what a pleasant surprise." Corinna ignored me, directing her comment at Jon. "I hope you don't mind if our walks converge for a few minutes."

Jon muttered polite assurances and, after a small nudge from Corinna, Cole nodded his own greeting, adding a cool, "Prince."

"Cole." Jon sounded equally distant.

Corinna clearly noticed their unease, since she inserted herself between them in such a way as to force Jon to offer her his arm. I relinquished my place beside him, and fell back slightly, ending up next to Cole.

The merchant's son made polite conversation easily enough but showed no real interest in me as a person. I felt sure that he wouldn't even have noticed if Sophie and I had traded places halfway down the path.

After the usual polite chit-chat, Cole steered the conversation toward trade. His subtlety far outstripped his father's, but he still displayed a focus on wealth that reminded me too much of my previous interaction with his sister.

And, as he questioned me further, I became even more uncomfortable. Although he never came out and said it, he seemed to be hinting at his family's interest in a direct trade alliance. But I had attended the first day of meetings and knew that Arcadia had made its position clear. All alliances would be officially sanctioned through the duke and occur with Marin as a whole, rather than on the level of individual merchants. My parents didn't want to risk establishing the wrong connections when we still knew so little about these new lands.

Nothing about Corinna or Cole had dissuaded me from my original stance. I didn't want their family included in any sort of alliance with my kingdom at all, sanctioned or otherwise. With that aim in mind, I took the same approach with Cole as I had with his sister, downplaying Arcadia's wealth and position within the Four Kingdoms. It was easy enough to do since we were neither the richest kingdom nor the strongest military power.

I simply omitted any mention of our significant size or the fact that, ever since my older brother had married for love six years ago, our kingdom had been thriving with bumper crops every year and increasing peace and security.

Cole's interest in me seemed to wane as the conversation progressed, and I congratulated myself on a task well done. Hopefully I wouldn't be bothered by either sibling again.

Sophie, who had been following the conversation with interest via my silent commentary, eventually rescued me and got us both back up to the palace. Once there, she went in search of Helena with a question about one of her dresses that still hadn't made it back from the seamstresses, and I decided to visit Celine. Our poor friend was still under enforced rest between Tourney events.

But, as I neared Celine's room, I picked up the soft sounds of suppressed crying. The noise emanated from a partly opened door, and I decided to peek inside, afraid it was one of the younger princesses from the Tourney.

I found the sitting room of a guest suite that looked identical to Celine's. Blanche sat on the low green sofa, a piece of parchment clasped in her hand and tears rolling down her cheeks. It looked like a letter, and I instantly felt guilty for intruding on her privacy.

Before I could move, however, she looked up and saw me. I froze, unsure whether to move forward and attempt to comfort her or to retreat. Enough seconds passed that I decided retreat was no longer an option, so I walked over and sat beside her.

"Are you all right?"

"It's just a letter from home." She sniffed, putting the paper down into her lap.

"Not...not bad news, I hope." My thoughts flew instantly to her father's poor health.

"Oh!" She seemed to follow my meaning. "Oh, no. Nothing like that. It's just my stepmother. She must be having the servants report to her, because she seems to know all about the current scores in the Tourney. She wrote to lecture me for not trying hard enough. Apparently I'm giving our kingdom a bad name or some such thing. Disappointing my father."

I stared at her. "But…" I paused, lost for words. "Surely she can't want you to win."

Blanche gave another big sniff, although she managed to make it sound scornful. "Of course she does. You should have seen the way her eyes lit up when we received the summons for the Tourney. Nothing would delight her more, I expect." She dashed the tears from her eyes as her expression turned angry. "But she can't fool me. I know my father doesn't want me to win. He wants me to come home." She scrunched up the letter and threw it across the room.

"I'm sorry, Blanche," I said, not sure what else I could offer in the way of sympathy.

She shook her head and straightened, drawing a deep breath. "Please, call me Snow. Everyone else does. And don't worry about me. I'm used to it by now. I just needed to let it out for a moment." She drew another deep breath.

"I just wish she hadn't sent the letter with Randolph," she added in a more normal tone. "He's one of her favourite guards, and I don't like having him here. He always looks at me with such black eyes. I feel like he's waiting for me to put a step wrong, and then he'll be judge, jury and executioner all rolled into one." She shivered.

"I'm sure he wouldn't actually do anything to harm you! No one here would allow that."

"No, I suppose not. I'm just being foolish, I realise that. Still. I wish he wasn't here."

"Why don't you write a reply to your stepmother? Assure her you'll try harder from now on. Then ask him to take it back for you."

Her face brightened. "That's an excellent idea. I'll write it immediately." She jumped up and took several steps toward a small desk, before pausing and looking back. "Oh, I'm sorry." She stepped back toward me, but I shook my head.

"No, you go. The sooner, the better, right?"

"Right!" She smiled at me and hurried over to the desk.

I excused myself and returned to the corridor. I just hoped my suggestion worked. From everything I'd heard, Snow had enough burdens already.

Distracted, I almost collided with a tall, hulking guard loitering near Snow's suite. He wore the colours of Eliam, Snow's kingdom, and one glance at his face was enough to confirm his identity.

I could easily see why he made her uneasy. His eyes held a look that made even me nervous, and he had no connection to me whatsoever. How long he had been out there, and had he overheard any of our conversation? Our plan would be ruined already if he had.

I could do nothing about it, though, so I hurried away and told myself my speed had nothing to do with a desire to stay as far as possible from the ominous guard.

CHAPTER 20

$\mathcal{W}$ e all lined up for the fifth event with much more confidence than we had ever done before. Hazel looked a little nervous, but no one seemed to fear serious injury now that we had entered the individual phase.

I entered the room last, as I always did, the duke immediately closing the door behind me. Instantly I knew something was wrong. The others hadn't moved toward the trapdoor as they usually did, but still stood crowded around the door.

No one spoke, though, and the silence resounded loudly.

"What's going on?" I asked, just as Sophie's projection reached me.

Lily! Opal!

Opal? How could the girl possibly have gotten into trouble before the trapdoor had even opened? I pushed some of the other princesses aside, moving to the front of the group. Shock washed over me.

For the first time ever, we were not alone in the room.

A large man stood on the far side, Opal gripped to his chest and a knife held to her throat. She trembled slightly, her giant eyes meeting mine across the empty space between us. Apparently all the action had happened in the few seconds it had taken for the entire line to file into the room.

"Silence. Now! And don't go making any sudden moves," the man said, pressing his blade threateningly against Opal's delicate neck. His eyes seemed to be focused on me, so I froze just like the others.

I rejected a momentary thought that this might be part of the next task. The challenges never involved other people; such a thing violated the requirement for secrecy. And the trapdoor still hadn't opened.

Pearl, standing next to me, whimpered, and a rustle moved through the girls in response to the sound. Our standoff couldn't last forever.

But the man had made no demands, and I couldn't think of a likely reason for his presence or his threat. Was he an angry Talinosian, simply taking advantage of the opportunity to find one of his kingdom's princesses alone and vulnerable?

"Randolph," whispered Snow behind me, almost too quiet for me to catch.

The name jolted my memory, and I recognized the Elamese guard who had been lingering outside Snow's suite. And now he was here, threatening one of the Talinosians. It still made no sense.

"What do you want?" asked Celine, uncowed despite her broken leg.

He looked angry at her defiance but must have realized the necessity to communicate with us. "Wherever it is you all go, I'll be coming with you. And this little thing with me." He gave Opal a small shake. "Princess Blanche will be winning this next task, and you all had better make sure of it if you don't want to see this little girl harmed."

Ten heads swiveled to stare at Blanche who had gone pale. "What are you thinking, Randolph? Let her go at once! You know it's not permitted for anyone to interfere with the Tourney. Don't you care for your life at all?"

"My instructions are clear." He seemed entirely unmoved by her arguments. "I'm to ensure that you win for the glory of Eliam and my queen."

"My stepmother. I knew it," Blanche muttered. "I can't imagine how she thinks she's going to get away with this."

"I'm guessing she expected him to try something a little more subtle," I said, equally quietly. Perhaps the Elamese queen had failed to notice the crazed look in his eye when she had given him such foolish orders.

"Doesn't she fear the magic of the Tourney?" Lilac joined our whispered conversation.

I shook my head slightly. "I bet she thinks she's safe enough since she's not directly involved. She clearly isn't too worried about him forfeiting his life. And he seems devoted enough not to care either."

"Enough!" Randolph spoke with enough menace to bring instant silence. "What are you waiting for? Let the task begin."

When no one moved, his knife nicked Opal's skin causing a single drop of blood to trickle down her thin neck. Pearl whimpered again.

Rage filled me. The trapdoor still hadn't opened, so the task would obviously not begin while someone else remained in the room. Which meant we needed to do something to rescue Opal, and fast.

I debated just opening the door behind me and calling for help, but I didn't trust that he wouldn't hurt Opal before anyone could reach him. And I now stood at the front of the huddled princesses, anyway. If I moved for the door, it would be more than obvious.

Sophie! Any ideas?

I'm trying! Sophie sounded frantic.

186

What if you distract him by pretending to open the trapdoor? If you can get his attention, I might be able to get behind him.

And do what?

I frowned. I hadn't thought that far. I glanced around the small room, but it was as bare as ever. If only I were armed. Any weapon would be better than none right now. But tradition definitely didn't support princesses wearing weapons to balls.

My eyes caught on Celine. She leaned, as always, on her crutches. Crutches that I had often heard her complain were far too heavy, carved as they were from a dense, solid oak of a type we hadn't encountered in the Four Kingdoms. Lilac had told us it had been used as a mark of respect, a status symbol, but Celine had grumbled to me more than once that she would have much preferred the use of light and practical pine.

I'm going to thwack him over the head as hard as I can with one of Celine's crutches.

A short pause followed, before Sophie sent her agreement. Really, it was the only plan we had so, like it or not, it had to do.

"Very well, then," Sophie said to him, her voice trembling convincingly. "We need to open the trapdoor."

"But…" Marigold's confused interjection, presumably to point out that the trapdoor had always opened on its own before, was quickly cut off by Sophie.

"Don't you see? We have to do what he says, or he'll harm Opal." She gave a significant glare at the other girls, and no one raised any further objections. I only hoped they understood enough not to interfere.

Sophie moved toward the spot where the invisible trapdoor lay, talking loudly about the process we had to use to open it. "It's a dance. No one else knows the moves but us." She glanced at Randolph. "A very complicated dance," she added, firmly.

"Yes, and a long one," agreed Millie, stepping forward to support her.

Lilac joined them. "Three of us have to do it. And if anyone makes a wrong move, we have to start again."

Sophie nodded. "Why do you think we're gone for so long each night?" She raised both of her hands over her head, and the other two girls followed suit.

You look ridiculous, I told Sophie as I sidled past the remaining princesses. *Are you trying to mimic the travelling merchants' dance? Because it really doesn't look anything like that.*

Thank you, Lily. That is extremely helpful. She had now started hopping from foot to foot in a complicated pattern. The other two tried to follow her steps with limited success.

I slid past Celine and tugged at one of her crutches. She released it instantly into my grasp. The briefest exchange of glances told me she understood exactly what was going on. As soon as I had moved past her, she began to call criticisms to the other girls. "That's not how you do it. You've got it all wrong. It will never open like that."

"Why don't you do it yourself, then?" asked Lilac.

"I would if I could!" Celine shook her head.

"She's right you know, that's not the right move," said Blanche, joining the argument on Celine's side. "You should have done five hops with your left foot before switching to your right."

"Fine!" said Sophie, stopping to put her hands on her hips and glare at Blanche. "You come and do it, then."

"Very well," said Blanche, moving to join Millie and Lilac. "It's like this." When she put her hands above her head and began to hop she looked almost elegant, her beautiful features intensified in concentration. When she spun around and swung her arms low, Celine snorted.

"You were supposed to spin the other way."

"No, she wasn't," said Hazel, finding the courage to join in. "You always get it confused."

"No, she doesn't!" said Marigold, glaring at her middle sister. "You're the one who always gets it wrong."

Millie sighed. "Marigold and Celine are right. Now we'll have to start again. Everyone back in position."

"Let me try again," said Sophie. "I was doing it right all along."

Several voices called protests about this over the top of each other.

Randolph's eyes jumped between them all with increasing confusion. The room now seemed overly full of complaining voices and bouncing princesses. In the confusion, I managed to circle around him and approach from behind.

I planted my feet firmly, adjusting my grip on the awkward shape of the crutch. I was only going to have one chance at this. As I carefully raised the implement above my head, my eyes met Pearl's across the room.

She hadn't moved at all despite the chaos that had broken out. Instead she stood rooted in spot, her terrified eyes never leaving her sister. Seeing me move to strike, she gasped loudly.

Somehow the sound penetrated the noise from the argument and the dance Sophie and Millie had begun. Randolph's eyes flew to Pearl, and then he twisted, following the trajectory of her gaze to look over his shoulder.

I had only the briefest second to act. Forgetting all about a good grip, I swung the long piece of wood down onto his head with all the force I could.

For a moment, our eyes met, his starting out with surprise, and then he dropped. His knife cut a long, shallow slice down Opal's arm as he fell, but she stumbled away from him, otherwise unharmed.

Emmeline, who had remained apart from the uproar and had made no move to help, flung open the door.

"Help," she called. "Intruder." She sounded calm despite the intensity of the words themselves. It was hard to believe it could have been fear in her case that had prevented her from assisting us.

Her cry brought an instant response. Soon the room became

even more crowded and chaotic than it had been a moment earlier and, before I knew it, we were all back in the ballroom. Unlike the usual quiet crowd waiting for us, the ballroom remained packed with the entire court. The music had stopped, but the confused couples on the dance floor suggested the ball had still been in progress before our interruption.

Jon and Gabe, who had responded so quickly they must have been lingering near the door, had dragged Randolph out and stood over him. And the duke himself had carried out a half-fainting Opal, Pearl clinging to her sister's hand.

Within minutes, doctors had arrived and were tending to the cut on Opal's arm, and Randolph had awoken to angry questioning from the duke. The guards who usually ringed the walls rushed forward to form a protective bubble around us, keeping back the shocked and curious guests. Only the delegation heads, along with Duke Philip and Duchess Aurelia of Marin, and Millie's parents, King Edward and Queen Juliette of Trione, had been permitted to stay within the circle. But with Jon, Gabe, Randolph and all twelve contestants in there too, it still felt like a crowd.

"Let me through, let me through. I want to *see*," called a small voice that I recognized. Daisy appeared to be trying to push her way through the resisting guards.

Despite everything, a small smile made its way onto my face. I would have felt just the same at her age. Teddy appeared and demanded the guards let him through, allowing Daisy to slip in behind him. Her triumphant grin made my own grow, fueled by my still-pumping nerves.

Emmeline explained what had happened in a most composed manner, and I wanted to shake her for caring so little about yet another danger that had confronted us all. At least if she seemed uncaring about the rest of us, she seemed equally uncaring about her own safety.

Outrage gripped everyone present at her story. Sullenly,

Randolph denied any involvement of King George and Queen Alida of Eliam. He had acted alone, he said, on his own initiative. Motivated solely by his pride in his kingdom.

I could see by the outraged faces of everyone inside the circle, that no one believed such an unlikely tale. But I could see also the immediate resignation. With no possible proof to the contrary, the duke would be forced to accept his story.

"You have risked your life by defying the sanctity of the Tourney," said the duke, raising his voice to be heard throughout the ballroom. "Who knows what taint may now strike you down. I will not risk anyone else by allowing you to roam free, carrying unknown darkness within you."

I could see the weight of the pronouncement in his eyes. A reminder that the people of this land were as much bound by this Tourney as Sophie and I. None of us had a choice in allowing this to play out.

A small squad of guards hauled Randolph to his feet and escorted him from the ballroom. The doctors, having finished bandaging Opal's arm, also left. Gabe helped his young sister to her feet and then started as Duke Philip ordered us to reform our line.

"But, surely...Opal..." He stared at the duke.

"I'm sorry, Your Highness." Duke Philip included us all in his gaze. "All of Your Highnesses, for the unacceptable interruption to the Tourney. The Elamese guard Randolph must have been hiding in there since yesterday given that ball preparations have been going on in here all day. I can assure you that the law will be upheld. Unfortunately, however, the event must go on."

Gabe looked like he wanted to argue, but Jon met his eyes across the small space, and he subsided. Slowly, we formed back into our allotted order and began to reenter the room.

As I inched forward, Jon approached me where I stood at the back.

"Are you all right?" he asked, concern filling his voice and face.

I could easily read how much the situation infuriated him, so I infused more cheer into my voice than I felt when I whispered back. "Of course. We are all of us unharmed except for poor Opal. And the doctors didn't seem to consider her injury serious."

"And once again, you're the hero." His eyes glowed. "Be careful in there, Lily."

The forward movement of the line carried me through the door before I could answer, but the approval in his gaze lingered in my mind all the way through the groves and across the lake.

When we each received our own parchment with instructions for another treasure hunt, I breathed a sigh of relief. If only everyone could avoid falling in the lake or tumbling down the stairs, we should be safe enough. We had certainly all had our fill of excitement for the night.

My body, at least, seemed confused as to whether it needed to remain in a state of heightened tension, or whether it could collapse in the aftermath of the previous burst of energy.

Somehow I forced myself to put aside thoughts of Randolph's attack and focus my attention on the challenge. A list of coded instructions directed us to a series of locations within, and possibly outside, the castle. Each location would yield a clue to the next instruction. My main concern was how it would be possible to pull ahead in such a competition. Surely we would all end up travelling from place to place in a group?

But, to my surprise, when the bell sounded, everyone scattered in different directions. A quick consult with Sophie soon revealed why. Our instructions were completely different. Did they all lead eventually to the same treasure? Or were there twelve buried prizes to be found?

Sophie and I split up, racing through our instructions with constant help from the other in deciphering our clues.

I just saw Celine hobbling past, projected Sophie.

Do you think we're ahead of everyone else?

I got no response, so I tried again. *Sophie?* And then again. *Sophie!*

Oh! Sorry! I had to count the panes in the top left corner window in one of the rooms on the second floor. And I can't count and talk at the same time. There were six panes, so now I need to go to the sixth room on the right up on the third floor.

My clues had already led me out to the lake, and I only hoped I hadn't missed some crucial piece of information and gone off in the wrong direction. Floating across the water gave me plenty of opportunity to help Sophie with the clue for the sixth room on the third floor. It was the hardest one yet, but eventually we worked out that the paneling was walnut wood, and that her next clue would be in the kitchen.

Two of the other coracles were already gone, I told her. *That gives me hope I didn't get something too horribly wrong.*

Of course you didn't. Stop fretting. Sophie sounded distracted again, so I assumed she had reached the kitchen.

Working together, I felt reasonably certain we were ahead, or at least keeping pace with the others. But unbeknownst to Sophie, I had a secondary concern. I needed to find my treasure before she found hers. Pulling ahead in the points without her realizing what I was doing was going to be a delicate process.

I grew more insistent asking for help on my next few clues, and slower to come up with assistance for her, but she still announced she had reached her final destination just as I began to dig beneath the largest knothole on one of the trees in the grove of golden leaves. Sophie was still back at the castle, so I couldn't imagine she would have to do any digging.

I threw myself into the task with increased fervor, but I had still only just uncovered the tip of a small leather bag when the bell rang out. For a moment, I hoped I had done enough to trigger it, but Sophie's triumphant projection told me she had found her treasure. I dug the bag up anyway, and when the rest of the princesses joined those of us already in the groves, I discovered Sophie and I weren't the only ones carrying bags.

Hazel looked even more dejected at her second prize than she had at her first, and Lilac and Marigold both remained unusually silent.

"I saw my bag," commented Emmeline, "but I hadn't quite reached it when the bell sounded. It dissolved away before I could retrieve it."

Did that mean the three of us who still had our bags had tied? I didn't have to wonder long. The scores soon proved exactly that. Hazel, Sophie and I had each received leading scores, with Emmeline close behind.

We all climbed the ladder to the trapdoor in silence. Sophie and I even refrained from projecting. We had succeeded in protecting Opal earlier but had now failed to protect Hazel. I could only hope the next challenge was less tailored to her strengths.

This second treasure hunt had taken much longer than the first and, as we filed out of the room, I noticed that dirt caked my dancing slippers from my efforts at digging. They looked incongruous against my pristine gown. What would Jon and the others make of them?

But Jon's eyes didn't stray down to my shoes. A larger group than usual awaited us, and we were each swept away quickly by guards from our own kingdoms. After the immersion of the challenge, the attack from Randolph seemed distant to me. But those who had stayed behind in the palace remained on edge, despite his arrest.

Jon met my eyes for only the briefest moment, before his focus centered on his sister. As was right and proper. But the fire that had leaped from his eyes to take up residence somewhere around my heart made me question if his sister held his full attention, after all.

CHAPTER 21

The next morning Sophie talked some sense into me. *You were a hero last night, Lil. And clearly Jon saw that.* You're *the one who was disappointed we didn't manage to overtake Hazel, not him.*

I smiled at her, grateful for her calm good sense. *You were pretty good too, you know. I particularly liked that dance you and Millie were doing to 'open' the trapdoor.*

Sophie laughed. *I can't believe it worked.* She sobered. *I just wish we'd done a little better at that treasure hunt. Maybe we need to brush up on our riddling skills.*

I've been hoping that the next challenge is entirely different. But you're probably right.

In consequence, we spent a significant portion of the next three days in the palace library. The large, airy room was beautiful, lined with floor to ceiling bookshelves, interspersed with equally tall windows, many of them opening out into the garden. But the pleasant environment only served to remind me I would rather be in the garden, and I often caught myself gazing out the windows, my book forgotten.

By the time the next ball arrived, however, I felt a lot more

195

confident about decrypting riddles, so the time had been well-spent. And Sophie had loved the room. She eventually admitted it made her feel at home. Libraries were familiar environments since we had been forced by our sister-in-law, Alyssa, to spend a lot of time in the one in our own palace while growing up. Alyssa had a firm belief in the power of books and had been in charge of our daily study schedule. Unfortunately.

When we arrived at the next ball, Jon was not in sight. Eventually I spotted him already on the dance floor with Emmeline, but the haughty Eldonian princess sparked no jealousy in me. She was infuriating and unhelpful in the Tourney events, but I couldn't imagine Jon being attracted to her. I could still feel the fire that had burned between us after the last event, and Emmeline was pure ice.

When he hurried over as soon as the dance ended, I scolded myself for the way my heart leaped. If I couldn't improve my self-control, it was going to end up broken.

"Lily!" He bowed over my hand. "Would a heroine such as yourself deign to dance with a lowly duke-to-be like me?"

I pretended to consider. "I suppose so, since no one else is available."

He grinned, looking significantly at the other young men standing around us before leading me into the dance. "I've hardly seen you the last few days," he said more seriously once we had settled into the dance. "I had started to think you were avoiding me."

"Avoiding you?" The suggestion startled me. "No, of course not."

A second later it occurred to me that perhaps I should have encouraged the idea. But he already looked more cheerful again, and I couldn't bring myself to say something cutting.

"Sophie and I have been...otherwise engaged."

"So I heard."

I glanced up at him. Had he been asking about me? Plenty of the servants had seen us in the library.

"I was all ready to challenge someone to a duel, until I heard it was just a bunch of books that had you so enthralled."

He said the words lightly, but I still flushed. Why couldn't I control my emotions around him long enough to push him away? I needed to try harder. Say something to put him off. It was for his own sake, after all. I could at least try to limit the heartbreak to myself.

The dance ended, and Jon reluctantly let me go. "I've promised to dance the next one with Blanche. But save me another one later?" His warm brown eyes compelled me to say yes. "Please?"

I tore my gaze away, determined not to be so easily swayed. "It's kind of you to think of me, but I don't anticipate having another dance available." I said the words with as much indifference as I could manage, not meeting his eyes. When I risked a glance up, I immediately felt guilty for the combination of hurt, confusion and frustration on his face at my unexpected turn toward cold formality.

"Perhaps I will have someone to challenge to a duel, after all, then." He kept his words light and kissed my hand again.

As he strode away, I couldn't stop myself from watching him disappear into the crowd. My hand burned from the pressure of his lips. I suspected he had meant to match my own formal disinterest, but his lips had lingered just a second too long.

I retreated back to the edge of the room, needing to regain my composure before reentering the dance. As I lingered there, I noticed a bright flash of color behind a large potted plant. I drifted over to get a better look. Peering through the greenery, I saw Daisy, looking despondent.

"Do you mind if I join you?" I asked.

She eyed me consideringly. "I suppose you can. Since we're friends now."

I rounded the pot, sliding down the wall to sit beside her. "You've picked a good spot here. Well-hidden but with an excellent view."

"Yes." She sighed, a heavy world-weary sound, and I hid a smile.

"What's the matter?"

She glanced up at me. "Do you promise not to tell? Not even Millie?"

"Not even Millie," I assured her gravely.

She grinned up at me a little impishly. "I begged Mother and Father to let me attend all the balls. They said I was too young, but I wanted to wear a big dress and be part of the fun. I told them I should be here to support Millie, so they agreed."

I suppressed yet another grin. I could easily imagine the tactics Daisy had employed to wear her parents down. "But now you're hiding behind a plant."

"Yes." She gave an even bigger sigh. "It turns out balls are *boring*. But I can hardly admit that now."

I nodded solemnly. "They can be, a little."

"At home everyone was always too busy to notice me much during a ball. In the summer, I would sneak out for a moonlit ride on my pony. And during the winter, when it was too cold, I would go down to the kitchen. The pastry chefs at home all like me, and they let me help ice the little cakes."

She shook her head. "I thought for sure the ball itself would be more interesting, though."

"Perhaps you'll find them more interesting when you're big enough to dance?"

She looked at me doubtfully. "I suppose. But I've been at six of them now, and they just seem to be about dancing with princes.'"

"You don't like princes?" I asked, struggling to keep a straight face at her accurate assessment of a royal ball.

"Princes are for ninnies! I'm an adventurer, remember?" She looked disgusted at my suggestion.

"What if you found a prince who was an adventurer too? Like Gabe. He seems daring. Doesn't he have a younger brother?"

She flushed slightly at my mention of Gabe, and I remembered Millie saying Daisy hero-worshiped him. But then she rolled her eyes. "Gabe's only daring because he lived with us. The rest of his family are afraid of everything, like the twins. And, anyway, Percy is *old*!"

I would hardly have called Prince Percival old at fifteen, but then I supposed it was all a matter of perspective. To an eight-year-old, fifteen must seem ancient.

"When I'm grown up, I want to do more exciting things than make eyes across a ballroom!"

This time I suppressed a sigh. I had been all too similar as a young girl. Desperate for a long dress and to be included with the adults, dazzled by the allure of a ball. But, at the same time, wanting adventures. It hadn't seemed at all contradictory either.

I didn't try to explain to her that growing up, for a princess, at least, meant responsibilities, many of them boring, and sacrificing adventures for diplomacy and alliances. Except for the sort of unpleasant adventures that were thrust upon you, like this Tourney. She would find out soon enough. Right about the time she discovered just how fascinating making eyes across a ballroom could be.

I thought of Jon walking away from me with hurt and confusion in his eyes and actually sighed aloud this time.

"Oh, I'm sorry," said Daisy. "I probably shouldn't have said any of that, since you like Prince Jonathan so much."

"Excuse me?" I twisted around to stare at her. Was I really that obvious, despite all my efforts to distance myself from him? I flushed, embarrassed and horrified. Did everyone in the palace think I was desperately pining away?

"Don't worry," said Daisy, patting my hand comfortingly. "He watches you even more than you watch him."

"What?" My eyes flew to Jon, spinning around the dance floor, on the other side of our leafy green screen. In the back of my mind I realized that I knew exactly where he was.

"I've been at six balls now," said Daisy. "I know all about how it works. If someone watches you all the time, it means they're interested. You know, in dancing and stuff." She wrinkled up her nose. "Unless they're old. Then they watch their children and the people their children dance with."

I didn't dare ask her what she considered old after her comment about Gabe's younger brother.

She seemed to take my silence as disbelief. "See." She pointed to where the baron and baroness waltzed past, their heads close together in quiet conversation. "They're always watching each other. Although they are old." She stopped to consider. "It must be because they don't have any children here. They watch each other all the time, when they're not watching you and Sophie, anyway." She pointed again. "And all those girls over there watch Prince Jonathan."

I examined the cluster of girls and recognized some of them as local nobles. It was true that they often seemed to watch Jon and me when we danced.

"I've heard them talking about how handsome he is." Daisy looked unimpressed. "And swooning over how he's a prince. But he's going to be a duke one day, so he won't even stay a prince. So that's just silly. I would much rather marry a knight on a noble quest."

I coughed. "Do you have a lot of those in Trione?"

She looked defensive. "I only need one."

This surprised a snorted chuckle from me, but I quickly returned my expression to solemnity. "Very true, excuse my foolishness."

"That group of girls watch Gabe, and those ones watch Teddy." She pointed out several more groups of courtiers. "Which is also silly, because who would want to marry *Teddy?*"

"Well, he is a prince. And he's good-looking enough, when you're not his sister."

Daisy shook her head skeptically, but continued her rundown of the ballroom. "That girl definitely likes Prince Jonathan. She's always watching him."

Leaning around a large leaf, I saw that she was indicating Corinna. The Marinese girl stood to the side of the ballroom watching the dance, her brother at her side. "What about him?" I pointed at Cole. "Who does her brother watch?"

"Oh, him? That's easy. He watches Celine. Even though she can hardly dance with her broken leg." Daisy frowned for a moment. "I don't like him. He has a funny look when he watches her. Kind of like the one the scullery maids get when they're trying to steal one of the best cakes while the pastry chef's back is turned." She lowered her voice. "Don't tell anyone, but I help them sometimes, and then they share the cake with me. But it's a funny look to give a *person*."

"That does sound odd," I said.

"And he had a conversation with one of the other nobles in front of my bush at the last ball. I couldn't exactly follow it all, but they kept talking about tributes and alliances, and they weren't saying very nice things about the duke." She looked over at me. "He's my uncle, you know."

I bit my lip. None of that sounded good. "Do you remember anything more about what they said?"

Daisy shook her head.

"What about who he was talking to. Could you point him out to me?"

Daisy scrambled up onto her knees and leaned forward through the bush. "There. It was him." She pointed at an older man deep in conversation with a small group of nobles.

I couldn't recall his name, but he looked familiar from the single day of meetings I had attended. *Sophie? Do you remember the name of that influential baron we met at those meetings?*

Ummm...no? Wait, yes! Baron Thurrgold. Why?

I quickly filled her in on my conversation with Daisy. She laughed at Daisy's childish insight, but sobered when she heard her comments about Cole.

It's one thing for Sir Oswald to disparage Jon and his family, but it doesn't seem like a good sign if the most powerful nobles are joining him. And if they think they have a chance of negotiating alliances around the duke, that's even worse. I think we need to tell Jon.

Well, I'm already dancing, she projected quickly. *You'll have to do it yourself.*

I rolled my eyes, easily seeing through her, but pushed myself to my feet anyway. "Thank you for telling me, Daisy," I said. "And for letting me join you. Could you let me know if you overhear any other strange conversations?"

"Of course I can." Daisy's eyes lit up. "I'm great at overhearing things. And I'm glad we decided to be friends."

I smiled at her. "Me, too."

"You should tell Sophie to visit me sometime, too. She always treats me seriously, and I like that. Even if it makes me a bit sad."

I had already started to step away in my urgency, but her final sentence made me pause. "What do you mean? Why does it make you sad?"

She frowned. "Princess Adelaide used to treat me like that, too. She never told me I was annoying and to go away like the others."

I stared at her. "Princess Adelaide?" The name did sound vaguely familiar, but how could there be another princess who wasn't here participating in the Tourney? Was she already betrothed? Or dead? That would explain Daisy's sadness.

"She's the Beast's sister. But she's nice, not like him. Or at least she used to be. No one in my family would tell me anything, they all think I'm a baby, so I had to ask the servants. Apparently she's disappeared, along with King Nicolas and Queen Ruby. Only Prince Dominic is left, and he's some sort of monster apparently."

She looked down and then up at me. "You don't think he could have killed his own sister, do you?"

I knelt down and touched her hand. "No! I'm sure he wouldn't have. Remember, we don't really know what's happened in Palinar. She might be fine. Maybe her parents took her somewhere to hide her away and protect her."

"I didn't think of that," said Daisy, instantly brightening. "I bet that's what happened! I bet they all ran away from awful Dominic. He was always too important to notice anyone else. His horse trampled my favorite doll after I dropped it one day, and he didn't even care."

She seemed cheerful enough with this theory, so I bid her farewell and hurried away in search of Jon. I didn't share her hopeful outlook on Princess Adelaide, but I was hardly going to say as much. I grimaced. Yet another awful mystery to add to the horror of winning the Tourney. What if the Beast had done something terrible to his family? Would his wife 'disappear' too?"

I paused on the edge of the dance floor to take a deep breath. I didn't have time to worry about a princess I'd never met. I had more urgent concerns. One of which was approaching Jon after I'd just told him I had no time for him.

The current dance ended while I was still thinking about what to say. My hesitation allowed the group of admirers Daisy had pointed out to approach him first, so he was surrounded by the time I arrived.

I considered retreating and waiting for an easier opportunity, but I didn't want to be cowardly. Not when I had such a clear sense that something was wrong in Marin. Swallowing my pride, I joined the group of girls around him.

He conversed easily with them, but I noticed the moment his eyes fell on me. He looked both surprised and something else. Only I couldn't quite pinpoint the other emotion. Was it pleasure at seeing me again, or resentment at my earlier words? Whatever it was, something had unsettled him.

"Don't tell me you've come to beg a dance, Princess Lily," he said with a laugh. It didn't sound as warm as his usual one. Maybe resentment, then.

The crowd around him tittered. I felt like a child again, surrounded by unfriendly faces at court. I wanted to tell him a princess of Arcadia didn't beg before turning around and walking away. But I hadn't come here for myself.

I forced a smile. "I would be honored, Prince Jonathan, if you have one free."

For a second I read in his eyes that he meant to pay me back for my earlier comment by refusing me now. But as his gaze lingered on me, something changed. Perhaps he saw my desperation. Reluctantly he held out his hand. "I would be the one who is honored."

Relief swept through me at the escape from public rejection. As his arm circled around me, a spark seemed to jump between us. Our circumstances had been nothing but complicated since we met, and yet the attraction between us persisted. I struggled to remember why I had come to find him as he pulled me close and leaned down, his face just above mine.

"You torment me, Lily," he whispered, and I forgot to breathe.

What does he think? Sophie's projection seemed to thunder through my head, pulling me out of the moment.

I pulled back slightly from Jon. *I don't know. I haven't told him yet.*

What are you waiting for?

I... The sound of the bell reverberated through the ballroom, saving me from coming up with an excuse, but also cutting short my dance with Jon.

CHAPTER 22

*H*e looked disappointed, but I wasn't sure if it was due to my withdrawal or to the bell.

"There's something I need to tell you," I said as he led me toward the small room.

He looked at me expectantly.

"No, not now, there isn't time. Tomorrow. Come find me."

I joined the line and entered the room without hearing his answer, but the curious look on his face assured me he would search me out the next day.

The hours of study proved to be worthwhile since we found ourselves facing the exact same challenge as in the previous event. Only the clues themselves were different.

"I guess the Tourney doesn't approve of ties," said Celine, her gaze fixed on her parchment. "Maybe if we can keep this up, the next ten events can all be treasure hunts. That wouldn't be so bad."

Ugh, I hope not, I sent to Sophie. *I'm not sure my riddling is good enough for that.*

We all scrambled up as soon as the bell sounded and scattered through the mirror palace. The clues were more difficult than the previous time, but Sophie seemed energized by our days of preparation. Even though I dragged out my responses to her clues, she still kept pace with me. I only hoped our teamwork, when combined with all our study, had enabled us to gain a lead on Hazel.

As the first tones of the final bell rang through the underground world, I lunged forward and managed to wrap my fingers around my treasure pouch. I exhaled and collapsed with exhaustion when it stayed solid in my hand. Another tie. Just.

"Wow, you actually managed it," said Celine when the whole group gathered on the far edge of the lake. "I don't know how you two can do everything with such coordination." She shook her head. "Like when that Randolph attacked. Makes me wish I had a twin."

I smiled weakly. I had been too distracted tonight, another excellent reason why I needed to do better at staying away from Jon. At least Sophie and I had gotten ahead of Hazel. We had tied only with each other.

All three of the Marinese princesses looked greatly relieved, especially when I read out the scores. Sophie and I once again led the Tourney, although Hazel wasn't far behind.

I slept late the next morning, but ate quickly once I was up. My meeting with Jon loomed in my mind and made it impossible to focus on anything else. I wished I had set a more specific time, but I hadn't known how the event would go.

Sophie knew exactly what I was thinking when I announced I wanted to stroll through the gardens. She rolled her eyes but didn't offer to join me. Apparently she still held on to her matchmaking intentions. I told myself I was disappointed not to have her company, but I didn't believe it.

Part of me had hoped Jon would be waiting for me at the beginning of the gardens, but I saw no sign of him. Wandering aimlessly, I eventually found myself surrounded by trees and tall bushes which shielded my view of the palace. I had just decided to turn back around, since Jon wouldn't be likely to find me this far out, when he appeared down one of the paths.

A small voice in the back of my head asked if he had waited for me to wander this far on purpose. Perhaps he didn't want us to be disturbed this time. I squashed the thought.

"Lily." He bowed over my hand, the formality making me think he might still be put out by our interactions at the ball. But he didn't let go of my hand, keeping it clasped firmly in his.

You torment me. The memory of his words drifted through my mind, but I thrust them aside. I hadn't come here to talk about us.

He drew me over to an ornate stone bench. "You have something to tell me?" He sounded almost hopeful, and I wondered what he thought I was going to say. I felt sure my actual news could only disappoint.

"I've been up all night from the curiosity, you know," he added, the laugh in his voice belying his words.

"Yes, that event last night was ill-timed. I'm afraid it isn't good news, though."

His face instantly dropped into a look of concern. "I'd ask if you've received bad news from home, but I know no ship from the Four Kingdoms has entered our ports."

I shook my head. "It isn't Arcadia. It's Marin."

His look sharpened. "What do you mean?"

I drew a deep breath. "I'm afraid it might be trouble for your father." And I proceeded to tell him the whole story, from my encounter with Cole to Daisy's report of the conversation she had overheard.

Jon's frown deepened as I talked, and he let go of my hand to run his fingers through his hair. "Baron Thurrgold, you said. Are you sure?"

I nodded apologetically. "I'm terrible with names, but I confirmed it with Sophie. And she never forgets a face."

"Baron Thurrgold has always been a strong supporter of my father."

"Perhaps he still is. We don't really know what's going on. Daisy might have completely misinterpreted the conversation. They might not be strategizing against your father at all."

"Perhaps." He didn't sound convinced.

He stared into the distance, and I stayed silent, not wanting to interrupt his thoughts. A sudden sound made him whip his head to the side and leap to his feet.

"Quick," he said, pulling me up and pushing me behind the bench and between two bushes. "Stay here and stay quiet."

He sat back down, while I stood frozen, blinking in surprise. What in the kingdoms had just happened? Had Jon hidden me in a bush? Whatever for?

I brushed some leaves out of my hair, slowly maneuvering myself around some sharp branches, trying to ease myself into a more comfortable position without making too much noise. I couldn't imagine why Jon had suddenly felt the need to hide me, but something had clearly startled him, and I wanted to see what it was.

Perhaps he felt my reputation was at risk from meeting him in such a secluded spot. Arcadia wasn't so strict, especially not on the palace grounds, but perhaps Marin was more old-fashioned about such things.

I peered through the leaves—Daisy would be proud. A second later, all thought of the young girl was driven from my mind by the appearance of Corinna, walking alone up one of the paths. She approached Jon with purpose, not making any attempt to make the meeting appear coincidental.

I bristled and had to remind myself that I had no claim on Jon. *Sophie,* I projected, *my walk just got interesting.* I sent her an image of myself in the bushes and Corinna approaching down the path.

What in the kingdoms? I got the sense that I had woken her up from a half-doze. *Tell me everything that happens.*

Very well, just be ready to come and rescue us if needed. I don't want to be stuck behind this bush for the next hour or something.

"Corinna," said Jon, rising, "this is a surprise."

"I need to speak to you."

Get in line, Sophie's amused chuckle accompanied her projection but, with a branch sticking into my arm, I wasn't finding the situation so humorous.

"By all means, what can I do for you?"

Jon was using his polite voice, and Corinna seemed to know it. "It's not what you can do for me, it's what you can do for yourself." She paused before meeting his eyes. "Marry me."

"What?"

What? Sophie's silent screech nearly sent me backwards into the garden bed.

"I'm sorry," Jon sounded dazed. "I don't understand. Are you suggesting we become betrothed?"

"For your own sake, yes," said Corinna. "And for your sisters."

"And what exactly is that supposed to mean?" Jon took a step toward her, but his stance looked menacing rather than romantic. "Is that a threat?"

Corinna sighed, sounding annoyed. "I'm doing you a favor here. I shouldn't be talking to you at all. My father and brother will be furious, which is why I had to wait until I could find you alone, somewhere remote." She glanced around the garden with apparent distaste.

Jon took a small step back, his angle changing enough for me to read his face. He looked concerned. "Why would your father be angry that you were talking to me?"

"The people of Marin are worried," she said, ignoring his question. "They fear they will soon have no food on their plates or fuel in their fires. Your father has done nothing to protect them or their future. In their fear, they've turned to my father for leadership."

I shook my head silently. Did she really believe that anyone had turned spontaneously to her father? Or was she just trying to whitewash the situation?

"What's that supposed to mean?"

"It means that your father won't be in power for much longer. My father has come up with a plan to save us all. All except for your family, of course." She frowned. "He's going to become a *governor*. Do you know what the daughter of a governor is called? Nothing. Nothing whatsoever. It's exactly like being the daughter of a knight. Worse, maybe."

Her gaze latched back onto Jon, and I recognized the same hunger I had seen previously. "But I don't want to be nothing. I want to be a princess."

Jon stepped forward and then back. "Corinna, what do you mean by your father becoming a governor?"

She ignored him again. "I've come up with another idea, a better one. And if you agree to it, I'm sure I can convince my father. You just need to marry me."

Jon grabbed her shoulders and spoke slowly. "Corinna, what are you talking about?"

She sighed. "Any day now, my father will have enough support from the nobles and merchants of Marin to demand your father relinquish his throne. Father will then execute a deal with the Lanoverians for Marin to become a province of Lanover. Apparently Lanover is the richest of the Four Kingdoms, even that Arcadian princess told us that. They can afford to feed us all while the duchy recovers its position in these lands. We just need to give them a motivation to do so."

My stomach roiled. I had never dreamed that my words to Corinna and Cole could come back to haunt me like this.

"My father will be the governor, of course," she continued, "and the alliance will be sealed with a marriage between Cole and Princess Celine. Cole will return to Lanover with his new wife, as a prince, and I'll be left to languish here as nothing more than the daughter of a governor."

Corinna shook her head. "Lanover doesn't have any available princes for me and, anyway, I don't want one of them. I want you.

I've always wanted you." She looked up at him with such an intense expression that he let go of her and fell back.

I could see him shaking but couldn't tell if it was from anger or shock. "Corinna, you cannot possibly think I would agree to marry you when you have just admitted your father is planning treason against my family."

"But don't you see?" She stepped forward, closing the gap between them again. "It's too late for you to do anything about it. What will your father do? Throw half the merchants and nobles of Marin into the dungeons? There would be rioting in the streets. And, even if he could, how will he feed the people once the summer is over?"

"We have stores..." Jon sounded shaken. "They'll last longer than that."

Corinna shrugged. "But they won't last forever. I'm giving you a way out, for both our sakes. I don't know what will happen to you and your sisters when my father takes over."

Jon stiffened at the mention of his sisters, and Corinna pressed the point.

"I can't guarantee your safety. Any of you. Unfortunate things happen in coups. Even ones that are intended to be bloodless."

Jon paled, his hands curling unconsciously into fists again.

"But," she continued, "if you agree to marry me, to work with us, I know I can change my father's mind. Your father would still have to abdicate, of course. And Cole would still marry Celine to seal the alliance, but we could negotiate for you to keep your rank. It's already only an honorary title. You could rule as prince and governor with me as your wife, and your sisters would be safe."

Jon barked an angry laugh. "You father would never agree to such a thing."

Corinna stepped even closer and looked up at him appealingly. "My father has only ever cared for my future, and my brother's. I can convince him, I know I can. Obviously he will be the true ruler of Marin. But I know he would agree to do it from the position of First Advisor, rather than governor, if it means his grandchildren will be princes and princesses. And he can train our son to take over as the next Governor."

A shudder ran through Jon at the mention of grandchildren, but Corinna's eyes glowed even brighter. She moved closer again. "I know you could come to love me. I know it."

Jon stepped back, and her face fell.

"You must be mad to even think such a thing. I would never turn against my father like this." He shook his head. "Hand Marin over to foreigners? Enter a sham marriage, just so I can become a puppet ruler with my sisters as constant hostages? Never!"

Her expression hardened into unbecoming rage. "Don't be so hasty, Prince Jonathan. Better hostages than dead."

He straightened, anger sweeping over his face, but she spoke again before he could respond. "I'll give you some time to think about it. You might not want to be so hasty next time we speak."

Turing on her heel, she stormed away, leaving Jon standing alone and in shock, and me still cowering in the bushes filled with horror.

CHAPTER 23

Once Corinna had completely disappeared, I struggled out from amongst the greenery. Jon moved to assist me, his expression haunted.

"Is she right?" I asked. "Can your father truly do nothing against such a plot?"

Jon sank onto the bench and put his head between his hands. "If Oswald has the support she claims..." He looked up at me. "And it doesn't look good given what you were just telling me about Baron Thurrgold. I'm sure he wouldn't turn against my father unless he truly felt there was no other option. And if he feels that way, how many others..."

I placed my hand tentatively on his shoulder, wishing I could offer more substantial support. But I had no idea how I could help Marin.

He shook his head. "I think she's right about the risk of rioting. My father has already told me he can't enforce rationing without risking mass unrest." He stood up and strode across the path, returning to the bench within a few steps. "I just don't understand how such a widespread plot could be underway without my father getting wind of it. Some of the city must be loyal to him still. He has served Marin faithfully his entire life."

I squeezed my lips together, not wanting to speak my thought aloud.

Jon noticed. "What is it?"

"Perhaps he already knows. But if there is really nothing he can do against Sir Oswald without destroying the duchy, perhaps he hasn't wanted to tell you."

"He wouldn't keep such a thing from..." Jon looked at me with shadows in his eyes. "I made this plan possible when I told the Emissary to bring delegations from foreign kingdoms back with him. And I did it secretly. Perhaps my father no longer trusts me."

"No!" I jumped up and took one of his hands, holding it between both of mine. "I'm sure he understands that you were only trying to help Marin." I remembered Sophie's earlier words about who really bore responsibility for the duchy. "He is still the duke, after all. And you're his son. I'm sure he's working on some alliance or plan of his own to save Marin, and he doesn't want to worry you when there's nothing you can do."

"What plan? What alliance?" Jon sounded bitter, but he didn't pull his hand from my grip. "You know Lanover much better than me. Do you think they would be party to such a coup?"

I frowned. "The Lanoverians are good people. But they are also shrewd negotiators. I do not believe they would assist in a coup. But if it had already taken place...If the nobles and merchants were all in agreement, and they came to Lanover pleading for salvation for their people?" I shook my head uneasily. "They are the richest of the Four Kingdoms and could afford to support Marin for now, in the hope of future gain. They might easily see the benefits of having a foothold in this land. It would certainly give them an advantage over the rest of the Four Kingdoms when it came to trade between our lands."

"Then we are lost." Jon closed his eyes and drew me in close, wrapping his arms around me. I didn't resist the embrace since he seemed unaware of having done it, reaching out instinctively for comfort. Our individual troubles had paled beside the scope of this danger to his family and duchy.

Oh, Lily... Sophie's voice in my head sounded small.

After a minute, Jon let go, stepping back and looking guilty. "I'm sorry. I had no right..."

I shook my head, cutting off his apology. "Surely there must be something we can do to help your father. There must be some way to save Marin without this!"

Jon eyed me, clearly hesitant. "I don't suppose you'd consider calling on your godmother? We could certainly do with such assistance about now."

"I'm sorry," I said miserably. "Sophie and Celine have both tried. But nothing happens. It seems Oliver was right and we are all on our own out here."

~

It was awful, I projected to Sophie as we sat together on my bed that night. *He looked so tortured. I can't bear the thought of him being forced to marry that awful Corinna.*

Sophie pulled me into a hug and patted my back. *I'm sure he won't agree to such a thing.* We sat in silence, each lost in our own sad thoughts.

I feel sorry for her, actually, Sophie projected at last. I raised my eyebrows disbelievingly, and she shrugged. *I'm not saying I hope he marries her or anything. But she's obviously in love with him.*

And with his title, I grumbled.

Well, yes. Sophie frowned. *But we have no way of knowing how we would feel about our rank if we hadn't been born princesses.*

You're too nice.

She shook her head. She hated when I said that. *You're nice too, Lily.*

I ignored her. *What are we going to do to help them? Could Arcadia make an alliance with Marin?*

Sophie bit her lip, and I could tell she had already thought about the possibility. *I don't think the baron would agree. I know Helena would be sympathetic, but Mother and Father charged them with the welfare of us and our kingdom. Not with the welfare of Marin. And with no trade coming through the duchy, Marin has nothing to offer an alliance.*

I sighed. *That's the problem. Sir Oswald is gambling on the fact that Marin has nothing but itself to offer. He's seen his opportunity to gain power, and he's seizing it.*

I don't know what sort of trade deals we could make when they have nothing to trade. Sophie squeezed my hand, her next projection reluctant. *And I can't see Mother and Father agreeing to a marriage alliance when it would put their daughter in such an unstable position.*

I could see she thought she was delivering a blow, but I had never expected to make a marriage alliance with Marin. Not with the end of the Tourney ahead. I couldn't tell her so, though, since she still didn't know about my determination to beat her.

The sudden toll of an alarm bell made us both jump up and rush toward the window. But our view overlooked the gardens at the back of the palace, and we could see nothing but darkness and stars.

Without needing to discuss it, we both raced across the hall to the Liltons' suite. We knocked, and the baron called for us to enter. He and Helena already stood by one of their windows, so Sophie and I ran to the other.

"Fire," Sophie breathed as we peered down into the city.

The bright flames stood out against the dark sky, illuminating a small crowd already gathered at the distant scene.

"The flames are so high already," I murmured, mesmerized by the dancing red, yellow and orange. I couldn't drag my eyes away from the terrible sight.

"You girls stay here, we're going down to see if we can help."

The baron's voice pulled me out of my daze, and I turned to find him pulling on a jacket.

"Absolutely not." Sophie spoke for both of us. "We're coming too."

The baron eyed us and seemed to know an argument would be fruitless. "Very well then. Be quick."

We flew back to our room, exchanging nightgowns for our most practical dresses and boots. Within minutes all four of us had joined the stream of people flowing from the palace toward the fire.

More alarm bells had picked up the call, and people poured in from all directions. I feared there were far too many of us to be of any help but, to my surprise, the crowd moved without chaos. I faltered and slowed as we reached the fire, overwhelmed by the heat and sound and the scope of the ordered activity around me.

Ash and smoke swirled through the air, and the fire roared hungrily. A large group of guards barked orders and organized the volunteers, with force if needed. They had already formed two long bucket lines between the nearest fountain square and two hand pumps located in front of the burning building. The volunteers at the end of the line dumped water into the wells of the pumps while more volunteers operated the pumps themselves, swapping out when anyone became too tired to pump at full speed. Guards directed the hard jets of water onto the flames.

Two men had arrived just in front of us, pulling a small wagon full of more buckets, so some of the guards began organizing a third bucket line. Young children raced along each of the lines, carrying empty buckets back to the fountains.

The windows of all the houses on the street blazed with lanterns and candles, fighting against the night and the smoke in their attempt to illuminate the efforts. A team of guards went from house to house away from the fire, clearing out the inhabitants before leaving one of their number to guard each front door. Whether they remained to prevent the occupants from returning for one last treasured item, or to guard from looters, I wasn't sure.

The central burning building appeared to be a large warehouse, but houses flanked it on either side, and the roofs of the two closest were already aflame. The buckets from the newly formed bucket line were soon used to douse all the closest houses, in an attempt to prevent any more from catching fire.

Clearly the people of Marin knew exactly what to do when it came to fighting fires. I felt out of place in the frantic scene, confused by the noise and the smell and the heat that assaulted my senses. I looked around trying to spot somewhere I could be of help. I had been unable to think of any other way to help Jon's duchy, but surely I could be of some assistance here.

One of the men at the pump staggered away, rubbing his arms, and the third man from the front of the nearest bucket line raced forward to take his place. Seeing an opportunity, I ran to take his position in the line, a bucket immediately thrust into my hands by the person behind me. I passed bucket after bucket along, coughing from the smoke, until a local dipped a scarf into one of the buckets and handed it to me, gesturing for me to wrap it over my nose and mouth. I tied it on as quickly as I could, already holding up the progress of the buckets.

A group of three guards strode past, their eyes on the fire that had taken hold of one of the neighboring houses. With a start, I realized that one of them wasn't a guard at all. It was Jon. Someone thrust a bucket into my hands, and I passed it on blindly, my eyes stuck on Jon's tall figure.

He looked strong and confident as he directed the guards at one of the pumps to abandon the main blaze in favor of dousing the smaller, neighboring fire. Just as the guards began to move the pump, the loud shatter of breaking glass and a piercing scream broke through the rush and crackle of the fire and the shouts of the guards and volunteers.

For a brief second everyone froze, and then further furor

broke out. I followed the sound and the many pointing fingers to see a young woman, half hanging from one of the top windows in the burning house, a baby clutched in one arm, and a young child hanging off her other hip.

Oh no. Sophie's quiet projection cut through the noise, when not even her shout could have done so. She had joined the third line, and I could barely see her.

I didn't even try to respond, my mind too full of the scene unfolding before me. Because Jon, upon hearing the scream, had run forward and, as I watched, disappeared into the burning building.

CHAPTER 24

My feet moved of their own accord, as if to follow him, but a bucket thrust into my hands made me stop. I could do more good here than standing uselessly in front of a burning building. I passed the bucket on, my arms burning by this point from the heavy water, and reached back for the next one.

In my head I counted the seconds, my eyes glued on the woman who still hung out of the window. The two guards who had been with Jon called instructions up to her, while several more ran forward carrying a large sheet which they placed on the ground beneath the house.

How could they stand the heat? I stood further back and could barely cope despite being dressed much more lightly than the guards in their heavy leather jackets. None of them faltered, however, and I took strength from their confidence.

The seconds ticked by, and still Jon did not appear. A prickling sensation crawled through my body, my fear mounting. Surely there had been enough time for him to reach the woman by now. I pictured him consumed by flames, and had to wrench my mind from the image before I was sick.

Another bucket came and went through my hands. And another.

Jon, where are you? my mind screamed.

What do you mean? Sophie's sharp question shocked me. I hadn't realized I had projected the thought.

He's here. He went into that building after the woman and children.

What? Sophie sounded appropriately horrified.

A shout went up from the men at the base of the building at the same moment as the woman pulled back, away from the window. What had happened? Had Jon reached her?

A second later, his head thrust out of the window, and he called down to the guards. Four of them each picked up a corner of the sheet, raising it well above the ground and stretching it tight.

They planned to catch the trapped people. *Sophie! Do you see?*

Can they do that?

I didn't answer, caught up in the unfolding drama, my hands mechanically passing along the buckets shoved into them. Jon pulled back into the house and reappeared with the young child in his arms.

One of the guards called something up to him, and I gasped as he let the child drop. I held my breath as the screaming girl plummeted down, landed on the sheet and bounced back into the air. The guards moved in coordination, keeping the sheet steady and at the right tension to catch the child again. I didn't breathe until she had rolled off and landed on all fours, crying hard. A woman from the crowd rushed forward and scooped her up, pulling her away from the fire.

My eyes flew back to the window. I could just see Jon and the woman, both trying to breathe the cleaner air outside. I couldn't hear anything from them, of course, but the woman looked angry or, possibly, hysterical. After a moment, I realized that Jon had taken the baby and was gesturing for the woman to jump out of the window and onto the sheet. She kept shaking her head and trying to grab the baby back from him.

I wanted to scream at her to stop fighting and hurry up. Every moment that passed saw the fire consume more of the building.

More buckets passed through my hands.

Finally, Jon pushed the woman away from him and bent down. When he straightened he no longer held the baby. Picking up the now screaming woman, he threw her bodily out the window. She fell into the sheet, like the child had done earlier, but this time my eyes remained on the window.

Jon bent down again and reappeared with a large bulge in the front of his jacket. Did he intend to jump as well?

But he didn't even stop to check if the woman had survived the fall. Taking a deep breath at the window, he turned and disappeared.

He's gone back inside. I couldn't quite believe my own words.

He doesn't think the baby will survive the fall. That must be it, Sophie whispered back at me.

The woman had rolled from the sheet, unharmed it seemed, and was now being restrained by two guards as she fought to rush back into the building.

I was reduced to counting again, my hands still passing the buckets, but my mind wholly focused on the numbers that kept rising in my head. How long could he survive in there? Had his passage been blocked by the flames?

A physical pain burst through my chest. I loved him. This prince who put even the smallest of his people before himself. The realization made my head spin. I could not bear for Jon to die. It took every bit of my willpower to stop myself running into the building after him.

And then a cheer roared from the crowd as he burst through the doorway, coughing but still on his feet, his shoulders and arms curled protectively around the front of his jacket. The woman and several guards rushed forward, blocking my view.

For a second I could see nothing, but I heard the woman's screams. I didn't know how she had any breath left for such a sound with all this smoke.

"He isn't breathing. The baby isn't breathing." The words passed through the crowd, yelled from person to person.

I waited for the guards to do something, but for once they seemed lost, milling around without purpose. The crowd cleared enough for me to see Jon, sitting on the ground, his head in his hands.

Lily! Sophie screamed in my mind. *Do something!*

I dropped the bucket I was holding and ran toward him. A guard grabbed me around the waist and I fought, kicking backwards and screaming Jon's name. He looked up and saw me, leaping to his feet and staggering in my direction.

He tried to order the guard to release me, but only succeeded in bringing on a coughing fit. The guard saw his gestures, though, and let me go. I ran to the weeping woman, who was cradling her baby.

I grabbed the arm of the closest guard and yelled for him to take the infant. The woman struggled blindly, but another guard held her back, shouting to her to give us space and let us help him. I placed one hand on the infant's head and one on his tiny chest. I could feel a few flutters from the soft spot on his skull, but no rise and fall of his breath.

"There's still a chance," I said, as loudly as I could. "We need to get him away from the smoke." I glanced back at Jon. "And him too!" I made eye contact with two other guards. "Drag him away, if you have to." The older one nodded at me, a determined expression on his face.

I looked back at the guard holding the baby. "Give him to me, and then run ahead of us. We need to get to the palace quickly, and I don't know the way well enough."

The guard hesitated for the briefest moment and then shoved the limp bundle into my arms. I cradled him in one arm, as several more guards appeared and formed a circle around me, clearing my path on all sides. We ran through the streets as I pressed hard repetitively with the fingers of my hand against the infant's chest. After a moment, I paused and lowered my head to cover his nose and mouth with my own mouth, exhaling a breath into his tiny lungs.

Step by step and breath by breath we moved away from the heat and the smoke. Until, finally, I raised my head to breathe and found myself gasping in clear air. We had reached the courtyard of the palace.

I lay the infant down on the ground. "Fetch a doctor," I panted, my focus on the baby, my fingers still pressing against his chest. I swayed, dizzy, and a hand grabbed my elbow to steady me.

"Whoa, careful there, Your Highness." I looked into a vaguely familiar face. "What was that you were just doing? With the baby?"

"Breathing for him. And compressions to get his heartrate up."

The man seemed to understand, thrusting me aside to take my place kneeling beside the baby. I finally placed him—one of the doctors who had assisted with Celine's ankle and Opal's cut.

I sank down onto the ground and put my head between my knees, still gasping in beautiful, fresh, clean air.

After several more breaths, my dizziness cleared, and I looked around for Jon. He sat on the palace steps. Two more doctors and a nurse surrounded him, but his eyes were fixed on me. I managed a weak smile, and a look passed over his face too intense to describe.

A sudden cheer went up from the small crowd around the infant boy. "He's breathing!" someone called out, and I heard the message passing back into the city. "He's alive! The baby's alive!"

My eyes were still locked on Jon's, so I saw the wonder that crossed his face at the news. He staggered to his feet, pushing the protesting doctors aside, and strode over to me. Crouching, he took my face in his hands.

"You saved that child," he whispered. "I was trying to save him, but I accidentally killed him instead. He was breathing at the window, but I wanted to protect him from the smoke, so I tucked him into my jacket. When I got out of the house and pulled him out, I found I'd prevented the smoke from reaching him, but no air had got through either. But you saved him."

"No." I shook my head. "We both did. He wouldn't have been so easy to revive from smoke inhalation." I leaned my head into his hands. His grip, strong but gentle, steadied me after the fear and shock.

"Lily…" The wonder hadn't left his eyes. "I…"

I desperately wanted to hear whatever he was going to say, this man who I loved. The word pulsed through my veins with each heartbeat. Love. Love. Love. Jon. Jon. Jon. But a sudden commotion at the palace gates distracted him.

He looked up, over my shoulder, and a moment later new arms encircled me.

"You did it! You did it!" Sophie cried into my hair.

I could hear more joyful sobbing close by and saw that the mother had arrived with Sophie, her older child in tow. The baron and baroness were close behind.

After that more chaos descended with doctors and nurses swarming us all. Jon and I were pulled apart and lost each other in the confusion of examinations and explanations that followed. I wanted to call out after him, to protest, but I knew I had no right to do so. My feelings had changed but the facts had not. Jon did not belong to me, or I to him. And we never would.

~

When I woke up the next morning, it was to a riot of color. Red and yellow and pink and white and purple and green filled our room.

"What in the kingdoms?" I murmured, still too sleepy to make sense of what I was seeing.

Sophie, who stood beside her bed, frowning down at it, looked up and grinned. "Good morning, sleepy head."

"Ugh." I threw my pillow at her, and glanced out the window. "It can't be that late."

"Maybe not." She grinned and gestured around her. "But your many admirers are already up and about."

I sat up. Flowers blanketed the room, every color and size imaginable. "What do you mean, admirers?"

"Apparently, they got the fire under control not long after we left, although it was only extinguished completely in the early hours of the morning. They didn't lose any more houses, either. But the real topic of conversation in the city is you and Jon and that family you saved."

"I did not save a whole family." I swung my legs out of bed. "Wait. Jon! The baby!"

"Relax. They're both fine. The family is still here at the palace; the doctors kept them under observation all night. They'll be here for another couple of days, apparently, but they seem healthy given the circumstances."

I ran a hand over my face, trying to chase away the sleep. Memories from the night before came flooding back. I blushed, remembering the feel of Jon's hands cupping my face.

"Lily? What is it?"

I opened my mouth to admit my nighttime revelation to her and stopped. I couldn't tell her, not when I planned to win the Tourney. It would break her heart on my behalf. And one broken heart between us was quite enough.

"I smell terrible," I said instead.

She grimaced. "Not as bad as these, I'm afraid." She gestured toward whatever she had been staring at when I woke up.

I walked over to join her, looking down at our two dresses from the night before.

"Oh dear." I turned my head away from the overpowering smell of smoke.

"I don't think they're salvageable." Sophie sounded resigned. "I'll give them to one of the maids to burn."

"I think the job's half done for them," I muttered, wandering over to examine some of the flowers. "Are these really from the people in the city?"

"Apparently. It looks like half the city raided their flower boxes for you. I wonder if Jon's room looks like this, too?"

I wanted to see him so desperately, I could feel the longing throbbing in my chest. I suppressed it. "You know I didn't do anything particularly brave or heroic."

"It was heroic enough. There's a note for you, by the way." She pointed to a silver tray resting on our small table.

I hurried over and opened it, hoping to see one particular name. And, sure enough, the note had been written by Jon.

> *Lily —*
> *I need to talk to you. Come to the infirmary as soon as*
>   *you have the chance.*
> *Jon*

I felt the ghostly pressure of his hands against my face and the echo of his words, broken off. What did he want to say to me? And, whatever it was, what could I possibly reply?

"It's Jon." I met Sophie's eyes. "He wants me to come to the infirmary. Do you want to come, too?"

She nodded, and we set off down the corridor. *I'll distract the doctors, so the two of you can sneak off together.* I didn't need to see her grin to hear it in her projection.

Sophie... I infused my own projection with tones of warning, and she rolled her eyes before slipping her arm through mine. But, thankfully, she said no more on the topic.

Our arrival in the infirmary caused something of a stir. The mother who had been rescued from the fire jumped up to thank me and had to be coaxed back to her bed by a nurse. Jon also hurried over to greet us, proving more resistant to the nurses' disapproval than the mother.

Two doctors were also present, including the one I had spoken to the night before, and they wanted to know more about what I had done.

"And how did you know to do it?" added Jon. "I've never seen such a thing."

"Some of the sailors claim to do a similar thing when they rescue one of their number from the sea," said the second doctor. "There has been some debate on the topic amongst the doctors here, and some of us have begun to train in the technique, but I have never seen it done on one so young."

"It is widely used in the Four Kingdoms for drownings and other such accidents," I said. "According to the stories, it originated with a woodcutter's third son, who decided to leave his family to seek his fortune. He found it as a doctor and introduced many new life-saving treatments. I suppose godmothers can give practical assistance as well as magical."

"If only our godmothers had not left us," muttered Jon.

I ignored him since I had no reply to that. "We have a family friend who is a doctor, and he taught me the method. Time is critical, and I wanted to be equipped in case no doctor was nearby."

"We would like to hear more details, and an exact description of the process, if you would be willing," said the doctor from the fire.

He was looking at me, but I had insisted Sophie learn the technique as well, so she stepped forward to answer their questions, giving me a slight nudge in Jon's direction as she did so.

Against my better judgment, I stepped toward him, eager to see for myself that he was truly unharmed.

"So, once again you're the hero, Princess Lily," he said quietly.

"No. This time that title belongs to you." I looked up at him, the newfound intensity of my emotions making me shy. "You were very brave to run into that building like you did."

He shrugged. "I acted on instinct." He grinned down at me. "Just like someone else once told me, if I recall correctly."

I chuckled and shook my head. "What a modest pair we are! Think of all the accolades we're missing out on."

"There's only one accolade I want," he said, his voice low and his eyes gazing at me with a shade of his wonder from the night before.

I shivered. "You wanted to talk to me..." I whispered.

He blinked. "Right. Yes. The doctors had been pestering me with questions which I've been entirely unable to answer. I thought it would be better if you answered them yourself."

I deflated. Had this been how he felt when I met him in the garden and started talking about possible treason? "Oh, of course. Sophie and I are happy to answer any questions they may have. Perhaps we can organize a medical exchange at some point. I'm sure there would be a lot to learn on both sides. And for the guards as well. I've never seen such impressive firefighting efforts."

"Thank you." Jon grinned. "I'm the official head of the Fire Squad, so I'll take the compliment."

"The Fire Squad?"

"Given that Marin is one giant city, we take the threat of fire extremely seriously. We have a squad of specially trained guards who direct all firefighting efforts. They're the ones you saw in action last night."

"They certainly seemed well-trained and capable. I'm sure my parents would love to speak with some of them about their methods."

"We're always seeking to improve." Jon grimaced. "And after last night, it's clear we need to add a couple of doctors to our number. I don't know why I didn't think of it before."

The nurse interrupted us then to insist that Jon needed to rest. He grumbled, but this time he complied, and Sophie and I left to give all the patients some peace and quiet.

I didn't see Jon again until the next ball when his appearance shocked me. He looked like a different person, grim and with shadowed eyes.

"What's the matter?" I asked as we danced, trying not to focus on the feeling of his hand on my waist. "Between us and your squad, we managed to save everyone. And with the help of all those volunteers, only two houses were lost along with that warehouse. You should be feeling proud of your city right now."

He shook his head. "My squad are experts on fire. They've examined the site in the daylight, and the news isn't good. We won't make the findings public, because we don't want to incite panic, but that fire was deliberately lit."

I gasped. "Arson? But why? And who would do such a thing?"

Jon's mouth hardened into an angry line. "Excellent questions. We haven't had an arsonist in the city for over a generation. So, I keep asking myself who stands to gain from such a disaster. And the answer is all too clear. That warehouse belonged to my father's most loyal adherent amongst the merchants, and Oswald's biggest rival. And it was being used to store grain and other necessities."

I gasped again. "You're saying he deliberately burned some of the city's supplies? But people could die." I paused. "People nearly did die!"

He sighed, and his shoulders slumped. "Oswald has just become the richest merchant in Marin. And with those supplies gone, the city will only last until the end of the summer. Without much hope of the usual harvest trading coming through, the whole duchy will be in hardship after that. I'm already hearing rumors, now that I know what to listen for. Since this disaster, Oswald has already won some of the previously reluctant nobles and merchants to his cause. The number of loyalists grows smaller by the hour."

"A masterful move, then. He has achieved several goals with one blow."

Jon spoke almost in my ear, so that no one would overhear us, but now his voice dropped even lower. "I haven't mentioned this to anyone, but I've been thinking. Oswald bought his position in the nobility here. Everyone knows that. He was originally from Palinar. When the kingdom was cursed, many people congratulated him on escaping well before the disaster. But I'm starting to wonder. All this time I've been concerned about the darkness creeping toward us on every side. But maybe it's already here, festering in the heart of the duchy."

My eyes flew up to Jon's as I tried to process his words. "You mean you think the darkness has taken over Oswald's heart? His actions with the fire certainly seem evil enough."

"I can only imagine it found fertile ground there," he said, bitterness in his voice. "The man has always been greedy and proud."

A sudden memory surfaced. "And remember what Corinna said? She asked how your father would feed the people once the summer was over. They were already counting on destroying those supplies." My stomach churned, and I fought the urge to be sick. "Perhaps you will need to accept her proposal, after all."

CHAPTER 25

I barely saw Jon in the two weeks that followed. And when we did cross paths, at the Tourney balls or in the corridors of the palace, he looked withdrawn and desperate. His haunted eyes always followed me, and I could feel their burning force, but he rarely approached me.

When I asked him questions he turned them aside, except to tell me that I had been right about his father. He knew of the conspiracy but had yet to devise a way to counter it. Some of his nobles and merchants remained loyal, however, so while Sir Oswald worked to gather more support, a delicate balance held, everyone pretending to devote their attention to the Tourney and the stalled alliance negotiations.

Occasionally I saw Jon's eyes following Corinna, and I feared that he was steeling himself to accept her offer. I couldn't bear the thought and now spent most of my time in the library, searching desperately for a solution. If I could only find something of value that Marin could offer the Four Kingdoms other than itself.

Millie, Teddy and Gabe couldn't understand my obsession and had just about given up on me. Sophie remained loyal, of course, but even she often chose to join our friends in the gardens instead. She had a greater love for books than I did, but she didn't believe we would find a solution for Marin within their pages. I was content to let her go, encouraged it even, because I had another purpose in the library. I studied in the hope that I would gain enough knowledge to pull ahead of my sister in the Tourney.

I studied mainly in solitude, undisturbed by the silent Keepers of the Library who flitted in and out. They had perfected the art of moving soundlessly around the room so as not to disturb visitors. With beautiful spring weather outside, I saw few others.

Celine had been wrong about the repeated events being due to tied scores. Rather it seemed that the Tourney liked to operate in threes. Three cooperative events. Three treasure hunts. The hunts were followed by three purely physical endurance events that left us all exhausted but favored Sophie and me as the oldest, excluding the injured Celine. I might have stopped visiting the library during those events, except that I still hoped to help Marin, and I had a lurking suspicion that puzzles and riddles would reappear in later events.

And sure enough, the next set of three were the least physically demanding events of the Tourney so far, involving a series of logic and number puzzles. My study gave me some small advantage, but I received an even greater one when Sophie succumbed to summer fever before the twelfth event. Her whole body ached, poor thing, and she struggled to sleep or think clearly.

Seeing her sick brought back a rush of my old fears, as it always did, and I longed to take my usual position at her bedside as nurse. But this time I forced myself to stay carefully away, in quarantine, even sleeping on a pallet in Celine's room. I could tell that both Celine and Sophie were concerned for me and my strange behavior, but I offered no explanation.

When the next ball and event arrived, I easily pulled ahead, catapulting myself to the top of the scores. When we saw the results on the parchment, Sophie peering over my shoulder, she looked green. I couldn't be sure if it was exhaustion from having to compete while sick, or guilt over falling behind. I didn't ask.

I had always tried to protect her, but I had never tried to separate myself from her like this. I kept waiting for her to demand answers, but the illness must have exhausted her too much to press me.

And after being forced to compete she had a relapse. I felt drained as I watched her suffer from afar, anxiety eating at me. I desperately wanted to be by her side, cheering her up and nursing her through it, but I kept reminding myself that I was staying away for her sake. She had properly trained nurses with her, so it was really only my company she lacked. And better she lose my company now, than be forced to marry the Beast. The slightly lost expression in her eyes when she looked at me only confirmed my resolution. My feelings for Jon didn't matter next to my need to protect my sister and the younger girls.

Yet, every time I saw him, my traitorous heart still leaped. And I did feel like a traitor. I had only known him a matter of weeks, but his distance felt almost as painful as my own forced withdrawal from Sophie. It made no sense. But my heart refused to listen to reason and continued in its erratic course.

The day after the twelfth trial, Jon's mother, Duchess Aurelia, threw a garden party for all the visiting royalty and nobles. The spring sun shone brightly, a light breeze keeping the day from becoming too hot, and Helena dragged me out of the library to attend.

"I don't know what has taken hold of you," she said, eyeing me suspiciously. "You were never one to hole yourself up in the library." She cracked a smile. "Not that Alyssa wouldn't be proud, but Sophie is sick and you must represent Arcadia. We're here to make a good impression and form alliances, remember?"

I agreed because I knew she was right. Between the Tourney

and the impending coup, I had almost forgotten our original purpose in Marin. An hour later, I entered the garden in my favorite afternoon gown. I knew I looked elegant, but I still felt half-naked. I never attended social functions without Sophie. I reached out to her in my mind but could tell she was asleep.

I looked around for Millie, instead, but could see no sign of her. Lilac, Snow, and the others were similarly absent from sight, with the exception of Emmeline and Giselle, who only made me turn hurriedly the other way, hoping to avoid a stilted conversation.

Taking a drink from one of the tables that had been carried out onto the lawns, I wandered through the flowers alone. I knew I was getting further and further away from the party, but I couldn't make myself care. It felt too nice to stop thinking and stop trying, and just walk and enjoy the beauty. Of course, that only lasted for about twenty minutes, until I turned a corner and almost ran into Corinna and two of her friends.

"My apologies." I stepped back hurriedly.

She sneered at me. "Just because you're a princess, doesn't mean you can walk all over us."

I said nothing, since such a comment clearly didn't warrant a response. But my silence seemed to infuriate her. She stepped up to stand directly in front of me, her face so twisted with anger, I feared she meant to physically attack me.

"You think you're so much better than me?" she whispered. "Well you're not going to have him. He's mine, do you understand? Mine!"

I stepped back, my eyes widening. "I…I don't know what you mean." My eyes flicked over her shoulder to her two friends who both looked bemused.

The slight movement seemed to remind her we weren't alone. She stepped back, taking a deep breath and regaining some calm. "Prince Jonathan will never choose some worthless foreign girl like you."

Rage boiled through me, but I kept my face still. I refused to let her know that she had succeeded in upsetting me. Especially when her comment was only a trigger rather than the cause of my true pain. The pain I had been denying for the past two weeks, shut up in the library.

Because it didn't matter if Jon would have chosen me or not. I was going to win the Tourney and marry a prince more beast than man. And all my efforts to save Jon from Corinna were only going to free him to inherit his throne and marry some other princess. It was still worth it, of course, to save him. But that didn't stop it hurting more than I had thought such a thing could.

Then, almost as if she could read my mind, one of the other girls spoke up. "Don't worry, Corinna. Haven't you seen the latest results? Princess Liliana is going to end up betrothed to the Beast."

She and the second girl both shuddered, but I could tell from their shining eyes and smiles that they rather enjoyed the second-hand fear. It didn't touch them, not really. I felt like I watched them from a great distance, so far separated by situation that we didn't really inhabit the same location.

Corinna, on the other hand, felt all too real. The venom in her eyes stung because she was playing the same high-stakes game as me. And she wasn't satisfied to see me dragged away involuntarily. She couldn't bear the idea that Jon might have chosen me if we were both free. I could read it on her face as clearly as if she had spoken aloud. But she couldn't say the words. Not now, anyway.

"It's a good thing you'll be going to Palinar," she said instead. "Because you'll never be welcome here in Marin."

"Corinna!" The second girl's shocked reprimand was undermined by her giggles.

I drew myself up to my full height, wishing it were more impressive, but hesitated. Did Arcadia's honor and good name require me to defend myself, or to leave before I insulted someone? Naturally I didn't care about insulting Corinna, but I didn't even know who the other girls were. Instinctively I reached out to ask Sophie, before remembering she was asleep.

"I think you must be confused, Corinna," an unexpected voice joined the conversation, and his tone sent a delicious shiver racing down my spine. I had never heard him sound so dangerous. "I decide who's welcome in Marin, not you."

She paled and fell back several steps as if driven by an invisible source. "P...Prince Jonathan. I...I just..."

"Yes?" He stepped into view, stopping just in front of me as if shielding me from her. "You just what?"

Corinna gaped at him, clearly shocked at his presence and his attitude. When the silence lengthened, she seemed to remember their earlier interaction, and her eyes narrowed into a glare. "Really, Jonathan. Is that whose side you want to take? Are you sure?"

Her friends gasped, but she ignored them, taking a step toward him. Jon didn't back down, stepping forward, instead, to meet her halfway.

"Let me make one thing clear." His words were low but clear, spoken slowly and with dangerous intent. "It doesn't matter what you do or say. I will always choose her. Every. Single. Time."

I swayed, unable to believe what was happening. Unable to take it in. I could read the rage and the warning in Corinna's eyes, and I knew Jon could, too, but he didn't falter for even a second.

The tense silence lengthened and then suddenly snapped. "Fine!" Corinna spun around and gestured for her friends to follow. "Have your foreign princess. But don't say I didn't try to warn you."

She stormed off, but her two friends hesitated. They glanced at each other and then dropped quick curtsies to Jon and me before scurrying after Corinna. We watched them go without moving. And then we were alone.

"Jon." His name came out half-breath, half-whisper.

He spun around and strode over, jerking me into his arms. His eyes devoured my face, hungry and tortured. "I don't care about consequences. I don't care about responsibility. I'm going half out of my mind." His low voice throbbed with passion. "All I want is you."

A small voice in the back of my mind told me that I, at least, couldn't abandon consequences and responsibility. My ailing sister was relying on me, even if she didn't know it. But the rest of my thoughts had fastened on the feel of his strong arms around me, the glow in his eyes and the shape of his mouth, so close to my own.

And when he groaned, pulled me even closer and crushed his lips against mine, those weak and traitorous feelings not only allowed it, they gloried in it. Because despite every barrier between us, despite everything, Jon had chosen me. And my heart wanted to burst from the joy.

PART III
SACRIFICE

CHAPTER 26

*W*hen Jon and I broke apart, it was sudden. Both of us falling back and panting, staring at each other with wide eyes. Every nerve in my body tried to pull me back toward him, but I resisted. Now that the first heady moments had passed, I remembered that I wasn't free to follow my heart.

"What are you doing?" I whispered. "I'm leading the Tourney, and you just threw away what might be your only chance to save your sisters." I hated the words even as they came out of my mouth.

He ran a hand through his hair. "I know." And then softer. "I know." He stepped closer, and I took a trembling step back. But he stepped closer again, reaching for me. I pulled away, but his eyes pleaded so desperately and eloquently that I stopped fighting myself and melted forward into his arms. He wrapped them tight around me and gave a deep sigh.

"I've been asking myself for the last two weeks if I could do it. If I could force myself to marry her for the sake of my sisters. And sometimes I almost convinced myself I could. And then I would see you again, and the illusion would be swept away.

"My whole life I have been nothing but responsible. And now, despite all my efforts, my duchy is about to be destroyed. I've tried and tried, and I cannot think of a way to save it. I told myself I could save the girls, at least. But I cannot marry Corinna. Not now that you're here. And for once I want to stop thinking about everyone else. I want to be selfish and think about just one person. You."

I laughed shakily. "You might need to take another look at the definition of selfish. I think you're doing it wrong."

He chuckled softly at my humor, and I immediately felt guilty for giving him hope. This time I did pull away, and his arms dropped to his sides, his face falling.

"It doesn't matter what either of us does, it doesn't change the Tourney," I said. "We are all of us bound by it."

He frowned and moved toward me again. I gave him a warning look, and he fell back with a sigh. "There are still five events to go. That's plenty of time for the scores to change. You might fall and break your ankle like Celine."

I wanted to shake my head at the sort of twisted situation that would make that a loving statement. A bigger part of me wanted to ask him who he hoped would win in my stead. Sophie? Hazel? But I refrained from any of it.

"Even if I don't win the Tourney, there's still the crisis in Marin." I took a deep breath. "My parents would never let me make a marriage alliance with the duchy in its current state."

A look of intense pain and shame crossed his face.

"I'm sorry," I whispered, wishing there were something else I could say. But I had nothing.

A long silence stretched between us, broken eventually by a distant voice calling my name. We both stirred as if awakening from a dream. I started to turn toward the sound, but Jon stopped me, gripping my shoulders and leaning toward me.

"I won't leave it at that. I can't." He pressed a fast kiss down onto my lips, and then disappeared around a hedge.

"Lily?" Helena appeared from the other direction, looking at me with confusion. "What's going on? What are you doing out here?" She looked around as if expecting other people to come bursting from the flower beds.

I still stood in the same spot, my fingers pressed to my lips, trying to hold onto the warmth of his kiss, knowing that, despite his words, it had to be the last one. For both our sakes. We couldn't torment ourselves like this.

"Lily? Lily, are you all right?" Helena laid a concerned hand on my arm, and I shook myself.

"Yes, oh, yes. I'm sorry, I was just daydreaming. I took a walk and got distracted by the beautiful flowers." I gestured weakly at the garden.

Helena relaxed, although suspicion still lurked in her eyes. "It is beautiful, isn't it? I'm sorry to pull you away, but I have some Trionians I want to introduce you to."

"Oh, of course." My feet followed behind her without conscious thought. I seemed to be floating through water, every movement meeting resistance, all sounds distant and muted. I must have said the right things, but I remembered none of it.

And when the event was over, I had to remind myself that Sophie, sick in bed, knew nothing of what had happened. My whole world had just shifted, and I couldn't tell my twin. It felt like another loss. When Celine fell asleep that night, I cried soundlessly into my pillow for half the night.

And yet, despite everything, life went on. Now that I had pulled ahead in the Tourney, I abandoned the library. I had given up hope of finding a solution for Marin there, and with Sophie in bed sick, I hated the constant solitude.

The doctors had finally given Celine permission to move around a bit more, and she had insisted on an excursion into the gardens. "I miss the gardens at home," she told me, and I realized flowers to Celine were like books to Sophie. A taste of home.

All the girls except for the Eldonians had been regularly visiting Celine in her suite to keep her company, and everyone shared the excitement at her release. As we all rushed around, ensuring every tiny detail had been considered, I realized it was the first time we had all been together without fear or tension hanging over us.

And I found I enjoyed it. Even Celine, despite her constant eye rolls and commands for us to get on with it, appeared to be appreciating the cheerful chaos. Perhaps it reminded her of growing up surrounded by her many siblings.

"Where's her shawl? There might be a breeze, and I can't find it anywhere," said Marigold, upending the room in her search for the missing article.

"Stop! You're destroying the room," said Hazel, asserting the superiority that came with being one year older than her younger sister. Except Marigold appeared not to recognize her sister's authority, and a squabble threatened to break out until Millie intervened.

Blanche meanwhile had quietly made her way around the room, straightening everything that Marigold had thrown around.

Celine ignored them all, distracted by Pearl and Opal who had decided to try on her collection of hats with many accompanying giggles. Celine had no great consideration for the state of her room, but she had a significant love for her wardrobe. A love that caused her to hover nervously near the youngest members of our group.

"Don't worry," said Lilac, who had ignored the dispute between her two younger sisters in favor of supervising Pearl and Opal, "I won't let them damage anything."

I suspected her responsible attitude came from her secret desire to make her own inspection of Celine's admittedly impressive wardrobe. I made no move to intervene anywhere, preferring to sit back and laugh at the others' antics and Celine's attempts to conceal her clothing-related anxieties.

At last Daisy burst into the room. "It's ready!" she called. Everyone dropped their various discussions and activities and rushed toward the door.

"What's ready?" Celine's eyes narrowed into suspicious slits as she observed the chaos fall instantly into order. "What's going on?"

"You'll see," I grinned at her.

We all instantly stopped our fussing and swept her out of the room, which only fed her suspicion. "I was right, you really were wasting time, the lot of you," she said, her voice full of fake outrage. "Waiting for Daisy."

"You'll find out soon enough," I said.

Daisy, who had raced ahead of us, turned as we stepped out into the garden and yelled, "Surprise!"

Several large rugs had been thrown across the closest lawn, and large cushions had been scattered liberally over them. Sophie, whose fever had finally broken but who remained weak, had already been carried down and sat in a dense pile of the pillows. Keeping her company were Teddy, Gabe and Jon. I carefully averted my eyes from Jon, scared of what I might see in his face.

A picnic had been laid out on the rug, and Gabe, stretched out full length on his side, his elbow propped on a cushion, had already begun on a plate.

"Gabe!" Daisy seemed to visibly swell in her outrage. "What are you doing? You can't start eating before the guest of honor arrives!"

"Can't I?" He grinned lazily up at us all, not bothering to rise in greeting as Teddy and Jon had done. "But it's such a lovely day, and the food looked so very delicious."

"Humph!" Daisy plonked down and continued to glare at

her hero.

He shrugged and smiled charmingly up at us. "My apologies, Celine." He pulled a second plate from amongst the pillows. "I did, however, save you a piece of cake."

"Save? What do you mean save?" Daisy leaped back to her feet. "Did you eat all the cake?"

"I'm sure he can't possibly have had time to do so," I said, soothingly, afraid she might actually explode.

"You underestimate him," said Teddy, grinning at his sister. "Daisy knows him better."

"What can I say? I'm a hungry man." Gabe took a big bite from his plate and then winked at Celine and me.

"Stop it," said Celine. "Leave poor Daisy in peace. I can see a large cake over there with sufficient slices for everyone."

Daisy glared at him again and marched off with her nose in the air. The younger girls all followed her lead, rushing to collect their own plates, while Millie helped Celine to sit, and I collapsed down next to Sophie.

It's good to see you up. I was worried you wouldn't be well enough to be here.

It's good to be *up. I was so sick of that fever and that bed, I could have screamed.* She tipped her head back to the sun and closed her eyes.

"I have to tease her occasionally," Gabe was explaining to Millie. "It wouldn't be sporting to do it to my own sisters." He looked a little sadly in the direction of the twins, and I silently admitted he was right. Pearl and Opal lacked the necessary spunk for such an endeavor; it would just be cruel.

Millie rolled her eyes and began to assemble her own plate. Soon everyone was eating happily, the silence broken only by the occasional comment on the food. I risked a single glance toward Jon, but his eyes were fixed on me, so I quickly looked away again, flushing.

What's going on? asked Sophie.

Nothing, I projected quickly, and she didn't press it.

A group of servants stood nearby ready to clean up the food, laughing and talking quietly amongst themselves as they waited for us to finish. Sophie nodded her head toward them. *It reminds me of the servants at our picnic on the hill. They seem to be having a good time. Remember what Alyssa told us?*

I nodded but said nothing. Our sister-in-law had taken us aside before we left to give us some advice. And one of the things she had told us was to make sure to watch the servants in whatever palace we visited. "If they seem lazy and disorganised and sullen, that tells you the rulers are weak and ineffectual. But worse is if they seem silent or scared. That means the rulers are harsh and cruel. Find a palace where the servants laugh and talk as they complete their duties, where they have time off, but where everything always seems to be done. That's the mark of a good ruler, both kind and effective. The sort of person you could trust." She had paused, tears in her eyes. "The sort of place you could call home. The state of the servants won't lie."

She'd hugged us both tight, then, one in each arm, although we'd grown as tall as her. I don't think she would have let us go at all if the baron and baroness hadn't been with us. She trusted them to care for us just as she and my brother would have done themselves.

I had felt so hopeful when she had given us the advice, but Sophie's reminder now merely twisted the knife that had taken up permanent residence in my heart. Yet another reminder that I had found the perfect home. A reminder of what could have been if not for the darkness consuming these lands.

"It will be nice when the summer begins, and we no longer have the Tourney hanging over us," said Lilac, wandering over to join us. The younger girls had moved away from the rugs and were throwing a small ball back and forth between them. "Everyone will stay on for a little while at least. I hope, anyway. Then we can do things like this all the time."

She smiled around at us all. Clearly she no longer feared winning the Tourney herself. Because, for one of our number, summer would only bring a worse fate than the competition itself.

"Except that someone will win, Lilac," Jon reminded his sister. I could feel his eyes on me, but I kept my own trained on the ground. He at least had not forgotten.

"Oh! Yes, I didn't mean…" her voice trailed off, and she sounded almost in tears.

I forced myself to look up and smile. "Don't worry, Lilac, I'm quite sure it won't be you or either of your sisters."

"No," said Celine, drawing out the word, her eyes drifting from Sophie to me. "I've had that distinct impression for some time." She knew what we had been doing, then. Not that I was surprised. I felt sure she would have joined us in the attempt if not for her leg and her low score from that first event.

A moment of silence ensued as everyone absorbed her words, and I couldn't resist taking a tiny peep at Jon. A growing horror crept across his face. His eyes slipped to mine, and I forced myself to smile. I mustn't have succeeded very well, though, since he only looked more tortured.

Sophie cleared her throat and changed the topic and everyone followed her gratefully. I tried to talk and laugh as if nothing was wrong, but I didn't know if I was fooling anyone. I didn't look at Jon again, and soon Sophie tired and needed to be helped back inside.

He stood immediately and came over to assist us, but I clung stubbornly to my sister. I could tell he was trying to pull me aside, but I refused to give him the opportunity. I didn't even move far enough away from Sophie for him to whisper in my ear. Only when we reached the door of the palace did I glance back to see him still standing where we had left him on the rug in the garden, staring after us.

CHAPTER 27

*N*ow that Sophie was recovering and no longer infectious, I stuck to her side, trying to make up for my earlier absence, while also protecting myself from any unexpected encounters. It worked until the next ball. As soon as we stepped through the doors, Jon appeared, just as he used to do.

"Dance with me," he said, and his voice made it clear it wasn't a request.

Sophie nudged me forward and, in a moment of weakness, I capitulated. I knew I had made a mistake as soon as his arms encircled me. Their strength felt far too appealing, and the fire that raced through me scared me. It was already hard enough holding everything together.

"You're planning to win, aren't you?"

I had no reply to his hard words, not one he would accept anyway. But we had only just arrived at the ballroom, so I had no expectation of being saved by the sound of the bell. When it rang out, we both stilled, staring at each other in confusion.

"Was that for the Tourney?" I looked around. "Are we even all here?" I counted the princesses in the ballroom as they started to move slowly toward our small door, clearly all equally surprised.

Jon laughed bitterly. "Just a reminder for us all that we are none of us in control." He released me abruptly and disappeared into the crowd.

Sophie appeared at my elbow, watching him go. "What was that?" She shook her head. "Never mind. Let's go."

After so many events without injury, we no longer trod in fear as we followed the now-familiar routine. Even Pearl and Opal chattered away as we walked through the groves. Of course, as the events ticked past, and everyone else grew lighter, I grew heavier. But it was a sacrifice I had chosen.

Except, when we sat down, no individual puzzles or instructions appeared on our golden plates. Only a single parchment in the middle of the table. The voices dropped away, as we all remembered we had now completed three puzzle events and were facing the unknown again. A shadow of our earlier dread reappeared. In an instant everything had changed, and it immediately seemed hard to understand how we had ever become comfortable in this mysterious and gloomy world.

At least now, after the three treasure hunts, it wasn't only the Marinese princesses who knew the mirror castle well. We had all explored its nooks and crannies, as well as the three groves.

But it turned out that our new challenge required none of that knowledge. Emmeline read out the instructions. "Return across the lake. In the grove of golden leaves, you will find a marked track. You must each take it in turns to race to the end of the track. Points will be awarded based on speed. If any part of your body touches the ground outside of the track, you will be instantly disqualified."

"A straight race? Well, that rules me out," said Celine.

I looked around the table trying to guess who amongst the other princesses might be fast runners. Certainly neither the twins nor Marigold had anything to fear with their short legs.

The bell sounded, and we all rose silently and crossed the lake. As soon as we stepped into the golden grove, we found a new path that branched away from the regular one. It glowed as if it, too, were made of gold, although the surface still looked like dirt in texture.

It wove away between the trees and out of sight. The finish of the race track, however, could just be seen connecting with the main path again at the other end of the grove. It must swing back around, then.

We all looked at each other, wondering who should go first. Eventually Celine shrugged and stepped forward to the line. As soon as she was in position, a small chime rang out, and she hobbled away, her crutches swinging.

She had been out of sight for a couple of minutes when the same chime sounded again. Before I could ask Sophie what she thought it meant, Celine flew out onto the path and landed hard, as if shot at speed from the other end of the race track.

I gasped and raced over to her. She had pulled herself up into a sitting position, and tears leaked out of her eyes as she clutched at her injured ankle. I kneeled down next to her, but she merely shrugged at me and grimaced. I reached for her leg, to check it, but she shook her head and pushed me away, gesturing for me to return to the beginning of the track. I hoped that meant she hadn't reinjured it despite the evident pain.

The others had watched our silent interaction with wide eyes, no one stepping up to run next. After a moment, Emmeline looked around at the rest of the group and then moved forward. She was taller than either Sophie or me, but my previous concerns about beating her time had faded, replaced by new ones as to what exactly this 'race' entailed.

She disappeared from sight much more quickly than Celine had, leaving the rest of us with no option but to wait and see what happened.

Did Celine seem badly hurt? Sophie asked.

I think she'll be all right. I hope so anyway. But there's nothing we can do to help her down here. And I'm worried about you getting thrown around like that. You're still weak from the fever.

You'll have to go first, projected Sophie. *You can tell me what to expect. Maybe I can avoid triggering whatever happened to Celine.*

I had originally planned to send her first, to give myself that advantage of foresight, but in the light of this unknown danger I agreed to her suggestion. Even with the extra help, she would still be slow so was likely to have one of the lower scores.

When the chime sounded again, we all flinched, our eyes racing to the end of the track. Sure enough, Emmeline came flying out, just as Celine had done. She landed hard, winced and pushed herself slowly upright. Thankfully Celine had managed to push herself out of the way before Emmeline's abrupt arrival, or the other girl would have landed on top of her.

Millie moved forward to take her place at the start of the race, a look of determination on her face. I was grateful to her for leading the way since strategy suggested I should wait until the end, in the hope I might be able to gain some clue to what was happening.

When her chime sounded, she followed the previous two, shooting out onto the main path and landing awkwardly. I frowned and met Sophie's eyes.

It's hard to tell time down here, but... Sophie started chewing on a strand of hair. *Do you think the chime is sounding after the same amount of time?*

I nodded. *It did seem like it. But the instructions didn't tell us there was a time limit for completing the track.*

She sent back a laugh that lacked humor. *They didn't tell us the ceiling would fall in either. Or to watch out for waves.*

She had a point. *Let's count this time.*

We counted steadily through the next three contestants and, sure enough, the chime sounded after five minutes each time. *So we need to finish the track in that time to avoid a painful exit,* projected Sophie.

I nodded but without much hope. If neither Emmeline nor Millie had managed it, I didn't see how Sophie would in a weakened state. Which meant it was up to me to give her enough of an advantage with my description of the track.

The group at the end of the track grew as the group at the beginning shrunk, until eventually only Sophie and I remained. No one had succeeded in outrunning the chime, and Pearl and Marigold were both crying from their falls.

Finally I took my place, springing away before the chime had faded from the air. The golden glow of the track made it easy to follow, and the path behind me was soon swallowed by the trees. It twisted and turned, and I soon came upon an obstacle—a downed tree across the track. I leaped over it, but had to slow my pace or risk serious injury if I came upon another obstruction too fast. I wondered uneasily if a few bruises from being flung from the path was the only thing making Pearl and Marigold cry.

I pushed them from my mind. I could do nothing to help them, and I needed all my attention to try to beat the race and leave Sophie forewarned. If she knew when to expect the obstacles, maybe she really could run faster than the rest of us and escape the fall. I kept up a constant projection to her, warning her of each obstruction and twist of the track.

My lungs and legs burned by the time the track turned back in the direction of the path. I continued to push myself, though, thinking of Sophie every time I felt my steps slow.

I've circled all the way back, I said to her, keeping up my account of the track. *I can actually see a stretch from the beginning of the track. I didn't notice it passed so close when I was running the other section.*

Thank goodness I didn't need my breath to project since I had none left. *Now I've made another turn and I still can't see the end of the track.*

It had been too much to keep count while also talking to Sophie, but I had a sinking feeling that five minutes must nearly be up. How could anyone complete the track in the allocated time?

I had no sooner finished the thought, than the chime sounded, and my feet slid out from under me. The golden dirt of the track solidified into a surface as slippery as ice, and the ground immediately behind me seemed to rise, the raised portion moving forward like a wave and propelling me down the slide that was thus created.

By the time it dumped me onto the main path, I had gained enough speed that it hurt. A lot. I lay there, not even attempting to sit up as I tried to regain my breath. I had five minutes to get out of the way, and I didn't see how Sophie could possibly finish in that time, even with my warnings. I had slid a long way.

Anger and frustration at the impossible task welled within me, buoyed by the pain from where I had landed. I took several deep breaths and made myself sit up.

Millie and Lilac appeared and held out their hands to help me up. I had just grasped the proffered assistance when they both looked over my shoulder, their eyes widening. I tried to twist around to look as well, but they dragged me quickly forward, not waiting for me to get my feet under me.

I finally managed to regain my balance and turn around just in time to see Sophie jog across the end of the track onto the path. As she stepped over to join us, everyone's voice was freed.

"That was so fast!"

"How did you do it?"

The other girls crowded around her, calling out questions, but my shock was too great to be put in to words. She laughed and shrugged. "I knew I didn't have the energy for a full run, and I would never have made it before that chime. So, when I saw another section of the track so close, I took a chance and jumped across. I ended up cutting out most of it, I think."

"Jumped it?" Marigold sounded half-shocked, half-delighted. "Are you allowed to do that?"

"It just said our body couldn't touch the ground outside of the track, it didn't say you had to actually run the whole thing. And once I'd done that, I found I was almost here."

"I'm impressed," said Emmeline. "I didn't even notice the track doubled back so close until I was on the second section."

"Me neither," said Snow.

"I didn't notice it either," said Celine. "But then I was already sliding by the time I must have come back past it."

Sophie met my eyes and grinned before shrugging again. "I was watching really closely."

I had to force myself to smile back. I had only wanted to protect her from injury, not to allow her to leap ahead in the scores as she would surely do now.

When we collected the scores, I was relieved to see that I had been the third fastest after Sophie and Emmeline. Emmeline now trailed Hazel closely, but Sophie and I still considerably outstripped them. I had lost most of the lead I had previously gained on my sister, though.

The usual small crowd awaited us when we emerged from the small room, but Helena's efforts focused on Sophie given her current frail state. I trailed behind them, still too tired after my intense run to offer any assistance.

"You're planning to win, aren't you?" The words, that I had already heard once that night, emerged from the shadows. I jumped. I tried to move away without responding, but his hand shot out and gripped my arm, pulling me into the shadows with him.

It's Jon, I sent to Sophie. *He wants to talk to me about something. I'll try to catch up in a minute, but give some excuse to Helena if you have to.*

Very well. I could hear her curiosity, but she refrained from asking me questions. Another area in which her virtues exceeded mine.

"Look at me." His voice was so anguished, I couldn't help but comply. "And don't try to hide it from me. I know you too well. You would never let someone else take on the responsibility. I can't let you do it."

I sighed. There was clearly no point denying it. "You can't do anything to stop me."

"Can't I?"

His intensity scared me. "No, Jon, you can't! The law is clear, remember? You can't get around the magic, your life would be forfeit. It doesn't matter who you are. Think of your kingdom. Think of your parents and your sisters. They need you. Especially now." I clutched the front of his jacket with both hands. "You can't do anything foolish. You'll only get yourself killed."

He pulled me closer. "I'm always responsible. For nineteen years I've been nothing but responsible. And I love my people. I just love you more. I've already told you—in this one thing I can't be responsible. I would do anything to save you."

"Don't say that," I said, my voice small. I looked up into his eyes and felt like I was suffocating. "I don't want you to save me at the expense of yourself. It would break my heart."

He leaned down so our faces nearly touched. "You're already breaking mine." His lips pressed down hard against mine, and his arms swept around me, locking me against his chest.

I embraced him back, I couldn't help myself, but silent tears poured from my eyes, and the salt water mingled with the taste of our kiss. Could you die from love and sorrow and pain?

Lily? Sophie's voice in my head made me stagger backwards from the kiss. *Helena's coming back for you.*

I mopped at my face, desperately trying to scrub away the tears before the baroness found me. Gentle hands reached out and gripped mine, stopping me, but I wrenched myself free and fled down the corridor.

"Lily," he called after me, his voice hoarse. But I didn't stop.

~

I could barely sleep, haunted by Jon's words. Sophie had instantly seen my distress, and this time had pressed me to explain. The encounter with Jon had broken down some of my carefully constructed defenses, so I had told her my most pressing fear—that Jon would attempt to interfere with the Tourney.

I could tell, though, that she didn't think it likely. "All of them get heated up, sometimes," she said. "But Jon is always the most sensible. If anyone was going to try, it would be Gabe."

Except that you succeeded, I wanted to tell her. We broke through his responsibility and restraint, just like you told me to do in that ballroom so many days ago. Only, we did it more than the little bit you were aiming for. And now I'm terrified he's going to end up destroying his life, and it will be all my fault.

But I remained silent, even in my mind.

The next morning, I refused to leave our room. "I'm saying in here until I come up with an idea," I told Sophie. "We have to think of a way to save Marin." If I could give Jon some hope for his duchy, perhaps he would give up whatever desperate plan he had hatched.

But no brilliant revelations came to me. Eventually, in desperation, I convinced Sophie to come with me to talk to the head of the Lanoverian delegation. "The Duchess of Sessily is shrewd, but she has compassion. Perhaps she will agree to help Marin." I lowered my voice. "Perhaps she would consider a marriage alliance between Celine and Jon, without requiring Marin to hand themselves over to Lanover."

"Lily! How can you even think of such a thing!"

But Sophie's horror didn't sway me. My desperation had grown as I spent the day cooped up in my room, and I knew that nothing would be so terrible as seeing Jon struck down by the magic that had destroyed Palinar and Prince Dominic.

Reluctantly Sophie accompanied me and listened in silence to my halting explanation to the duchess. I told her of Marin's troubles and their need, but I didn't mention the coup. I thought she might be more likely to offer Lanover's help to the duchy now if she didn't know a better offer might be coming. Although, given the noblewoman's reputation, I considered it more than possible she already knew, anyway.

"I'm sorry, Lily," she said when I had finished. "The duke and duchess seem like good rulers, fallen on hard times through no fault of their own. But I serve Lanover's interests, not theirs. Marin is smaller than all the kingdoms of this land and only a duchy. I could not, in all good faith, recommend a marriage alliance with them over Talinos or Trione."

Her face softened slightly and she gave a small sigh. "If love were involved, that would be a different thing. We still serve under the High King's laws, of course. But I have seen no sign of that between the Marinese prince and Celine..." Her voice trailed off, her eyes gentle but all too knowing.

I fought to hold back tears. I had never meant to doom Marin's only chance by attracting Jon's attention. I had always imagined that when I fell in love it would be something beautiful, a pathway to peace and prosperity for many. This reality was nothing like I had pictured it.

I excused us both then, Sophie still not having said a word, too dejected to attempt conversation. But at the door I paused, looking back at the older woman. I tried to make my voice light, keeping my face clear of emotion.

"Oh, I've been meaning to ask you. Has Sir Oswald approached you at all? I'm afraid I may have encouraged him in your direction in my efforts to avoid the younger members of his family." I wrinkled my nose as if it was no more than a matter of my less-than-deft dealings with an unwanted suitor.

A veil seemed to descend over the duchess' expression, reminding me that while she had something of a soft spot for me and Sophie, she was also a master diplomat. "He has, as a matter of fact. He is a man full of passion for his business. I was forced to remind him that the king and queen of Lanover have made their position clear. Like Arcadia, they wish only to make treaties through the rulers of this land. While Duke Philip rules, all alliances with Marin must go through him."

"Apologies, Your Grace, for putting you to that trouble." I gave her a respectful nod, as seemed appropriate toward someone below me in rank, but well above me in age, experience and wisdom, and shut the door behind me.

Well, that was clear enough, said Sophie.

Yes, she definitely knows about the plans for a coup. And her position is exactly as we suspected. She won't aid it but, if they succeed, she'll profit from it.

Perhaps we should have told her about Sir Oswald being behind the fire? Sophie twisted her hands together. *About what sort of ruler he would be. If she expects it to be a bloodless coup, with the support of all the nobles and merchants, she may even think it's a good thing.*

I shook my head. *How likely is she to believe us, when we have the information from Prince Jonathan? If Duke Philip had any evidence, he would have arrested Sir Oswald for conspiracy to commit arson by now. It would have been a nice solution to his problem, in fact.*

Sophie slammed her hand against the stone wall. *This is infuriating!*

I haven't given up hope. There's still time. But maintaining any optimism was getting harder and harder.

CHAPTER 28

*A*fter my reaction last time, and my weakness in the corridor, I didn't trust myself to dance with Jon at the next ball. I caught Teddy as we were walking in and had agreed to dance with him before he knew he had asked.

Despite the lack of any real danger in the race challenge, we still passed through the groves with a far more somber air than three nights before. The events had returned to more physical challenges, and we all remembered the dangers we had faced before. And something about Sophie's surprise win had unsettled everyone. A reminder, perhaps, that the unexpected could still happen with the scores.

And, sure enough, the instructions for the challenge were far more detailed than usual. We had to race to the tallest tower of the mirror palace, a different structure from the high keep we had visited in the first challenge and, once again, take a piece of jewelry. Only this time, the winner would be the one to bring back the superior piece.

When Opal timidly asked what that was supposed to mean, no one had any answers. And, to complicate it further, we were only to be allowed to leave the table one at a time, with the princess with the lowest rank leaving first. A list of our current ranks had been provided, and a series of bells would indicate each princess' release.

"It looks like the Tourney is giving us an opportunity to even the scores," said Celine. "It won't make much of a difference for me, though, given it's another race."

I ground my teeth together. After all the hard work I had put in to gain my lead, it seemed I would have to continue to struggle to keep it. But the scared faces around the table reminded me why the effort was worth it. Hazel, in particular, looked terrified at being given the chance to catch up.

"Opal, it looks like you're to leave first," said Celine, just before a chime sounded through the room.

Opal froze, panic taking over her face, but her twin gave her a shove and she leaped from her chair and rushed from the room. Pearl, only a few points in front of her, almost immediately received the chime signaling her own release.

One by one, princesses fled the room, the table emptying until only a handful of us remained. My leg jiggled beneath the wood, the tension rising in my middle. I kept picturing them all gaining ground, and the images made it hard to sit still. Celine had long gone, and soon only Sophie, Emmeline, Hazel and I remained. Sophie kept sending me reassuring projections, in an effort to calm my tension, but the other girls wouldn't meet our eyes. Despite this challenge, we were the four most likely to win the Tourney, and I could only assume they were both hoping it would be anyone but them. As usual, our voices had been silenced.

Then Emmeline was gone, and soon afterward Hazel. The next wait seemed interminable, though in reality it must have been less than a minute. When the next chime sounded, Sophie leaped to her feet and raced from the room, with a single backwards glance for me. *Calm down! Our scores are close enough that your chime will sound any second.*

She was right, of course. The final chime released me within moments. I jumped up so violently that my chair clattered to the ground behind me. I ignored it and dashed from the room.

Sophie still hadn't regained her full strength from the fever, so I quickly overtook her. And I easily remembered the path to the tallest tower since three of my clues had been located there during the treasure hunts. The room at the top was accessed by a long spiral stone staircase that wound through the center of the tower, and I hoped to pass most of the girls struggling up the endless flights of stairs.

I kept reminding myself that it wasn't a straight race, either. It all came down to our choice of jewelry, and none of us knew what sort to expect, or what might be considered significant.

I passed Hazel on the first stretch of stairs, and Celine not long after, struggling up with her crutches. I sent her a sympathetic smile but didn't slow. Pearl and Opal were next, despite having left first, and then Giselle. I kept expecting to see Marigold but saw no sign of her.

I was panting hard and wondering how much farther when I passed Blanche and, shortly after, Emmeline. Like me, she had gained a lot of ground, but now seemed to be struggling to catch her breath.

Still, I wasn't far ahead of either of them when I burst into the room. A table filled the center of the small space, and Millie stood beside it staring down at an array of crowns. I hurried over to join her. Only eleven items lay on the table. I looked around again, as if Marigold would suddenly emerge from one of the walls.

Have you seen Marigold? I asked Sophie who I guessed would be more than halfway up the stairs by now.

No. Why?

I didn't pass her at all. But there's already a crown missing.

Oh, they're crowns are they?

Yes. I kept my answer short, my mind divided between

concern for the mysterious disappearance of Marigold, and confusion over which of the crowns I should take. Millie seemed to share my indecision. Twice she reached out a hand only to draw it back again.

When I gazed at them more carefully, my eyes caught on one in particular. One so familiar, I didn't know why it hadn't leaped out at me immediately. Sitting on the table of this strange mirror tower was an exact replica of the Arcadian royal crown worn by my father at important functions and state occasions.

Now that I knew what to look for, I easily identified the others. Arcadia, Lanover, Northhelm and Rangmere were all represented from the Four Kingdoms. And I had spent hours on the voyage on the way over learning about the local kingdoms of this land. I recognized the crowns of Eldon, Eliam, Palinar, Talinos and Trione easily enough. The table even included the circlets worn by the heirs of Palinar and Talinos.

Which meant Marigold, if she had indeed been and gone already, had taken the crown of her own duchy. A statement of loyalty regarding the superiority of her home. Despite my love for Jon and his home, it wasn't the crown I would have chosen in her place.

But what was? Did superior mean largest kingdom in land size? Or most powerful? Or richest? And could I even be sure how they all ranked in these areas? I knew how each of the kingdoms compared to the others of their own land, but it was a little more difficult to compare between lands.

Before the mysterious curse, Palinar had been the largest and richest kingdom of these lands, although Marin held the greatest prestige. I suspected, now, however, that the smaller island kingdom of Trione would have to be the richest. But all of them were threatened by the encroaching darkness, so surely the Four Kingdoms, currently in one of their greatest ever periods of prosperity and peace, would have to be considered superior.

And Lanover was the richest of the Four Kingdoms. So

perhaps theirs was the crown I should take? My hand hovered over it as I reached out to Sophie, still toiling up the stairs, to explain my dilemma.

So, do you think I should take Lanover? I concluded.

Let me think for a minute.

I waited impatiently for her answer.

I've had a thought, she projected after several long beats of silence. *What if the crowns don't represent the kingdoms, but their rulers? The Princess Tourney is all about finding the perfect match for each ruler, after all. So, the winning score is supposed to go to the princess who best matches the one who called the Tourney. And surely that girl would consider the ruler in question superior over all others. Which means the superior crown belongs to Palinar.*

Brilliant!

My eyes latched on the Palinaran crown before veering off to the side. It had been Prince Dominic, not King Nicolas, who had called the Tourney. So it was the heir's circlet I should take. One of the least-imposing crowns present. That realization made me feel certain of my decision. This was the test.

I snatched it up. Millie, eyeing me sideways, seemed confused by my choice. After a moment she also chose a crown—the Lanoverian one I had nearly taken earlier. Did she even recognize our crowns? Or was she taking her cue from me?

It didn't matter now, we had both made our choice. Emmeline and Blanche burst through the door, almost colliding with one another in their haste and hurried over. We stepped back to give them access to the table. I watched their faces, waiting for the moment of understanding as they recognized the pieces. But they were both difficult to read.

Sophie darted into the room, her eyes raking the table. For a brief moment she looked disappointed before snatching up the Palinaran crown. Had she attempted to lead me astray on purpose, hoping to take the heir's circlet and the winning score herself?

She staggered back to lean against a wall gasping in deep breaths. Millie, Blanche and Emmeline all stared at her in surprise, but she ignored them.

She chuckled silently. *I've really confused them all now. Did you find Marigold?*

No. The question of the crowns had momentarily distracted me, but my earlier confusion now returned. How could the younger girl have gotten so far ahead, and how had we not seen her? *We should go back down. Perhaps we'll find her back in the Throne Room.*

Millie followed our lead, and the three of us left just as Lilac entered. We passed Hazel, Giselle, Pearl and Opal at the top of the stairs, and Celine some way below them. She grimaced at us, and hopped her way up another stair.

We all winced in sympathy. When we reached the throne room, we found it empty. I bit my lip and glanced at Sophie who shrugged. Millie frowned questioningly at us, and I pointed at the chair where Marigold had sat, raising my hands in a question.

She squinted at the table, clearly struggling to build a mental image of who had been sitting where. I could see the moment she remembered and, seconds later, the confusion when she realized we hadn't passed Marigold at all.

I crossed back to my chair and placed my chosen crown on the golden plate. A chime sounded, identical to the ones that had released us. Millie raised her eyebrows and copied me, Sophie not far behind her. Two chimes sang out.

I stood behind my chair gripping the back, tired from my dash up the stairs, but too restless to sit. Sophie mimicked me, but Millie chose to sit.

She must have taken another way. I'm sure she'll turn up any minute. Sophie tried to calm me, just as she had before the event began.

Did you see another way? And, anyway, one of the crowns was gone when I arrived. If she did take another way, she should have been back by now.

The other girls trickled into the room, following our lead and placing their crowns on their plates. When ten chimes had sounded, the bell signaling the end of the challenge rang.

"Oh, thank goodness," said Millie. "I thought that stupid bell was going to make us wait for Celine to hobble all the way back down."

"Perhaps she's just taken the last crown," said Blanche.

"Where's Marigold?" Lilac sounded as worried as I felt.

"Exactly what I want to know." For once I didn't try to shield the other girls from the fear in my voice. I felt a dreadful certainty we were right to be afraid. "I didn't see any sign of her, and one of the crowns was already gone when I arrived at the top of the tower."

I glanced over at Millie who frowned. "It was gone when I arrived, too, and I never saw her ahead of me."

"You know her and the palace better than any of us," I said to Lilac and Hazel. "Is there another way up to that tower?"

The two sisters shared a look. "You don't think she would have...?"

"Of course she would." Lilac sighed and looked back at me. "There's an uncovered stairway that circles the outside of the tower. She's never been afraid of heights, or deterred by our parents forbidding her to use it. It's much quicker to get to it from here than getting to the base of the tower inside the palace."

"Then it also should have been quicker to get back," I said grimly. "Lead us there."

Hazel and Lilac ran, and the rest of us followed, somehow finding new reserves. My pulse drummed so loudly I wondered if everyone could hear it, my breath scraping loudly past my ears.

We were out of the mirror palace and circling the outside wall within a few steps. Lilac had pulled ahead, so it was her piercing scream that rent the stillness.

CHAPTER 29

Somehow, impossibly, I found a final spurt of energy. I sprinted around the final corner, the horrible sight unfolding before me.

Marigold lay still at the base of the wall, her small body sprawled unnaturally across the ground. Her pale face stood out horribly against the stream of bright red blood that cut across it. The Marinese crown lay a short distance from her outflung arm, as if it had rolled from her fingers after she hit the ground.

In my peripheral vision, I noticed a small segment of one of the steps had crumbled away well above my head height. I dropped onto my knees next to Lilac, Hazel close behind me. Both of them were crying.

"Can you do that thing you did for the baby?" Hazel sobbed. "Breathe for her?"

I leaned over Marigold's comatose form and then sat back up. "I don't need to. Her heart is beating, and she's breathing on her own. We need to stop her bleeding and check for any broken bones."

The rest of the girls had arrived by this time, forming a loose circle around us, several of them crying almost as much as Marigold's sisters.

"She's not dead," said Sophie. She eyed off the others consideringly. "And Lily needs your scarf, Blanche."

Blanche quickly complied, handing it to me so I could create a makeshift bandage. I wadded it against Marigold's head, where the blood appeared to originate.

"Lilac, press down here. I'm going to check her."

I looked up at Sophie, and she dropped down to her knees to help without my having to ask. *What do you think?* I asked.

She gently ran her hands along the younger girl's legs. *I'm not sure. I wish Aldric or Matilde were here, they would know what to do.* She named our medical friends at home in Arcadia.

We don't know how long she's been lying here, but it looks like she's lost a fair amount of blood. I don't like that she's still unconscious.

Sophie met my eyes but didn't reply, as aware as I was that it wasn't a good sign.

"We can't find any breaks," I said, at last. "But we're far from experts. We need to get her back to the palace and to some doctors as quickly as possible."

"There's no point. She should have regained consciousness long before now." Emmeline's emotionless words set off more rounds of tears.

I glared at her, but she simply shrugged slightly. "I'm just stating the facts."

"Well, please don't," I snapped, before rearranging the bandage so I could tie it around Marigold's head. Then I looked up at Sophie. "We'll have to take turns carrying her."

Emmeline stepped forward. "I'll carry her to the boats." I wanted to push her away, but I took a deep breath and reminded myself that her cold words had done no actual harm to Marigold. That had occurred long before any of us arrived. And she had only said the truth Sophie and I had kept silent. In fact, Emmeline had never actually done anything against any of us. Maybe her and her sister's minds simply worked differently than the rest of ours. A lack of emotions wasn't exactly a crime.

"Thank you," I made myself say, helping to steady Marigold as the Eldonian crouched down and gently lifted her limp body. Emmeline didn't respond.

Laying the still-unresponsive form into a boat alone felt completely wrong, but there was nothing else we could do. The coracles would only bear the weight of one. Celine finally arrived as the rest of us were loading ourselves into our own boats.

"What's going on?" she asked before catching sight of Marigold and falling silent.

Millie, Sophie and I each carried her through one of the groves, her slight frame growing heavier with each step. Millie took the last turn through the grove of silver leaves, so I took the parchment of scores, tucking it into my dress without bothering to read it, and climbed the ladder first. Sophie followed but stopped halfway, and carefully Millie handed Marigold up. Once I dragged her into the room, I lifted her into my arms again.

I could barely wait for poor Celine to crawl up, two of the others helping her, and for the trapdoor to close and melt into the floor. As soon as it had disappeared, Hazel thrust open the door and staggered out, calling for a doctor through her still-falling tears.

I only just made it through the doorway before sinking onto my knees and placing Marigold down upon the ground. Her family gathered around her, screams and shouts filling the mostly-empty ballroom. Someone I couldn't see helped me to my feet.

A tingling rushed through me at the contact, my body somehow recognizing the feel of Jon's hand, even if my eyes couldn't see his face. I wanted to collapse into his arms, but I held myself back. This was his family's tragedy, and I didn't deserve to be the one seeking comfort.

Sophie approached, and we clung to each other, just outside

the circle of action. Watching and waiting. And hoping still, however feebly.

"M...Mother?" Marigold's soft, frail voice somehow cut through all the sound to reach our ears. Sophie went limp beside me.

"Oh, thank goodness," she whispered. "I thought..."

The doctors quickly confirmed our hasty diagnosis. Marigold had suffered no broken bones, the concussion and bleeding her only injuries, although serious ones.

Once she had been carried off, her family around her, the rest of us drifted to bed, still half in shock. I kept feeling her dead weight in my arms and hearing her shallow, halting breaths. It took me a long time to fall asleep.

~

The next morning, Helena woke us to the news that Marigold was expected to make a full recovery. "She's awake and alert," she told us with a broad smile. "She will need rest and lots of fluids for the next three days, but she will recover."

We all exclaimed joyously, no one commenting on why three days was the limit given to her recovery. But after Helena left, I sat on my bed, my arms wrapped around my legs and my chin on my knees.

It doesn't make sense, I projected to Sophie, thoughtfully. *We saw how far she fell, and how much blood she lost.*

Sophie chewed on a strand of her hair. *I've been thinking the same thing. She was unconscious for far too long.*

I'm delighted, of course...but she shouldn't have recovered. Certainly not so quickly and easily.

I think it's good news for more than just Marigold, Sophie projected. *I think it proves our worst fears have been groundless. Especially when you also consider Giselle in the third event. I don't think any of us can actually die in the Tourney.*

I didn't quite share her optimism. *All we can be sure it means is that things don't follow the same rules down there. And that can go either way. Remember how sick the water made us. There's no way that was natural.*

Sophie sighed. *Well, whatever it was, in this case at least, I'll take it and be glad.*

It soon became apparent that a stark contrast in perspectives existed between those of us who had made that long, silent trek through the groves, listening desperately for each shallow breath, afraid it might be the last we heard. And those who had merely seen me burst through the door carrying a deathly-injured child.

The competitors all saw it as a miracle, the joy of relief lightening everything else. The princes, however, were angry and afraid. Of course, we could not explain to them how much worse the situation should have been. And I doubted that would have comforted them. We had become somewhat inured to the dangers of the Tourney in a way they had not.

For me, seeing their reactions drained away any lingering pleasure from Marigold's recovery. Her accident could only fuel Jon's deadly desire to interfere with the remaining three events. Especially since my guess had been correct. I had received the highest number of points for Palinar's circlet, Sophie close behind me with the Palinaran crown.

Tension permeated the Marinese palace. Duke Philip had made no progress in undermining Sir Oswald. Without an alternative plan to save Marin, more and more of the influential members of the city reluctantly swapped their allegiances.

Summer seemed to be approaching far too fast, and the reality of the end of the Tourney, with its inevitable betrothal, had cast a pall over anyone untouched by the planned coup. The ball before the fifteenth event had a more subdued tone than any of the ones that had preceded it.

Sophie and I had each danced our single obligatory dance with nobles of the Marinese court and then refused all other offers. We stood by the long windows, clutching glasses but not drinking. Too tired in body and mind to do anything but wait for the bell.

"Lily! Sophie!" A small figure approached us at speed.

"Daisy? I haven't seen you for a while."

"No, I've been busy, like you told me." The mood of the court didn't seem to have touched the young girl. Her shining eyes and bright face were a breath of fresh air cutting through the stale tension.

"Busy with what?" Sophie looked between us in confusion.

Oh dear, I sent to Sophie, and then, "What have you overheard?" to Daisy.

She leaned in dramatically. "It's Gabe."

I exchanged a glance with Sophie. "What about him?"

"He says he's not going to stand by to see any other young girls carried out of that room. He says he's going with you all, to protect you."

I paled and dropped to my knees, heedless of my gown, so I could look her in the eyes. "Daisy, tell me exactly what you overheard."

She did. And any hopes that it had just been talk, more blowing off steam, evaporated. He really meant to do it. And tonight.

"Daisy," I said. "You know that if he tries to interfere, he'll die, don't you?"

Her face dropped. "He said that other guard didn't die, he's just ill, and that maybe he can get around the magic."

I wanted to scream at such foolishness. "The guard is deathly ill, Daisy, they don't expect him to survive."

Her whole face fell, and her lip began to wobble.

I spoke quickly to cut off any tears. "But it's not too late. We can still save him. Daisy, I have a very important task for you. Do you think you can do it?"

She stared at me with wide eyes, and I knew she saw all this as an adventure, unable to fully understand the consequences.

"I need you to watch Gabe. Don't let him out of your sight. I'm going to go get something. When you see me return to the ballroom, come and find me. Can you do that?"

"Of course!" Daisy sounded almost scornful. "That's not difficult."

"Thank you." I stood and grabbed Sophie's hand, dragging her along without pausing to explain first.

I don't know how much time we have, I projected over the music as we pushed through the crowds near the door. *The bell could go at any moment.*

I can't believe he's actually going to try. There's no way he could hide himself in that tiny room.

Yes, but he doesn't know that. He doesn't know what's in there, or where we go, or how any of it works. And he's been building himself up to this for weeks, even before Marigold. It doesn't help that he knows Pearl and Opal are the most likely to be injured of all of us.

So what's your plan? asked Sophie, running beside me down the corridor away from the ballroom.

The infirmary. I recognized something when we were in there after the fire. I kept berating myself for not seeing this coming. Sophie had even told me it would be Gabe who tried something, but I had been too distracted by fear for Jon.

The infirmary was deserted, which made my task a great deal simpler. Opening a tall cabinet, I located a large bottle. *Can you see an empty one anywhere, something smaller?* I didn't want to lug the large one around, and I didn't want anyone to notice it was missing either.

Sophie managed to find two small vials, and I carefully filled them from the main bottle. *Come on, let's go.* I took off as soon as I had finished, tucking them both into my dress.

Every second I expected to hear the bell, but it had yet to ring.

We slipped back into the ballroom and started looking for Daisy. She appeared almost instantly at my elbow, as if from nowhere.

"He's over there." She pointed to the far side of the room. "With the others."

The three princes stood in a huddle, clearly waiting for the bell to sound. I knew from Daisy that they planned to open the door for us, and that the other two would shield Gabe from view while he slipped inside. With the number of people usually milling around the door, they trusted that no one would notice his disappearance.

It was a terrible plan.

As the princesses knew from Randolph's attack, the trapdoor wouldn't open with someone else in the room. Which meant that even if there had been cover in the room—which I knew there wasn't—his presence would be discovered before he had any hope of doing good to offset his sacrifice.

Thankfully, I had previously set Daisy to work as a little spy, and she had an especial interest in Gabe. I hoped that one day he would realize his mistake and thank her. But it wouldn't be today. Because I had no intention of letting him find out his errors when it meant destroying himself in the process.

Seizing a goblet of wine, I emptied one of the vials into the dark liquid.

"What's that?" asked Daisy.

"Don't worry," said Sophie. "It's just a sleeping draught."

Daisy's eyes grew round. "Are you planning to drug him?"

"We have to." I met her eyes. "It's the only way to save him. You don't want him locked away forever, do you?"

"No…" She eyed the drink uncertainly.

"It won't hurt him," said Sophie. "We promise."

I didn't wait to hear my sister's reassurances, hurrying across the ballroom toward the princes instead. Jon stepped forward to meet me, but I sidestepped around him, stopping in front of Gabe.

"Gabe." I laughed and shook my head. "I've been assured that you're parched and in need of a drink. And a dance. With someone more than four feet tall." I gestured over to where Daisy still stood beside Sophie, watching us with a fascinated expression.

"Ah." Teddy clapped Gabe on the back. "Your youngest admirer strikes again."

"You have to drink it, you know." I thrust the goblet into his hand. "Or you'll hurt her feelings."

He rolled his eyes but tipped his head back and drained the wine. I tried not to follow his movements too eagerly. Once he had finished, he thrust the empty goblet at Teddy and held out his hand to me. "And a dance I believe you said. This is the sort of tyranny I could get used to." He flashed his charming smile at me. "A refreshing drink and a dance with a beautiful woman."

I shook my head but accepted his hand. He led me away, punching Jon lightly in the shoulder as he went past. "Sorry, old fellow. I'm under orders."

I glanced up at Jon through my lashes. He was glaring at his friend, his hands once more in tight fists at his sides. But then his eyes moved to me, and for the briefest second before I looked away, I saw that it was pain, not anger in his face.

I had sidestepped him without acknowledgement and gone straight to Gabe, laughing and joking. In fact, I rarely ever looked at him now, let alone initiated conversation. I wanted to drop Gabe's hand and run to Jon, I wanted to tell him that if I had the choice, I would spend every moment with him. I wanted to wipe away all that agony of longing in his eyes.

But I didn't. I entered the dance with Gabe instead. I laughed and chattered, until his eyes began to droop. Then I carefully maneuvered us to the far side of the dance floor, out of sight of the other two princes. I pulled him closer, so that his head could drop onto my shoulder as we reached the edge of the floor. I felt glad for all those times I had helped the younger princesses or hoisted Celine up the ladder. I could maneuver his weight more easily than I could have done before, given all the strength I had gained from so many weeks of events. Making one last turn, I deposited him into a chair which Sophie and Daisy had tucked behind one of the large potted plants. He blinked at me twice in confusion, and then his head dropped and lolled to the side.

"That was neatly done," said Sophie admiringly.

The bell finally rang through the ball.

"And just in time, too." I sucked in a relieved breath.

"I'll stay here and watch him," said Daisy, sitting cross-legged on the floor. "But, don't worry." She smiled conspiratorially up at us. "I won't tell him what happened. I'll just say he got very sleepy and decided to have a nap."

Sophie snorted, but I pulled her away before she could argue. We rushed into line and pushed at the other girls impatiently. I could see Teddy and Jon looking around in confusion, and then the door closed. I sighed in relief.

"Goodness, what's the rush?" asked Giselle, looking mildly put out.

I shrugged and didn't answer.

The burst of fear, the rush through the palace, and then my hastily executed stratagems had left me buzzing with energy. I funneled it into the challenge, a different kind of race from the previous two.

It took place in the mirror palace's library, the room stocked with books for the first time. We had to race against each other to find answers to a series of questions. After all my hours spent in the library, I thought I would easily win. But Sophie had spent large amounts of my study time just wandering the room, browsing the titles, so she had an excellent sense of where to go to find a book on any particular subject.

In the end I kept my lead, but only just.

I led us all back through the groves at a near-run. The others kept giving me strange looks, but I ignored them. I wanted to reassure myself that Gabe had woken up without incident.

For the first time, none of the princes waited to meet us in the ballroom. I overheard Queen Juliette telling Millie that Teddy and Jon had gotten into some sort of argument with Gabe and they had all left immediately after the ball. Daisy, standing next to her mother, gave Sophie and me an exaggerated wink. I interpreted it to mean Gabe was fine.

"That girl is a true treasure," said Sophie, trying to hold back a smile.

"Absolutely," I agreed fervently. Then I glanced sideways at her. "But I'm glad she's not *our* little sister."

Sophie snorted and Helena shook her head in confusion. "That event was one of the shorter ones and, thankfully after the last one, injury-free. So let's get the two of you to bed."

CHAPTER 30

*S*omething changed for me after that. The fifteenth event had marked the end of the second stage, the last of the individual challenges. All that remained was the group competition on the final night of the Tourney. The first day of summer, the last day of my freedom, was only three days away, and I couldn't get out of my head Jon's expression as Gabe led me off to dance.

I slipped out of bed early, careful not to wake Sophie, and went for a solitary walk in the garden. Jon appeared so quickly, he must have seen me leave the palace and followed me. And not for the first time, either, I suspected, given how often we had stumbled upon each other amongst the leafy green paths.

He looked surprised and then delighted when I didn't try to avoid him. Falling into step beside me, he kept the conversation light. But once we had exhausted the beautiful weather, the gorgeous flowers, and our plans for the afternoon, the topic inevitably turned to the coup.

"We've had word they have it planned for immediately following the Betrothal Ceremony. The ceremony will take place the day after the final event, and is the true end of the Tourney.

They don't wish to risk disrupting the Tourney and bringing a curse onto Marin, so they won't act until it's finished. But, as soon as the final words are spoken, the ancient laws will be fulfilled, and then they will have the ideal opportunity." He sounded bitter. "It couldn't be more perfect, really, with all the notable members of the duchy gathered ready, along with witnesses from all the kingdoms."

"How do you know all this?" I asked.

"Some of the servants remain loyal even though their masters have felt obliged to change allegiances."

A shiver ran through me. "Do you hate them for it? Does your father?"

He rubbed a hand down his face. "No. How can we? What alternative do they have? To leave things as they are and see their people starve or freeze come winter?" He growled suddenly. "Oswald, on the other hand, is a different story. And a couple of his closest supporters. They clearly have no concern for the people, they are merely seizing power while they can."

I placed a hand on his arm. He looked down at it and then up at me. I could see it took all his willpower not to take me in his arms. With a shuddering breath, he tore his eyes away and continued. "We know that some of the more senior nobles have their own plans. They're going along with Oswald now to secure the alliance and the aid, but then they plan to petition Lanover to have one of them replace Oswald as governor."

He shook his head. "Apparently Oswald has promised that after my father and I have abdicated, our family will be merely imprisoned. These nobles plan to smuggle us to Trione and bring us back once Oswald has been ousted."

A bubble of hope filled my chest. "That doesn't sound so bad."

He gave an angry bark of laughter. "No, indeed. It is a pretty story to salve a throbbing conscience." He looked sideways at me. "But you saw the fire, and you heard Corinna. If any of us so much as make it to the dungeons, I will be astonished." His voice dropped. "I'm hoping I'm wrong, though. I'm hoping they'll spare Mother and the girls. There's a chance they will, since she was originally a princess of Trione. Maybe they will even let her take my sisters back home with her."

I shuddered at the awful picture he painted, my bubble easily burst. Now that he had said it, it sounded all too likely. Jon and his father, at least, were too much of a threat for Sir Oswald to keep alive. And he had already demonstrated his lack of concern for the lives of others.

My voice trembled. "Perhaps it's not too late to take up Corinna's proposal?"

He was shaking his head before I had finished the words, stopping and pulling me into his arms without care for who might be nearby. "No. I won't do it. You know I won't."

"You may not have a choice." I hated how small my voice sounded. And how much I craved the comfort and safety of his arms. I tried to tell myself to pull away, but my body didn't move.

The threat of my impending forced betrothal had made me cling to my last days of freedom. I knew I needed to cut Jon off completely, to free him to save himself, but when I saw the look in his eyes, I simply couldn't do it.

"Oh Lily," he breathed, looking down into my face. "How I have missed you." He leaned down to kiss me, but I turned my face away.

"Jon!" I scolded. "Anyone might see!"

"Let them." He tightened his arms around me.

I shook my head and lightly pushed him away.

"Very well, then." He took my hand. "Let me show you some much more lovely parts of the garden." His eyes grinned wickedly, and I knew I should scold him again but, instead, I let him tug me along. Laughing, even, because of the giddy feeling of holding his hand.

When we reached the secluded spot where Corinna had confronted me, and then Jon and I had shared our first kiss, he stopped. "This," he said, gesturing with his free hand, "this is my personal favourite spot."

I groaned, but he just laughed and tugged on my hand again, reeling me in toward him. He pulled me in gradually, his eyes on my face, and a delicious tingle shot through me. When he finally pressed me against his chest and lowered his face slowly toward mine, I didn't even think of resisting.

As our lips finally met, I melted, his arms tightening to support my weight. I couldn't think of anything at all, except to agree with his assessment, that this beautiful spot might just be my favourite place in the world.

For once he was the one to pull away, groaning and cradling my face into the crook of his neck. "Do you think, just for a few hours, we could pretend that there is no Tourney and no coup. That the Emissary just sailed into the harbor one bright Spring morning and brought me my heart's desire, no strings attached."

For a brief second, I thought I should be responsible and say no, but the thought dissolved before it had fully formed. After weeks of being responsible, surely I could let myself have a single morning.

I pulled out of his hold and stepped back. His face fell, but I smiled up at him and swept my deepest curtsy. "Greetings Your Highness, and thank you for your hospitality. They call me Princess Lily."

A grin lit up his eyes, and he bowed equally low. "The pleasure is all mine, Princess Lily, I assure you." He took my hand and pressed his lips passionately against each knuckle.

My knees began to melt again, so I pulled my hand away, giggling. "You would never have done such a thing when we first met."

He pulled me close. "Only because I'm too much of a fool to instantly recognize the love of my life."

He tried to snatch another kiss, but I pushed him away. "I

would like to walk amongst these delightful gardens, Prince Jonathan."

"Then it would be my pleasure to show them to you." He tucked my arm into his, and we strolled along the closest path, content in our companionable silence. After a while he asked about the mare he had found for me to ride, and I ended up telling him about my beloved pony. He squeezed my hand, confessing that he, too, had once had a much-loved childhood mount, and that he had cried when the animal died.

"It comes from having three sisters," he explained gravely. "It makes you very in tune with emotions." He glanced at me, his eyes dancing and his mouth twitching upwards. "It's what makes me such an excellent catch. I can assure you that not even tears are enough to dismay me. I've won over many a lady, old and young, with my handy handkerchief and complete lack of terror."

I laughed, and the sound echoed back from the other side of one of the hedges.

"Quick," said Jon, "someone's coming."

And the next thing I knew, we were both of us hiding behind a tree, Jon with his back pressed against the trunk, and me tucked into his chest.

"What in the kingdoms are we doing back here?" I tried to peer around him and the tree. "Is there some reason I don't know about why we can't be seen?"

He looked down at me and grinned. "None at all. I just wanted an excuse to do this." And before I could realize what he meant to do, he pressed his lips down over mine.

I swatted him away. "If you had done that on the day we met, I would have turned the ship straight back to Arcadia. Or maybe just on to Trione," I added, unable to resist teasing him a little. "I hear their prince is a nice enough fellow, and they make excellent allies."

"Lies. All lies," said Jon promptly, trying to kiss me again.

I giggled and wriggled out of his grip, the other voices long since having faded away. "That's funny. I could have sworn *you* were the one to…"

"Oh, look! Shall we take a rest on that lovely patch of grass?"

I shook my head, but followed him over to it, and even let him lie back with his head in my lap.

"I think I deserve all sorts of credit for my nobility," he said, once we were settled. "Praising Teddy like that."

"Certainly," I agreed soothingly. I felt a spike of fear that he would ask what had happened to Gabe during our dance, but he said nothing.

We fell into a peaceful silence, and my hand reached out of its own accord to stroke his hair where it rested against my gown. He sighed and closed his eyes.

After some time, he spoke. "The truth about the tree, is that, just this once, I couldn't bear to share you. Not even for a minute. Not this morning."

I felt a warm wash of contentment at his words, and the feeling scared me. My fingers stilled. "This is so unlike us," I said. "Both of us. Being irresponsible and foolish. Do you think someone put something into our breakfasts this morning?"

He sat up. "If they did, I'll have to request they do it every morning."

I shook my head, the magical bubble I had somehow enclosed myself in disappearing and exposing me to cold reality again. "Our responsibilities won't go away simply because we wish to be free of them."

"But we could be together," he said, his eyes burning into mine. "And surely, together, we could find some way to save Marin."

"But the Tourney," I whispered.

"There's still time. You don't have to win."

I shook my head, saying nothing. There was nothing helpful to say.

He stood up abruptly, paced the length of the grass, and then dropped back down with a growl. "I think I will go mad at the idea of you going off to Dominic. I can't bear the idea of the Beast being anywhere near you, let alone getting to call you his."

His pain tore at me, but I liked the idea no more than he did. This had always been nothing but the lesser of many evils.

He read the answer in my eyes and sighed. "There's nothing I can say to convince you, is there?"

"I'm sorry, Jon."

He looked away. "It's horrible, but I feel so jealous of Sophie sometimes."

I frowned at him, startled and displeased to hear him say such a thing.

He ran a frustrated hand through his hair. "I love that you have each other. But I hate that I can't get through to you, no matter how many words I use. And yet, the two of you only need to look at each other, and you seem to arrive at perfect understanding."

His words surprised a laugh out of me. "Hardly." In all these years I had never told anyone the truth, but the words fell from my lips now with surprising ease. It felt right to share every part of me with Jon. "We use as many words as anyone else. You just can't hear us."

"I…I don't understand. What do you mean?" His brow crinkled in adorable confusion.

"At our Christening, our godmother gave us a gift. 'A greater bond than ever twins have shared before.' We can, sort of, *project* our thoughts to each other. Silently, and regardless of our physical location."

He stared at me in disbelief. "You're telling me you can read each other's minds?"

I shook my head quickly. "No. No mind reading. We can only hear what the other chooses to send. Like talking, but we don't use our mouths or our ears."

"So…" He paused, clearly struggling to wrap his mind around

my revelation. "Right now you can project your thoughts to Sophie. And she to you. Even though she's…"

I nodded. "Exactly."

"Are you talking right now?" He stared at me with wide eyes.

I shook my head again and then realized the truth of my denial. I had just made one of the most momentous decisions of my life. I had shared my darkest secret, and with a foreigner, no less. And it had never even occurred to me to reach out to Sophie for her opinion. Despite how much it affected her. Guilt filled me, but also a strange exhilaration. I had always shared everything with my sister. Had always been glad to do so.

But now I had something that was all my own. Jon and I might never be together but, when it came to Sophie and me, he would always be mine rather than ours. When I was with him, I wasn't a twin, one half of a whole. I was just Lily.

It struck me that I had always been a little bit afraid. Afraid that our godmother had gifted us such closeness because she had known from the beginning that neither of us was a complete person on our own. That, without each other, we were both deficient.

But, in this moment, nothing about me felt deficient. And my new sense of freedom brought back my earlier bubble of hope. Only, this time, it was hope for my sister. That once I was gone to Palinar, she, too, would discover she didn't need me to make her whole. She could stand on her own and make a life for herself without me.

Lily? Her voice sounded as if in response to my thoughts. *You've been gone all morning. Where are you?*

Just in the gardens. I'll come in now.

"You're doing it aren't you? Talking to her, right now." Jon sounded excited. "You get a sort of faraway look on your face, sometimes, as if you've mentally detached from your surroundings. I always wondered what you were thinking about because you sometimes do it at the oddest times." He seemed proud of himself.

I stood up and brushed myself off. "Yes, that was Sophie wondering where I am. I should go in."

He leaped up to accompany me, ready with a constant stream of questions about our gift, many of which I couldn't answer. When we neared the palace, I swore him to secrecy. Telling Jon was one thing. That didn't mean I wanted to tell everyone. And certainly not without Sophie's agreement.

CHAPTER 31

*O*ver the following days, I no longer avoided Jon, but neither did I leave my room again without Sophie by my side. I treasured our stolen morning together, and the feel of his lips on mine, and I craved his presence, but my heart could only take so many tragic kisses. I needed to start thinking of Jon as nothing more than a friend. However hopeless a task that seemed now.

Each hour that passed after the fifteenth event seemed to bring all my worst fears closer. When I spent time with Sophie and Jon, I could smile, but the gesture didn't reach my heart. In my heart I felt only panic.

The day before the ball, I convinced them both to join me in the library, in one last, desperate attempt to come up with a plan.

"You really love books, don't you?" Jon sounded bemused.

I grinned. "I like books well enough. But it's my sister-in-law who's the true fanatic. She believes that the answer to any problem can be found in a book somewhere. And, admittedly, she's managed to solve some pretty big problems in the library. I figure it's worth a look."

"It certainly can't do any harm."

But once we were in there, none of us knew where to start. We wandered down the shelves aimlessly, calling out the names of books, in case they sparked an idea. Sophie pulled a book off the shelf and started reading it, so I wandered over to peer over her shoulder, hoping she'd found something of interest. It was a book on fabric and clothing design.

I raised one eyebrow at her, and she shrugged. "They have a very large section here on cloth and fashion. I was curious."

Jon looked over. "My mother brought many of those with her when she married my father. Trione is known for its fabric, and many of the garments throughout the Four Kingdoms originate on the island. I believe she had a great interest in it as a girl." He ran his hand over the spines of the books. "My ancestors have lived here for too many generations to count, each one growing this collection of books, building this duchy. I just can't believe it's all about to be ripped away from us."

"There is still hope," I said, although the words felt increasingly empty.

A gravelly voice spoke from the far corner of the room, startling me. "Some of us still remember how many generations it has been, my lad."

"Albert!" Jon strode over to greet the old man who rose from a deep chair, half hidden in shadows. "I didn't expect to see you here today." He turned back to Sophie and me with a wide smile.

"Albert here used to be our Keeper of the Library, although he retired many years ago. He had endless patience for a serious young boy wishing to make his father proud."

"And proud he is," said Albert, clapping Jon on the back. "Never you doubt it. We Keepers always know what's going on."

"Do you?" The shadow had dropped back over Jon's face. "And do you have the answers I seek this time?"

Albert sighed and slowly lowered himself back into his seat. "Not all answers can be found in a library. Some you must search out for yourself."

"That sounds like the sort of cryptic thing a godmother would say," said Sophie.

"Godmothers, hey?" Albert looked her over with a sharp eye. "And what would you know of godmothers, young lady?"

"My apologies," said Jon, ushering us both forward to join them. "This is Princess Sophie and Princess Lily, Albert. They are part of the delegation here from the Four Kingdoms."

"I know who they are, boy." He sounded testy and not at all impressed by our rank. He watched us silently for a moment and then shook his head. "I did not think I would live to see our lands united again. Or to meet someone from the Old Kingdoms."

"The Old Kingdoms? I haven't heard that name before," I said, just as Jon said, "What do you mean 'again'?"

Albert looked between us. "I knew that no one here cared to remember, but I have often wondered if anyone in the Old Kingdoms remembered those they had lost." He seemed to sink into his memories for a moment.

"We would like to remember, if you would be willing to tell us," said Sophie softly.

He looked up and a light came into his eyes. "It does me good to hear you say so, my girl. I have stories in me still, for those who care to listen."

"Haven't I always listened to you, Albert?" asked Jon.

Albert gave a bark of laughter. "Oh, aye, you did your best. But young boys are restless by nature."

Sophie giggled, and he smiled at her. "Girls, too, if this one's sisters were anything to go by."

"Yes, we gave our governess plenty of grief as children," said Sophie.

"Not that she didn't deserve it," I muttered. Sophie gave me a reproving look.

"But we never learned anything about this land," I said to Albert. "And yet, you seem to have heard of ours."

Albert nodded. "Have you not wondered why we speak the

same language? Why so many of our customs are similar? Many generations ago, the rulers of the Four Kingdoms lost their way. They forgot the directions of the High King, and they ceased to rule their kingdoms with love. A group of nobles collected a band of citizens who wished to live by the old ways. They built a flotilla of mighty ships and sailed off in search of a new home. They found these lands, pristine and untouched, and founded the kingdoms we have now.

"They called on the High King to protect them from their old rulers, and he set up a wall of storms to keep them safe. But they still remained fearful. So they asked the High King to choose their queens for them. To ensure that true love always ruled their lands. He assured them that his godmothers would always be there to help them. But it wasn't enough. They didn't want to trust to the godmothers, and the trials that seem to accompany them. They wanted an easier, surer way.

"They begged and pleaded and, at last, he agreed and made the Princess Tourney for them. He warned that any such system had the potential to become twisted, but they insisted upon it anyway. And for generations it served them well.

"Until a generation arose who wanted to make their own alliances without influence from the Tourney, or the godmothers, or even love. They worked against the Tourney, and they ceased even to call upon their godmothers."

The old man spread his hands wide. "It seems they got their way, and now we all suffer for it. Because, I ask you, who has seen a godmother in their lifetime? Who is coming now to aid us in our trials?"

None of us replied.

"But I see that the Four Kingdoms have found their way again. And the godmothers help your rulers to find true love, bringing good to all the kingdom."

"Things weren't going so well for a while," I said. "But then my mother's godmother gave her a pea. Things began to turn around after that, kingdom by kingdom."

"A pea?" Jon looked as if he thought he must have misheard.

"Well, there was also a bargain in Northhelm, and a curse in Lanover..." Sophie trailed off. "It's a long story."

Albert barked a laugh. "It always is once the godmothers get involved."

"I'd like to hear the whole story one day," said Jon, his eyes on me.

I turned away with a weak smile. I still had hope he would survive to hear the story, but I didn't expect to be the twin around to tell it to him. I withdrew from the conversation a little after that, and we left the library without having found any solution to Marin's problems.

I didn't see Jon again until the final ball, and it arrived all too quickly. Helena had instructed us to save our most elaborate gowns for the Betrothal Ceremony the next day, and we made no protest. After the many different events we had endured, we couldn't even guess what this final group competition might entail, and we wanted to be dressed as practically as a ball would allow.

We did, however, wear our favorite colors — pale gold for Sophie and pale blue for me. A small gesture of comfort and familiarity as we faced our fate. And, at the last moment, I tucked the second vial of sleeping draught into my gown. I had taken it to the last ball without need; Gabe had not even attended. But I would rather have it again and not need it, than find myself having to run back to the room.

I danced the first dance with Jon, and when the music ended he made no move to let me go. "I don't care what anyone says. If this is to be our last night, I won't leave you."

I could resist neither the sentiment, nor the passion in his eyes. And so we danced and danced, sometimes spinning, sometimes merely swaying in each other's arms. This ball seemed long and, after a while, I laid my head against his chest, uncaring about the other people that filled the ballroom.

His arms tightened around me as we swayed to the music. "Don't be afraid," he whispered to me. "Albert was wrong. There will be someone to help you in this trial."

I jerked up and stared at him with wide eyes. "What's that supposed to mean?"

He looked back at me in stubborn silence, refusing to say more. But I didn't need him to speak, I could read the truth in his eyes.

I let him pull me back down against his chest, but my mind raced frantically. He meant to try to follow us as Gabe had intended to do. To find out where we went and aid in the final challenge.

Another song passed and then I made myself speak, voice light. "I'm thirsty."

We stepped apart, and he tucked my hand into his arm. "Let's find you some refreshment, then."

I smiled back at him, forcing my expression to stay calm. As we approached a table against one of the walls, I called out silently for Sophie. *I need your help!* I recounted our conversation, and she soon appeared, Teddy in tow.

The two of them engaged Jon in conversation, leaving me to choose our drinks. I turned my back to them, hiding my hands as I chose a glass for myself and a goblet of wine for Jon. I needed something dark and strong enough to hide the draught. My hands shook as I poured it in, trying to hurry.

Pasting my smile back on, I turned and handed Jon the goblet. His eyes conveyed so much affection as he took it from me, that I had to fight the waves of guilt.

You're doing this to save him, projected Sophie, instinctively understanding my feelings. *You don't have a choice.*

Jon led us all to a place by one of the windows. We stood between two large potted plants and observed the dancers, talking only fitfully. I kept glancing surreptitiously at his goblet. When was he going to drink it?

"I have to admit I'll be glad not to have to attend a ball every three days," said Teddy.

Jon laughed and raised the goblet to take a sip. I looked away, hoping he hadn't noticed my interest.

Sophie made a teasing reply, and he sipped again.

Calm down, she sent to me. *He's going to realize something's wrong.*

She was right. I stepped away a little, going to her side and putting my arm around her and resting my head on her shoulder. She tipped her own head sideways to lean against mine. I forced my anxious eyes to look away from Jon for a full twenty seconds.

I'm not at all interested in your drink, I'm not at all interested in your drink, I repeated to myself silently.

What? Sophie projected. And then, *Are you projecting your thoughts again without realizing?*

Sorry. I sighed.

Look, he's finished it now.

I couldn't stop my eyes from flying to his hand, relieved to see the empty goblet. He reached out a hand for my glass as well, and deposited them on a nearby table. "Dance with me again?" he asked.

I nodded, not trusting my voice, and returned to the dance floor. But within minutes, his movements slowed. "I'm sorry," he said, rubbing at his face. "I've been suddenly overtaken by exhaustion. I don't know what's the matter with me."

"Nothing is the matter with you," I said firmly. "You're just tired and stressed. Come over here, and we can sit down quietly for a few minutes."

He protested but allowed me to lead him over to two chairs in a secluded corner of the room. I guided him into the first one, against the corner, and then took the other.

His head began to nod, and he apologized again, mumbling his words. Then his head dropped completely, coming to rest against the wall.

"I'm sorry," I whispered, dropping a kiss on the top of his hair. "This is for your own good." I rearranged his arms into a more comfortable position before leaving to find Sophie.

CHAPTER 32

He's asleep.

Good. Surely the bell will ring any second now.

It didn't, however. Two more songs passed before it finally sounded. We both hurried over to the small door and took our places at the end of the line.

Only when the door closed on us all, and I looked around to reassure myself we were alone, did I breathe easily again.

"Well, whatever happens tonight, at least this will be our last time down that beastly ladder," said Celine, sounding almost cheerful at the thought.

I looked over at her and frowned. She looked different somehow. "Celine! Your crutches!"

She smiled broadly at me. "The doctors have finally declared me healed. I'll have to work to rebuild the strength in my leg again, but I can walk freely, at least." No wonder she looked pleased.

And she was so far behind in points that, even with the best will in the world, she had no hope of overtaking my lead. A small, guilty part of me felt sorry for it. Celine at full strength would have been capable of taking on this Prince Dominic, however monstrous. But such a thought did me no good. It was Sophie who closely trailed me in scores, and Hazel was behind her. Either of them could still find themselves the winner after tonight. I glanced at Hazel's pale face and drew a determined breath.

The trapdoor had swung open while we talked, and Celine eagerly took the lead, no longer needing assistance. The rest of us followed more slowly, Marigold pushing Lilac away and declaring she needed no help. Her older sister still hovered solicitously, though, and I understood her concern. Marigold looked even paler than her middle sister and much frailer.

Pearl and Opal came down last, and Opal had barely stepped onto the ground when she cried out in alarm and twisted around. I stepped back to her.

"What is it?"

"My dress. Something pulled at it."

I stared at her dress, now hanging smoothly in place, and then doubtfully at the ladder. "Are you sure? It must have caught on the ladder."

Opal looked like she wanted to argue but then glanced at Pearl and nodded meekly. I sighed and returned to Sophie. Not that I *wanted* her to dispute with me...but I could see what Gabe meant about his sisters.

We all trod the path toward the palace for a final time, and I found myself gazing at the incredible leaves with something of the wonder I had felt the first time. Still, despite their magnificence, I hoped never to see them again after this night.

When we crossed the lake, Opal's boat seemed to lag behind. I watched it floating sluggishly along and wondered if some of the magic of this place was tiring as the Tourney reached its conclusion. That was fine with me, just as long as it lasted long enough to get us back across the lake again. I didn't like the idea of swimming back.

For the last time, we took our places around the table in the

Throne Room. When the parchment appeared, Celine leaned forward, snatching it up before Emmeline could do so. "A queen must possess compassion, cunning and strength. Behind this palace, you will find a garden. And in the garden you will find three tasks, designed to demonstrate these traits. Once you have completed the tasks, you may claim the crown in the center of the garden. The first to do so shall end the challenge and claim all the points for this event."

We all looked at each other. Our final three tasks of the Tourney, in one big event. Most of the attention focused on me, Sophie and Hazel. The number of points assigned to this event wouldn't matter if any of the three of us claimed the crown. Our current differences in position were small enough to ensure an overall win for any of us.

"Well, this is it, then," said Celine. "Avoid any dangers we encounter in this mysterious garden, complete these tasks as best we can, and we can all leave this place forever. It says the bell to start the challenge will sound once we all reach the edge of the garden."

I bit my lip. I hadn't even thought of dangers in the garden. But I couldn't rule it out. Not when I remembered the first event.

And it seemed Celine's fears had merit. As we crossed the palace toward the doors that would lead us out to the garden, or at least the doors that did so in the real palace, the ground began to shake. The tremors were only gentle, but we all exchanged nervous glances.

Sure enough, the mirror palace was now accompanied by gardens that mirrored the ones aboveground. Hazel knew them better than me, of course, but I thought I had spent more time in them than Sophie. And any advantage might make the difference in the end.

We all assembled on the lawns outside the palace, glancing nervously at one another. The all-too-familiar bell sounded, and Celine smiled at us all and took off running. I think she was just glad to be able to do so, but we all followed her lead, scattering quickly in different directions.

Nothing gave any indication of where the tasks might be located, and I soon slowed to a less headlong pace, trying to guess where they might be. A rustle behind me made me spin, heart racing, but nothing was there. Not long after, a twig cracked loudly, and I turned again, sure I must have crossed paths with one of the other girls. But, again, I could see no one.

In fact, whether by coincidence or some magic of this place, I didn't see any of the other competitors at all. My feet led me to the fountain in the center of the garden and, sure enough, a silver crown glimmered on its rim, bright with jewels. It was hard to tell from this distance, but I thought it looked like the crown worn by the queen of Palinar. I walked toward it but found a soft invisible barrier prevented me from approaching too close. It seemed that the Tourney wouldn't let me near it until I had completed the tasks.

I found one! Sophie's voice made me start and turn but, of course, I couldn't tell what direction it had come from.

Where are you? What is it?

I'm in the rose garden. Of course she was. *And it's archery. Celine will be pleased.*

I raced in her direction, moving quickly now that I had a destination. *Which trait is archery supposed to demonstrate?*

Strength, maybe? It's a big bow, and the apple we have to hit is far away.

An apple? How do you know that's the target?

Her projection sounded dry. *You'll see when you get here.*

I had taken a slightly circuitous route, figuring I would move faster overall if I stuck to the paths rather than crossing through the gardens directly. I ran but not at full pace, needing to conserve my strength, and so I was moving slowly enough for my eye to catch on a small side garden. One I recognized from my wanderings with Jon. My feet slowed on their own, and then I noticed something out of place. The corner of what looked like a table. I changed course.

Sure enough, a small desk had been tucked into the garden. I read the parchment I found there. A riddle.

I grinned. What a stroke of luck that I had passed by and noticed it. All that time in the gardens at the true palace had given me an unexpected benefit now. I read it over and then read it over again.

> *I hide myself, an armored creature*
> *With no beauty in my features*
> *Though I seem to bring no pleasure*
> *I may conceal a hidden treasure*

I considered asking Sophie for assistance but hesitated. I had to assume she would be presented with the same riddle. And I didn't want to give her any help. In fact, I didn't even want to tell her where it was.

If only it had been another riddle I already knew, like the one from my childhood about my own name. That thought sparked another one, and I chased it down in my mind. Names...princess names...Pearl!

I considered it from every angle. It certainly fit. I looked around for a pen.

This is hard. Sophie sounded frustrated. *And where are you? I thought you'd be here by now.*

I'm on my way, I projected, distracted. And, I was, in a very roundabout fashion.

I found the pen but wasn't sure where to put my answer. In the previous event, we had written our answers beneath the riddle itself, but I didn't want to leave the answer there for Sophie and the others to find.

No other option presented itself, however, so I lowered the pen to the paper to write *a pearl*, and then pulled my hand back.

Wait. The pearl was the hidden treasure, not the armored creature. Which meant the answer was an oyster, not a pearl.

I took a deep breath and tried again, my hand trembling slightly at the near mistake brought on by my distraction. As soon as I had finished the word *oyster*, a soft chime sounded, and the letters dissolved away.

What was that? asked Sophie.

She had been able to hear the chime, then. I didn't reply but started running toward her again.

I did it! she cried, just as a second chime sounded, and then added, *So that's what it means. Someone else has completed a task then.*

I stayed silent, picking up my speed slightly. But when I entered the rose garden, there was no sign of Sophie. In the center of it, I found a small table holding a tall bow. Picking it up and taking an arrow from the quiver beside it, I looked around for a target.

A large silver apple, hanging from a tree on the edge of the garden, instantly caught my eye. I understood immediately what Sophie had meant. The apple glowed like the leaves in the silver grove, clearly not a real piece of fruit despite the way it hung from the branch above it.

A place to stand had been marked out next to the table, so I drew a deep breath and centered myself on it. Sophie and I had similar skills with a bow so, if she could do it, I could do it. It took all of my strength to draw back the bowstring, and in the back of my mind I wondered if Hazel would even be able to do it. If she couldn't, it meant one less competitor for me to worry about.

I let the arrow fly, and it missed. By a lot. I groaned and selected another arrow. And another. And another.

Ugh. You're right, this is hard. We should have taken Celine more seriously and brushed up on our archery skills.

She'll be so pleased when she sees it. Sophie sent a giggle. *But do you think she'll actually be able to hit it?*

I laughed too. *She's not that bad.*

No, but she's not that good either.

My shots were getting closer, falling first to one side then to the other. At least no wind blew down here, but the continuing tremors in the ground, however slight, were throwing me off. I could feel the tension rising in me again, making me jittery. Two more chimes sounded, and I had no way of knowing which tasks and which princesses. I wanted to be moving again.

At least I assumed that Sophie would have told me if she had encountered another task. I shot another arrow, and another. I'd used them all now so had to trek across the garden to collect them.

The movement eased the jitters slightly, and I forced myself to take several deep breaths before trying again. I closed my eyes and tried to put the Tourney and Jon and Sophie and the Beast and everything out of my mind. I lined up the shot, feeling myself slip into a more confident stance. A certainty crept over me that this one would hit. I pulled back the string, tighter and tighter, and…a sudden crack behind me made me jerk and the shot went wide.

I screamed in frustration and spun around. As before the garden remained empty except for me. I shook my head and collected another arrow, grumbling to myself. My irritation made me rush, not worrying about centering myself or carefully lining up the shot. Instead I simply pulled the string to my ear and released.

The arrow flew above the roses, smashed into the apple, and sent it hurtling to the ground. A chime rang through the air, and I dropped the bow in my shock.

Was that you? Did you do it?

Yes! I called back. *I can't believe it! Where are you?*

Lily, tell me the truth, she projected, unexpectedly. *Were you that first chime? Did you find another task on the way to the rose garden and not tell me?*

I stayed silent, not wanting to confirm it, but not wanting to lie outright to her either.

She sighed. *I thought so.*

I'm going to win, Soph. I'm not letting you go off to that Beast.

This time she was silent.

Sophie? Are you mad at me?

Not mad, no. Of course not. But you know I can't just let you do that.

I considered her words. *You've found another task haven't you? And you aren't going to tell me what it is.*

No, I'm not. She sounded sad. Another chime sang out.

The tension, released by my success with the apple, flooded back. We were even again, then.

I headed away from the rose garden in the opposite direction to where I had found the riddle. I still hadn't seen anyone else, and it made sense that the tasks must be spread out. I had presumably completed cunning and strength. Which just left compassion.

I knew Sophie had also finished strength but not which of the others she had found. Or who the other chimes had belonged to. Three more rang out while I searched, but Sophie remained silent. I could only hope that meant neither of them had been her.

I stumbled upon another fountain and decided to pause for a brief rest. Wandering aimlessly didn't seem to be getting me anywhere, I needed to think. I sat on the edge of the fountain and closed my eyes, trying to clear my mind and focus.

As the tension drained away, my shoulders relaxed. Until a long, low growl ripped through the quiet stillness. My eyes flew open. A golden shape hurtled toward me, mouth wide and teeth glistening.

Before I could do more than register the threat, an invisible force slammed into me, throwing me sideways. I hit the ground hard, a large weight landing on top of me. The lion sailed over me and into the fountain.

Its growl cut off as it fought to escape the water. I struggled to move away from the fountain, pushing against the unseen force that held me pinned to the ground. It lifted suddenly, and I scooted backwards, feeling about me for a stick or some other weapon.

My questing hands found nothing, and I took a breath, ready to scream. But before I could, unseen hands pulled me to my feet and unseen arms closed around me. My vision filled with dark cloth in every direction as I found myself inexplicably encircled by a cloak and crowded against a familiar chest. I choked on the scream.

"Jon! What..?"

Struggling to understand what was happening, I tilted my head up to see his face. But he wasn't looking at me. His head was shrouded in the hood of the cloak, his eyes fixed on the fountain. He seemed to have wrapped me in both his arms and his cloak.

In the midst of all the chaos, my mind caught on an irrelevant detail. I had successfully spoken aloud. Understanding dawned. A magic cloak, then. Somehow it was shielding both me from the restraints of the Tourney and Jon from sight. And, I hoped, from the magical notice of the Tourney as well.

He continued to ignore me, his eyes focused on the lion. The animal had managed to climb out of the fountain and was pacing the path next to us. It seemed confused, however, so I could only guess that I had become invisible as well.

It stopped to sniff the air, weaving its head from side to side in confusion, before starting to pace again.

"When I count to three, you need to run behind me," Jon whispered. "I'll draw my sword and take it down."

"No!" As I watched the animal, something niggled at the back of my mind. "Give me a second to think."

Jon moved impatiently but said nothing. I watched the way the lion walked. It seemed to be limping slightly, favoring one of its front paws. If there was a lion in this underground realm it had to be significant, a part of the event. I had already completed the tasks for cunning and strength or, at least, I thought I had. Which left compassion...

"Look at its paw." I kept my voice quiet.

"I'm a little too focused on its teeth and claws," said Jon, in a strained voice.

I didn't want to tell him it was a task, since he wasn't likely to do anything to help me win. But I needed to convince him to assist me. I tried to think of something else to say. Something that was true, since it wouldn't be convincing otherwise. "Listen to me. You had no choice but to kill the bear on the hill that day. But I've felt terrible about it ever since. Whatever is happening in these lands, it isn't the fault of the animals."

He shook his head. "And that's why I love you. But did you notice that this one attacked you, too?"

My heart thrilled at the word love, but my mind remained focused on the event. "I think it's in pain."

"What?"

I sighed. "Look at its paw, like I said. I think it's injured. I need to get a closer look."

"You what!?"

I tried to come up with options, but there didn't seem to be many. "We're invisible, right?"

"Yes, that's why it hasn't attacked."

"So it's going to be very surprised when I step away from you and reappear."

"You're not doing that." His voice sounded flat.

I ignored him. "While I confuse it, you approach and knock it out with the hilt of your sword. Be prepared for it to take a couple of blows. You'll still be invisible, so it shouldn't be too dangerous."

"Lily..."

"All right. That's the plan." Without giving him any more

chances to protest, I pushed myself away from him hard, stumbling out from under the magical protection of the cloak.

The lion turned toward me, confusion slowing its movements, and Jon cursed under his breath, his voice already sounding further away from me and closer to the beast.

The animal stepped toward me and then stepped again, its rumbling growl sounding through the clearing. My plan seemed a little less appealing at this point, and I wished I'd taken the chance to arm myself. I backed slowly away.

The lion gathered itself for a leap, and I prepared to spin and run. Just as I began to pivot, however, the lion crumpled to the ground.

I took a deep shuddering breath and reminded myself that its unconsciousness might not last for long. I hurried toward it.

"That was very dangerous." Jon's voice sounded eerie, emerging from an empty patch of air. I shrugged and gestured to my throat as I dropped to my knees. Hopefully he would understand that the normal prohibition on our speech extended to the events as well.

He must have realized my meaning, because I felt heavy material settle over me. He reappeared kneeling beside me, awkwardly holding his cloak over my head.

I tried to ignore the lion's open mouth and glittering teeth as I picked up the paw it had been favoring. At least I could speak now. "Why are you here? How are you here?" I asked, the curiosity overpowering me.

"I've come to save you from yourself." His serious expression broke for a minute. "And from that lion, too, of course."

I didn't smile back, pausing for the briefest moment to glare at him instead. "Don't you understand the risk you've taken? Are still taking. And that's just for yourself. What about the Tourney? Someone has to win it. Who have you decided you're willing to sacrifice in my place?"

"No!" He looked like he wanted to shake me. "You're the one who doesn't understand! How do you think I got here?"

I had found a thorn in the lion's paw and begun tugging at it, but his unexpected question distracted me. "I have no idea. It makes no sense. I put a…" I trailed off, not sure I wanted to admit to drugging him. "How *did* you get here?"

He grinned a little. "You're adorable, you know that, right? And also that I'm not an idiot? I wasn't going to drink anything you gave me at that ball. Not after what happened to Gabe. I wasn't really asleep when you left me."

I bit my lip, embarrassed and focused back on the thorn. It was long and deep, but I thought I nearly had it free. It was a task I had great interest in completing before the animal woke up.

Wonder filled Jon's voice as he continued to talk. "I asked you a while ago if you had called on your godmother. It never occurred to me to call on mine. I didn't even know I had one. But talking to Keeper Albert gave me a sliver of hope along with my desperation. And it was enough to make me try." He shook his head. "And one actually came. She told me that everything depends on Marin. If Marin falls to the darkness, then eventually the kingdoms will fall, as well. Even Trione. But, if Marin stands, we will have turned the tide. The other kingdoms will have a chance. She gave me this cloak, and she said I'd know how to use it."

He smiled, his face full of excitement. "I've been here with you the whole time."

Jon's godmother. The shock made my hands fall still again as I remembered Opal's comment about something pulling at her gown. It must have been Jon, stepping on it. And the strange noises, they must have been him, too.

Jon, apparently unaware of my distraction, continued his story. "At first, after the godmother disappeared, I felt like such a failure. I couldn't understand what she wanted me to do. And then, suddenly, I realized. What does every tale tell us? What have the godmothers always fought for? True love! If we're together, then Marin will survive. And we can help fight the darkness in Palinar. We can help whoever wins. As long as we're together."

The thorn popped free into my hand, and I looked down at it and then up at Jon as a chime sounded, and the lion stirred. Jon started and staggered to his feet, pulling me up with him and away from the animal. It shook its head, lumbered to its feet and wandered away. If the chime hadn't already confirmed the task successfully completed, the lion's strange behavior would have.

I had completed the third task. I needed to go. I tried to pull away from Jon, but he held me tight, looking down at me, his eyes shining with hope. "Don't you want to be with me?"

I opened my mouth to tell him no, but I couldn't speak the lie. "More than anything," I admitted, my voice a soft whisper.

He leaned down to kiss me, his face alight, but I turned my head away. I needed to hurry, but I couldn't bear to leave him without an explanation. I spoke quickly. "But I'm the one who's right. And you're the one who doesn't understand. You've seen the scores. It's not just anyone we would be sentencing to the Beast. It's Sophie." I took a deep breath. "I'm sorry, Jon. I love you. But she's my sister. And I can't abandon her now."

I took a steadying breath. "And did you hear that last chime? The third task was compassion, and I think I just finished it."

I didn't wait for my words to sink in. Shoving him hard in the chest, I turned and fled back toward the center of the gardens. Three chimes sounded in quick succession as I ran. Had any of them been Sophie?

Just as I thought her name, I rounded a bend in the path and collided with her. We hit so hard that we both fell backwards onto the ground. For a moment we lay there, panting and staring at each other.

I know you want to protect me, she projected. *Just like you always have. But I'm not a little girl anymore. Neither of us is. And it's time for me to protect you.* Her eyes met mine, strong and confident.

Have you completed all three tasks? I didn't see how anyone else could have gotten past the lion. I had only succeeded with Jon's help.

She nodded wordlessly.

But how did you knock it out? I still couldn't believe it was true.

Knock it out? She frowned at me. *What do you mean? Of course I didn't knock it out. The task was compassion, and the poor thing was injured. I just approached it gently, and it calmed right down.*

I stared at her in shock. I had spent most of my life trying to keep my sister safe, and she had decided to approach a crazed, wild animal *gently!*

You're not the only one who's allowed to sacrifice for the people she loves, she projected, easily reading my expression. *And I won't do anyone any good here. But you can. Together you and Jon might have a chance of saving Marin. You've been tormenting yourself over him, don't think I haven't seen it. But there's a simple solution to your problem, and it's obvious to everyone except you.*

It took me a moment to understand her meaning, distracted as I was by the crunching gravel behind me. Jon, once again invisible, had followed my flight.

Sophie had held my eyes the whole time she spoke, her body relaxed against the ground, so I had no warning when she suddenly leaped to her feet.

Sophie, no! I thundered the projection at her, but she had already started running. I scrambled up and took off after her, but we were too evenly matched. No matter how I pushed myself, my lungs and legs straining, I couldn't gain any ground.

She looked back at me as she approached the fountain, meeting my eyes. *This is for you, Lily. I love you.*

I screamed a protest, reaching a useless hand toward her, as she snatched the crown from the fountain rim. A loud bell rang through the gardens. She stared down at her fingers, tightly clasping her doom, and then up at me.

CHAPTER 33

I walked the last three steps to stand before her. Looking into her face, I wondered how my identical twin could seem to tower over me. I had expected to see fear, or perhaps determination, but she looked almost radiant.

"I remember I used to feel so angry at life sometimes," she said, "when we were children. But you were always there for me. A sister who knew me completely and loved me better than I loved myself. You were always so strong, Lil. You taught me how. And now, finally, it's my turn to help you."

Her eyes moved to the empty air next to my shoulder where I could feel the warmth of Jon's presence. "Both of you." So she knew everything then. I shook my head at the foolishness of believing I could keep such a secret from her.

"But how can I let you go to face this Beast alone?" I gripped both of her arms. "I couldn't bear it."

She tapped her forehead and even managed a smile. "You're forgetting that neither of us is ever really alone. You'll be coming with me, even if you can't do so physically."

"Maybe I can." Why hadn't I thought of it before? "I'll come with you, and we'll face this Beast together."

The other girls arrived in a rush before she could respond, and I flicked a warning glance at Jon, hoping he knew better than to give himself away at this point. The others looked from me to Sophie and then to the glowing crown she still gripped in one hand. How many of them still couldn't tell us apart?

"Princess Sophie," said Emmeline without inflection. "What a surprise."

I blinked at her. After so many weeks of the Tourney, I still didn't understand either of the Eldonian princesses. But apparently Emmeline, at least, had been paying attention after all. Did that mean they weren't as detached as they seemed?

"Sophie." Celine came forward to embrace her. "I thought…" She glanced at me.

"I know," I said, still in shock. "So did I."

An awkward quiet fell, silent tears dripping down several faces. I couldn't tell if they were tears of relief or tears of sorrow for Sophie. I felt Jon move behind me and remembered we still needed to get him safely away. I didn't want to take the risk of any of the others seeing him.

"Come on," I said, my mind whirling. "It's time we left this place for good."

We formed a sort of honor guard around Sophie as we made our way around the palace and down to the lake. I let everyone else board their coracles first, taking the last one and watching the disturbed water where Jon slipped into the lake beside me. I could feel his weight dragging down one edge of the small boat, and assumed he had gripped the side and was letting it pull him along.

Now I knew why Opal's boat had lagged behind on the way over. I only hoped he had the good sense not to let his head go under the water.

The others had waited for me on the other side, and when we resumed walking it was in the same tight huddle. Still no one spoke, so when a crack sounded, like someone snapping a twig, it startled me, loud in the silence. The tremors, which I had almost ceased to notice, picked up and my body shuddered with the vibrations traveling through me from the shaking earth.

No one said anything about it, but we all hurried our pace. We had almost left the grove of gold when another snap sounded, followed again by an increase in the shaking of the ground beneath our feet. Several of the girls staggered.

"Let's hurry," I said, and we all took off at a half-run.

As Emmeline, who was leading us, stepped out of the silver grove, a third snap sounded. This time we all staggered as the ground rippled beneath us, and distant crashes began to sound from the direction of the palace. "Run!" I screamed, snatching the final parchment from its customary place and herding the other girls toward the ladder.

Two of them had made it up the ladder before the first of the trees came smashing to the ground. Pearl, on the ladder at the time, slipped and was only just caught by Celine.

"Hurry," said Snow, her white face stark in the gloom.

More trees fell behind us, and the crashes from across the lake grew louder. Lilac almost propelled Marigold up the ladder, Hazel following on her heels.

I could barely stand from the powerful quaking by the time I was the last one left. Last except for one. "You go first," I whispered at the empty air, not sure of Jon's exact location. "It might close behind me."

A rush of air moved past me, and I followed behind it. My hands, grasping for the next rung, kept colliding with his invisible boots, so I knew he was definitely ahead of me. I crawled over the edge of the trapdoor into the room and spun around, still on hands and knees to stare back down into the hole.

The earth itself was dissolving now. Falling away in great chunks. Several of the others pulled me away as the trapdoor closed with a deafening bang.

Some stood, some sat, but we all stared at each other, loud pants filling the small room as we processed our narrow escape.

"I think that might have been the last Tourney," said Sophie softly. "Surely there are limits to its regeneration."

I counted heads for one final time. "I hope so." I dragged myself to my feet. "Personally, I never want to see this room again."

Someone, I didn't see who, pushed open the door and slowly girls drifted out. Eventually only Sophie and I remained.

"Please tell me you weren't responsible for those snaps we heard." I addressed the air.

Jon's head appeared, floating eerily above the ground. He looked guilty.

I sighed. "And let me guess. You took something from the table after we left. When those first tremors started."

He pulled back his cloak to reveal his hands holding a golden goblet, and three twigs bearing leaves of silver, gold and diamond. "You were in a hurry when we spoke down there." He paused. "I didn't get the chance to tell you the whole story."

I took a deep breath. "Well how about you tell me now?"

"I went down there to save you, to save us. I meant it when I said that. I just had another purpose." He winced. "I didn't realize it would happen so fast, though."

"You meant to destroy it?" I raised both eyebrows. "Isn't your family tasked with protecting the Tourney?"

"We were. Back when the Tourney was something good. But it's changed, it's been twisted. You should know that better than anyone after everything you seem to have experienced. And my godmother explained why. Each Tourney is shaped by the ruler who calls it. When the cursed Prince Dominic called it, he created an opening. A chance for the darkness to infect the Tourney. When I told you that the darkness was already in the heart of our duchy, I didn't know how true it was."

I trembled. Nothing he said surprised me. Not really. Not after struggling for so many weeks against the Tourney.

"It wasn't completely corrupted, though," said Sophie. "There seemed to be enough good magic left to keep us alive at least."

"And thank goodness for that," said Jon, stepping toward me as if to take me into his arms.

I shook my head, and he stopped. "But *how* did you do it?"

"With this cloak and with these," he held out the goblet and the twigs. "The Tourney has always operated under a veil of secrecy. My godmother explained it to me. Although she was a little cryptic, and it took me a while to work out what she meant." He paused and frowned. "Are they always like that?"

"Pretty much," said Sophie.

I shook my head at both of them. "What does secrecy have to do with anything?"

Jon shrugged. "The cloak let me get in and out, unseen by the magic. And I brought evidence out with me. I made no contract with the Tourney at the opening ceremony. My lips aren't sealed, like yours are. My presence, and finally my escape, disrupted the very fabric of the Tourney."

I looked at him and then across at my sister. "So...if the Tourney is destroyed...does that mean...?" I let my voice trail hopefully away.

Jon winced, avoiding Sophie's gaze. "I wish it did. But while the Tourney has been destroyed, the ancient laws remain. The final task was completed, the betrothal contract stands." He gestured toward Sophie's hands. I followed with my eyes and realized she still clasped the crown, as solid as it had been in the underground garden.

"I suspected as much," said Sophie. "But I, for one, am glad the Tourney is gone regardless of my betrothal. Jon, put that cloak, or whatever it is, back on. I assume you're safe enough from the magic now, but you don't want to give the enemies of your family any reason to claim you violated the law."

He disappeared instantly, and I slipped a weary arm through Sophie's. "Come on. I'm sure the others have spread the news about your win by now. Everyone will be waiting to see you."

She closed her eyes, took a breath and nodded. "Let's go."

∼

I was right, of course. And it looked like most of the guests from the ball had stayed this time, too. Sophie shuddered once at the sea of gaping faces, but then the baron and baroness surrounded us. The Duchess of Sessily and Celine joined them, and together we formed a small shield around her.

I knew the delegation heads wanted to know what had happened, and I saw more than one surreptitious glance thrown at me, but they knew better than to ask. Helena kept sniffling, but she held herself together when she asked if we wanted her to spend the night in our suite. We both shook our heads. We didn't want outside company tonight.

I climbed into bed beside Sophie, neither of us wanting to be parted. Surprisingly, she fell asleep quickly. I, on the other hand, lay awake, listening to her breathing. I would go with her. I was determined, now that the idea had occurred to me. We would face this beastly prince together, as we had faced everything else.

I just wished I had such a solution for Marin. Jon had risked everything to help me in the Tourney. I had failed Sophie, I could not bear to fail him too.

But the next day I didn't even have a chance to speak to him. It seemed the winner of a Princess Tourney needed to begin her preparations for the Betrothal Ceremony first thing in the morning. Jon's mother had sent a team to assist us, but we turned them away. We wanted Arcadians, our own people, around us now.

Celine slipped in at some point, and we let her stay as well. She felt as much like home as any of our own delegation. Our hair had been arranged and pinned, and our dresses chosen and

laid out, before everyone else went for the midday meal. Helena
didn't want Sophie and me to risk leaving the room and being
mobbed by curious locals, so she ordered us to stay. Celine
elected to keep us company.

"I'll find something and bring it back for you," Helena
promised.

We had hardly been alone for a minute, however, when the
door opened again. I turned around and froze, my mouth dropping open. Millie had stepped into the room, her face downcast,
but she gave me a strange look when she saw my open astonishment.

"Celine!" I managed to squeak out my friend's name.

Celine spun around and gasped. "Oh, my..." She came
forward, her eyes locked on Millie's gown. "What is that?"

"It's beautiful," whispered Sophie. She sounded, if not happy,
at least distracted.

Millie looked at us all in confusion and then down at her
dress. "My gown, you mean?"

"I've never seen anything like it," said Celine, circling her.
"The colors are incredible. And they change!"

I had never seen such stunning and dramatic material. It
shifted under the light, changing from blue to green and
almost to gold as she moved. It slid softly against her skin as
she walked, making it look as if she was clothed in the ocean
itself.

"How have we not seen this before?" Celine asked, still
circling, her eyes wide.

Millie looked amused at our admiration. "This fabric is traditional dress here for Christenings, betrothals and weddings, but
we rarely wear it otherwise. Apparently it used to be extremely
popular, but it's now considered rather..." She wrinkled her nose.
"Old-fashioned."

Celine shook her head. "You're all of you mad."

Millie laughed, apparently unoffended, and then glanced

between us all in confusion. "You all look astonished. Don't you have silkworms in the Four Kingdoms?"

"Silkworms?" Now it was Celine's turn to laugh. "We have silkworms, but they don't produce anything like that. Are you telling me the thread comes out of them already colored?"

"Of course it does! Doesn't yours?"

I shook my head, too dazed to speak. A thought was forming in my mind, and it demanded my full attention.

"Oh!" Millie looked thoughtful. "Perhaps it's because of their diet. They consume—"

"Celine." I cut Millie off. "Just how much would one of your sisters pay for a dress like that?"

"Forget my sisters," she said, a grin spreading across her face. "I'm not so sure I want to share."

I turned to Millie. "Does the fabric come from Trione?"

She nodded, still looking utterly bemused at the stir over her dress. "The silkworm colonies live on our island. Some merchants tried transporting them to the other kingdoms, but they didn't produce silk anywhere else and quickly died. It used to be a very profitable business for us, but those days are long past. Few people buy new gowns like this now. They just wear old ones when tradition demands."

Her face turned thoughtful. "In fact, I seem to remember my grandfather gave the silk farms to Aunt Aurelia as a wedding present when she married Duke Philip. Because of her interest in fashion. My father said she brought half a library of books on the subject here with her, as well. Although I find that hard to believe since we seem to have enough of them left in our own library." She shrugged. "I don't think owning the farms has done her much good, though. I believe all the silk they have produced in the last few years has simply been transported here to Marin and stored somewhere in the palace. I sometimes hear Aunt talking about ideas for rekindling interest in the fabric, but it has yet to catch on. Perhaps her grandchildren will bring it back into fashion again." She smiled at us.

And I smiled back at her. "Thank you, Millie. You may have just saved everything."

"Everything?" She looked startled.

"Well, not everything," I conceded. "Just Marin. But that's enough for now." I looked around the room. "I'm going to need all of your help."

CHAPTER 34

*H*ours later, a trumpet processional sounded. I stood next to my sister outside the true throne room. I couldn't help thinking of the many times we had rushed in and out of the mirror version of this room. And then farther back to the first time we had stood here in this hallway, facing these double doors, mere hours after our arrival.

So much had happened since then that the memory felt distant and foreign. I looked sideways at Sophie. She looked terrified and brave at the same time.

Ready? I asked.

Ready, she replied.

We didn't wait for the herald to announce us but stepped forward together onto the long red carpet. A gasp and a hush raced through the crowded room. We stepped forward, eyes straight ahead, but I wished I could see us as they did. I think I would have fallen silent as well.

It should have only been Sophie proceeding down the carpet. I should have been waiting at the front with the other royals. But, instead, two identical princesses walked in perfect unison. Both dressed in magnificent gowns of betrothal white.

Apparently even here the betrothed herself wore white to the ceremony, rather than the changing fabric worn by all the guests. We had wrapped our waists in sashes of the Trionian material, however, the long ends draping down to the ground and fluttering as we walked. Sophie's rippled like the colors of a sunset, while mine appeared like a constant stream of water rushing down the front of my gown.

My eyes, which had been fixed on the duke, shifted slightly to where his son stood at his side. Jon was staring at me, his eyes wide with shock and awe. He, at least, had no trouble telling us apart. For a moment my mind flitted back to the horror in his eyes the first time I had trod this carpet. I had thought that emotion strong, but the love I saw shining on his face now made it pale in comparison.

He had been nowhere to be found before the ceremony. I still wasn't sure if he even knew what was going on.

The silence held as we reached the front of the room and knelt before Duke Philip. Sir Oswald, seated in one of the front rows, stood as we went down.

"What is this?" he called in a loud voice. "There was only one winner of the Princess Tourney. Which of them is Princess Sophia?"

I wanted to smile at the nerves in his voice, but I kept my face solemn. We had planned for utmost drama because there was still a chance this might not work. We needed to shock and awe the audience.

Duke Philip stared silently at the knight-merchant until he finally sank back into his seat. Only then did he speak. "I have joyous news for us all. We are here today to witness two betrothals, not one."

He looked out over the crowd, his face bearing a broad smile. "Today I also have the joy of announcing the betrothal of my son, Prince Jonathan, to Princess Liliana of Arcadia."

A choking sound beside the duke made my eyes fly to Jon. A

small smile flashed across my face. So he hadn't known then. His father must have decided to surprise him.

"This double Betrothal Ceremony will seal an alliance between Marin and the Kingdom of Arcadia in the Four Kingdoms." He paused, and I could see his eyes picking out certain individuals in the crowd behind me. "As part of this alliance, Marin has agreed to give Arcadia exclusive trading rights amongst the Four Kingdoms to all silk produced by the silkworm colonies which are located in Trione but owned by the Marinese royal family. In exchange, Arcadia will provide livestock, grain and other necessities to Marin."

A murmur rushed through the crowd, shock breaking through the formality of the moment. The Duchess of Sessily turned a forbidding look on Celine who maintained such a convincing expression of innocence that even I almost believed it. Celine's role in our frantic negotiations had been to keep the head of her own delegation as far away from them as possible. The duchess wouldn't be too pleased at Lanover's exclusion from the trade deal.

Duke Philip allowed the sound to swell and then break, ebbing back into silence. Jon came forward to kneel at my side, and a proxy in the place of Prince Dominic knelt beside Sophie. And then the duke began the ancient and official words of a Betrothal Ceremony. We had been instructed in how it would proceed, and I could only assume I said the right things. It passed in a blur, however. I felt so many emotions, I could hardly absorb any of them.

Despite every barrier that had stood in our way, I was binding myself to the man I loved. But my beloved twin stood beside me binding herself to a man she had never seen. A monster who presided over a cursed kingdom. And through it all, ran tension. Would Sir Oswald still attempt his coup? And, if he did, would he succeed? I had bound myself to that now as well.

The duke pronounced a final blessing over us and invited us

all to stand and face the crowd. We did so in another moment of hushed silence. And then loud cheers rolled through the room, reverberating from the ceiling and filling the space. They went on and on, the release of tension palpable.

Into the chaos marched ten guards, their faces grim and their hands resting on their weapons. I knew the plan, but I still swallowed and surreptitiously reached out my hand for Jon's. He clasped it strongly.

The guards' boots trooped down the carpet that had so recently passed beneath Sophie's and my slippers. The sole remaining pair of slippers that had been made for us by the palace shoemakers to last us through the Tourney.

The guards stopped in front of Sir Oswald. The cheering died instantly away.

"Sir Oswald," said Duke Philip, his voice carrying easily through the silence. "You are hereby arrested for treason against the crown."

"This is an outrage," cried Sir Oswald as the guards dragged him to his feet. His eyes flew around the room, and I held my breath. But one by one the nobles and merchants presented him with stony faces. As we had hoped, the majority of them had no desire to follow Oswald now that the duke had found a way to save the city. And those who might have been loyal to him regardless, clearly saw the general mood and remained silent to protect themselves. The duke could deal with them later, as needed, now that the threat of rebellion had been broken.

Two guards also pulled Corinna and Cole up from their seats beside their father, and all three of them were escorted from the room. When the doors closed behind them, more cheering broke out. How many people had wondered in private about the cause of that fire? It was as if the whole room had been freed from a shroud of fear.

I looked up into Jon's face and found he was already staring down into mine. The gold in his eyes seemed to glow as he devoured my face with his gaze. I smiled at him and it cracked his last restraint.

Scooping me into his arms, he carried me behind the throne and kicked open a door with his boot. I put my arms around his neck, a small thrill racing through me. He carried me as easily as if I weighed nothing, and I had no desire to be put back on my own feet.

Still, his behavior seemed outrageous, so I managed a small protest. "Jon! What are you doing? The Ceremony has only just finished. The whole court is still out there."

"I know," he said. "That's exactly the problem." He kicked the door closed behind us and gently put me down, cradling my face in his hands. "I thought they might be shocked if I did this, but I couldn't wait a second longer."

His lips came down over mine, and I met them eagerly, twining my arms around his neck again. He deepened the kiss, letting go of my face to snake his arms around me and pull me tight against him. I let go of the torrent of other emotions and allowed myself to feel only the joy. And I could feel it all the way down to my fingertips and toes.

When he broke the kiss, panting and resting his forehead against mine, I sighed. A small, happy sound of contentment.

He smiled. "Happy, my beautiful wife-to-be?"

"Blissfully." I sighed again.

"Well you deserve it. You've somehow saved us all. At some point, very soon, you're going to tell me exactly how you did it." He pressed the lightest kiss against my mouth. "Always the hero, it seems."

"Don't forget you saved me first."

He laughed. "I'm perfectly willing to spend the next, oh, sixty or seventy years arguing with you about who's the more heroic. But I should warn you, I'm hard to convince."

I shook my head. "Shocking, my prince, shocking."

The warm light came back into his eyes, and he leaned down

to put his lips against my ear. "That's right. Yours and yours alone."

He would have kissed me again except the door burst open, and we were forced to break apart to receive a stream of excited congratulations. My eyes fell on my sister, and all the less pleasant emotions from the ceremony came rushing back.

She was the true hero, her face alight with happiness and joy for me, as though her life hadn't just been destroyed. Our gazes locked.

We will face this beast together, I projected to her across the chaos. *We will find a way to free you, and then we will come back together. Because I'm not getting married without you by my side.*

She smiled, and this time it reached all the way into her eyes.

EPILOGUE

J sat on a bench in the garden. I was supposed to be planning how Sophie and I would travel to Palinar, but the bright sun and beauty of the day made it hard to focus. I had been in almost constant meetings since the Betrothal Ceremony, and this had been my first opportunity to escape outside.

I hadn't told anyone of my intention to accompany Sophie yet, which is why I wanted to come up with a convincing plan before I broke the news. It didn't help that Prince Dominic had sent another missive. He had demanded that his betrothed, whoever she might be, join him at one of his castles in Palinar. And he had demanded that she come alone.

The baron had been horrified but, thankfully, no one had been willing to accede to that demand. "Neither the ancient laws nor tradition require such a thing," the duke had said firmly. "We will not even consider it."

But who exactly should go with her had become a matter of much debate. Guards would certainly be needed. But how many? And while they debated, it gave me time to come up with an excellent argument.

Except the golden rays falling around me kept luring my mind into a state of pleasant stupor.

"Have you heard about Celine?" Jon sat beside me.

I felt a twinge of curiosity. "No, what about her?"

"Emmeline and Giselle have invited her for a visit to Eldon, and she's accepted."

He had my full attention now. "That's odd."

He chuckled. "Of them or her?"

"Both."

"Well, Celine thinks it's odd, too. I think that's why she accepted. She told me there's something strange about them, and she's going to get to the bottom of it."

I considered his words. "Well, she always did like the idea of adventures. And if anyone can face that icy kingdom it's Celine."

Jon grinned. "She does seem fiery enough to melt them all." He shook his head before pausing. "Oh, wait. I almost forgot. Where's Sophie? My father wants to discuss arrangements with her."

"She's in the library. I tried to convince her to come out here with me, but she wanted some peace and quiet. She figured no one would be in there on a beautiful day like this."

I smiled into his golden-brown eyes and trailed my fingers down his arm. I still couldn't quite believe that he was mine. His muscles jumped under my light touch, and he put his arm around me, tucking me into his side. I felt small and delicate. Cherished.

It struck me as humorous that I had learned to stand apart from Sophie, only to choose to once again become half of a whole. Perhaps that had been the lesson, after all. Not that I could stand alone, but that I could be more than one person. Sophie's twin. Jon's fiancée. Myself.

"I just looked there and couldn't find her. She must have gone somewhere else."

I leaned back into him, feeling drowsy in the warm sun. Had the Tourney only finished three days ago? I relished this calm between storms. I wanted to soak up every peaceful minute before we had to face new dangers in Palinar. "I'll ask her."

Sophie? Where are you now?

In the library. I told you, remember?

"She says she's there. You mustn't have looked very well." I chuckled. My father had never been able to find anything either. It had always been a source of great amusement to my organized mother.

Jon's arm around me tightened just the tiniest bit. "No." I couldn't quite read his tone. "I looked thoroughly. She wasn't there."

I sat up, ripping myself from his arms and meeting his eyes. But it wasn't him I called to. *Sophie!* I poured all my panic into my projection. *Sophie, where are you?*

She replied with a sigh. *I'm sorry, Lily, but I'm long gone.*

What? No!

I wanted to say goodbye, but I knew you would never let me leave.

I leaped to my feet. *Not alone!*

You know what Prince Dominic's message said. "I cannot stop you sending an escort, of course, but only my betrothed is guaranteed safe passage." I couldn't risk anyone else, least of all you. I'll be safe. He has sworn it.

He's a monster! A beast! You can't trust him.

He is also my betrothed. I must trust him. Him and the magic of the Tourney. The duke said it will protect me until my marriage, remember. Not even the one who called the Tourney can disrupt the subsequent betrothal. We are all *of us bound by it.*

I collapsed back down into Jon's arms, my legs giving way and tears pouring down my cheeks. He held me tight against his chest and stroked my hair while I pleaded with Sophie for an hour. But she would not turn back.

"I'm going after her," I said at last, when I realized she could not be swayed.

Jon's arms tightened. "You most certainly are not."

"You can't stop me!"

He buried his face in my hair. "Oh, Lily. You know you can't go. You'd never make it, and then Sophie would be truly alone."

I stilled in his arms. He knew me too well. He had used the one argument that could break through my panic.

"She asked you to trust her. To let her go. To allow her the chance to protect you for once. You have to let her. And you're needed here, in Marin. The tide is turning for our land—you did that. But the darkness is still strong and deep. We need to stand against it here, so that Sophie can have some hope of standing against it there. But there is hope for her. Hope for Palinar. And if the day comes that she needs us—if she calls—we'll be ready to go to her."

I wanted to tell him he was wrong, that she needed me now. But I couldn't. Because he was right. Sophie had sacrificed herself for me, and I couldn't reject her gift. I would fight with her from Marin, but I would not follow her into the wastelands.

I'm here, Sophie. I put all the love of seventeen years of sisterhood into my projection. *I will always be here for you.*

I know. Her projection didn't waver, full of all her own affection and love. *I can do this, Lily. All those years ago, our godmother gave us a gift. You never said it, but I know you feared she did it because she saw a weakness in us. But I've always known that couldn't be true. Because you, at least, have never been weak. And I realize, now, that it was strength she saw in us. A strength that she knew would one day be needed. She equipped us for a fight that has to be fought. A fight I know I'm strong enough to face because I carry you with me wherever I go. A friend, a sister, a fellow warrior. I can defeat this Beast; I can free Palinar. So don't worry. I'll be coming back. But not until I can bring the light with me.*

To find out what happens to Sophie in Palinar, read *A Tale of Beauty and Beast: A Retelling of Beauty and the Beast*.

And to discover the story of the twins' childhood, read the first book in The Four Kingdoms series - *The Princess Companion: A Retelling of The Princess and the Pea*.

To be kept informed of my new releases, please sign up to my mailing list at www.melaniecellier.com. At my website, you'll also find an array of free extra content.

Thank you for taking the time to read my book. If you enjoyed it, please spread the word! You could start by leaving a review on Amazon (or Goodreads or Facebook or any other social media site). Your review would be very much appreciated and would make a big difference!

MAP

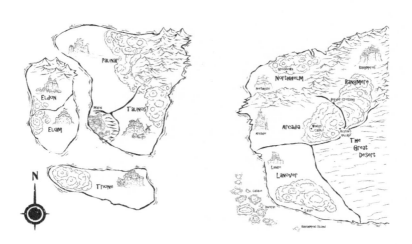

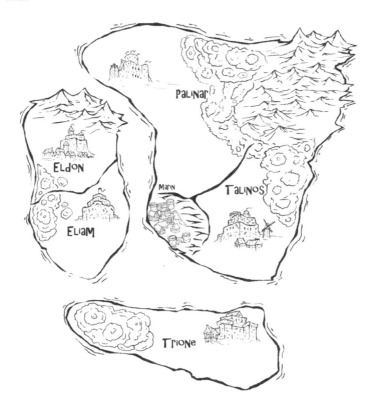

ACKNOWLEDGMENTS

This book has felt like a long time coming. Ever since I first wrote about the twins in my first novel, The Princess Companion, I've known they needed stories of their own. But I needed to wait for them to grow up and, in the meantime, there were some other characters needing happily ever afters first.

And now that the twins are finally getting their turn, I've also introduced a whole new set of kingdoms and characters to join them in their adventures. And, as always, I rely on the support of so many people to make these books a reality.

In the time I've been publishing, my appreciation for my team has only grown. My beta readers, editors, friends and family go above and beyond in helping me with every aspect of my writing.

In particular, I want to give a huge thanks to my faithful beta readers: Rachel, Priya, Katie, Greg and Ber. They promptly read each book I send them and give thoughtful, considered feedback. You guys are seriously the best and, as always, you've made this book better.

My editors are incredible and greatly improve the finished product. In particular, a huge thanks to Mary who has only recently come on board as one of my editors but who has brought so much enthusiasm and expertise to my series. I appreciate your insight and encouragement immensely.

And also a big thanks to my other editors, my dad and Deborah, who graciously worked within my schedule with limited notice.

I am also incredibly grateful to have found my new cover designer, Karri. She is talented, professional and easy to work with, and produces incredible covers. I love my cover for this book, and am excited about the upcoming covers for the rest of the series.

In terms of ongoing support with my life while I was buried in this book, there are so many people to thank including friends on- and offline, but the biggest thanks goes to my husband, Marc. Being married to an author means he has to put up with a lot, but he remains incredibly supportive of my writing. And he's willing to do all the nappy changes and wiping of sticky fingers that is the practical outworking of that support. These books are a team effort!

My life has changed in so many ways since I started writing this book, and I'm so grateful to God for opening up a new season for our family. Now I can't wait to see where the adventure of this series will take us!

ABOUT THE AUTHOR

 Melanie Cellier grew up on a staple diet of books, books and more books. And although she got older she never stopped loving children's and young adult novels.

She always wanted to write one herself but it took three careers and three different continents before she actually managed it.

She now feels incredibly fortunate to spend her time writing from her home in Canberra, Australia where they don't have a beach but they do have kangaroos hopping down the streets. Her staple diet hasn't changed much, although she's added choc mint Rooibos tea and Chicken Crimpies to the list.

Her young adult *Four Kingdoms* and *Beyond the Four Kingdoms* series are made up of linked stand-alone stories that retell classic fairy tales.